In a Place Like No Other

A Novel
by
Ed Touchette

Copyright© 2002 Ed Touchette
All rights reserved including reproduction in any form
except passages excerpted for review.

First Printing

ISBN 0-9741220-0-9

Library of Congress Control Number: 2003093198

Design: Ed Touchette Design
Cover art: Detail from a painting by the author titled A Gloucester Summer.

Printed in the U.S.A.

Published by
Uncle Ham's®, Gloucester, MA U.S.A.

Orders may be sent to:
Uncle Ham's
Box 477
Gloucester, Ma. 01930

or placed through
www.unclehams.com

or by calling
1 800 986 2534

Uncle Ham's is a registered trademark and the property of Ed Touchette Design.

Illustrations

A Gloucester Summer	Cover
City Hall, Gloucester	Page 13
Beauport	Page 25
Rackliffe House Original Cupola	Page 39
The Aviary	Page 55
St. Ann's Steeple	Page 109
Ten Pound Island Lighthouse	Page 137
Garland Building	Page 169
Our Lady of Good Voyage	Page 224
The Universalist Church	Page 268
Cupola	Page 295

The people and events described in this work are fiction. Any similarities to anything or anyone living or dead are coincidental.

Billy and Nick. Not a day has passed . . .

Ed Touchette

Prologue

Sanctuary is a magnet. Solace and sustenance attract the weary and forlorn. Provide respite for the traveler, escape for the ravaged, and recuperative spirits for the weakened - all at a reasonable price - and you'll pack a place.

Les Moor

Les Moor, an unknown beat poet, proposed these maxims after he'd visited Gloucester, Massachusetts seeking an audience with literati laureate Charles Olson. Although Moor'd failed to establish contact with this earthly god of the written word, he'd extended his stay to avail himself of the solitude of this sleepy fishing village and complete a first draft of his posthumous autobiography <u>Dead Beat</u>. The appendix of this voluminous account of a life wasted contains the following poem composed by Moor subsequent to this visit.

> The artists have
>   plucked her beauty and remanded it to paper.
> Oh Gloucester, my Gloucester. Oh
> The fishermen have
>   hooked her fish and devoured them in their bellies.
> Oh Gloucester, my Gloucester. Yo ho ho.
> The tourists tan their faces and bask in her bisques.
> The bankers hike profits beyond their wildest wish
>   es
> The sailors drink her rum and swallow her ale.
> Arrest these mothers and put 'em in jail.
> Sing polly wolly doodle all the day -
> Oh yeah.

Analogue

April 4, 2009

    For the fisherman and the sailor, Gloucester has, for centuries, meant shelter from the wrath of the North Atlantic and welcome respite from the labors of the sea. Proximity to that piscatorial gold mine, Georges Bank, brought the Vikings, the English, the Dutch and some French to Cape Ann hundreds of years ago. Native Americans, who'd been planting and fishing here for years, greeted them all. Then the Italians and Portuguese arrived to chase the cod, flounder and haddock, adding to the cosmopolitan flavor of the community, and Gloucester became the greatest fishing port in the world. In the Twentieth Century, though, a spate of groundfish curbed her growth as one of the world's major suppliers to the protein dependent.

    Some of the financial benefits from harvesting the seas off Gloucester resurfaced as the migratory route of the Blue Fin Tuna wound close to Cape Ann. Sport fishermen found their way into the harbor and enjoyed their summer months on the water as they chased the tuna by day and the ladies by night. As well, a taste for Blue Fin attracted the followers of a Far Eastern guru and they, too, reaped the rewards to be had from the export of this delicacy.

    This religious group encountered strong resistance from the locals, among whom were quite possibly descendents of the English who'd first made their way to New England to escape civil and religious strife in the motherland. More to the point, the first settlers to erect their fish stages on the high granite of the western shore, were dissenters from the Plymouth Colony's collection of dissenters, banished over a dispute involving interpretations of the scriptures. Was the haven for the persecuted of the persecuted fostering intolerance? Not really.

    This coastal mecca was and is highly valued by another sect - sun and fun loving inlanders. The population of Gloucester blossoms during the summer months; the beautiful beaches and rocky coastline attract thousands. Cool breezes off the Atlantic mitigate the sun's heat so its disciples can tan in comfort, enjoying its warmth without suffering the stifling temperatures and humidity of the cities. The sandy beaches at Good Harbor, Wingaersheek and Niles ease the masses into soothing salt waters.

The granite coastline also affords exquisite siting opportunities for those whose fortunes warrant a second home where they can relax and regenerate. During the nineteenth and twentieth centuries, wealthy industrialists and financiers came to Cape Ann to erect more testament to their successes. Their twenty and thirty-room summer cottages still stand along the shores.

Artists and writers needing to escape oppressive urban environs found the harbor's scenic beauty and variety as appealing as its mild summer climate, and the sail lofts on Rocky Neck supplied ample studio space and access to the array of activity associated with the industry of the harbor. They still come today to merge their talents with the profusion of pigment awash in the atmosphere and the panoply of activity into marketable commodities. Understandably so, as visitors to Cape Ann will agree that the aura of Gloucester is noteworthy. At sunset, majestic.

Through these allurements, Gloucester has gained her most prized possession - an eclectic assemblage of fishermen, laborers, businessmen, entrepreneurs, writers and artists who cohabit and present an intriguing patchwork. Immersed in the littoral setting, this amalgam exudes its own tantalizing aroma attracting throngs. For the bewildered and confused, this conglomerate of life-styles and a congenial ambience proffer a unique opportunity to regroup and take new direction - or not. For the day tripper and the weekender, it presents a plethora of photo prospects, ripe for picking and preservation in the family album. In redressing this influx, hotels, motels, inns and pubs have become essential.

Early in the twentieth century, magnificent grand hotels began to line the shores to accommodate the flocks of thousands. Along Eastern Point to Niles Beach and Rocky Neck, grand dames of dining and decorum decorated the coast.

All hail the Colonial, a marvel indeed. Affixed to the granite of Eastern Point, her 175 rooms, casino and furnishings welcomed the weary - but only for four years. Fire reconstructed all of her, including her portico

In a Place Like No Other

magnifique, to rubble and ruination in a matter of hours.

The Hawthorne was a multi unit structure located on sumptuous acreage just north from Niles Beach. Mid-career, fire downsized this campus to a bar and some out buildings which held a mere few guests depending on the nightly rates. Sold in the 1980's for kindling, condominiums sprouted from this magnificent site abutting the harbor.

The Fairview Inn, of more modest cottage construction, rested on a knoll across Eastern Point Road from the Hawthorne. Its location endowed visitors with an unobstructed view of the harbor from the roomy porch that fronted the building - much the same as in 1884 when Rudyard Kipling began his book <u>Captains Courageous</u> on a summer visit to Cape Ann.

There were and are other retreats, yet in size and popularity, local lore attests that none, including the aforementioned, approached the stature of the grandest of the grand, Rackliffe House, located on Rocky Neck, the granite promontory just to the west of the East Gloucester hills. A small piece of Rackliffe House stands today - a failed condominium development on the verge of modification to low income housing. A dearth of recorded testament bars verification, but a few East Gloucester elders regularly bespeak her magnificence.

They say: A hundred years ago, this edifice occupied approximately five acres on The Neck and housed almost a thousand visitors in hundreds of rooms. Guests strolled along the harborside pathways and chatted in the gazebo that topped a large granite outcropping jutting into the harbor. Here many Brahmin and their get watched sails flutter as friends and family delighted in the offshore breezes that would carry them to Marblehead and Manchester for afternoon tea. From here, Gloucester natives cheered Captain Marty Welch and *Esperanto* as she sailed against all odds to capture the first International Fisherman's Cup. Undoubtedly the pastoral frontage of Rackliffe House inspired artists to render the ubiquitous white gowned lady with sun hat and parasol, gazing thoughtfully at the cat boats gliding across the harbor.

They also say: A protégé of Henry Davis Sleeper, the noted designer whose eclectic mix of styles created Beauport, his home and a renowned piece of American architectural history, conceived and contrived Rackliffe House because, like Beauport, Rackliffe House grew organically. Her basement, a labyrinth of dens and closets, storage rooms and ingenious service devices, supported three floors of casinos, dining rooms, lounges, posh libraries and guest suites, all conjoined by an intricate web of passages so convoluted even the most experienced staff members brooked befuddlement in their daily travails - truly indicative of the clever master designer's remarkable precepts and indelible sense of humor. Although inadmissible, this hearsay cultivates an appropriate image of Rackliffe House.

More anecdotal evidence supports the belief that Rackliffe House was the brain child of the builder of Beauport or a close counterpart thereto. In 1930, the remains of a Philadelphia lawyer who'd gained fame by disassembling the empires of wealthy industrialists were found slumped in the corner of the antechamber of a suite of basement rooms which, until this grim discovery, had never been opened to the public, or, in fact even known to the hotel's staff. Ossified, his hand clutched a spigot that drained a series of oaken channels ingeniously disguised as structural elements and decorative trim. The cache of bootleg whiskey found stored in those concealed trenches rivaled the volume of that confiscated and dumped by the Untouchables at the height of their activities in Chicago, Illinois. Oddly, the official report forwarded to the deceased's next of kin cited confusion as the cause of death. The coroner had deduced that the victim had somehow stumbled upon this room as a consequence of a wrong turn in the Gordian knot, the bowels of Rackliffe House, and as egress was provided only through a secret panel masterfully disguised as a book case, never left because he was too dissipated to read.

Unscathed by this scandal, Rackliffe House sailed on and again made headway when the Federal Government rescinded Prohibition in 1933. As her repute approached Olympian status, her coffers belched the magic elixir in such volume that many nearby residents avowed silver certificates insulated her walls and the down of the golden goose stuffed her pillows.

Encomium graced her from courts far flung and heads of state regularly bestowed extravagances to her inestimable collection of finery. Her crowning jewel, a 24" diameter, 24k gold plated aluminium ball, delivered by diplomatic pouch, capped her loftiest point, the lightning rod which topped her observation deck, a two story cupola, crowning the center most guest wing. An architectural oddity in itself, this cupola featured a roof design never before seen. The winged gables that curved slightly upward from the center, where the lightning rod roosted, traced a concave line to the outside peaks. At great distance, they tendered the bearing of the flukes of a whale. A cherished sea story tells of a senile Nantucket skipper in pursuit of his last great fortune, who entered the harbor one cold grey morning only to find himself coming about in hurried fashion to avoid rolling waves of granite.

That fish tale is more than likely just that; what follows, though, may explain what we see today. As sometimes is the case, a simple gesture can have far reaching effects, and a simple mind even more so. Had the hotel engineer realized that the addition of the ball to the lightning rod would likely negate the intended commission of Benjamin Franklin's ingenuity, he might have suspended it from the cherry wood rafters in the sumptuous casino or have placed it on a granite pedestal amidst the waterfront walks to provide meditative respite for generations to come. But he did not and an immense conflagration reduced Rackliffe House in 1934. A bolt of lightning struck the cupola and as it exploded, like that on Fillipo's Florentine marvel some 500 years earlier, it spewed forth burning timbers that ignited a hellish blaze. A full ten days hence, when the fire storm had subsided and the smoke had cleared, the gathered multitude gazed unbelievingly: All but the center most guest wing of the once proud Rackliffe House had been razed.

That wing, sans its gabled crown, was scarred but deemed structurally sound. It was refurbished almost immediately and the cupola restored to its winged glory. With new furnishings installed and the charred remnants of the behemoth hauled off as land fill, planning commenced to reconstitute from the ashes of this Shermanesque debacle a pavilion of heretofore unseen pleasures.

However, the owners, a consortium of well intentioned investors, discovered ineptitude and negative acumen made an odious combination. A paucity of insurance failed to cover even the haulage fees for the rubble, so the acreage which the grand dame had so gracefully occupied, had to be sold as house lots. Fewer than fifty guests (based on double occupancy) could now frequent Rackliffe's grandeur. Thoroughly dismayed, disappointed and disoriented, the syndicate agreed to sell to the highest bidder, or even one who might come close, this stunted Rackliffe House. She was purchased at auction in 1935.

Valiant attempts were made to rejuvenate the old girl's glory years. None succeeded. Her reputation attracted dreamers but never again was Rackliffe House able to generate the cash flow needed to cover the principal and interest on her selling prices. Finally, the 1970's-1980's interest rate hikes coupled with the efforts of a notable mismanager finished what the blaze of 1934 could not. Rackliffe House succumbed to the developers' shovels in 1985.

On the cusp of her demise, Rackliffe House made one last bid to secure her rightful claim to the uppermost rung on the ladder of hostelry history. This spa, whose salubrious powers had gained world renown, housed one of the most popular bars on Rocky Neck and became the core of the Gloucester scene. Her doors opened to all who knocked and she cleared her deck to cater to as diverse a crowd as the imagination could fathom. From the disenfranchised to high end professionals, rich and poor alike gathered nightly, to bask in the waning glow of the sunset, sip their beers and cocktails and salute the impending bender.

Any further attempts at describing this ultimate debauch lie fallow juxtaposed to the facts. A Gloucester Summer, a poem included in poet Moor's collection written in 1968, tried but failed miserably. Suffice to say, this taken from the police notes of *The Times*, adumbrates the magnetic force that was Rackliffe House in the 1970's: "An employee's spouse told investigators it was an 'unfuckingbelievable scene.'"

Here our tale of woe commences - not Norman's, not Thatcher's, but Frank's; and aptly so, for this was his first contact with the most interesting city in the world. Into her harbor have sailed the obscure, the illustrious, and even the famous. Out o' Gloucester have come some incredible tales.

Part 1

Travelogue

Chapter 1

A centrifuge of turmoil had forced them to the fringes. Proximity to new gravities would consummate their separation. The laws of nature are incontrovertible.

Dogs in a Rain Storm
Les Moor
1968 The Aviary Papers Publishers

He thought as he drove: "Did I pack underwear?" He remembered: A month ago, April, 1975 - he'd decided to leave. She'd asked why. He'd told her, "It's patent, even obvious, it's time to get the fuck out of Dodge."

She didn't know Dodge, but she'd been polite. "Try not to get too involved with people that are crazier than you, Frank. It'll only make you worse off than you already are."

"Thanks," he'd said. "That's good advice."

"And remember what your father taught you about the birds and the bees, dear."

"Actually, it was Sally who taught me about the birds and the bees. Remember? Dad left."

"What?" she'd screamed. "Frank, how could you? This is embarrassing. Sally Barber? She's my best friend's daughter. Damn, I never knew. Does she know?"

"Sally? I suspect she does. She was there."

"Oh, you ass, Francis. You know what I meant."

"I don't know. You'll have to ask Mrs. Barber. We've never talked about it."

"Oh, I'm mortified. What shall I say?"

"I don't know. It happened years ago."

"Oh, Frank, she's my bridge partner."

"Who, Sally?"

"No, Mrs. Barber."

This morning as he'd packed the car, she'd asked again why he was leaving? What was in Gloucester? He'd told her that like the Abenaki, he was headed for the coast to fish and plant seeds for the summer; he'd be back in the fall. She'd grabbed his shoulders and just as when he was a child, covered his forehead with her palm. She'd gazed up, begging resolution with her eyes and groaned, "Frank, what's an Abenaki?"

He'd hugged her, said "Good bye, Mom," and left.

Frank Noal headed for the New England coast. Left behind: the oppressive humidity, his Adirondack Valley, the perennial overcast. Frank loved walking in the mountains. He heard a voice: "You can't have everything, Frank." He made notes to himself as he drove with the sun at his back: To Gloucester, a new opportunity. Work at Rackliffe House. Part time bartender, part time maintenance man. Jack Carson, his former college roommate and son of the owner, Senator Maynard Carson, had hired him.

He drove through the Green and the White Mountains. He got confused. "It's spring green everywhere," he whispered to no one. By mid afternoon, he'd dropped into the coastal plain. He could almost feel the sandy soil as he glanced at the embedded refuse beneath the guard rails. The landscape flattened. He sensed the ocean in the distance. When he reached Beverly, he hugged the shoreline along route 127. Tudor mansions snug in the carapace - high stone walls and wrought iron spikes. Jack called it the Gold Coast.

He first glimpsed the harbor at Gloucester from the Magnolia shore on the west side: white sails gamboling; reds, blues, greens and yellows of brightly painted fishing draggers plowing the water; rolling hills, to the north and east speckled with houses - large Victorian and Federalist mansions, revived Greeks and Gothics, Italianates, chateaus, saltboxes, arts and crafts, triple deckers marching up a hill - mechanic style. Architectural Styles in America 101. Dr. Gruntel would be impressed. Rows of brick walls grew from the water. Spires saluted the gods. He crossed a small drawbridge and cruised a wide boulevard, passed a patinated statue. "Gorton's," he mumbled, squinting into intoxicating sunlight.

"Find the causeway and cross the tidal mud flats that connect Rocky Neck to the rest of the cape," Jack had told him. Frank followed signs. In a narrow street, a badly weathered one read: "Rackliffe House Hotel. Enjoy the sunset from our deck overlooking beautiful Gloucester Harbor." A possible arrow indicating a turn was worn to bare wood. At the curb, he lowered the window to check with a pedestrian and an acrid odor, a mix of fish gurry and the mephitis of low tide, stung Frank's nostrils. He coughed and thought of the mills. "Ahemm. Rackliffe House down that way?"

The passerby, a woman wearing a pink pillbox hat and a leopard coat, lowered her head to eyeball Frank over the aviator sunglasses that had slipped to the end of her nose. Pointing with a heavily carved walking stick, she grunted "Ayeah," tugged up a gray wool knee sock that had bunched at her ankle then ambled on oblivious to Frank's "Thank you." Frank noted the woman's scuffed brogans, one black and another brown, both with lime green laces tied around her ankles.

An historical marker under a tree read: "Samuel de Champlain sailed into Gloucester Harbor in 1606 and called it le beau port." The coincidence and caustic smell followed him along the causeway onto Rocky Neck. Up a hill following another sign, he'd decided it was a good omen.

Frank changed his mind quickly when he first glimpsed Rackliffe House. This remnant of a much grander era on Boston's North Shore perched on a granite outcropping overlooking Gloucester's outer harbor. Scarred clapboards and missing roof shingles spoke to years of neglect. Several shutters on the dormers that dotted the top floor hung precariously at odd angles. Door and window screens had holes the size of a woolly mammoth's footprint. Frank groaned. "Stately location . . . maybe all it has left," he thought. Clouds of gulls circled and cawed above him.

Jack had sent a brochure on Rackliffe House so Frank already knew some of its history. He'd hesitated when he'd seen the knotty pine paneling and the orange shag rug in photographs of the typical guest quarters and now he could see even more architectural blasphemies. He wished he'd hesitated longer.

A translucent fiberglass awning covered a sun deck that overlooked the pool and the harbor beyond, suffusing everything beneath it in a sickly grey-green. The bowed deck's railing ran parallel to the back wall, denying access to its extremities. The curvature of the deck reflected no other architectural or landscape feature. It seemed as aberrant as the alternating aqua and white panels of the awning.

The lobby still boasted a few original features - the leaded glass entry, a superbly crafted granite fireplace, and a magnificent crystal chandelier. Finely detailed wood work had been repainted so often the dentils around the fireplace mantel and the bull's-eye corner moldings had mostly flattened. Photographs lined the mantel - mostly sailing ships. Frank read the names inscribed in pencil - *Esperanto, Endeavor, Henry Ford, Bluenose II, Gertrude L. The.* "Gertrude L. the what?" Frank's eyes couldn't see through the smudges.

Paintings with business cards jammed in the corners of their frames cluttered the lobby. "The Rocky Neck galleries," he surmised. Mixed among these contemporary offerings were a few smaller older canvases, yellowed from years of tobacco and wood smoke. One small watercolor bordered by a faded water-stained mat rested under cracked glass. The top right corner of the frame was separated.

Frank walked to a gold flecked formica counter and tapped on a bell. Tinkling echoed, then faded. A minute or two passed and no one appeared, so Frank slapped the bell harder. Then he walked back to the fireplace to discern 'the what' that Gertrude L. was.

"I'm coming. I'm coming." A voice sang behind him. A short rotund man stumbled through a passageway leading from a flight of stairs, one shirt tail half stuffed into his twisted belt overlapped the other - stuck in his zipper. He fumbled with the top buttons of his shirt as he perused Frank. His curly blonde hair was as disheveled as his clothing but his soft blue eyes were warm. He pursed his lips and they quivered as he chimed in a mellow tenor, "What can I do for you?"

"I'm Frank Noal, the bartender slash maintenance man. I just got here and wanted to check in."

"Oh, you don't have to register, dear. Aha. You'll be living in the cottage."

"I see," Frank said looking puzzled.

"Ha, ha, ha, ha!" the man chortled, tossed his head to the side and closed his eyes. His heavily wrinkled forehead flushed to match his ruddy cheeks. "That just cracks me up." He bent, slapped his knees and then straightened. "Gotcha." He reached up to poke Frank's chest with his chubby index finger.

"I'm Harley, Harley Fenton." He extended his hand, palm down as if presenting his rings to be kissed. "I'm the desk clerk from seven in the morning until seven at night seven days a week. Seven is a very lucky number for me. I'm also the bell captain and the bell boy. I schedule the wait staff and the kitchen staff, too. On occasion, I justify the previous evening's bar receipts and register the deposits in the hotel checking account - only when the regular bookkeeper isn't here."

Frank shook Harley's hand and was about to speak when something made him glance back to the passageway. A young man sauntered through the lobby, heading for the exit door. A sweet musk followed him.

"See ya' darling," the young man said as he strutted past and blew a kiss toward Harley.

"Bye bye," Harley responded.

The young man, pausing to primp in a mirror hanging on the wall by the door, carefully rolled up the sleeves of his tee shirt then turned sideways to check them in profile. Returning to a front view, he inhaled deeply, shifted the buckle on his belt to center it and slicked back his hair. He grasped a lock above his forehead and twisted it to fall just above his left eye. He looked again. Satisfied, he turned and ogled Frank from head to toe. "Someone I should know?" he asked Harley.

Harley frowned. "Slut," he muttered and shooed him with a wave of his hand. The young man shrugged and left.

Harley continued. "Sorry for that minor indiscretion, Frank. Let's see. Oh, yes. I always get here a little early to be sure the morning kitchen staff has started a pot of coffee. If you're up by six, feel free to join me for coffee. We have tea, too." Harley giggled, "Oh my wouldn't that be delightful - tea for two." He whistled the tune and tapped his toe as he glided a few steps toward the sundeck and then back. "Sorry," Harley said. "I do love my music. OK, ahh, yes . . . Dear me, where was I?"

"Coffee or tea."

"Yes. Yes, I recall. OK. If it's raining or foggy, I'll usually light a fire and read the morning papers here in the sitting area." He swung his arm as if featuring prizes on a game show. "If it's sunny, I have my coffee out on the deck with music - piano concertos and string quartets mostly. On occasion, a touch of Edith Piaf." Harley cooed as he pirouetted to a sliding door that led to the sun deck. "Remember, at seven o'clock sharp, I commence with my duties."

"Thanks," Frank said. "It's nice of you to offer. I'll join you for coffee some mornings . . . when I'm up that early."

"Terrific!" Harley wheeled back. "Follow me, Frank. Jack is next door in the cottage. He's expecting you. He told me to send you right over when you arrived. Do remember, if you need anything at all, let me know. I'll be happy to give you a tour - the kitchen, the dining room, the bar or, oh, of course the guest rooms. When you're ready, let me know."

"Thanks again," Frank said walking across the driveway. He mulled Harley's offer and chuckled, "I'm sure you would."

Jack Carson had been Frank's roommate for two years at Crandall College. Jack's father had bought Rackliffe House in 1964 and Jack managed it during the summers. Jack had often asked Frank to work at the hotel but Frank had stayed at International Paper. He told Jack, "Summers on Lake Champlain suck, but the money's fantastic. I joined the union."

No one answered Frank's knock on the cottage door, so he turned the knob and let himself in. In a sitting area, he saw magazines strewn on the floor, a stereo and a pile of album covers; a pocket mirror and wine glasses graced a battered coffee table. Then footsteps shuffled down a set of stairs as Jack Carson tugged at his belt and wriggled his foot trying to arrest an uncooperative loafer.

"Hi, Jack, I made it." Frank reacquainted his eyes with his former roommate. The tall gaunt figure spewed forth self assurance from steel blue eyes and those perfect dimples formed in his tanned cheeks. One confident snap of his head and the lock of straight dusty blonde hair that had fallen to his forehead fell back in place with elegance. Frank smirked and nodded toward Jack's lower extremities and Jack crumbled, frantically grabbing his pants zipper. Frank laughed.

"Frank, great, terrific, yeah. You made it. Fabulous. Hey, get your stuff. Make yourself at home. Second bedroom down the hall." Jack pointed quickly. Then a lock of blonde hair flopped over his eyes as he tried to refocus on his zipper. "Two waitresses are sharing the big room. At the end. Kim and Pam . . . ugh, damn . . . Bristol and Sharp. I'm upstairs." Jack tugged at his zipper and looked up at Frank. Then: "Aw shit." Jack doubled over.

"OK." Frank struggled not to laugh. "Hey, Jack. Cool it. Relax. Go back to whatever you were doing and I'll unload my stuff."

"Great," Jack said turning away.

" Where's a good place to park when I'm finished?"

Jack bounded back to the stairway, then hesitated. He scratched his head for a second then shrugged his shoulders. "Anywhere. Park anywhere in the lot for now. Look, unpack your stuff, get settled and we'll get together for dinner."

"No problem," Frank chuckled. "See you in a while." Leaving the cottage, Frank heard feet shuffling overhead and a woman's voice shrieked, "Jack, where's my fucking bra?"

Jack looked at Frank sheepishly, then vaulted up the stairs. Frank heard Jack: "Wait. I'm coming."

"Not today," Frank heard.

Frank smiled as he walked to his car. "A hot afternoon on Rocky Neck. Like those lazy Sundays with Allie, in bed at the apartment," he mumbled inwardly. "History."

Frank had everything placed in his room, a couple of books and an old clock radio on the table next to his bed and his clothes in the small closet. He checked his appearance in a full length mirror hanging behind the door. He sucked in the slight paunch and tugged his jeans higher. "Gotta start swimming again." He stepped back to gauge the upper extremities of his six foot frame and swiveled his head left to right as he ran his fingers through his wavy brown hair. "Not too bad," he thought as he moved closer and rubbed around his eyes. "The circles are gone. They're actually white again. Goes better with the blue than the bloodshot look." He scrunched his nose with an index finger and smiled. "Almost straight," he whispered, remembering a tumble down two flights of stairs in a drunken stupor.

Frank walked over to a window and drew back the curtains. The harbor glistened in the sun and he admired a gazebo on a granite ledge down by the water. "Nice view," Frank thought, "Allie'd like this place. The ocean. Beautiful."

Frank folded a duffle bag as Jack knocked sheepishly on the door frame. "Great to see you, Frank. Glad you finally got here. Sorry about what happened. Caught me at a bad time."

Frank laughed. "I suspect it was a good time, Jack."

"Whatever," Jack said, "Hey. You're going to love it. If you're settled in, let's head down The Neck. Have a few beers before dinner. Come on, Frank, it's on me. You'll get a taste of what it's like. Hey, Frank, getting a little heavy?"

Frank thought, "Y'shoulda seen me twenty pounds ago," then asked if he had time to shower and change. Jack told him to hurry because he had to meet someone later on. Frank pointed to the ceiling. "Make up for this afternoon?"

Jack smiled, walked over to the window and looked out into the harbor. "No, Frank," he said, "someone else. You'll see." Jack turned and smiled at Frank. Those steel blue eyes dilated and danced, the dimples formed and the sly grin greeted Frank on the steps to the Quad -

Hey Frank, Farnsworth gave me an A in International Affairs and I never made a class.

How's Sally, Jack?

Good. She's coming tonight to tutor me. I'm taking her European Politics this semester.

Frank reconnected as he listened to what he called classic Jack:

"There'll be a ton of women hanging around this place in a couple of weeks, Frank. Some regulars, others just visiting with one thing in common. They all want to get away and get laid. Who am I to say no?"

Frank shook his head and said, "Nothing changes."

Jack thought for a second and looked out the window again. "You know, Frank, we're both the same. Neither of us can handle a relationship. The difference is, I accept it and move on. You keep trying to change. Maybe, though, just maybe . . . that bullshit with Allie finally woke you up. Took long enough."

Frank headed down the hall for the bathroom. "Maybe he's right," Frank thought as he remembered Sunday morning showers with Allie.

"The piano bars on Rocky Neck attract big crowds," Jack told Frank as they strode down Rocky Neck Avenue. "Gay, straight, young, old, men and women - they all circle the grand pianos and sing until the bars close. Lot of fun. Places get packed. The tourists love it. But the Galley's different. Great food. Wild. You'll see. We'll have a couple of beers there and then go to dinner." As they passed a small saltbox, Frank recognized the woman in the pink pillbox hat. She sat on a stone wall, whittling her walking stick with a jackknife and humming. He asked Jack about her and Jack said, "That's Ruthie, she walks up and down The Neck carrying those sticks. She carves 'em and sells 'em to the tourists. Makes a shitload of money doin' it, too." The woman lowered her head and peered at them over her sunglasses.

Ed Touchette

Jack and Frank walked into the Galley and the crowded bar said hello to Jack. A couple changed seats so Jack and Frank could sit together. They sipped beers and Frank read the covers of movie posters and show bills that lined the walls and low slung ceiling. When he sniffed and said, "Garlic," Jack replied, "Mussels." Then Jack spoke louder to be heard over the busy chatter: "This place is unreal. Most of these people are regulars, but in a couple of weeks it'll be packed with tourists. Unbelievable reputation. Great entertainment."

Frank looked around while Jack talked. "The piano player bangs out show tunes and ballads all night long but nobody sings except Polly. She's the owner. There she is over there at that window table."

Jack pointed to a tall stunning fortyish woman with flowing platinum blonde hair, wearing an evening gown, carrying a sequined purse and tapping the deck with an ivory and silver handled cane as she strolled from table to table. Large round pearl framed sunglasses, studded with glistening stones slipped to the tip of her button nose as she backed away from a table, threw her arms wide and bellowed a song title. In the dim light, the candle on the table cast vaudeville shadows on the ceiling. Somebody tapped a glass with silverware and quiet suffused the room. Then the piano player rattled through an intro and Polly belted out *Fever*, tossing the cane dramatically from one hand to the other, spinning gracefully to face another table, then popping a table top to punctuate her phrasing or wake a groggy diner.

"Thaaaat's Polly," Jack shouted over the clanking upright piano. Frank strained to hear: Polly'd been an actress in New York and the wife of a tug captain. He'd bought her the restaurant as an anniversary gift fifteen years ago. According to Jack, she'd decided to move here when her career waned. "Now she manages the place full time. During dinner, she sings and dances. Does medleys from her favorite musicals while customers plow through bisques." Jack sipped his beer and nodded to direct Frank's attention to a photograph with a lengthy inscription hanging near the mirror behind the bar. Frank squinted but didn't recognize the face. Jack continued: "Polly's cousin. If he's doing a stint nearby, he'll stop in and sing along." Frank shrugged and asked Jack how he'd gotten to know Polly.

"The Neck is small, Frank. We're all in it together - sort of. The old man and Polly were partners. Remember the ferry deal?"

"What ferry deal, Jack?"

"Frank, I told you about it."

"If you did I don't remember, Jack."

"Yeah, they invested a ton of money and raised more from some friends. Started a ferry service from Boston. Trying to boost traffic here. It failed. Miserably." Jack smirked and sipped his beer.

"Why?"

"They didn't have a clue about advertising. You know the old man. Cheap prick. They lost a shit load of money." Jack rubbed the label on his bottle as he weaved through the details of a debacle. His father and Polly had tried to assuage angry investors with an end of the season party that bombed, too. A sword boat crew with pockets full of money from a good trip had joined in what should have been a private party and when the ferry departed for Boston, the crew departed the Galley. "Unfortunately," Jack said, "they'd stripped to the skin in the men's room, then they ran through the dining area and jumped over the railing into the harbor screaming, "Wait for us." The crowd here went numb with shock but the crowd on the Lobsta Pot pier cheered and howled, and the band playing there joined the mayhem." Jack claimed that a couple of buxom women from the ferry decided to join the fishermen, stripped to the waist and dove into the water. Before it was over, the ferry captain, flustered and shaken, had backed into the moorings across the cove, crushed a yawl and sank it. "The band played *Taps* as the boat settled to the bottom." Jack's hand slowly descended to the bar, animating the sinking.

A familiar gleam of delight filled Jack's eyes as he plunked his bottle on the bar and snickered. "Polly was ripped. She stood at the porch railing screaming, "You guys are banned for life." A waitress chucked their clothes over the railing."

Frank stared at Jack in disbelief then roared. "Come on, Jack?" Frank rubbed his side.

"No shit, Frank. I was here. I saw it."

Frank held his sides at Jack's details then Jack laughed, too. Polly strolled through the dining room, twirling her cane, headed to the bar.

"Hi, Jack," Polly said. She kissed Jack on both cheeks. "I didn't know you were back. When are you going to open for the summer?" Polly paused, looked at Frank and asked gruffly, "Who's this and what the hell is so funny?" She tapped the bar with her cane and the bartender delivered a Manhattan.

Jack introduced Frank and told Polly he'd just told Frank the story about the ferry. Polly started to laugh. Then she stopped abruptly, removed her sunglasses and looked straight into Frank's eyes. Under the layers of heavy mascara, liner and deep violet shading, her silvery-blue eyes lurked like barracuda in a coral reef. She wet her lips, then yowled, "Those dumb bastards cost me twenty grand - y'know. If they ever dare show their faces in here again, I'll denut the mothers and send 'em screaming over the railing again." Polly jerked her thumb toward the porch. "This time," she said gratingly, "their voices'll be a lot higher." Polly gulped her Manhattan and slid the glass down the bar without losing eye contact with Frank. "A lot higher," she barked.

Frank laughed harder. Jack spoke with Polly speculating about the fortunes of the season. Then Jack suggested the Loft for dinner. Walking back up the neck, Frank was still laughing at Jack's story when he said, "That place is wacko."

"It is. The whole town is. I don't know for sure why, but it is. It seems like people come here and let go of everything. Everybody's on vacation, laid back - except the restaurant and hotel people; they've only got a hundred days to make any money. But everybody else just wants to sing their troubles away and relax in the sun."

After a quick dinner at the Loft, Frank and Jack said good night. Jack said that he might not get to the hotel until late the next morning so Frank should take a look around and write up a list of projects. Then Jack left in his car to meet "someone" and Frank went to the cottage. He listened to music and read a story. He heard the chugging of diesel engines so he shut off the table lamp and glanced out the window. A parade of draggers, masthead lights beaming, putted toward the vast dark of the open ocean. A search light swept at the night and a red light blinked its warning. Frank wondered where he was headed.

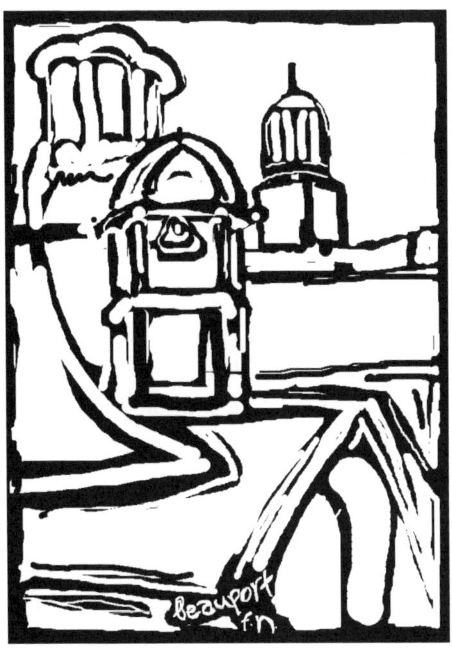
Beaufort
f.n.

Chapter 2

*Fog. It's common here.
There's a lot of water around.*

A Gloucester Summer
Les Moor
1968 The Aviary Papers Publishers

A dense salty mist shrouded Frank's first morning on Rocky Neck. He sipped a cup of coffee as he walked the grounds to get acquainted. A lot of things needed immediate attention: "dead privet - get that out; railing around the swimming pool - needs bracing." A pathway led to a gazebo sitting precariously on a granite boulder. Along the way, he noted the precision of the cut stone in the dry granite walls that held the gardens.

The gazebo needed almost everything. "Posts rotted, steps rotted, floor and seats are OK but the railing's gone." He looked up to check the roof. "That sucks," he thought as he scribbled in his book.

A fog horn sounded at regular intervals. "Keeps the ocean going from reaching shore in an unsafe manner. Wonder how many don't make it?" Frank thought as he surveyed the collection of flotsam lodged in the smaller rocks that sat at the base of the boulder. "Clean up debris at gazebo," he wrote and closed the notebook. A bell buoy, somewhere out in the harbor, clanged.

Looking back, he could vaguely see the building through the heavy mist. It disappeared, then reappeared as the cloud of moisture thickened and thinned - an image in a lens as the focus is adjusted. All but the gabled wings of the cupola vanished into the rolling brume. Frank noted the cupola. "A little more than unusual," he thought.

"Ah, she must have been grand. A few hundred rooms on three floors - stretched all the way across." He eyed the property from one end to the other. "Hundreds of people enjoying the grounds - crisp white linen slacks and fluffy white cotton dresses, parasols and straw hats. Painted every spring - glossy white, black shutters, white porch railings rippling across

In a Place Like No Other

her facade. Up on the roof, the patterned slate would have accented the scalloping of the cedar shingles that still covered the dormers. The brick chimneys and their caps must have looked like decorations on a wedding cake - connected her to the sky."

He glanced at a single bench planted near a bed of hosta. "The back needs new boards." He imagined a couple holding hands and gazing out at the harbor, planning and dreaming. He turned to assess their view. The fog restricted this, too, to dreams.

Frank walked slowly. When he heard, "Frank, is that you?" Frank answered, "Yeah. That you, Harley?"

"Yes it is. Come in for coffee."

"OK." Frank walked toward the steps. The closer he got the more impending chores he noted in his book. He crossed the sundeck to enter the lobby, the deck creaking and groaning under his weight. He noted: "Fix that today." He opened the door to dulcet tones and saw Harley pouring coffee.

"Good morning, Frank. Coffee's ready. Sugar and cream? Sugar no cream? Cream no sugar?"

"Black's fine. Harley, this place needs some instant attention. Where's the nearest lumber yard?"

"The Building Center will have what you need. We have an account. But clear it with me or Jack first. We have a strict budget."

"OK. I need about thirty feet of decking, a bunch of two by fours and some . . ."

"Slow down, Frank. Write it down on a slip of paper and I'll look at it. Let's savor this rapturous music."

"Sure."

Frank watched. Harley sat in a Queen Anne wing chair near the fireplace. His head rested against the back of the chair and he'd closed his eyes. He held his cup in his left hand and his right arm was slightly raised. He conducted an imaginary orchestra with a slight tilt of his head, first in one direction, then another. His extended index finger marked the time.

"Rudolph Serkin," Harley said, suddenly. "Beethoven's Emperor. Masterful. Perfect."

Frank opened his mouth to speak but Harley shushed him.

"Please, Frank, I must concentrate. It's almost over and there's a hellish passage."

Ed Touchette

Harley laid his head back and closed his eyes as the orchestra came in and the piano subsided. Harley placed his coffee cup on the floor and demanded a bigger crescendo, sweeping his arms in a circle. As the piano ran through its final flurry, he rose to his feet, leapt with his arms high above his head then landed on the floor. The orchestra sounded its last chord and Harley crisply lowered his arms. Impeccable timing found him dropping his hands almost to the floor as he bowed to the wall.

"Bravo! Bravo!" Harley screamed as the speakers crackled. He sat down in the chair and applauded with a few patters of his hands. "I'm exhausted but I love it."

"That was great."

"Well, it's almost seven, Frank. Sorry we didn't have more time to talk."

"No problem, Harley. I'll talk to you later. I'm going to check out the basement. Bye."

"Bye bye, Frank." Harley busied himself behind the desk.

Frank walked down to the basement and the maze of hallways and rooms, closets and storage areas instantly baffled him. He ducked to avoid colliding with bare incandescent bulbs dangling from cloth wrapped wire. In the dimly lit passages, dust particles danced in intermittent shafts of light from clerestories. He coughed and sneezed as fetid fumes, seeping from floor drains, pricked his nostrils.

Alligatored paint coated most of the wood. Opening a door, he saw shelving extending from floor to ceiling. He grabbed the lip of a shelf to check its strength and the entire unit spun around, ball bearings clicking, exposing another set of shelves. "Clever," he thought, then he choked on the putrescence of a rodent that had been trapped in the mechanism.

Some of the rooms he entered had more than one egress. One had a door that opened into a concrete wall. At the end of a long hallway, he entered what he thought was the tool storage area - the sign on the header read "Tools." Inside, the clutter of listing stacks of cardboard cartons, opened packages of napkins and tablecloths and note pads, reeking of mildew, bided in a veil of cobwebs.

He walked up a set of stairs and found himself in the kitchen where another set of steps led down. He took those and found himself at the point from which he'd just ascended. "Bizarre!" he muttered.

Frank meandered through several more dens and storage rooms, made notes when he found the circuit breaker panel, and in the actual tool storage area - an old shower - he checked the inventory of screw drivers, hammers, saws and wrenches. He opened a small vented door labeled "Fasteners." Shelves of glass jars coated with dust and grime overflowed with screws, nails and bolts. What Frank thought was the skeleton of a cat, lay across the bottom of the closet. He closed the door and ducked instinctively as a dust cloud billowed from the door vents. Coughing and wheezing, he stumbled into the hallway.

At a different flight of stairs, a wall sign read "Kitchen," and he went up, thinking he could use another cup of coffee. At the top of the stairs was another unfamiliar room. He looked: hand painted wall paper, brass sconces, gold framed portraits, a sterling tea service on a sideboard. "What the hell is this place?" He closed the doors and walked down yet another set of stairs, thinking he'd end up where he'd started, but he landed somewhere else. "Where the fuck am I?"

He opened a door to a room labeled "Trunk Storage." A cot with a thin mattress stood against the far wall. A wool blanket, folded neatly, lay at one end of the cot and a pillow at the other. No sheets. A small table with a lamp and an electric clock sat against another wall and tee shirts and jeans hung in a small, open metal locker that stood against the wall by the door. Frank thought he smelled incense. "Somebody's living here?"

When he turned to walk out, his exit was blocked by a large swart man with straight black hair that brushed shoulders spanning the door frame. Coal black eyes - deep set in a countenance that might have been carved with a few strokes of an adze - offered no clues. A black tee shirt stretched across his massive chest and clung to his biceps. Tucked tightly into jeans held up by a braided leather belt, it hugged the ripples in his abdomen. An eagle soared on the belt's silver buckle. As Frank's eyes fell to the floor, he noticed the man's bare feet and fiery crimson toe nails. Frank introduced himself and reached out a hand.

The man nodded.

"I'm the new maintenance man and bartender," Frank offered.

The man nodded.

"Do you live here?"

The man nodded and stepped around Frank into the room. Frank stepped out. The man walked to the cot and lay down on the mattress. His feet hung over the end. "Nice to meet you," Frank said as he walked away.

Frank wiped sweat from his brow and mused. "Friggin' weird." He tried to gauge his location. He recounted his last steps and decided he was only a few feet from the lobby stairs, so he walked toward a storage area that looked familiar. He entered - another wrong turn; he went back into the hall. He tried another unfamiliar set of stairs. Finally, he opened the door at the top and stepped into the lobby. Harley was writing feverishly behind the front desk.

Frank opened the doors to the deck, breathed the fresh salt air deeply, turned and complained: "Christ, Harley, I was lost as blind drunk down there! What the hell goes on down there? And who the fuck is that giant?"

"Oh, Frank, don't worry. you'll get used to it," Harley sang. "You must've met Patrick. He lives there - in the basement. If he needs a few bucks, he works in the kitchen or helps with deliveries."

"Does he ever talk?"

"He doesn't say much, Frank. He only talks when he has to. He's all right, Frank. He keeps to himself. If you need a hand with something, just ask him."

"Yeah, right, Harley, and how would I find him?"

"You'll get used to it, Frank."

Frank shook his head as he walked to the kitchen for a much needed cup of coffee. Then he went up to inspect the guest rooms. In one, he caught a glimpse of the orange shag rug he'd seen in the brochure. He slammed the door and walked toward the other end of the corridor. He saw a padlocked door with a sign above it, "To the Observation Decks." He tried to jimmy the lock but it was secure, so he went to the lobby to get a key from Harley.

"Yeah, it's safe," Harley said, handing Frank the key. "Jack wants it locked to keep the crazies out."

Frank marvelled at the view from the top level of the observation deck. The fog had lifted and the harbor looked surreal - sails off in the distance and fishing boats like toys. A few hundred yards across the water sat a small island with trees alive in the wind. A lighthouse graced one end of it. Beyond that, a hill of green spotted with houses lined the other side of the harbor and rolled lazily to a rocky point at the mouth. The Atlantic slapped at the granite shore - white crests tumbling over the sandy brown. Above the tree tops, he could look down on the neighborhood roofs and below them, figures on the street walking in slow motion.

He unlatched the door that led out to the widow's walk and climbed out on the deck. Its stability surprised him, as did the railings' when he tested those. He noticed a circular pattern in the roofing below him and realized that the slates around the widow's walk were less weathered than those covering the rest of the roof. He looked at the island again; the trees wavered. The breeze smelled fresh and tasted salty.

"Frank is that you?"

Frank recognized Jack's voice. "Yeah, Jack," he said, "I just wanted to check this out." Then he climbed down the circular stairway and walked out into the second floor corridor. "Unreal!"

"Yeah, it is, Frank, but we've got to keep it locked or some bozo will try to sneak up there. We don't need any sky divers climbing out on the widow's walk and screaming at the pedestrians. It happened once and the neighbors called the fire department thinking the guy would jump. The chief was pissed and threatened to yank our permits." Frank frowned quizzically and Jack said, "No kidding!"

"What's the little island out there?" Frank asked. "Is it private?"

"Ten Pound Island, Frank. You can take a boat out there but they say it's infested with rats. Homer used to paint there. Lived in the light house."

"Winslow?"

"Yeah."

"No shit. That's amazing."

"Yeah, Frank, Patrick lived out there, too. Harley told me you've met him."

"Yeah, if that's what you call it. The guy didn't say a word."

"He doesn't say much, Frank. He's OK. He lived on Ten Pound for a couple of years - built a shack out of drift wood. I think he might have been a junkie. He'd row in at night and scavenge for food and clothes. Never bothered anybody but he sure scared the shit out of people who didn't know him. Then the city threw him off the island so we let him live in the basement. He helps out once in a while - washes dishes, cleans the kitchen. We pay him a few bucks. You'll see."

"Yeah, I know, Harley told me that."

"What else did Harley tell you, Frank?"

"Not much, just that I'd get used to it."

"You will." Jack smirked. When he reached the head of the stairs,

Jack turned and looked at Frank. Frank rubbed the back of his neck and stared at the door to the observatory. Jack chuckled to himself, remembering the night Frank walked to Barbara's and stood knocking at the door for forty minutes not realizing she was with Jack.

Frank quickly developed a daily routine. Coffee in the morning with Harley until seven and then the *Boston Globe*. He started his repairs and maintenance chores at eight. He worked until early afternoon, painting doors and window sashes, repairing screens and broken shutters. He cleaned the swimming pool and checked the pump filters. On Wednesdays, he mowed the grass and trimmed the hedge at the front of the hotel. From four to five, Frank napped in his room after a quick dip in the pool. Then he made himself a sandwich, showered and headed off to tend bar until closing at 1 A.M.

Jack had offered a tour of the bar, a converted storage area in the basement, during the orientation. The ceilings were extremely low because the reinforcing needed to support the addition of the sundeck above, borrowed from what little head room there was. Frank had to bend often - especially getting in and out of the back closet. It took some getting used to.

Jack had explained that the navigation maps of famous harbors decorating the walls were a cheap way to cover the homosote that had been there for years. He'd pointed with pride to his selections - Newport, Nantucket, St. John's, Block Island. Then he'd pointed to the entry and told Frank that the newest map covered a hole in the wall board a couple of fishermen had made during a disagreement about who should leave first. "They made a new door and left together," he'd said and laughed as he remembered the brawl. Jack said the menus on the ceiling gave the really drunk something to look at as they passed out.

"That bell at the end of the bar is a nice touch," Frank had said.

"It's for last call. You announce it at quarter of one and ring the bell. No bar service after one."

Frank had noted other enhancements to the nautical motif: a porthole in the door, glass topped, ship's wheel tables, captain's chairs, glass balls and fish net. A row of jalousie windows ran along the poolside wall where the grade dropped off to the pool apron. They reminded Frank of Florida but he eventually discovered their real value. "In the morning," he'd later written to a friend on the back of a postcard, "the stench of alcohol, soggy cigarette butts and mildewed carpet is wicked." When he worked in there repairing tables and chairs, Frank cranked open the windows and took deep breaths. Behind the highly polished mahogany bar, a seamless mirror reversed the entire room. On busy nights, Frank would cringe as he gazed into the mirror and saw himself as a silhouette in a sea of bobbing heads. A Lautrec poster.

Frank didn't open his bar until six because most nights, the cocktail crowd stayed upstairs on the deck watching the glorious sunsets. The sundeck adjoined the dining room so Jack and a couple of waitresses worked from the service bar. The spectacle of a Cape Ann sunset attracted throngs to Rackliffe House; Frank was never very busy until after eight o'clock.

While he stocked coolers and shelves, crushed ice and polished the mahogany bar, Frank enjoyed the few regulars, mostly fishermen and other locals who came in early and talked colorfully about Red Sox baseball, new government regulations, cost of fuel. Fishermen liked telling Frank where the best places were to meet women other than on Rocky Neck. Women fancied Frank's boyish smile and often invited him to the after hours parties they frequented. They'd leave an address and some secret code to be sure Frank could get in. One night Frank went to an after hours party, knocked at the door and said, "Hello," and a voice replied, "That's the password. Come on in."

The first night he'd opened, Frank had met Donna Pearce. "Born and bred right here in Glosta," she'd said before she'd introduced herself. Then she'd shoved her blunt-nailed, long-fingered hand out over the bar and said, "Hi, I'm Donna Peeahrs. Who're you?"

Frank introduced himself but Donna, tugging at a strap on her green tank top, had already resumed her story: "Moved ovah the bridge to Bevlee for a yeahhr then up to Rahllee. Hole in the wall but OK. Folks run a dinahr theahr. They used to cut fish at Gahrton's but they saved some money and bought the dinahr so they could make more and send me to college. Moved back here after I quit. College, y'know. I'm a native so why not. Rent 'n apahrtment ovahtown - Portugei Hill. Waitress at the dinahr during the day to help the folks out. Usually go out. The Neck in the summer. New faces. Some of the locals I see every summahr but the othahrs change. Fun place. Meet all kinds." She'd adjusted the other strap on her tank top and wiggled on her stool as she tugged at her tight jeans.

Donna'd been an art major at Bristol Hall in upstate New York but she'd left after a year because she thought it was a waste of money. She'd told Frank math and history were useless when all she wanted was to paint. "And," Donna'd said, "I really got sick of those dip shit rich girls who did nothing but fuck, drink and look for a husband. Pains in the ahs and full a shit. All they talked about were the tags on their clothes - designahr names inside, prices outside. Like some of the ahsholes up on the deck. Y'know, Frank?"

"Nice to meet you," Frank had said.

Donna, in a tank top and a snug pair of blue jeans, exuded an understated but enticing sexuality. Her warm brown eyes wanted. But her short straight brown hair bouncing with the twists, tilts or nods of her head that punctuated her stories, always seemed frivolous. Her stride in clopping work boots downplayed her lush curves, and her gruff speech contradicted her femininity. "Hello. Frankie boy," she'd say as she straddled a bar stool. "Gimme a beahr." Donna'd ignore Frank's hello, bolting along, dispensing with any further civilities. "You know, Frank," she'd say, "well maybe ya don't, so I'm about to tell ya." Frank had to listen as Donna'd harangue about something - anything - presently on her mind.

Frank liked the "Glosta" accent - as severe as most he'd heard - beahr, idehr, lobsta, Glosta, ahshole, but often, Donna'd correct herself mid-phrase. She told Frank that she worked at losing it but sometimes she slipped. And Frank noticed how Donna sipped a beer: pursed lips, tilting her head, her eyes glued to her reflection in the mirror behind the bar. "Like she's checking to make sure she's here," he'd told himself. She'd run her hand back through her hair and cock her head to one side. "Challenging something." Then she'd talk and he'd listen.

The Friday night of Memorial Day weekend, Frank came in early to stock extra bottles near the speed racks and make sure the beer coolers were full. He brought an extra tub of ice down from the kitchen and left it on the back counter. He was polishing the bar when Donna bolted through the door and mounted her usual stool. She waved Frank over. "Gimme a beahr. Quick, Frank," she heaved.

"Sure, Donna. Everything OK?"

"Fucken A, Frank, don't those ahsholes make y'nuts when they come

In a Place Like No Other

down here after the sunset. I mean, ahh, y'know, the gold coastahs." Frank listened closely as Donna ripped through the preppies, partying up on the sundeck in their bright pink, green and blue Izod shirts with that little alligator over the left nipple and the color coordinated cotton sweater over their shoulders - a knot in the sleeves; Madras shirts, pressed khahkis, penny loafers and Docksiders and Bermuda shorts. Donna snickered as she described the knee socks - always black - that went with the shorts. Then she complained about the girls in their flowered dresses and skirts and said, "If they had an ahs_*ass*, they'd wear tight white jeans. Most of 'em don't though." She paused and swigged her beer, coughing as she continued to talk before she'd swallowed, "Big straw sun hat with a colored ribbon and sunglasses. Oh yeah. Almost forgot - those friggin' pink or lime green pumps with the basket weavin' around the bottom."

Frank said, "Espadrilles," and Donna gawked. Her eyes widened then she screwed her mouth and asked, "How'd y'know that?"

"History," Frank said.

"Anyway," she continued, "some nights that deck looks like a box of salt watahr taffy. It's like a cult thing. They all stand around and sip white wine spritzahrs or drink Heinekens and talk about travellin' or whatever. Then when the sun goes down, they all come down here, listen to music and dance - if that's whatcha call it. Jack, that jerk, hires this band that plays nothing but oldies 'cause that's what Bippy and Muffy like - and Jack likes boppin' Bippy and Muffy. If I hear that Beach Boys medley one more time, I think I'm going to puke. They stand round impressin' each other with the bullshit about where they've been and who they've been with. Big deal."

"Well, it's a big deal to them. What the hell, if it makes them happy," Frank said.

"Yeah, I suppose. Maybe. Probably you're right but sometimes it really pisses me off."

"What do you mean?"

"That peckerhead Richie Barnes."

"Is he up there now?"

"Yeah, saw him when I walked in."

"OK, I get it," Frank said.

"You get what, dickhead. Don't interrupt. I'm talkin' here." Then Donna burst into a description of a hot night she'd spent with some guy named Richie Barnes last August. They'd been dancing at the Party Boat Lounge and decided to go to Richie's family home on Eastern Point to swim in the pool. Richie had pot so he and Donna got high and hot then Richie's grandfather caught them "bahreass naked and ripped to the gills," Donna said. Richie'd told his grandfather that Donna had brought the pot her fisherman boyfriend had given her, and that he'd only been experimenting. Donna cringed, then she pursed her lips to imitate Richie's grandfather. "Well, Richahrd, let that be a lesson. Yawhr a Hahrvahd mahn. Mix with yawhr kind. He had one of those fake English accents or somethin', Frank. You know what I mean?"

Frank nodded.

Donna continued saying she got dressed and had to walk three and a half miles back to her apartment because Richie's grandfather wouldn't let him drive. She'd only gotten to the stone pillars at the end of Eastern Point when Richie screeched up and woozily told her his grandfather had fallen asleep, so he'd come to give her a ride home. In the car, she saw Richie didn't have any pants on so she asked what he was doing and he said he wanted sex. Donna's frown changed quickly to a broad smile as she slapped the bar and yelped, "Know what I said, Frank. I said 'Richie you can't. You ain't got any balls.'" Donna paused and swigged her beer. Then: "What time is it, Frank? I gotta get goin'. I can't risk bein' here when the friggin' Strahwberry Alahrm Clock starts playin' - that'll make me shithouse."

Frank laughed. He didn't want Donna to leave. "Hey Donna, what about those guys?" Frank motioned toward two men at a table with a jerk of his head. "Tell me about 'em. I like your style."

"Locals, townies, like me. Wear jeans and tee shirts or tank tops. Guys like 'em 'cause it shows their muscles. Girls like 'em 'cause o' . . . " Donna paused, brow furrowed, and placed both hands under her breasts. She lifted and exclaimed, "These!"

Frank sniggered.

"You laughing at my tits?"

"No. They're nice." Frank blushed and turned away. Then he turned back, smiled and said, "I just like your . . . "

"Fucken A. They ain't bad, are they?" Donna pushed more; her nipples almost broached the neck of her blue tank top.

"Not at all."

Donna shot a quick glimpse to the mirror. "Anyway, sometimes the guys like to wear those luau shirts but only if they got more hair on their chest than a friggin' poodle. They unbutton it down to their balls and the gold chains'll clank together like they were carrying the incense in a church parade." Donna sighed and took a swig of beer.

Frank watched: she scratched at the label on her beer bottle and looked at her reflection; turned her head and brushed a wisp of her hair back, over her right ear; nodded to herself in the mirror. "Take the aht _art types. Hippies, I guess. They're up there on the deck with the sunset crowd, too. Probably trying to snuggle up to some of 'em with bucks so they can get famous. Bunch a dogs."

Frank turned and looked into the mirror at her reflection. "What are you looking at?" he asked.

"Oh, nothing. Just that . . . oh, damn, it is. Shit! Split ends." She grabbed a lock of her hair and pulled it around to her crossed eyes, then pushed it back. She glared at Frank. Then she continued with her description of the artists: torn sweaters and sweat shirts, paint globbed all over, Earth Shoes or sandals. She nodded her head at a couple that had just walked in and were holding hands over a table in a dark corner. "Ovahr there. See what I mean! She's got it down - frayed collar, sandals. Turquoise earrings dangling to her shoulders. Nice touch. Real original. He's splashed paint all over his jeans and, oh man, the shoes. Beret's nice, too. Check those shoes."

"Earth Shoes?"

"Yup."

"Artists." Frank proudly inflated his chest.

"Whoaaa, Wait a minute, Frankie boy. Almost missed that. Friggin' Greek fishahrmens' hats. Nobody from around here would be caught dead in one of those. Nobody I know. They gotta be from the city. Probably staying in Rockport. Here to make the scene. Probably work at an ad agency. New Yahrk. Y'know, spend a couple of weeks hanging around with ahrtists, get their creative juices restored. Crock a shit. Five bucks says their drivin' a Caddy."

Frank looked carefully, turned to Donna and said, "Maybe. Maybe not. Maybe they're just like the rest of us, Donna. Just here for a while to lay back; figure out a next move. Maybe they don't care about a next move. Maybe they're just here to escape."

"No way! That's like tryin' to convince me the tourists come here to relax. Ha. You see 'em every night wearin' suits and ties and evening dresses. You can't get down and dirty in that shit, Frank. It'll cost you a fortune to clean it - especially those leisure suits the guys wear. Y'know those, Frank? Tangerine's my favorite color. White belt and white shoes, shirt collahr ovah the lapels. As much gold as the altar boys. Saw a bunch of 'em walking toward me one night last summer. One guy in lime green, one in raspberry and one in baby friggin' blue. Can you believe that? I ran like hell. Thought it was a science fiction movie. Y'know "Invasion of the Killer Popsicles" or somethin'. Geeezuz, Frank, I know I had a few beahrs but they looked like they'd had a bad run in with a pie truck or somethin'."

"Geez, Donna, what happened to the sixties? Do your own thing. Peace. Love. Brotherhood of man. All that stuff."

"You forgot one, Frank."

"What's that?"

"Here come da judge," Donna quipped. She slapped the bar and winked at her reflection, then raised her right fist above her head and yelled, "Right on, baby!"

Frank laughed. He scanned the bar and saw someone seated over by the windows. "OK, Donna. How about that one?" He pointed with his chin.

Donna turned and glanced at a man in a yellow Nehru jacket with gold chains and beads around his neck, torn jeans smudged with paint, and sandals. He had long reddish hair tied back in a ponytail and aviator sunglasses. Donna chuckled, "Ruthie's brother maybe. I don't know. That's what I'd call a real fashion fart. Here one second gone the next."

Frank had to turn away and walk into the passageway. His belly ached from laughing so hard and he could barely hear Donna. Then she called hoarsely, "Come on, Frank, I got time for one quick story, then I gotta go. You gotta heahr this one. It's a beaut."

Frank wiped his eyes, walked back and asked Donna if she wanted another. She looked around. "Yeah, sure," she said, "But drag it. With my luck Wayne Newton'll show up."

A couple of fishermen at the bar clamored for beer. "Wait, Donna. Right back."

When Frank came back, he opened her bottle and placed it on the bar before he realized that she was in the middle of another story about a singer Jack had hired last summer. "It's hot as hell in here and he's wearin' Frye boots and a leathahr suit with those silly thin sunglasses," she said. "Then he does the long version of *In-A-Gadda-Da-Vida* and he's bangin' away on his guitar and the fishermen are booin' and hissin' and the guy stops and says he's gonna do *American Pie* and somebody yells out "The long version?" and he says "Yeahhhh," in a low voice like he's at a Holiday Inn or somethin' and the whole place just freaks. Everybody runs for the door. Jack goes nuts because the first drink was free that night, he wanted a big crowd. Well he got one, but they all beat it. Jack was bullshit. Nobody spent a dime."

"What happened? Jack fire the guy?" Frank asked.

"Didn't have to. The guy walked over to Jack and said 'I'm an ahrtist. I don't need this shit.' Packed up his stuff and left."

Frank grinned. The sounds of chairs and feet scraping the deck filtered down. Donna slapped a few bills on the bar. "Sun's down. I'm outta here. Keep the change. See ya soon. It's fun talkin' to ya."

Frank nodded, hoping he'd see Donna soon.

Chapter 3

Intimate: conversations under the covers.
Talk to friends. Bang your lovers.
Ishmael and Queequeg were gay.

Call me Ahab
Les Moor
1968 The Aviary Papers Publishers

Saturday night, the fog horn moaned as Frank crossed to the bar from the cottage a little after six in rain driven by cold onshore winds. A little late but Frank figured the weather would slow things down. Donna, arms crossed, hooded in a yellow slicker, shivered under the awning. "Glad you could make it," she said. "I thought maybe you'd headed back to N'Yawhk or something. I'm freezin' my ahs, I mean *ass* off here waiting for you, Frank." The buoy out by Ten Pound Island clanged.

"New York!" Frank pushed the door open and walked to the bar. "Sorry, Donna. Draggin' a little today."

Donna close behind said, "Don't let the rawr weather get you down, Frank. It'll blow out. Cats and dogs only lasts a day or two. It's the wintahr nor'eastahs y'gotta watch out for. Bury you alive." She shook her slicker and tossed it over the back of a bar stool.

"It's not the weather, Donna," Frank groused slamming the cash drawer. "It's my folks. They want to visit." Frank fumbled with ashtrays and bottles then handed Donna a beer. "War's on again." He wiped the bar.

"Viet Nam?" Donna asked and Frank said:

"No, the friggin' family war. They're still bustin' my ass about quitting my job. I moved in with them when I went back to work at the mill. Big mistake. All they did was bitch about me not using my education, wasting my life. You've got no goals. You on drugs like the rest of your hippie friends? Use your degree. Make something of yourself. Get a real job. All that shit. When it got really bad, they'd say no wonder Allie left. Loser." Frank stared at his reflection in the mahogany as he kept at the bar. Rain drops splattered on the deck above.

"You have a degree?" Donna said.

"Yeah, I graduated a few years ago and had a job. That sucked. I made a lot more money at the paper mill."

"Who's Allie?"

"A woman at school. We were pinned. Then we lived together."

"Pinned?"

"Yeah, I gave her my fraternity pin. We were steady - kind o' like engaged."

Donna's sarcasm was obvious as she quipped about how she'd been pinned a few times: a linebacker named Teddy from Dartmouth, on her dorm floor; a hockey player from R.P.I. in his MGB; and a swimmer from Union but she couldn't remember a name or where.

"Sport fucking," Frank sniped.

At first Donna scowled. Then: "Crack me up, Frank! Not bad. You are funny sometimes, Frankie boy. Was she smahrt and beautiful with a closet full of Pucci?"

"Who?"

"The girlfriend who dumped you, Frank. Try to keep up. OK?"

"Yeah."

"Espadrilles?"

"Yeah."

"Ahhhh."

"What?"

"Nothing. Ask her to marry you?"

"No." Frank eyed Donna more curiously. "I really wasn't thinking about it, yet."

"What happened?"

"She moved in with my best friend, Chuck. I called him one night and she answered the phone. She said she'd have told me sooner but she didn't know how."

"Bullshit! She was hedgin' her bets. Wanted to be sure ol' Chuckie boy was really interested before she gave you the pink slip."

"Could be. I kind of suspected. She was out late a lot of nights. Came home smelling of Chanel and I'm allergic to it. I knew something was up."

"Yeah, Chuckie!"

"Funny." Frank grimaced.

"I owed you one. Couldn't resist. Hey, look. That really sucks but hey, you'll get ovahr it. She was just following the pattern."

"What pattern?"

"You know. The pattern. You grow up thinking life's going to school, graduating, getting married, getting laid and having babies. You don't think about it. You do it. Everybody does it so that's what you do."

"I don't know. Maybe she was in love with Chuck not me."

"Nahh. Were you doin' it?"

"Doin' what?"

"You know, Frank, doin' it. Were you two screwing?"

"Yeah, but, hey, keep your voice down, will you. We've got other customers here." Frank paused and looked around. Donna stared at the mirror and twisted the ends of her hair. The groan of the fog horn permeated the room as Frank whispered, "OK. Go ahead. What's screwing got to do with it? Everybody does."

"Right, Frank but things changed. The getting laid and getting married parts of the pattern got reversed. You could get laid before you got married. See?"

Donna studied her reflection and rushed on. "Listen, Frank. If you were getting laid before you got married, then the getting married and getting pregnant part of the pattern became optional, not like before, y'know. Then you were married or you weren't getting any." Frank wiped at his cheek where a spray of beer had landed.

"So, Frankie boy, if you were living together and getting it regularly, she left because for her the last parts of the pattern weren't optional. She had to do it."

"Or she wanted to. She was in love. Changes everything."

"Franko, get your head outta your ahs_*your ass*. A woman can screw around unless she's in love. Women can't be in love with two guys at once. Oh yeah. I know they say, "We're liberated, I am woman," all that happy horseshit, but take it from me, they can't. Men can. They do it all the time. Just 'cause a guy's in love with you, it doesn't mean he can't screw around. But if a woman's in love with you, she can't screw around. So, Frankie boy. If she was doin' it with Chuckie at the same time, then she wasn't in love with Chuckie, she was just fitting him into her pattern."

Frank stared blankly into the room, unconsciously wiping the bar. He noticed the splattering of rain on the deck had abated to torturous drips from the awning. The faint clanging of the bell buoy drifted past.

"So, what was really going on? Are you ready, Frank?"

"I guess." Frank kept polishing.

"Was she screwin' Chuckie while she was screwin' you?"

Frank stared into emptiness, twisting a towel around his fingers.

"Well, Frank! Was she?"

"Shit, I don't know. For all I know, they could have been sitting around talking. I never asked. I just left, I guess . . . "

"Oh, man, Frank, you're screwed. Either she was or she wasn't. Now you'll never know. You should have asked then. It's too late. Now all you can do is forget about it and move on. Don't think about it 'cause it'll make you nuts."

"Uhh," Frank mumbled.

Donna didn't seem to hear. She scratched at the beer bottle, glanced into the mirror and then looked sternly into Frank's eyes. "Here, Frank. Listen. There's a ton of women here all summer. You're decent looking enough. Sorta tall, kinda cute with those blue eyes and wavy hair. Not a bad ass, either." She leaned across the bar and leered; Frank twisted and looked down to check his buttocks. "Yeah, why not. You could get laid every now and then. So just forget about it. Fuck your brains out. Get your head straight."

The bell buoy clanged as Frank reeled - whipsawed. He shook his head, leaned back and bounced as the small of his back hit the edge of the shelf. He staggered a little, then serviced some customers who'd just walked in. Donna kept talking: "unless of course you're one of them." Frank snapped his head to look at her. "What?"

"Them," Donna nodded at two men sitting at a table behind her.

"What about them?"

"A fag."

"Oh!" He peered past Donna. "How do you know?"

"Hey, Frank, most of the time a girl can tell. Look at the clothes."

"Here we go! Donna's fashion assessments. Can't wait."

"You asked didn't ya? Look. Look at the old one. Clean cut, shirt just pressed, expensive shoes, more jewelry than Aht's."

"Aht's? Who? What Aht's?"

"Christ, Frank, been off The Neck? It's a jewelry store ovahtown."

"OK. I get it."

"Look at the younger one. James Dean."

Frank nodded. "Could be. I saw him with Harley."

"See."

"What about women? Can a girl tell if a woman's a lesbian or not?"

"Sure," Donna said. "so can men."

"I can't."

"Sure you can, Frank. What about me?"

"I don't know."

"Come on Frank!"

"I don't know."

"Hey, Frank, you got ten seconds or I'm ovah that bahr and you're black and blue."

"No!" Frank put his hands up.

"Right," Donna said, grinning.

"No, I meant, no, don't jump over the bar."

"Right. Like I said, good thing you got it right or I'd be really disappointed, Frank," Donna said. Gazing at her reflection, she tossed her head to one side, then demanded. "Are you or aren't you?"

"I thought a girl could tell, Donna."

"Well, yeah . . . sometimes. But some guys are really good at covering it up." They listened as the deck above creaked and groaned with movement and Donna said, "A quick story then I gotta go before the honeymoonahrs get here. They'll come early. No sun tonight."

"OK, you don't need my say-so, anyway."

"Ahh, right, Frank, you're starting to get it. See, this guy, Drew, you'll meet him, comes every year. Nice guy. Likes to talk just like me. Right here at the bar, I get talking to him. No ring so I figure he's single and I'm getting a little interested. See, he's kind of good looking. So we talk . . . " And for the next ten minutes, Donna told Frank about an Atlanta salesman who'd stumbled into Gloucester one summer and had fallen for another man at one of the piano bars. He came back every year to spend time with his lover. He had a wife and kids but never told them. "I mean like he's really good lookin', Frank." Donna's voice rose. "And I'm sittin' heah gettin' hot and he's tellin' me he's gay!"

"So are we," the men behind her said.

Frank chuckled. Donna stood and punched him in the arm. Then she turned and said to the gays, "I'm telling a story. You mind?" The men laughed and Donna turned to Frank and continued. "You'll meet 'em, Frank.

They're here every summahr. Some of them are year rounders. It may not be obvious. They keep pretty much to themselves. The world being what it is and all."

"Judgmental, Donna?"

"Yeah. Right. You got it, Frankie boy."

"Like you and the preppies and the artists and hippies and gays? Christ, Donna, everything doesn't happen according to your pattern."

"No, that's not the same," Donna said sharply. "Richie Barnes is a complete ahhshole and the rest of them are, too."

"Why, because they're different?"

"No. Because they're ahhsholes."

"Wow! I'm sold. Real ahhhssoles."

"Well, kiss my Glosta ahs, you sahrcastic bahstahrd. I was only trying to help. You don't know shit about me. Somehow I knew you could really piss me off, Frank. Now, you have." Donna threw a roll of bills on the bar. "Here," she yelled, "stick those up your ahs and rotate. Give y'self a cheap thrill. And by the way, dickhead, you never told me if you were gay." She bolted for the door.

Frank counted the money and yelled, "You got the cheap part right."

"Fuck you, Frank."

"You'd like to," Frank said.

"Well!" the two gay men said.

Frank looked at them and said, "I'm not gay."

"Too bad," they responded.

"You might as well be." Donna slammed the door.

Frank looked around the bar. Customers stared at him. "She gets a little excited," he said but the braying fog horn muffled his words. He forced a grin. Nobody laughed so Frank turned and shrugged at the mirror.

When Jack came into the bar, Frank, still bewildered, shook his head. Jack saw the look on his face and asked, "Everything OK, Frank?"

"Yeah," Frank said. "Minor altercation."

"Fight? Who? Should I get Patrick?"

"Nahh, it's OK, Jack."

The bar started filling up. The chatter rose, the fog horn groaned as someone dropped a quarter in the juke box and Blind Faith couldn't find their way home either. Two women hopped up on stools at the far end hollering, "Hi, Jackie." Frank thought, "Tough night for the sunset crowd."

"Frank. Hey, come here. Meet a couple of friends," Jack said, gesturing. Annie Barnes was a tall dark, green eyed brunette with perfect cheek bones and pouty red lips. Missy Dahlgren was a perfect contrast: short, plump, blonde hair, big blue china doll eyes. The two women each reached out a hand.

Frank took Annie's hand first. "Nice to meet you," he said. They giggled, speaking in unison, "Nice to meet you, too, Frank."

After Frank had taken their orders, "Cape Codders," they giggled again. Jack, as usual, took over the conversation and told the girls how glad he was that Frank had finally made it out to Gloucester. "I've told him a hundred times what a great place it is, and finally he listened," Frank heard as he returned with the drinks.

"Best place in the world to spend the summer," Missy said to Frank. "After the winter in New York, this place is such a relief."

"What do you do in New York?" Frank asked.

"Graphic design," Missy said fluttering her mascara laden eyelashes.

"She's incredibly talented," Annie said running her finger around the rim of her glass. She was speaking to Frank but smiling at Jack. He winked at her.

"Oh, Annie," Missy giggled. "You're so cute. You always say the nicest things to me. You're such a sweet friend. Isn't she cute, Frank?"

"Very," Frank said. The two women looked at each other and giggled.

Then Jack asked Annie if she still needed a brochure to send to her friends and when Annie said she did, Jack told her to come up to the lobby and he'd find one. She asked about a deposit and Jack said, "A hundred'll cover it, Annie," so Annie borrowed fifty dollars from Missy saying she'd left her checkbook at home. After Annie followed Jack, Frank and Missy talked about how beautiful Gloucester was in the summer. Minutes later, Annie came back to the bar flashing the brochure. Missy asked when her friends were visiting and Annie shrugged. Missy nodded and turned to Frank. "Jack seeing anybody special this summer?" Frank said he didn't know and she winked at Annie. Both she and Annie smiled.

"What do you do, Annie?" Frank asked.

"I'm still in college. I have one more year at Bristol Hall. I'm a dance major."

"Oh," Frank said. "Donna Pearce was here earlier. She was at Bristol.

You know each other?"

Annie looked down. Missy stared into the mirror.

"Know her?" Frank asked again.

"Well . . . ah," Annie said. "I guess. I mean, once when I was a sophomore, she walked up to me and introduced herself and said she was from Gloucester. But I don't really know her. Besides, she's not really from Gloucester. She's from Rowley."

The band had set up their equipment and Frank took them a few beers. As he slid back behind the bar, Missy said, "Don't you just love these guys, Frank? They're the best. They know every great oldie there ever was. The Beach Boys! The Neil Diamond songs they can do! Fabulous!"

"I love the Beatles," Annie chimed, swaying a little. Her hand slid back and forth along the mahogany bar as her Docksider tapped against the brass foot rail. The guitar player heard her, riffed through the opening of *Day Tripper* and Annie got up to dance. She gathered her brown waves into a ponytail as the drummer and bass player raised the volume. Then Annie swirled on her long legs, head back, eyes closed, hands above her grasping for the rhythm in the air. She twisted her torso then flowed in a new direction. Her arms, liquid, beckoning, enticed a couple of onlookers. They jumped to their feet as Annie passed but she spurned their jagged steps and flailing arms and spun away.

Frank said to Missy, "I've never seen anyone dance like that. She's unreal!"

"Isn't she," Missy said. "Just darling. And that skirt. Lilly Pulitzer - so cute."

Now people streamed into the bar and the room became a mass of writhing sweating bodies cloaked in a haze of cigarette smoke. Frank had turned to grab a bottle from the shelf. He could hear Donna's fashion appraisals as he watched the mirror full of bobbing heads and waving arms. Voices roaring with delight nearly overwhelmed the band.

More men tried to get Annie's attention, but she ignored them with a snap of her head. They ducked as her long ponytail whipped around. "She's got every guy in the room fantasizing about her," Frank thought to himself as he watched a couple of women shrug, then jab their partners in the ribs to refocus their attentions when Annie danced by. Over by the juke box, he saw a couple of guys doubled over in agony. "Must have been a little too fixed on Annie," Frank chuckled to himself.

When the band took a break, Annie danced to her seat and sighed, "God that feels good. I just love to dance. Do you, Frank?" Annie focused on her reflection in the polished mahogany.

"Yeah, sometimes, but you're out of my league, Annie. You're incredible."

"Isn't she just marvelous," Missy sighed.

"Jack's a great dancer," Frank said.

"I know," Annie said still fixated on her image in the bar. "We went dancing a few times last year. Earl's, downtown. Had a great time."

"I love dancing," Missy said. "I wish I could dance like you, Annie. Men go wild when they watch you."

"I don't even notice," Annie said, still staring into the mahogany. "I'm in my own little world out there." Annie got up and told Missy she'd be right back as she sauntered to the rest rooms. Two men walked into the bar and over to Missy.

"Hi, Rich," Frank heard Missy say.

Frank offered service. "What would you like?"

Missy took the opportunity and introduced Frank. "Frank, this is Annie's brother, Rich . . . "

"Richie," the man said, interrupting Missy.

"Nice to meet you," Frank said as he reached out his hand. A sweet aroma drifted across the bar. "Grass," Frank said to himself.

"And this is Peter Foster," Missy said.

Frank nodded and took their orders. Richie asked for a Stinger and Peter ordered a Heineken.

"Right away," Frank said. He turned to get their drinks.

"Where's Annie?" Richie asked Missy.

"She's in the girls room, Richard."

"Into the candy already?" Richie asked.

Missy looked puzzled. Richie grinned at Peter.

"Here you go," Frank said as he placed their drinks on the bar. "Let's see, two seventy five for the stinger and a buck fifty for the beer. Four and a quarter'll do it."

Richie handed Frank a five dollar bill and Frank put seventy five cents change on the bar. Richie picked up two of the three quarters and put them in his pocket. Frank watched as Richie checked out the room and sipped his Stinger. The conversation caught his ear.

"Could be some action tonight," Richie said to Peter.

"Yeah," Peter said. "Check out the two chicks over by the windows."

"Whoa! Couple of townies. Look at the set on the blonde. Love those tank tops."

"What do you say, Richie?" Peter asked.

"Give it a few more minutes, Peter. Let them get an eyeful first."

Annie came back from the ladies room. Peter stood to offer the seat.

"Where've you been, princess?" Richie said "Powdering your nose?"

Annie ignored her brother but when Peter guffawed, said crisply, "Fuck you, Peter."

"Your place or mine, Annie?" Peter said.

"Make it yours," Richie said. "Hers is a mess. Tissues all over the floor. The maid bitched to Grandfather, but I covered her ass and told him she was making decorations for the dance at the yacht club."

"Funny, Richie," Annie said. "Blow it out your ass."

"Do you have a cold?" Missy asked her friend.

"A little," Annie said.

"Speaking of blow," Richie said. "Got any extra with you, Sis? We could probably use it to score those chicks."

"Richie, get a life. You want it, you buy it just like I do. Don't be such a cheap prick."

"Fuck you, Annie."

Frank walked over to check on his customers.

"We're cool," Richie said.

The band cranked up their amplifiers and announced, "Everybody's favorites, The Beach Boys." The drummer banged out the introduction to *Surfin' Safari* and the floor filled. Heads bounced and arms jerked up and down. The cacophony rolled across the room and Missy hooted "I love it," as she jumped to the floor. Frank watched as she pumped her arms up and down in that exaggerated milking motion called the jerk. Her head bobbed forward and back and her knees pumped up and down as fast as the arms. She looked like an arthritic Tennessee Walker, as awkward as Annie was graceful - but she smiled broadly as she motioned to Annie to come join her. Annie declined.

Frank watched her curvet a while longer then glanced across the room at Rich and Peter escorting a couple of girls to the dance floor. The women danced wildly and Peter and Rich were even more ungainly at the boogaloo or whatever it was than Missy. Then Richie and Peter turned to face each other and acted like they were strumming guitars.

"What the hell's that?" Frank asked Annie.

"What?" Annie said.

"Richie and Peter - watch."

"They call it air guitar," Annie shouted over the music. "I call it boys pretending to have a dick. They'll get over it . . . in ten or twenty years. Not to worry, Frank."

Frank laughed. "Annie, do you want another drink?"

"Sure," Annie yelled back, "another Cape Codder."

"Right," Frank shouted back.

Frank placed it on the bar for her. He grabbed a couple of bills from the pile she'd left there and brought back change. Annie watched the dancers and Frank watched Annie. "She's beautiful. She must dance in her sleep. Wouldn't mind her dancing in mine," he thought as she swayed gracefully. Frank slowly walked to the other end of the bar to take an order from a waitress.

Jack was back at the other end of the bar when the band took their final break at eleven thirty. They'd start up at midnight to finish the evening. Jack watched the crowd and talked to Annie and Missy. Frank looked over at them. "Jack looks happy," Frank muttered to Pam when she picked up a tray of drinks. Pam scoffed. Rich and Peter departed the haze with the two townies.

Frank was heading toward Jack and his friends when the door opened and a group of three men and four women walked in. Frank stopped mid-stride, leaned forward and gawked. One of the men had a stainless steel halo bolted into his head. It stood on stainless steel rods fastened to leather pads that rested on his shoulders. Underneath the framework: a shaved head, a full, red beard and black rimmed dark glasses. A tall leggy redhead in a very short, very tight black cocktail dress strutted close behind him.

The man's arms were held out from his shoulders at a ninety degree angle by a cast that covered him from his waist to his neck and out to his elbows. His forearms dangled as he walked through the room. People said, "Hello, Bobby," and he had to twist his torso each time to return their greeting. He flapped his forearms and hands in a feeble wave. Trailing by a step, the redhead bowed intermittently; her mound of frizzed hair bounced and shimmered.

Frank whispered to Jack, "What the fuck? He looks like a scarecrow auditioning for the *Wizard of Oz*. A straw hat and he's in."

"You're about to meet the infamous Bobby Crosby," Jack chortled. "You'd better make him a drink fast, Frank, before he sobers up and sees how much pain he's really in."

Jack whispered to Missy and Annie; Frank walked over to wait on his new customers. "What can I get you, folks?" Frank asked.

"Folks?" Bobby Crosby queried. He removed his dark glasses to uncover deep green eyes that darted up and down and sideways - endlessly. "We, my friend, are not folks. We are hip. New York hip, by the way. Folks, my dear boy, are country people. Farmers, truck drivers, the like. We, on the other hand, are urbanites - sophisticated city dwellers."

The entourage twisted and twirled, giving Frank a fuller picture than he needed. The tall redhead turned sharply several times, offering profiles and full front and rear views. Posing a glimpse of her stunning bottom, she cocked her head back and scrutinized Frank with sassy green eyes, chin resting on her shoulder. Winking, she stretched a strand of her tightly curled hair to her mouth and nibbled; Frank admired appropriately: smacked his lips, raised his eyebrows and nodded. Then he looked directly at Bobby Crosby and said, "Whatever you say. Let me rephrase that. What the *fuck* can I get you folks?"

The entourage sniggered. "Fabulous, fucking fabulous," Bobby Crosby howled. "Yahoo! Jack's finally hired a bartender with a fucking sense of fucking humor. Great!"

The entourage applauded. "Fantastic. Super. Stupendous. Marvellous," they chimed.

"I'm Bobby Crosby." He straightened a finger intending a hand shake.

Frank took it and introduced himself to the group. The redhead breathed, "You're a cutie, Frankie," as she scanned him again from head to toe. "What's going down?" Then, she covered her mouth with her hand and giggled through crimson nails, "Ououou. Oh me oh my. Maybe me, if I'm not careful."

"That's enough of that shit," Bobby Crosby said. "Come on, Frank, get us refreshments."

"What'll you have?" Frank asked.

"Six White Russians and two Martinis straight up, three olives," Bobby ordered.

"You got it."

Frank passed the drinks down the bar and they toasted, "To The Neck," and sipped their drinks. Bobby had a finger around the stem of his Martini glass when he yelled, "Help me out here, will ya?"

The redhead jumped. "Sure, Bobby," she said, picked up the glass and poured the Martini into his mouth.

"Yeeeeeha," Bobby yipped after he'd swallowed. "Come on baby, olives. Gimme olives."

The redhead carefully placed the toothpick with three olives between Bobby's teeth. He clamped down on them and dragged them into his mouth one by one. "Deeeelicious," Bobby hollered and dropped to sit on the edge of a bar stool.

"Come on baby, hit me again," he said.

The redhead picked up the other Martini and turned to face Bobby. When she did, her breast brushed Bobby's face. "Sorry, honey," she said.

"Not to worry," Bobby said. "I'll need another mouthful of that after my next drink. Let'er rip, baby."

The redhead obliged and when she'd finished, Bobby leaned as far forward as he could and stuck his face into her cleavage. He gave each breast its own Bronx cheer. When he'd lifted his head, Bobby said, "I could live in there for a month, darlin'."

"Why don't you try, then," she said, easing her chest toward his face.

The entourage cheered wildly.

When the band tuned up for their last set, Bobby Crosby lamented. "Balls! It's the Beach fuckin' Boys. Drink up gang. We're outta here. Into the night. To The Neck."

The entourage gulped and followed as Bobby twisted and turned his way through the crowd. At the door, Bobby turned and cried out, "Be True to Your School, Frank. Back soon."

Frank waved good bye, walked over, mouth agape and looked at Jack. Jack roared with laughter.

"I know you said the place was nuts, Jack. That was a friggin' freak show," Frank said.

"I told you, Frank."

"What's the story?" Frank's bewildered look grew more so.

"Bobby Crosby's a trust funder from New York. Family's loaded. He rents a room here every summer. He comes here for two months to drink and carouse. He's always drinking and he's always with a big group. I'm surprised he didn't try to screw the redhead right here. Polly banned him for life when he jumped up onto a table at the Galley last summer, dropped his pants and mooned the entire dining room. She had him arrested."

"Holy shit! Why'd he do it?"

"That's what the judge asked him. It was in the police notes. He told the judge, he shot the moon because he couldn't shoot the singer. "She sucked." Polly was ripped when she read it in the paper and called an attorney. She came up here looking for Bobby. She wanted to punch him out. I had to calm her down. It took almost a quart of gin, but I finally got her settled. Then Bobby walked into the lobby and when he saw Polly he flipped her the bird and said "fuck you Polly." They got into a fist fight right here." Jack pointed his finger up toward the ceiling to indicate the upstairs. "There were guests registering and one of them said, "My, what an exciting place this seems to be." I'll never forget that."

"I guess. What's the thing on his head, Jack?"

"He broke his neck last summer in the pool."

"Diving?"

"Yeah. He walked out to the pool one afternoon with nothing but a bikini bathing suit and a Martini. Did a perfect back two and a half off the board. When he came up, he was still holding the Martini glass with the olives in it. The crowd around the pool went wild so when he got out, he shimmied and dropped his bathing suit. A couple of guests were horrified, demanded a refund and Harley had to get them a room on the back shore. The others loved it.

Bobby went back to the board for another dive. Still had the glass in his hand. This time he cracked the back of his neck on the board as he went into the pool. I thought the bastard was dead. He ended up at Mass General and a month later he's back here drinking in the bar with that halo on. He had to wear the thing for six months."

"So why's he still wearing it?"

"Frank, did you notice the body cast? His wife caught him screwing one of the maids in their apartment in New York. She beat him senseless with a squash racket and shoved him down a flight of stairs. Reinjured his neck, broke four ribs and both arms. Cracked a collar bone."

"He's one crazy son of a bitch."

"Yeah. I heard it was Viet Nam. A mortar round or grenade or something went off real close to him. He almost died, I guess. He's still got metal in his head. Just be careful when he's in here, Frank, the guy's a lightning rod for trouble. Usually good natured but he can manage to get into it sometimes so keep your eye on him when he's around."

"What a fucking mess."

"What?" Jack asked.

"His life. That friggin' war. Everything, I think."

"Oh shit, Frank. Don't get going on the war. Please."

The band quit at twelve forty five. Frank had already given last call at the bar and he rang the bell for the others in the room. The place emptied out slowly but by one thirty, he'd closed down and locked the door. Some nights, he'd walk down to the gazebo and sit for a while watching the harbor. Tonight the rain had ended but it was still cold and raw so he went to the cottage. The fog horn blared.

Jack sat next to Annie Barnes on the couch in the living room. Annie, head back, eyes closed, muttered something about "great shit" and wiped at her nose with a tissue as Jack slid his hand under her skirt. Frank walked to his room and closed the door. He read a few of his favorite stories and then he took out a notebook and scribbled a few words: 'The scarecrow was the single most crazy person I've met -so far.'

Frank closed his notebook and turned off the light. Footsteps. Clambering up the stairs. He dozed off when the draggers started heading out; their puttering engines syncopated the creaking of the ceiling.

Frank danced through his dreams with Annie Barnes until Donna's voice shouting, "He's gay!" startled him awake. Then he tossed and thrashed to the clanging of the buoy and the droning fog horn. Figures drifted in and out of his fog bank wearing Bobby Crosby's halo. "Lucas!" Frank sat upright in bed.

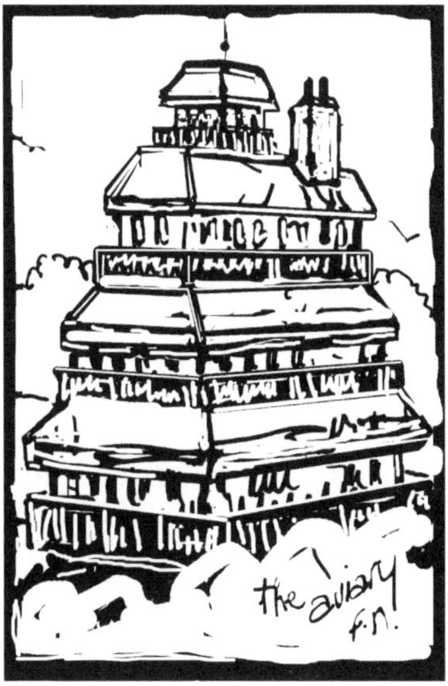
the aviary
F.N.

Chapter 4

Sounds of the city ringin' in my eahrs.

A Place Like No Other
Les Moor
1966 The Aviary Papers Publishers

Sunday morning, Frank sipped coffee on the deck and realized Donna was right - the front had moved off and the sun was bright. He had the day off so he decided to walk down The Neck and look around. Down the street, Ruthie sat whittling in front of a shack - garlands of fish netting draped over its cladding of weathered gray cedar shakes; colorful buoys accented the motif. The sign above the door read "Native Carvings." Ruthie'd donned a purple silk scarf to augment her customary ensemble. Frank watched as a man in a straw hat, luau shirt and shorts, and a woman in a flowery muu muu walked up to Ruthie and engaged her in conversation as she carved. When Ruthie reached down to tug on a sock, the couple whispered to each other. Then Ruthie handed the woman the walking stick and the man handed Ruthie a fistful of bills. Frank smiled and waved at Ruthie as he passed. She lowered her head and glared at Frank over her sunglasses.

Walking toward the Loft, he peeked through the windows of a couple of galleries, marvelling at impressionistic interpretations of the harbor and ocean. One painting caught his eye, a winter scene of a cove with ice blocks piled high at the shoreline. A boat was trapped in the ice, snow covered the houses in the background and children were running along the shore, jumping from one block of ice to another. A brass plaque was screwed into the frame. Frank read: "Running Buckolinos by Sam Murray."

A badly weathered red barn sat on pilings over the water. On the peak of the roof, a line of gulls yakked and screeched, defending their roosts from poachers. A sign over the door read: "Rooms by the week or month. Inquire within." "Might be nice to sleep over the water," Frank thought as he walked past. Then he noticed how the floor of the building sagged between beams and the battered porch railings undulated. "Maybe not," he concluded.

The sidewalk skirted the cove. Floats darted out from every building on the water; boats bobbed alongside. On the other side of the street, houses perched along the hillside to take in the sights. Turning at the Loft, Frank passed a few cottages resting precariously on the side of a knoll. Past a dilapidated shack, the harbor glistened. The road turned a corner to parallel the water, ending a few hundred yards away where a brick factory sat on a granite ledge. Its brick chimney with a bulbous cap rose forty feet above the ground. As Frank got closer and saw the detail of the brick work he reveled in the craftsmanship. His eyes searched along segmented arch windows that offered a panorama of the harbor to anyone inside, and he relished the detailing: brick corbeling at the eaves - masonry dentil work. "The building oozes sense of place," he thought as he read a plaque on one wall: "Tarr & Wonson Paints."

Frank decided to sit down for a while and watch the harbor. Fishing boats lined the piers on the opposite side; reflections of their brightly painted hulls slithered across the waves. Brightly painted buoys dotted the waves. An engine fired off and a puff of black smoke drifted up dissipating long before it reached the puffy whites scudding eastward. Frank listened: the high pitched whir of a grinder, the throaty roars of diesels, the fluttering and snapping of sails as yawls and sloops bounced through the wakes of power boats - all peppered with the forlorn cries of gulls swarming in a cloud around the stern of a dragger heading into port. Higher up, more gulls cawed and screeched as they glided, tilting their heads to gauge opportunities.

"Absolutely beautiful," Frank thought soaking up the sounds and colors as he surveyed the skyline he'd seen when he first drove into the city. He recognized landmarks he'd read about in a guide book he'd found in the hotel lobby: the green dome of City Hall sat on its sand colored clock tower, flanked on the left by the red cap on the white spire of the Universalist Church and the charcoal pyramid on the white steeple of the Trinity. To the right stood the aluminum steeple of St. Ann's capping a massive stone tower and the two blue domes atop the stucco facade of Our Lady of Good Voyage. Frank remembered: the locals called it the Church of the Fishermen. All of these sprung from an array of brick, granite and painted wood embedded in rolling verdure - their hues ricocheted across the water.

A gravel voice halted Frank's meditation, "Terst?" Frank turned and

Ed Touchette

saw a man and a black dog of indeterminate ancestry walking toward him. Frank said, "Hello." The dog turned back and sniffed his way down the road. Frank noted the age lines on the man's face, his grayed hair and a thick gray moustache under which drooped a moistly masticated cigar. The old man gnawed and puffed while he sat on the rock and spoke to Frank. He'd close his eyes and purse his lips, exhaling smoke in short bursts of grayish white puffs.

A small lobster boat came close to shore and the lobsterman reached into the water with a long gaff and grabbed a brightly colored buoy. The old man started telling Frank about his fifty two years as a lobsterman. The old man talked and Frank watched: a line got wrapped around a winch and a string of wooden traps came up out of the water. The lobsterman cleared each trap, added new bait and tossed a few small lobsters back.

"See," the old guy said, "Not much heahr this time a yeahhr." Then the old man yelled at the lobsterman, "Hey, Hackey, don't be so gawhd damned lazy. Get outside." The lobsterman waved, cranked the wheel and the boat moved off toward the other shore. The row of pots, lined up along the gunwale of the boat, slid down the rail and back into the water. A gull dove into the wake of the boat and snatched a morsel.

"Black back," the old man said, "tough bierd."

"Hard work?" Frank said.

"Ayeah," the old man replied. "But it's yahr own time."

They sat silent for a while and then Frank noticed a slew of draggers rocking alongside a motley array of weathered wooden buildings. Men worked around the boats and he wondered what was going on. He asked the old guy, who seized the opportunity to rattle on about the waterfront.

"The Fahrt? That theahr's the Eyetalian Fahrt."

"The what?" Frank was puzzled.

"The Fahrt. Put it up after Louisburg to keep the Frenchies from filchin' the fishin'. Then it kept the British out when we got sick a workin' for them. Fish whahves, now. Dealahrs buyin and sellin' fish theahr."

"Oh," Frank chuckled to himself. The man had meant "fort." The old timer continued: "The 'pahtment buildings behind the whahves was for immahgrint werkers. S'why they cahll it the Eyetalian Fahrt, now. The towahr with the red roof, that's Clahrnce Berdseye's building. Ben freesin' fish theahr a long time." The old man pointed as he talked and Frank's eyes followed storing details.

In a Place Like No Other

The old man expanded on what Frank already knew about City Hall and the churches. "Thaht theahr schoonah top the City Hall's whut made this place, I'll tell ya. And them churches give ya the faith ya need to keep fishin'. That one theahr, Saint Ann's, that ain't th 'riginal tawhr y'know. Hit by lightnin or somethin' while back. Now the Universalists mowahr pract'cal. Got faith and all but still got a lightnin' rod. See it theahr, on that little red cap on top. Ovahr theahr on, Portugei Hill, ayeah, the two blue domes. Church of the Fishahmen. Lady o' Good Voyage. All them houses going up the hill, well, that's wheahr a lot of the fishahmen live."

"Do you live there?" Frank asked.

"Nope."

Then Frank asked about the expansive concrete warehouses that lined the waterfront and about the freighters that were tied to their piers. Several lined the base of what the old guy called Portugei Hill.

"Jap freytehrs," The old man answered. "Fill 'em up with frozen fish and bring it in heahr to ship all ovahr the country. Some're Icelandic boats or from Eurpe but those big ones, like that, ah the Japs. Lotta fish sticks in theahr. Gahtons, ya know. Sells 'em all ovahr the wahld. Evahr have 'em?"

"No," Frank said, "but I've had Gorton's Cod Fish Cakes. I liked those. I recognized the fisherman when I drove past the statue."

"That ain't Gahton's. That's the man at the wheel. A memorial to remembahr all the fishahmen died at sea."

"I didn't know that. It sure looked like the guy on the Gorton's can."

"Ayeah, s'pose." The old man pointed. "Right over there. See them big houses up on the hill." He pointed more to the west. "Yeap. Them with the cupolas and towahrs risin' above the trees. Lots of houses like that 'round heahr. See," he said pointing toward the church steeples and City Hall in the middle of the harbor side. "Theahr's some theahr, too. Rich men made from the fishin' and tradin'. Lot of 'em gone, too. Too rich for the blood nowadays. A few still belong to families but lots of 'em bein' turned into 'pahtments and offices. Too much keepin' up."

A pulsating whir in the distance grew louder until it obliterated the sounds of the port. A helicopter skimmed over the hill at their backs and circled across the harbor. "Coast Gaahrd," the old man yelled through cupped hands. It landed in front of a brick building directly across from them, idled its engine and the conversation returned to a normal level.

Ed Touchette

"What are they doing?"

"Probably picked up some day sailahr fell off his yacht. Maybe a fishing boat went down. Some accident." The old man pointed. Frank saw flashing lights, an ambulance.

"Rescue?"

"Yup, could be anything. Those guys always get called. They always go. Good friends of mine, let me tell ya. Lost my engine once. They plucked me up before she smashed in the rahcks. Dangerous business, rescue work. Good bunch in my book - cep when they go out crackin' down on quotas and makin' sword boats dump a haul they think got smuggled in from the Canucks. Makes no sense to me, I tell ya."

They sat and looked out at the harbor. The helicopter lifted off and flew away. The old man smiled and waved as it passed over them. Then he got up and said, "Gotta get on." He looked around and hollered, "Come on, y' old dog."

"It was nice talking to you," Frank said. "Thanks for the tour. I'm Frank, by the way."

"Ayuh," the old man said as he turned away.

In a while, Frank decided to explore more of The Neck. At the end, he poked around the boat yard where a fishing boat had been hauled out of the water. Supported by thick, creosote and oil soaked timbers and blocks under its keel, it rested on a platform that slid along rails. Men chipped paint from rusted metal, chinked seams and rolled paint along the wooden planking. Sparks flew as a welder secured a brace to the side of a metal pilot house. Orange dories sat upside down on the tops of some of the pilot houses. "Orange caps," Frank thought. "Phew, diesel fuel and old fish!"

He walked to the end of a wharf and looked across the cove. Dozens of boats were moored - lobster boats, sail boats, power boats and dories. "No wonder the ferry rammed one."

On the other side of the cove sat a row of houses, old piers and more wharves. Some of the houses had walkways down to the cove where boats were tied to floats. Behind the houses, a wall of shrubs and trees rose sharply. Frank followed the flashes of cars between the houses as far as the causeway at the head of Rocky Neck. He was standing at the other end of the finger.

Several large homes dominated the rise across the cove. A white Georgian mansion marked one end, its precise symmetry paled for want

In a Place Like No Other

of paint. Four tiers of weather faded yellow rose to the south. Frank stared. "Probably in worse shape than the hotel." The front of the yellow house was half an octagon. Three floors, each fronted by a roofed porch. The roofs look like the visors on the pilot houses of the draggers. The windows were blackened with plastic coverings that flapped in the breeze. An ornate bannister wrapped a glassed cupola that sat at the top. A glass balled lightning rod sparkled. The edifice cantilevered from a granite ledge. "It looks like a birthday cake."

Plump green leaf clusters softened the houses. Above, billowy white puffs floated in a sea of bright azure. A broad violet swathe of lilacs rolled across the hillside below, underlining the granite outcropping. Tufts of wildflowers popped up through the rock. "Carved out of stone. Lucas would've loved that," Frank thought. He gazed at the spectacle a while longer then decided to go for a swim back at the hotel. He started back then paused and looked through an alley. He could see the house that looked like a birthday cake up on the hill.

The traffic on Rocky Neck Avenue had increased from an hour ago. People strolled in and out of the galleries and shops. Polly was putting a sign out in front of the Galley. "Hi, Polly," Frank said as he walked up.

"Oh, hi, ahh wait. Now don't tell me. Frank. See, I'm not that old yet. How 're you? How's Jack?"

"Great! We're doing just fine. It's been busy, I guess. At least it seems it to me."

"Well, come on in and have a beer. I like getting to know the people who are around all summer. You never know, you know. Say, we're opening for lunch. I'll treat you to one of my famous sandwiches."

"OK. Sounds good."

After talking a while, Polly left for the kitchen to order Frank lunch. He chatted with the bartender until Polly came back and said, "Hey, Frank let's sit on the porch before it gets crowded. We can shoot the breeze for a minute or two."

"Sure." Frank picked up his beer and followed Polly to the porch that sat over the water.

"This place is beautiful, Polly. Gorgeous."

"I know, Frank. The first time I saw it, I wanted to live here. I love it. I really don't miss New York at all. It's terrific . . . even if it's a little crazy at times."

"Yeah, I met Bobby Crosby last night." The smile quickly left Polly's face. "Sorry. I didn't mean to ruin your day."

"Jack told you that story, too. Boy, Jack just loves featuring my grief."

"Yeah." Frank smiled.

"That asshole. He's crazier than anybody I've ever had the displeasure of knowing. He just doesn't give a shit. It's too bad, too. I knew him when he was a kid. He'd come in here with his mother and father. Sweet boy. Funny. Charming. Well groomed, y'know. Now he's a friggin' fruitcake. Changed his name."

"Jack said it was something to do with the war."

"Yeah, whatever. This place sure collects the crazies. Ruthie, Phil, Bobby."

Frank said he knew Ruthie but not Phil and Polly said, "The old guy. Ruthie's husband. Wears a pea coat all summer, pipe stuck between his gums. They live across the street. He's got stories." Polly leaned toward Frank and whispered. "Phil had the hots for some woman painter, but I heard she liked the girls more than the boys. Good thing 'cause if Ruthie caught him she'd a beat him senseless with a walking stick. Anyway, Phil's told me stuff that'd just blow your mind. Opium, bath tub gin, you name it. Wild times in the old days, too." Polly shook her head and stared out at the cove. "No wonder he goes and blows his brains out in a double suicide with some other wacko he's having an affair with."

"Who? Phil?"

"No, Frank, some guy Phil met. Some writer or poet or something? Incredible story. Phil told me once."

"Wild," Frank said as his eyes wandered over the cove. Then he asked, "Hey, Polly, what's the story with those houses?" Frank pointed to the hill across the cove. "The yellow one that looks like a birthday cake up on the top of the hill. It's sure different."

"They call it the Birdhouse or Birdbath or something, Frank. Some famous woman owned it. They say she raised pigeons or parrots or something like that. She was sitting down here on The Neck having dinner one night with her husband. Staying here for the summer. She told him she wanted the house and he bought it for her birthday."

"Maybe it's the Birthday Cake," Frank offered.

"I don't know, Frank. Who cares? You hear all these stories around here all the time and they go around so much after a while it just is. Nobody knows except maybe people like Phil. He was here, but he's so friggin' old, he forgets what side of the street he lives on. Geez, I had to hire a kid last summer just to keep Phil out of the men's room. He'd come in here thinkin' he was home and go in there with a book and not come out for an hour and a half. We had to break the door down twice when he fell asleep in there. That's why I hired the kid. It was cheaper."

Frank chuckled but kept staring at the hill. "Anybody live there now?"

"I don't think so, Frank. I heard the woman in the yellow one died."

"What about the others, Polly? They look deserted, too."

"Could be. I don't know, dear. Who does? Nobody really keeps track of stuff around here, Frank." Polly smiled at Frank. She looked to the front of the dining room and said, "Oops. Customers. I'm the welcoming hostess. Enjoy your lunch, Frank. Nice talking to you."

"Thanks, Polly. Stop in some night and I'll buy you a drink."

"I'll be sure to do that, soon, Frank."

Walking after lunch, Frank stopped whenever he found a clear view across the cove and looked up at the houses on the hill. Then he crossed the causeway and walked along the street parallel to Rocky Neck. Now, when he glanced through openings between buildings he saw the Loft and the Galley and the boat yards. Frank walked by houses on East Main Street. Potted geraniums on doorsteps, window boxes overflowing with nasturtiums, ivies and petunias, small picket fences that enclosed orderly gardens, well kept houses. Queen Anne-style cottages. Gambrels. Neat, no weeds, freshly trimmed hedges, fresh, spring green grass. "Signs of life." Frank felt buoyant.

He came to a point just below the old houses on the crest of the hill and mounted granite steps overgrown with shrubs and briars that scratched his arms as he waded through. Halfway up, the steps disappeared but he continued anyway, through a pile of rubble and more vines and caught his foot in a rusted fence that was buried in the tangle of branches. "Shit, what a mess," he thought. He felt a powerful shove from behind.

Lucas'll get me through it.

Put your hand there, Frank. Step up on that ledge. Don't worry, Frank. I'll get you there.

Ed Touchette

The rubble gave way. Lucas pushed harder. It's not far now, Frank.
Sitting on the rock looking down at the lake.
We call this the Crying Rock, Frank.
Is this a special place, Lucas?
Yes. It's where my people bring Frenchmen to kill 'em.
Lucas' laughter echoed.
You look scared, Frank.

Frank pushed through a thicket of lilacs, stopped and looked up. The four dingy yellow tiers rose above him - ominous, deserted. Inscrutable. Proximity gave him a better chance to appraise what he'd already suspected. It needed attention but the widow's walk sat an impressive fifty feet above. "Still awesome."

After he looked around, Frank continued to the crest of the hill on steps more solid from here. When he reached the top, an expanse of unmowed lawn reached a few hundred feet back to a line of trees. When Frank turned to look at the harbor, the vista struck him dumb. "Incredible!" He breathed deeply, taking in the life that blossomed from the shores and almost tasting the sweetness of the lilacs.

He gazed outward. Rocky Neck sat directly below. Rackliffe House stood to his left, the gabled wings of the cupola resting on a wave of green that rolled toward the hill. The Loft, the Galley, the Lobsta Pot in the center; and at the end, men scurrying to work on the fishing boats. He could see over the trees that enveloped the roof tops of Rocky Neck to the Fort beyond. "Birdseye's tower," he muttered when he saw the red hipped roof. White hulls bobbed on the ultramarine of the cove. The multicolored draggers shimmered. Beyond, across the deep purple of the harbor, the city rose from the water: City Hall, the churches, Portugei Hill with the fishermen's church and dozens of three story apartment houses. "Which one's Donna's?" he wondered. The top of the hill thick with trees.

Mesmerized, Frank sat on a granite ledge between the two houses. He could look down from here on some of the gulls that had glided high above him. They cawed and squawked as they cruised. A pair of ducks had set their wings to land in the cove.

Lucas watched as an osprey glided below them and then swooped down to the lake to snag a fish. Hey, Frank, you know why there's a lake down there?
No, Lucas. Tell me.

It was born when the great god of the north walked from the north pole to the south pole and left his footprints, and the Indian girl, Sacca, who was running from the French to lead them away from her village hid in the bushes and watched as the French stumbled and fell off the cliff. Sacca walked to the edge of the rock and cried so many tears of laughter that she filled the footprint of the great god of the north and it became a lake. Every year the lake freezes over because the great god of the north blows cold air because he's angry that Sacca created such a beautiful lake but didn't remove the bodies of the dead French soldiers so the lake can't make fish for the people to eat because the dead French pollute the water.

Bent with laughter, tears streaming down.

Come on, Frank. I'm just kidding. Don't be scared.

I'm not scared, Lucas. I'm laughing so hard I'm crying.

See, Frank, it's true.

More ducks flew past, yakking as they settled into the cove. A Canada goose honked somewhere to the north. "I miss the mountains," Frank thought.

"Private, you know."

A woman's voice startled Frank. "I'm sorry, Ma'am. I didn't . . . "

"Well, it is, young man." The stubby woman snorted.

Frank stood and started for the steps.

"Well, nevahr mind. You can stay awhile, I guess. You don't seem to be botherin' anything."

Frank sat back down on the ledge and the woman joined him. Years were burrowed in her face. A black Labrador sauntered across the lawn with a springy step that belied his grayed chin whiskers. He circled and nested next to the woman.

Frank smiled at her image: silver hair caught in a loose bun; cheeks, round, red and smooth; a forehead furrowed with age and concern; and coal black eyes that squinted in the sun. She held a straw sun hat. A full length calico duster, stained and smudged, covered her checked print dress. Bright yellow rubber boots caked with mud, stopped just below her knees.

She looked at Frank. Her eyes darted up and down, scanning his face. Her pudgy nose twitched as she spoke. "Don't be pokin' around the house."

"Thank you, Ma'am. I won't. I was just curious about the view from here and saw the steps so I walked up. It looked deserted and I . . . "

"She left it that way and it'll stay that way . . . at least 'til I'm gone."

Frank considered the house. All of the window shades were pulled down. Bare wood everywhere. "The view must be something to see from the second or third floor. Does it have a name?" Frank craned his neck eyeing the cupola.

"What are y'lookin' at so curious, boy?"

"That house. It's huge. It must have been beautiful, once. Now it's kind of run down."

"Nobody wants these big old things anymore. It'll sit heahr and rot 'til it falls down. It's a shame but ain't sellin' to no greedy landlords."

"Do you live here?" Frank asked.

"Back theahr." The old woman pointed behind them to a cottage that sat behind the trees at the end of the lawn.

"Too bad. I mean, too bad nobody wants these places. This is a beautiful view. What exciting homes they'd make. Magnificent."

"Excitin', ayeah. Lived heahr m' whole life and nevahr got tired of it. Used to watch Henry's boat come sailing in - right from heahr." She peered sharply at the harbor looking for something. "Ya know when the fleet was in you couldn't see town for all the sails. Saw the *Gertrude L. Thebaud* sail out of heahr more times than I can count. Was sitting right theahr when Mahrty Welch and those boys took *Esperanto* up to Novi and whooped them Canadians." She made a fist and threw a sharp upper cut at the horizon. "Two straight, ya know. And he'd a whooped *Henry Ford*, too, but there was no wind and *Elizabeth*, oh well, she was a beauty but she was no *Esperanto*. The anniversary yeahr. That man was a sailin' fool if there evahr was one. Henry said he was the best."

Frank just nodded. He had no idea what she was talking about.

The woman's face softened as she gazed out over the harbor. "Some days, I'd just sit here on the rocks and watch the fish dry. The whole whahrf down theahr was flakes, y'know." She pointed directly below to an old wharf that was rotting into the water. "Drying cod in the sun. You ever eat any salt dried cod?"

"I don't think so."

"Ayuh, 's all frozen now. Get some fresh when I can. Not easy. 'S all changed now, for sure. I get some salted at Christmas, though. Great stew. Like the Guineas make. Best evahr."

They sat and watched the harbor. Frank scratched the dog's ears.

"We used to sit here at night and watch the bootleggahrs runnin' in and out of the harbahr," the woman blurted out. "I always told Henry they's bootleggahrs and he'd laugh somethin' fierce. Funniest thing, everybody talked about it but nobody ever seemed to get caught. I wondered if it all wasn' just another story. Henry always said it was 'cause the guys doin' the doin' were the only one who knew and if they were smahrt 'nuff to do it they were sure as Moses smahrt 'nuff not to talk. That's what Henry said. And I'd say, then, Henry, how come there's always a story goin' round 'bout smugglin' this and bootleggin' that and Henry'd say 'cause everybody likes a good story now 'n then. Just like the house. Boy, that's got some. That's for sure."

Frank looked at the house and thought, "I'll bet it does." Then he asked the woman about Henry. The dog studied Frank.

"Was married to him for fahrty six years. Finest man anywheahr. He took care of me fahrty six years. Fahrty six years."

"Your husband?"

"You're a bright one. Of course he was my husband. I'd a nevahr spent fahrty six years with a man who wouldn't marry me."

"Is he dead?"

"I believe so, young man, otherwise he'd be sitting heahr talking with us, wouldn't ya, Henry." The dog looked up at the woman. "No, boy, he's not a comin'. Just an old woman thinkin' out loud. Lie down." The dog rested his head on the grass with a sigh.

"What's this place called?" Frank asked.

"Glosta."

"No I mean where we're sitting - right here."

"Oh. Ha ha." She pointed to a rock outcropping and said, "Go look. Right over theahr. You can still see the bottom of the flag pole. Used to raise a big American Flag every important holiday. Fahrth of July, Armistice Day all of 'em. Flew for a week, half mast when the *Lusitania* went down. Go on and look. It's chiseled right in the rock."

Frank walked over to the rock where she'd pointed. The rusted metal base of a flag pole clung to the rock and just below, two words had been chiseled into the rock. "Banner Hill," he called back to the lady.

"I know that y'fool. Been heahr all my life." The old woman shook her head in disgust.

Frank walked back to where she sat. The dog was rolling on his back, luxuriating in the cool grass. Frank thanked the woman for letting him stay. "I'm Frank Noal." He offered his hand. "I'm here for the summer, working at Rackliffe House down on Rocky Neck."

"Ayuh." The woman got to her feet and waved at something out in the harbor. The dog jumped to his feet and looked out. Then the Labrador sat.

Frank looked at the dog. "Nice to meet you, too." Frank reached for the dog's paw. The Labrador barked and lifted his paw.

"His name's Euripedes," the woman offered as she turned and started across the lawn. Then she asked, "Haddie Bakeahr, there yet?"

"What?" Frank said.

"At Rackliffe House. Haddie Bakeahr comes every summahr from Chahhrleston. She there yet?"

"I don't know. If I see her, should I tell her who's asking for her?"

"Ayuh." The old woman walked away, the Labrador followed.

Frank watched as they disappeared behind a faded yellow picket fence and a hedge of privet. He studied the house again and wondered: "What kind of stories?"

Chapter 5

Cast your net wide. Fish for sole.

Dogs in a Rain Storm
Les Moor
1968 The Aviary Papers Publishers

The last weekend of June, with schools closed for the summer, and Gloucester celebrating St. Peter's Fiesta, the hotel and The Neck filled to capacity. The bars overflowed and Jack, anticipating a big crowd for the fireworks, asked Frank to open a little early on Saturday. Donna surprised Frank when she clopped in and straddled a stool two hours before sunset. Her face more deeply tanned, glistened even in the dimly lit basement. Her canary tank top shimmered against her dark skin. Already set up, Frank stayed and talked when she ordered a beer. Frank thought he noticed blue eye shadow as he said, "Nice to see you again."

Donna stared at the mirror, tossed her head to swish her hair, then glared at Frank. "Look, Frank," she said. "Let's be friends. Bury the hatchet. Don't get on my case again or I'll bury it right in your friggin' fahrhead."

Frank offered his hand over the bar and Donna shook it. Frank noticed she'd painted her fingernails. They laughed. Donna asked Frank if he missed her and he said, "Yes," but then observed it'd been too busy to miss much.

Donna snickered. "Just wait, Frankie boy. Y'ain't seen nothin' yet."

Frank, chagrined, listened: "Tonight 'll be a zoo. Fiesta. The place'll be hoppin' with wackos. Listen." Donna pointed to the ceiling - boisterous voices and shuffling feet careening along the sundeck.

Frank said, "Yeah, Jack told me. What's it all about?"

Donna colorfully laid out St. Peter's Fiesta for Frank: the gaudy altars in the fishermen's homes, the spicy foods and flowing drink had Frank leaning closer for every detail. He sniffed as she described the fried dough and sausages at the carnival at the Fort. There was a dazzling altar where the Bishop said mass and a parade through the streets with a statue festooned with paper money. Frank could almost hear the blaring marching bands as Donna went on about the procession that wound through the city and ended at the St. Peter's Club in a flurry of balloons and confetti and screams of "Viva San Pedro!" Donna said, "Y' got Sunday off, Frank. Y' otta go see the blessing of the fleet at the Fishahrmen's Memorial and the seine boat races and the greasy pole down Pavillion Beach."

Frank rubbed the back of his neck. "What's a greasy pole?"

"Form a birth control."

Frank jolted upright. "What?"

"Just kidding, Frank." Donna snickered and swigged her beer. "See. They got this pole on a platform. Sticks out over the water. Slap a ton a axle grease all ovahr it. These guys all try to walk out on the pole and grab a flag nailed at the end. Boats anchor out in the harbor to watch this. You gotta see it. These guys get buzzed and try to run out to the end of this pole and grab that flag. Slip and slide and fall in the watahr. Sometimes they get that pole jammed right up theyahr nuts. You can heahr the crowd groaning for miles when that happens."

"I bet."

"Then some guy gets all the way to the end and grabs the flag. The crowd goes wild. Boats blast theahr horns. Sirens are blaring. You'll heahr it. They all swim to the beach and carry the winner on their shoulders through the streets and he's a hero for a yeahr. Then they go to the bahrs and get more plastered. Fun."

"Sounds wild," Frank said.

Donna laughed and told Frank it was Rackliffe House's bar that got wild. The clamor above swelled. "See what I mean." Donna pointed upward. Then she continued, insisting that Rackliffe House had the best view of the fireworks that were shot from Stage Fort Park. "Tons a people come from ovahtown to watch 'em. They go down to the gazebo or just stand around in the parking lot. Caused a nasty brawl a few of years ago. Couple a guys. The first big boom surprised the shit out of this guy and he jumped out of his seat. Some fisherman laughed at him and the guy smashed a bottle over his head. They wrestled around for a while and Patrick came and broke it up. Those two had bruises and cuts all ovahr. When the fisherman found out the guy was a vet he felt real bad and apologized so they shook hands and bought each other a coupla rounds."

"Bobby Crosby?" Frank asked.

"Yeah, how'd you know?"

"I guessed. He was in the other night with a bunch of friends. Craziest bastard I've ever met. Jack said he'd been wounded in Viet Nam."

"World class crazy, Frank! Gonzo. Two years ago he went out fishing with some guys. They were out by the breakwater when Bobby dove overboard and started swimming for shore. Kept screaming something about the boat blowing up. The guys he was with ran the boat alongside to make sure he didn't drown. The closer they got the faster Bobby swam. I heard he made it from the breakwater all the way to Ten Pound. Patrick jumped in and pulled him out. He was exhausted."

"What a fucking mess," Frank said. He stared out the windows then asked, "Donna, what's the story with Patrick? I haven't seen him since the first day. What does he do?"

"I don't know, Frank. I just know he stays here and if ever there's trouble Patrick usually comes in and breaks it up. Not a lot of fights, I'll tell you. That guy's friggin' huge."

"No shit."

Two men sat at the bar and ordered rum and coke. One in a suit and tie caught Frank's attention and after he'd served them, he walked back to talk to Donna and mentioned it. She eyed the new customers and told Frank she thought they looked out of place.

"Why?" Frank asked.

"Cheap suit for one thing," Donna added.

"Boy," Frank groused, "for somebody who bitches so much about women and their tag fetishes, you sure know a lot about clothes."

"Be careful, Frankie, you're on thin ice here."

"OK. Forget it." Frank rubbed the back of his neck. "Why don't you stay for a while?"

"Absofuckinglutely not, Frank. The friggin' beach party's coming and I'm gone."

Frank said she should come back to watch the fire works. Donna said she might.

Frank checked his customers then busied himself with the bar. Washed a few glasses. Dried a few glasses. Wiped out a couple of ash trays. Frank glimpsed one of the men at the bar checking the mirror and tying his long red hair into a ponytail. He lifted the collar on his denim jacket and tugged at his tee shirt. His friend used the mirror to scan the crowd filtering in. Then the man in the suit spoke to Frank. "Good summer?"

"I guess," Frank said. "Everybody seems satisfied."

"What's it like?"

"Pretty crazy, at times. That woman I was talking to, she's got some unbelievable stories about this place. She's a native. Seems to know everybody. Pretty funny stuff."

"Great. She ever mention a guy named Ryan? Ducky Ryan. Old friend from school. Haven't seen him in years. Be great to see him again."

"I don't know the name. Maybe Donna does. I'll ask her when she comes back in."

"Great!"

"Who should I say was asking if he turns up?"

"Oh, he won't remember me. Just tell him and old school chum was in town on business and was asking for him."

The men finished their drinks and stood to leave. Frank swept their change from the bar and said, "Thanks."

"No problem," the guy with the ponytail said, donning a pair of aviator's sunglasses. Then a rush of vibrant colors and the bar overflowed with dancing and pounding rhythm. His friend asked, "What happened?"

"Sun set," Frank said. "They're getting primed for the fireworks."

"Let's hang out for a while," Frank heard the man say to his friend. "Maybe we'll get lucky." The two men sat back on their stools and ordered another round.

Frank watched as they scrutinized the crowd. The one with the ponytail checked out the women strutting their flowery frocks and tight white jeans. The other man kept an eye on the door. A couple of buxom well tanned girls walked in wearing tight blue jeans and bright white tank tops. Gold graced their necks and wrists. Frank glanced, then turned to the waitress station and told Kim to check some ID. Jack walked in and asked Frank how it was going.

"Probably the busiest night yet. The bar's getting packed and the waitresses are having a tough time getting through to serve the customers. I don't know if that's good or bad," Frank said.

"Great," Jack said.

"You going to help out?" Frank asked.

"Can't. I'm busy. Pam's working upstairs. I'm going to send her down. She's been bugging me for extra hours."

"You're the boss."

"Do me a favor, Frank. If she asks where I am, tell her I'll be back tomorrow. Tell her I had to go to Topsfield to talk to the old man about something or other. You know, Frank. Make something up."

Frank nodded. Jack said, "See ya tomorrow."

Frank chuckled to himself thinking he'd count the number of times he'd covered for Jack, then mumbled to himself, "Pointless." Frank saw the man with the ponytail turn to his friend and whisper, then jerk his head toward the door. He stood, dropped more bills on the bar and left. Then the man in the suit followed as the band set up and tested their mics. Frank smiled and sang along with the Rolling Stones.

"Vodka Martini," Frank heard from the waitress station. He turned to grab a bottle, filled a tumbler with ice and vodka and sang "I can' get no - I can't get no. No satisfaction."

Kim looked at Frank and laughed as he placed the glass on the tray. "You could if you tried, Frank." Her hips swayed as she delivered the drink. Then she paused and glanced coyly over her shoulder and winked at Frank.

When Pam came down, Frank asked her to take care of the drinks at the waitress station. She said she would, then grabbed Frank's arm and pulled him closer to whisper in his ear. Frank bent to listen, then said, "Kim?" as he jerked upright.

"Yeah," Pam said. "She's been hot for you for a month. She'll be pissed, Frank. You'll see."

Donna came back when the fireworks started. She plowed through the throng outside. Frank saw her, opened a bottle of Schlitz and waved it above his head. Donna put her head down and elbowed into the bar.

"Thanks," she said. "I need one."

Pam spoke to Kim at the waitress station, then she turned to Frank and said, "Hey, Frankie, we're going out to watch the fireworks. OK?"

"Sure, but get back in here before they do." Frank jerked his thumb at the door. "It's going to be nuts."

"Not a problem, darling," Pam said as she brushed past Frank and pinched his ass. Frank snapped a wink at Pam.

"She friggin' pinched your ass, Frank. What the fuck was that all

Ed Touchette

about?" Kim growled.

"Nothin'," Frank said.

"Yeah, if I come back there and pinch your ass you won't say it was nothin'," Kim quipped.

Frank laughed then turned to Donna. "How was the Galley?"

"What, Frank, you lookin' to bang Kim Bristol? She's the biggest slut on The Neck. World class, Frank. Better get a shot."

"Nah. Pam's just tryin' to piss her off. She caught Kim with Jack last night upstairs in the linen closet. Payback, y'know. How was the Galley? Big night?"

"I listened to Polly's Music Man. I've heard it fifty times but I really like the way she sings so I sit through it a few times every summer." Donna scratched at the label on the bottle. "Hey what did you mean we'll see?"

"Nothing, Donna. Was it crowded?"

"Friggin' zoo. The line was out into the street and the dancing at the Lobsta Pot shook the pier. Geezuz, when I passed Ruthie, the tourists were standin' in line to buy her walking sticks. Seems the crowd this year is more wired than ever. I'm getting worried that this place is gettin' too popular. It'll kill it for sure."

"The owners love it. It's a short season and they need the bucks."

Donna nodded in agreement as she swigged her beer. "But," she managed as she swallowed hard, "if they start making a lot of money, this place'll attract more businesses tryin' to make a lotta money and get ovahr crowded. Change completely."

Donna nodded at her reflection but snapped her attention to Frank as he added quickly, "And if they don't, these places will go out of business and somebody'll come in with a lot of money and buy up everything cheap and build something else. Either way it changes, Donna. It's normal."

"Fucken A. That's scary, Frankie boy."

"That bothers you?"

"Change doesn't bother me, Frank. You actually made sense. That scares me."

Frank laughed as he wiped the bar. The boom of the fireworks rattled the windows and flashes of light outlined the crowd against the darkened harbor. Whoops, howls and shrill whistles marked the explosions. "If you want to go see the fireworks," Frank said, "I'll keep your beer in the fridge. I can't leave the bar."

"No. I've seen them before."

Frank remembered the two men who had been there earlier and he asked Donna if she knew Ducky Ryan. Donna bit her lower lip and checked her reflection in the mirror. "Why?" she asked, eyebrows raised. Frank mentioned the guy in the cheap suit.

"Yeah, I know him. Biggest sleaze ball in Glosta. He'd steal anything from anybody and sell it. Bad news. I know he deals drugs when he gets the chance."

"That guy knew him from school."

"Reform school, maybe. Must be, narcs. I heard Ducky was into some shit. Somethin' about hashish fish sticks."

"What?" Frank chortled. "What are you talking about now?"

Donna spoke directly to her reflection in the mirror. "I'm telling you, Frank, Ducky Ryan's an eef. Had a scam going. Turned into hashish fish sticks. That's what I heard."

"Donna, are you for real?" Frank asked. "Never mind. You got me. What happened?"

"I can tell you this, Frankie boy, it couldn't have been hard. The last time they squared Ducky's I.Q. it changed signs. Anyway, y'know those freighters tied up at the piers, well they carry tons of frozen fish blocks. The lumpers go into the holds, pile the blocks on a pallet, and then a guy in a crane lifts it out. Sometimes it tips and falls into the harbahr if it isn't loaded right. Some days you can look in the harbahr and you see boxes of frozen fish bobbin' around like gulls. Ducky Ryan used to row around in his dory and collect 'em. Sold 'em or gave 'em to his friends. So Ducky's rowin' around one day pickin' up blocks and when he gets home and thaws some out he finds some stuff frozen in with the fish. Now Ducky, see, is thinkin' it's some kind a breadin' or something to coat the fish so he's thinkin' fish sticks. So he coats the fish. Then he goes around to his pals at the restaurants and says he's got the premo fish sticks for sale. So they buy 'em and the stuff is sellin' like crazy. People want 'em bad. More they eat the more they want. The restaurants run out right away and call Ducky to get more so he makes another batch. Then a couple of straight laced customers get wise to what they are and they complain to the cops so the cops bust the restaurant owner for sellin' hashish fish sticks. The guy gets off though. Evidence was consumed. Evahr since, the cops been keepin' a real close eye on Ducky."

Ed Touchette

After a good laugh, Frank shook his head. "How did the stuff get into the fish blocks, Donna?"

"Gee, Frank, I wonder. Somebody trying to smuggle something in? Naw. Not heahr. Sure as hell wasn't the first time somebody tried smugglin' somethin' in a load of fish, you can bet your ahs on that, Frank."

"Where's Ducky?"

"Disappeared, Frank."

"Guess that's why they call him Ducky?"

Donna glowered at Frank, shook her head and checked the mirror.

A wild volley of booms and flashes followed by a boisterous synchronized blaring of boat horns and whistles accompanied the crowd filtering back into the bar. Frank saw Missy and Annie and walked over to say hello. Annie ordered a Madras. Then one of the waitresses had a large order so Frank had to rush to help Pam. Donna yelled down the bar, "Beeahhhr!"

Frank brought Donna's beer and nodded toward Annie Barnes. "You know her? She's a dance major at Bristol. She vaguely remembers you."

Donna glared down the bar and then snapped her head to look back into the mirror. She snarled at Frank, "Vaguely? Vaguely! My ahs! That dog knows who I am. That preppie piece a shit and her brothahr can kiss my Glosta ahhhs. Who the fuck does she think she is? Vaguely! Huh. She told people I wasn't from Glosta that I was from Rahlee. Well, I told you, Frank. I was born heahr. I'm from Glosta. My folks are from Glosta. My grandparents are from Glosta. The only people more from Glosta are the friggin' Indians who were heahr when my great great great grandfather moved heahr from friggin' England. She's not. She's been heahr a few summers but it doesn't make her from Glosta. If you weren't born heahr you ain't from heahr."

Frank clanged the ship's bell at the end of the bar and bellowed "last call" as Donna finished her diatribe. A couple of late arrivals, disgruntled, griped to Frank that they'd just gotten started. They wanted another round. Frank checked the clock and said, "Sorry. After one."

The men grumbled and then one of them threw his beer bottle, smashing it into the wall behind the juke box and obliterating the compass rose on the chart of Martha's Vineyard. Frank wished the surly customers good luck with the tuna the next day and asked them to leave. Donna warned

Frank to be careful but Frank told her he could handle it. The two men looked at Frank and laughed.

"Fuck you, asshole," one yelled. "We'll leave when we're ready."

Frank walked out from behind the bar, opened the door and said, "We're closed." Then Frank ducked as another bottle ripped through the harbor at Newport. When Frank moved toward them, they jumped to their feet and ran out through the door. Frank looked back to the bar, inflated his chest and hitched up his jeans. Donna giggled, howled, then slapped the bar. Then she wrapped a cocktail napkin around her index finger and dabbed tears from her cheeks, directing Frank's attention to the passageway behind the bar with her other hand. The top of Patrick's head brushed the ceiling as he loomed, arms akimbo, in the doorway.

"Thanks, Patrick," Frank said. "Can I buy you a drink?"

Patrick shook his head, "No." He ducked as he turned to walk back through the passageway.

"I guess you showed 'em, Frank," Donna wailed.

Frank locked the door and cleaned up as he talked with Donna. She drank another beer and Frank listened patiently to her maudlin recollections of her first love. As Frank turned to shut the door to the passage, he heard her say something about her fifteenth birthday, then a choked sob. When he turned back, Donna nervously searched her jeans pockets for money, whisked her keys off the bar and bolted through the door. As he locked the bar, Frank heard tires squeal out the parking lot.

Chapter 6

*Mersey dotes and dosey dotes and little lambsy divey.
Kiddle dee divey, too. Wouldn't you?
The mind of a child is a terrible thing to waste.*

Cooked to Perfection.
Bobby Crosby
1971 The Aviary Papers Publishers

Wednesday. Cold. A persistent rain kept Frank from his outside chores so he hung a couple of mirrors he'd refinished in the second floor hall. Harley was writing at the desk when Frank walked down into the lobby and deplored the weather. Harley laughed. "It'll be a lot better in August, Frank."

"Harley, in June you told me it would be better in July."

"I know, Frank. Just trying to be optimistic. A couple more rainy weekends and we're screwed. Good thing we have some regulars. Wow!" Harley leaned closer and peered into the guest book. "Haddie Baker. She must be eighty now. This will be her sixtieth summer or something like that. Can you believe it?"

Pensive, Frank rubbed the back of his neck. "Wait, Harl. I met a woman, Emma Wilkins. She asked if Haddie Baker from Charleston was here. She lives up there on the hill by that big yellow house, looks like a birthday cake."

"The Aviary. The place where the woman who raised parakeets lived. Yes, Emma lives in the cottage. She'll be down to visit Haddie. They're old friends."

"Is that what they call the house, Harley? The Aviary."

"Yes, Frank. That's what I said."

Jack walked out of his office and asked Frank if he'd take some brochures over to a couple of the motels along the back shore. "Drive out to Niles Beach and then around the back shore. When you get to Moorland, turn left up the hill, past the golf course then come back down Mt. Pleasant Avenue. These places are along the way."

"Mt. Pleasant?" Frank asked.
"Yeah," Jack said.
"Goes right by Emma Wilkins' house," Harley said.

Frank delivered the brochures and was driving back along Mt. Pleasant Avenue approaching the hill leading down to East Main Street. He hit the breaks hard to avoid a grey-chinned black Labrador crossing the street to slop through a puddle. "Euripedes," he yelled, rolling down the window, "You should be more careful. I almost hit you." The dog acknowledged Frank's reproach with a turn of his head and then crossed back again through another puddle and ambled up a drive. Frank watched the dog then noticed the Aviary, soft in the heavy mist. He decided to stop and tell Emma Wilkins her friend was coming to the hotel.

Frank parked on the street and walked down the drive. The rain had mostly subsided. A small sign on a fence read "Private Way;" Frank kept on. Two small cottages surrounded by arborvitae sat on either side. Frank walked to the steps that led up to the porch of one where Euripedes reclined. The dog barked but didn't move. Frank looked down the drive. Through the heavy mist rumbled Emma Wilkins wearing a long dark green oil skin coat and a sou'wester. Her bright yellow boots slapped wetly against her shins. She approached Frank, checking him from head to toe.

"Hi. Remember me?" Frank winced. "I, ahh, was here a few weeks ago." Euripedes sniffed a pant leg and Frank reached down to scratch the dog's ears.

Emma eyeballed Frank carefully. She squinted, rocked closer and sniffed. She walked around Frank and surveyed him from the back and sides, then, in front of him again, she looked him square in the eye. "Nope," she said, "can't say's I do. What're y'sellin'?"

"I'm not selling anything," Frank said. "I was just driving by and wanted to see if you were here. Thought I'd say hello. And tell you . . . "

"Well, since I live here, young fella, y'weren't far off now."

Frank laughed.

Emma stiffened. "Well, hello," she said. "Lotta walkin' just for that."

"No, wait. Your friend Haddie Baker is coming this weekend." Frank hesitated. Then: "To Rackliffe House."

"How do you know?"

"I work there. Remember?"

"No, if I did, I wouldn't have asked."

"Oh, boy." Frank moaned, looking down at the dog. "Well, anyway, I was on my way by and I thought I'd stop by and tell you."

"Well, thank you, young man."

"How've you been?" Frank asked. "Guess you can't do much outside today . . . I mean with the rain." Frank looked over the fence that lined the drive. A few dozen rose bushes filled with blooms sagged under the weight of the water. More tidy perennial beds dotted the yards. "Looks like you keep busy, though."

"Say, young fella. It might be somethin' you like, standin' round talking on a rainy afternoon. Nothin' bettahr to do. I got plenty to keep me busy - leaks and all, so I'll be gettin' to it. Kids broke another window. Gotta get some more plastic and covahr it before the rain ruins the floor."

Frank offered to help and Emma chortled. "Nice a ya, young fella, but I'm not helpless. Been here in hurricanes and blizzards, y'know."

"OK," Frank said.

Emma snarled, "Welllll?"

"Oh, ahh yeah, well I guess I'll be going now."

"Aayeah."

Frank turned and walked back toward the street as Emma walked up to the steps of her cottage. She stopped suddenly, rubbed her chin and looked toward the house at the crest of the hill. She eyed Frank, looked back at the house, then perused Frank again. "Young fella, say, ain't feared a heights, ahre ya?"

"No." Frank said and turned back.

"Not afeared a ghosts, I hope?"

"No." Frank chuckled. "None that I know."

Emma hopped and clapped her hands. "Yippee! You wait right heahr and I got something for you to do. Been needin' this done for a time now."

Frank had a puzzled grin on his face as he watched the stout little figure bound up the steps and into the house. Frank talked to the dog while he waited. When she walked back onto the porch, Emma carried a stepladder and a roll of heavy plastic. The handle of a staple gun stuck out of the pocket of her raincoat.

"Come with me," she commanded, leaning forward and trudging down the drive. Frank followed. Euripedes followed Frank.

She walked to the side of the yellow house and out toward the crest of the hill. The breeze carried a heavy mist through which wavered a few old pilings, ghosts of hulls, a few tree tops and an eerie jingle of halyards slapping at masts. The fog horn bayed.

"Hey, com' heahr. Let's get movin'," Emma insisted.

"Sure. What do you want me to do?"

"Look up theahr." Emma pointed to the top of the of the house - almost invisible in the cloud. "Theahr. The cupola. See it?"

"Yes."

Emma explained how to access the cupola and how to apply the plastic and then said, "Come on."

Frank followed through the side door of the house. She put her finger to her lips and shushed him as they walked down a hallway toward a circular staircase. Frank looked around and noted the absence of furniture. The walls marked only with shadows of missing frames echoed each squeak of Emma's boots. Plastic sheets covered the windows - rattling along with the panes of glass when a gust struck them. Emma led him up the stairs and stopped on the second floor landing.

"OK," Emma whispered, "Keep going up to the third floor. If you heaaahr footsteps, get down quick and run like a deer. I'll wait for you heaahr or down the drive. Depends." She pushed the roll of plastic and the ladder at Frank. Then she clasped her hands together, rubbed them and whispered, "Boy, oh boy."

"Depends on what?" Frank asked.

"On whether r'not you heahhr the footsteps."

"What footsteps?"

"Just do as I tell you, boy. If you heahhr 'em, run. If you don't, just take this plastic and cover the windows. Be quick."

Frank started up the stairs to the third floor.

"Wait, wait, wait!" Emma insisted. "Here take this, you'll need it." She reached into her coat pocket and pulled out the staple gun. She walked halfway to the stairway, leaned forward and reached as far as she could to hand the staple gun to Frank.

Frank reached the third floor landing and looked around - closed doors, no windows, more frame shadows. He saw a trap door above his head, opened the ladder and climbed. He raised the hatch cover and glanced around. When he raised himself to stand inside the glassed in cupola, he bumped his head on the ceiling as he straightened. The cupola was barely wide enough for Frank to stretch out his arms. He looked out and saw a wooden deck with a railing that was barely knee high. He searched for an access to the deck and noticed a latch on a window frame. He turned it; the window creaked open. A rush of salt air filled his nostrils as he stooped to get through. As he shifted his weight through the window frame, the decking cracked and groaned but felt firm. Frank stepped out and stood erect. Fog encased him. "Bummer," he thought. "This must be unreal on a clear day." The clinking of the halyards cut through the fog.

Frank looked toward Rackliffe House; the winged gables of the cupola sat on the tree tops above the fog bank. To his right he could see the very peak of the green dome on City Hall. The fog bank masked everything else.

Frank stepped back inside, took out his knife and began cutting the plastic to cover the windows. He unrolled the sheet and doubled it over and it was exactly the width he needed. He stapled it to the window frames and mullions, wrapping it completely around the cupola. He could feel air pushing through the gaps where the glazing had fallen out. When he'd finished, he looked around and grimaced at the dire condition of the roost.

He opened the hatch and stepped onto the first rung of the ladder. He took one last look around the cupola. A small wire bound notebook lay against a corner. He reached for the notebook and his shifting weight rocked the ladder. He grabbed for the edge of the hatch as the ladder tumbled to the floor. He couldn't hold both the notebook and himself so he released his grip on the edge of the hatch and crashed to the floor.

"You OK?" he heard Emma shout.

"Yeah," Frank said.

"OK. Good. Now get down heahr and let's get out. You nevahr know when it's going to come back."

"What?"

"Never you mind now. Just get down here and I'll tell you all about it. Come on now."

Frank got up and brushed his clothes. He coughed and waved at the dust dancing in the air. Then he picked up the step ladder and folded it closed. He opened the notebook and saw pages of poetry. He mumbled as he leafed through the pages and read: "A summer's day - I write to you - you do not read. I sing to you - You do not listen. I die. L M"

Frank leafed through more of the notebook, then stuck it in his pocket.

Emma called impatiently, "Don't be dillydallyin."

"I'm not. I just have to get the ladder."

Frank picked up the ladder and the plastic and started for the stairs. When he got down to the first floor, Emma paced in the hallway, grousing about secret somethings. She saw Frank and blurted, "Let's go, and don't be tellin' anybody you're up theahr."

"OK," Frank said.

"Come on there, What's your name? Frank? C'mon."

Frank followed down the drive to her cottage. Every few steps, Emma looked back over her shoulder toward the house and twitched. When they'd reached the steps to her porch, Emma thanked Frank for his help and asked him if he'd like a cup of tea or coffee before he left. "Least I can do, after all. That's a load off my mind."

Frank said, "Sure," and followed her into her cottage. Euripedes sprang up the steps to the porch after them and Frank held the door for him. The dog stepped over the threshold, stopped and shook the water from his coat. Small dots of moisture spotted the walls in the entry.

"Take off your coat and sit down," Emma said.

Frank took off his slicker and slung it over the back of a chair. The staple gun fell to the floor and startled Emma.

"Sorry," Frank said.

"What's that?" Emma screamed.

"The staple gun. I forgot I had it in my pocket." Frank picked up the staple gun and handed it to her.

"No. That." She pointed to the notebook sticking out from Frank's other pocket.

Frank handed her the book of poems. "I found this up in the cupola and I thought it was interesting. I wanted to show you."

"Hmmm, L M." Emma fingered the edges of the cover, then opened it and leafed through the pages. Then she slapped it closed and drummed the cover with her fingers. "Poetry. Hmmm. Interesting. Up in the cupola? Hmmm. For yeahrs people have been saying they keep seein' someone up theahr. Weahrs a black cape and a red bandanna. I keep tellin' 'em I know nothin' about it. They keep saying it's the poet that was in love with her and jumped from the cupola. I say theahy're crazy."

"That one?" Frank pointed to the notebook.

"Could be. Geee willickers! Strange. I know she used to have a lot of friends here - ahrtists, writeahrs and the like. Some of 'em poets. Never saw anybody running around in a black cape and a red bandanna. Henry always said it coulda been the Wells boy. He wrote poems for her. Cute boy. Sweet. Henry thought he was a little light upstairs though. Know what I mean? Henry said the boy was handlinin' with his thumbs."

Emma got up and walked into a room off the kitchen. Frank asked her why the house was called the Aviary and Emma called back from the hallway, "I guess because it sits up high with all the birds, Frank. But I'd a called it the Birthday Cake." Frank laughed

When she came back and showed Frank a photograph, Emma pointed to images and said, "Ahrtists. That's Bill and Theresa. Let's see. Gordon. Phil and Ruthie. That's her, the tall striking one and those two were friends from New Yawhrk. Lotta money. And that's the little boy. Name was Wells. Used to visit all summer."

Frank stared at the photograph thinking he recognized the young boy but he couldn't place him. He thanked Emma for the coffee and stood to leave. Then he asked if he could come up sometime when it was clear so he could see Gloucester from the cupola and Emma frowned.

"Did you ever go up to the top to look out, Emma?" Frank asked.

"Stopped goin' up after a while, when she died. Bad luck."

"Are you afraid of ghosts, Emma?"

"You be gettin' along. Y'heahr?"

Frank grabbed his slicker and headed for the door. He looked back at Emma. She stood at the window dragging her finger on the glass, making the sign of a cross.

"See ya." Frank waved. Emma didn't respond.

"I'll be sure to tell Haddie Baker I met you, Emma," Frank added.

"Yes," Emma said. "Please tell her I'm still heahr. I hope to see her."

Back at the hotel, Frank walked into the lobby and saw Harley sitting in a chair by the fireplace. Frank warmed his hands over the fire as he told Harley what had happened. "Crazy shit, Harley. This place is bizarre."

"What gave you your first clue, Frank, - Bobby Crosby, Polly, Jack?"

Frank looked at Harley as he sat in the chair with his head resting against the back. "Rudolph Serkin," Frank thought. Then he asked Harley if he'd ever heard about a poet haunting the Aviary and Harley chuckled as he said, "Frank, let me tell you, Emma Wilkins has been around for years.

She knows a lot of stories about this place. She won't say much, though. Just forget it, ghost stories are pretty common, especially in old houses. She still got that black dog, Frank?"

"Euripedes! Yeah."

"Nice dog," Harley said.

Frank missed Donna; she hadn't been in for a few nights. That evening while he wiped the bar and stocked coolers, he thought, "She's usually sitting here by now." He checked the speed rack to be sure he had full bottles. The door opened and he looked up. He did a double take: Donna, in a sheer pink silk blouse and a short black skirt walked through the door with a man. Frank recovered and nodded a greeting as he glimpsed the shape her legs took from the lift of her strapless open toe high heels - not to mention her breasts, braless, under that flimsy blouse. They sat at a table in a far corner and Donna called across the room, "Couple a beahrs, Frankie boy."

Frank glared at her. "Sure. You want me to run a tab?" He placed the bottles on the bar and chirped, "No waitress service until seven."

Donna walked over and picked up the beers. She slowly clasped the neck of one bottle, stroked it then, squeezing it gently, winked at Frank. He didn't see it; his eyes were glued to Donna's manicured fingernails - the deep alizarin crimson matched her painted lips. Then Frank sniffed and thought, "Canoe" as he looked up and Donna said, "Good to see ya, Frank." She winked again, preened the curls that touched her cheekbones and spun to saunter back to the table. "She's wearing eye shadow," Frank thought. Then ogling her from behind he muttered, "Hope she dumps the work boots for good."

Frank continued to prep the bar and kept an eye on the table. He watched Donna pat the man's arm and whisper in his ear. Frank interrupted, "All set or do you want a couple more beeeaaahhhs?"

"What?" Donna asked.

Frank repeated the question and Donna said, "Yeah, ahhh sure."

Frank brought the beers to the table this time. Before he placed the bottles on the table he wiped it down with a towel he'd draped over his right arm. "Theah y'ahhhhh," Frank said.

Donna looked at Frank then introduced her friend. "Frank, this is Augie. Augie Campo, Frank Noal." She grabbed her friend's hand and held it up. The man, nodding with closed eyes, never looked up at Frank.

"Today's Augie's birthday," Donna told Frank. "I take Augie to the Galley for dinner on his birthday. We just stopped in to say hello."

"Great. Nice to meet you, Augie." Frank noticed that Augie barely breathed. As he turned back to the bar he wondered: "Shit faced on two beers? Where'd she find him?"

When Donna came to the bar to pay the bill, Frank asked if she was driving. Whispering through a puzzled grin, she offered, "You don't think Augie can drive, do you? He hasn't had a license in fourteen years -since the last time he parked his pickup in Judge Bailey's vegetable garden."

Frank smiled and said, "Another story I'd like to heahh, Donnerrr."

"Maybe you will," Donna said and picked up her change. She stared briefly at Frank then said, "See ya."

Frank watched as she put her hands under Augie's elbows and lifted him from the chair. Taking Augie's right arm and putting it over her shoulder, she shuffled him out the door.

The night wore on and Frank, distracted as he poured drinks and opened beer bottles, kept glancing at the door. He noticed the man in the cheap suit and his friend with the ponytail sitting at a table with a couple of women. One of the women wore a Greek fisherman's hat. The other sported a beret. Frank laughed. Annie Barnes came through the door and said hello to Frank. Before she ordered she told him she was meeting Missy to go dancing.

Frank poured the drink and looked at the back of Annie's head as she watched the dancers and swayed gently to the music. Frank went to place her drink on the bar but she turned too quickly and knocked it over. "Fuck," she groused.

Frank noticed her trembling hands. "Don't worry about it, Annie. I'll get another."

"Never mind. I gotta go." Annie fumbled through her purse and threw a few bills on the bar. She stood and stammered, "Tttell Mmissy I'll, ahhh. meet her there."

"Sure." Frank grimaced as he mopped the bar. Then, shaking his head he turned to the waitress station to ask Kim if she needed anything.

"How about a nice, slow, passionate fuck, Frank?"

"Shit. Jack forgot to tell me to order those. Look, I'll talk to him and we'll get some soon. OK?"

Kim laughed.

Frank walked to the other end of the bar to wait on other customers. He saw the man with the ponytail and the woman with the Greek fisherman's hat leaving arm in arm. He looked over at the table where he'd seen their friends. It was empty.

Richie Barnes and his friend Peter walked straight to the bar. "Hey, Frank, come here. You know where I can score some stuff?" Richie asked.

"I'm not following, Richie."

"Pot, coke, pills, anything."

"No, I don't have a clue. Not interested."

"What? Christ, Frank everybody gets high. It's the national pastime. What are you, a narc or somethin'?"

"No, I did my time with the crazies."

"Geezuz. A friggin' straight bartender. Fuckin' world is goin' t' shit." Richie moaned as Frank laughed and shook his head.

The band had quit for the night. Frank checked his watch. Kim had an order waiting so he walked to the waitress station.

"Two Absoluts, please. Oh, Frank did I mention. Straight up."

Frank smiled. "No, but I could have guessed."

"Am I that obvious, Frank. Gee, I better cool my jets or you'll think I'm . . . " Kim glared at the door. "Well, oh, my. Speak of the devil - townie sluts. Well, well."

Frank looked in the mirror and saw Donna walking in. She took a seat at the end of the bar. "Gimme a beahr, Frank."

"It's beer." Frank spelled it out for her, "B-E-E-R!" Then he leaned over toward the waitress station and said something to Kim. She laughed and winked at Frank as she turned to deliver her drinks.

"So?" Donna said when Frank came back.

"So, what?"

"So beahr." Donna then spelled the word correctly.

"So, why do you say beahr when it's beer?"

"Hey, Frank, y' gotta stick up your ahs or somethin'. I been sayin' beahr all my life. Everybody heahr says beahr, same way . . . like they say Glosta. It sounds right. You've been hearin' it for a month. All of a sudden you're on my case 'cause I say beahr. Y' never said nothin' before."

Ed Touchette

Frank didn't answer. He walked to the other end of the bar and made a White Russian for one of his customers. He stopped to check on Richie and Peter. They were still nursing their first drinks. Kim came over to talk to them and Frank heard her tell them she'd meet them outside after the bar closed. She looked at Frank as she started to walk away and said, "Might as well. Frank's got his head up his ass over some townie." Frank walked back to Donna. She was glaring.

"Everything OK?" Frank asked.

"What, Frank, you flirting with Kim. You are lookin' to screw her. I knew it. Go ahead, bang Kim Bristol tonight. Keep her record in tact as bein' a world class whore. Hope the old health insurance is paid up, dickhead. She's screwed everything that's come down 128 including a couple a . . . "

"Geezuz, Donna. Spit it out, now. Don't mince words." Frank laughed and looked down at the floor. Then he looked at Donna. "Funny."

Donna slapped a few dollars on the bar. "Gimme my change. I'm outta this shit hole."

"Whoa," Frank blurted as he reached over the bar and grabbed Donna's arm. "Wait."

Donna yanked free. "What's with you, Frank? You've given me shit before but you've never been friggin' rude like you were tonight. You're pissed at me for something. Is it Augie, Frank?"

"No. Not really. Hey, did I tell you how nice you . . . "

"Cut the shit, Frank, if it's Augie, you better get a clue. He's an old friend of my dad's and he works around the dinahr. Poor bastahrd hasn't been sober since 1964. I like him and every year I take him to the Galley for dinner on his birthday. He gets a big kick out of it. Trouble is he never stays awake long enough to enjoy his steak. This year, though, he managed to make it through his chowda before his face hit the salad."

Frank felt ashamed of himself. "Hey, Donna, yeahh, look. I'm sorry. OK? I didn't really mean anything by it. Forget it. I might've been a little bent out of shape seeing you walk in with Augie. But, well, ahhh, you're one of my favorite customers. I, ahh, well, didn't want to think . . . "

Donna cut Frank off with a stab of her index finger. Then she crooked it and beckoned him closer. Frank leaned toward her as she whispered, "Frank, listen to yourself. Come on. Spit it out. We're all friends here." She raised her voice. "You're full of shit, pal. I knew it. You're hot for me.

Fucken A. My instincts are good as evahr."

Frank smiled.

"Outstanding, Frank. I knew it. Now, look. From heahr it's real easy. Just don't get nuts."

Frank roared. His laughter quieted the bar until Donna said, "Just told him the one about Ducky's fishsticks." The crowd at the bar nodded and went on drinking and talking. Donna smiled at herself in the mirror.

Frank walked down the bar telling everyone it was almost last call and that if they wanted one for the road they'd better order. He mixed a couple of Martinis and placed a Budweiser in front of a fisherman.

Donna barked at Frank, "Beeeeeerrr, please."

Frank laughed. He walked over to Donna, looked at her and said, "Hey, maybe you ought to pass on this last one. You've got to drive home."

"Not if you ask me to stay."

"What about Augie?"

"He'll be fine. He's asleep in the back of my car. He's not gonna wake up for hours and by then I'll have him back in Rowley. He'll be all right. Frank, enough with the friggin' questions."

Frank reached into the cooler and grabbed a beer, popped off the cap and put it in front of Donna. "Here, knock yourself out, Glostaaaa girl."

"I'll take that as an invitation."

As Frank walked away to start breaking down the bar Donna whispered, "It's about friggin' time, ahhshole."

Frank turned, briskly. "I heard that."

"Well it is."

Frank locked the door to the bar and they left. Donna grabbed his hand and said, "Let's go for a walk." Frank agreed and they started down the hill. Then Donna stopped and removed her shoes, grousing that she'd feel more comfortable walking barefoot. Frank told her how sexy she looked in heels, and added that he liked her hair. Donna griped about taping the curls to her cheeks for four hours. Then she saw Kim Bristol walking with Richie and Peter so she jabbed Frank in the ribs and said, "What'd I tell ya, Frank." Frank looked at them, smiled, and reached back to slap Donna on the ass. "Just shut up and walk," Frank said. Donna laughed.

They walked down The Neck past the Loft and the Galley. Ruthie sat on a stone wall whittling a walking stick and peering over her sunglasses at them as they passed by on their way to the boat yard. Frank wondered why she was there at this hour and Donna said, "Best time. Some shit faced ahshole will buy one to impress his date."

It was two o'clock and some of the fishermen were pulling their trucks into the yard to load up for a trip. Frank recognized a couple that had just left the bar. "Must be tough bastards," Frank said, "drinking all night at the bar and now they're going out to fish all day."

"They'll sleep for a few hours on the way out, before they fish," Donna said. Then she and Frank walked to the end of a pier and sat dangling their legs over the edge.

"I love living near the ocean," Donna said. "The sound of the water calms me."

Frank laughed. "When?"

"Gimme a break, Frank."

Draggers creaked and groaned against their mooring lines. Fishermen cursed and joked as they loaded gear. The cool air, ripe with fish and diesel fuel, filled with music and laughter from a party at the marina across the cove. They heard a loud splash and then: "Nice dive. Woulda been a bettahr if you'd a kept youhr legs togethahr." A woman yelled, "A lot a things would've been bettahr if I'd a kept my legs togethahr." Frank and Donna roared.

Donna looked up at the night sky and talked about the stars. Sea gulls glided past - ghostly white flashes against the night. "Probably scared by a noise or whatever. They fly off - probably out to Thatchahr's or someplace," Donna explained. Then she asked Frank to tell her more about his life. Frank did. He sniffed and grumbled that a gust of wind here could fill his nostrils with a smell worse than the paper mills and Donna laughed. She told him to close the windows. Frank laughed. Then, when Donna laid her head on Frank's leg, he paused. Donna said quietly, "Keep talking, Frank. I like the sound of your voice."

Frank looked up and saw the Aviary, faintly outlined in the ambient light. He told Donna he'd met Emma Wilkins. Then he thought he saw a light in the cupola but when he asked Donna if she saw anything she said, "No," so Frank went on about the poet and the black cape.

"Oh, man, Frank. Get real. Every house in Glosta that sits up on a hill and is dark at night has stories like that. They're always haunted and somebody always died a strange kind of death there and all that shit. None of it's true. Once you get to know your way around, though, you'll cut right through the bullshit - I hope. Afraid o' ghosts, Frank?"

A diesel on one of the boats shuttered then thundered to start and Donna jumped to her feet. "Keeerist," she screamed, grabbing Frank's arm. "That freaked me out." She looked around.

Frank laughed and Donna punched him in the arm. "I wasn't scared about the story, Frank, I just didn't expect that."

"I hear that every morning," Frank said. "I like the sounds of the draggers leaving. Some nights I watch the parade through my window. A line of red and green lights sputtering out a . . . "

Frank couldn't finish his sentence because Donna had bent over and planted her lips firmly on his. When she caught her breath, she said, "Frank, shut up. Let's make love."

Frank hesitated, then mumbled, "Make up your mind, Donna. You just told me to keep talking."

"Yeah, Frank and now I want you to shut up and make love to me."

Frank looked around then he grabbed Donna and kissed her. "Yeah, I'd like that," he whispered in her ear, "but not here. Geezuz, you could get splinters in your ass from the wharf."

Donna grabbed Frank and kissed him again. She laughed, then squeezed his ass and whispered. "What makes you think you'll be on top?"

They left for the cottage.

The next morning, Frank got out of bed and told Donna to meet him by the pool. She asked where he was going and he said, "Coffee. We can take a quick swim and drink coffee there. Wear one of my tee shirts and a pair of my gym shorts. See you in a minute."

Bright sunlight warmed the deck where Harley sat reading the *Globe*. When Frank walked by with two cups of coffee and said hello, Harley forced a grin then watched as Frank walked toward the pool. He wondered what was going on when Donna walked over, kissed Frank, took a sip of coffee and said, "Let's go." They dove into the pool.

"Oh, dear," Harley whispered as he snapped the paper open.

Chapter 7

Old:Cheese, Wine, Bones.

The Minimalist
Les Moor
1968 The Aviary Papers Publishers

Frank liked doing maintenance around the old hotel. Most of it was routine and simple and it relaxed him he'd told Jack. He'd found a crate full of old gas light fixtures in storage in the basement and with Jack's approval, he'd converted them to electric and reinstalled them in the lobby and in the hallways upstairs. Harley had waxed poetic on their grace and elegance and what authentic detail they added. The day that Emma Wilkins came to see her friend Haddie Baker, she'd told Harley they looked just like they did forty years ago. Haddie Baker had agreed.

Frank'd repainted the entry door and added some decorative touches that made the door look more like it did in a photograph he'd found in Jack's office. The leaded glass needed more attention than he could manage; he just cleaned it, very carefully with vinegar and water.

He'd told Harley his favorite project was the gazebo. He'd replaced the rotted posts and floor boards and rebuilt the railing. The seats that lined the hexagon were in good condition so he'd just had to paint them. Jack was delighted when saw it. "Geez, Frank it looks fantastic," he'd said. "I wish we'd get the whole place looking this good. That scrolling you added is terrific. If we ever had a great season and there was enough extra cash, we could do something with the sundeck or the pool."

Frank had asked, "Like what?" and Jack had said he'd always thought the pool apron would look great with inlaid tiles. He specifically mentioned some Italian tiles he'd seen on a trip to Florence. He'd talked about adding some landscaping to give the pool a little more privacy and maybe even getting some more chairs like the ones from up where Frank was from. "Adirondack," Frank had offered.

A few days later, Frank was measuring the pool apron and checking the sides as he paced off an area around the apron. Jack had just returned from the bank and walked over to say hello.

Frank spoke without looking up. "Jack, privet would make a nice boundary here."

"Frank, what're you doing?"

"You know, Jack, the updating here in the pool area. Great idea. But what this place needs is some serious rehab. When I was checking around the storage shed under the porch, I noticed the posts under the deck are rotted at their bases. You'll need new posts and concrete piers by next summer."

"I know, Frank, but just worry about the cosmetic stuff now. We can't afford any major improvements. Just keep it looking good for the guests."

"I am not talking about improvements, Jack. I'm talking about necessities. Things are going to start collapsing."

"They already are, Frank. If the season doesn't pick up between now and Labor Day, we're going to have a tough time making it through the winter. So, for right now, we need to keep costs down. Spend as little as you can. Just keep the place looking presentable."

"I'm confused, Jack. A few days ago you were hinting at pricey, Italian tiles and Adirondack chairs. Now you're saying don't spend a dime. What gives?"

"I was dreaming, Frank. Sometimes I think out loud about what this place could be again. I'd love to make big improvements but I doubt that we can."

Emma Wilkins and Haddie Baker sat talking in the lobby on a sunny, Saturday afternoon while Frank replaced a cracked glass light in one of the French doors in the dining room. He could hear their conversation: the great place Rackliffe House had been when: the *Henry Ford* sailed in and out; the drives in Henry Wilkins' DeSoto to blueberry up above Bass Rocks; picnics on the rocks. Haddie recalled that painting by that wonderful Mr. Benson from Salem, then she conjured up Samuel Baker strutting through the lobby - cane and bowler in hand - bowing as he introduced himself to Mrs. Wilkins and her friend Haddie Brown. "Oh my," Haddie said, "what woman could have said no to such a man? Off we went to Charleston and what a wonderful life we had."

Frank smiled, listening to the old ladies reminisce. "Must have been great," he thought. He'd finished with the glass, had polished the brass knob and hinges and was returning the polish when Haddie Baker asked him to move a piece of furniture.

"That table, young man," she said as she pointed to a small drop leaf stand leaning against the wall near the fireplace. "It should be over here and opened full for our tea cups."

"There?" Frank pointed to a spot on the floor near their chairs.

"Yes," Haddie nodded.

Frank moved the table. He opened the leaf and secured it. Haddie Baker said, "Oh, that's just fine. There." She placed her saucer and tea cup on the table.

Emma looked up. "Oh, don't I know . . . Oh, yes, Frank's the boy who helped me with the cupola," she said. "How are you, Frank. Say, you're quite handy."

"I'm just fine, Emma. How's Euripedes?"

"He's a good dog."

Frank returned the can of brass polish to the front desk. Harley watched then whispered, "Frank, be careful about moving stuff around for them. They'll have you rearranging furniture and pictures until they think the place is what it was fifty years ago and that isn't going to happen."

"Frank. Oh, Frank," floated across the lobby. Frank turned and Emma beckoned with her index finger, suggesting that Frank move the magazine stand to a more convenient location. "There." She wagged her index finger at a spot on the floor near her friend.

"Too late," Harley said. "Good luck."

Frank relocated the stand. Then Emma and Haddie suggested that Frank rearrange the photos of the ships on the mantel. "They really should be in order," Emma said. "OK? Good. Now: *Gertrude L. Thebaud* should be after *Blue Nose* but ahead of *Blue Nose II* and *Henry Ford* should go next and then *Elsie* and then - no, sorry. *Esperanto* should always be first. Then *Gertrude*, then *Henry Ford* and *Blue Nose* and so on."

"No, Emma, I don't care what you say. *Elsie* should be before *Henry Ford*." Haddie Baker grumbled. Frank moved the photos.

"Haddie, you know nobody knew these boats like my Henry and he always said *Henry Ford*, then *Elsie*, but *Esperanto* was the best." Frank moved them again.

"I know that, Emma, we've never argued that. *Blue Nose* should be second, though, it's only fair," Haddie said. Frank waited to see the outcome of the discussion.

"Now, Haddie, I know about your uncle and all, but that just isn't right, you know, putting a Canadian boat up there so close to *Esperanto* and ahead of *Henry Ford*."

"Emma, she was the better ship."

"Well, Haddie, I always deferred to Henry on those things and he said, "No," flat out "No," and that is that." Emma locked her arms across her chest and threw her chin up.

Haddie said, "Well," and mimicked Emma's gestures. Then she added a great guttural "Hrumph," and peeked to see if Emma was watching her.

Frank waited. Then he started to walk gingerly out of the lobby.

"Stop right there," Emma demanded. "This is not finished by a long shot, Frank." Emma glared at Haddie.

Frank stopped in his tracks. The two women sat staring at each other. Finally, Haddie Baker relented. "OK, Emma, if you're going to make such a big fuss about those silly boats, well, well. Oh, just go ahead, son. Put them the way she says Henry wants them. Henry, Henry, Henry."

Frank reordered the photographs again. "OK?" he asked.

"No," Emma shrieked, "son, you have to pay attention. *Gertrude* then *Blue Nose II*."

"That's how they are," Frank said. "*Esperanto, Henry Ford, Elsie, Blue Nose, Gertrude L. Thebaud, Blue Nose II*." He pointed to each photograph as he said the name of the ship.

Emma got up and walked to the fireplace. She raised her head and scrutinized the photos. "Why that's not right. Haddie Baker, come look at this. That picture of *Elsie*. Why she'd a never flown a pennant like that one. My word. What have things come to?" Frank groaned.

Haddie smiled. "Well, Emma, we just have to do the best we can. It certainly is not like years ago. Remember?"

Emma walked back to sit in her chair. She lowered herself slowly as she shook her head. Then she closed her eyes, leaning her head against the back of the wing chair. "Those were wonderful times at Rackliffe House, Haddie. My father would take me to the casino and I'd watch those games. Such fun." Emma's eyes were still closed and she smiled.

"And the dining room - oh my - so elegant. Those boys all dressed in white. So polite." Haddie pined.

"They were," Emma said. "They knew their places then. That Indian boy remember him, Emma. Such a handsome boy and quiet, too. Always said, yes, Ma'am. No, Ma'am. Yes, sir."

"I do, Emma. I do. And that doorman, Roosevelt, he was my favorite. Always said, "A good day to you, Miss Haddie." Such a grand smile. Always pressed trousers and his shoes, oh those black patent leather shoes. So shiny."

The scratchy old voices murmured on as Frank slipped quietly down into the basement. He left his tools on the bench to go for a swim. Walking out, Frank saw a door that he'd not noticed before. His first inclination: "Shit, I'm lost again." Then the door opened and Patrick stepped into the hallway.

"Hi," Frank said. "What are you doing?"

Patrick grunted. Frank watched as the giant closed the door and reached into a pocket in the wall, grabbed a wooden panel and slid it to cover the door. Then he nudged the panel bottom with his foot and it popped out, flush with the moldings at either side. Frank looked up and down and sideways but could'nt detect the slightest clue that an opening was ever there.

"Pretty clever," Frank said.

Patrick nodded.

"What's in there?"

Patrick turned and walked down the hallway.

Frank waited for him to disappear and then tried the panel, running his hands along the moldings searching for a handle or button or whatever might dislodge the panel. He nudged the bottom with his foot. Nothing. He pushed up, down and sideways. Nothing. Frank stepped back and looked for a clue. Nothing. He walked away, thought for a second and walked back. Now he couldn't even decide which panel Patrick had closed. He shrugged then found the stairs to the lobby.

When he asked Harley about the secret room, Harley said he didn't have any idea what Frank was talking about.

"Christ this place is bizarre, Harley."

"I know, Frank."

Since that night at the railways, Donna met Frank regularly after the bar closed. Their mornings - Donna called it swim time - became part of the daily routine at Rackliffe House. On Sundays, though, when they both had the entire day off, they'd lie in bed until nine or ten. Then they took long walks to the breakwater or around the back shore. If they went around the back shore, they'd spend the rest of the day at Good Harbor Beach lying in the sand, napping and talking.

This Sunday, under the sheets, planning a day in the sun at Good Harbor, they listened as the door to the cottage crashed open and Harley shouted, "Frank. Quick. We've got an emergency. Get up to seventeen and shut off the water in the bathroom."

"Fuck, Harley. What happened?"

"We don't know. Mr. Sanchez came running into the lobby and said he can't shut off the water and the tub is almost overflowing. Hurry, Frank."

"Shit. Can't they read?" Frank dressed. "Donna, I'll be back as soon as I can."

"See ya," Donna said. "I'll be here."

Frank ran across the drive to the hotel, grabbed some tools in the workroom and headed upstairs. In the bathroom in seventeen, Mrs. Sanchez was wallowing in a bathtub overflowing with bubbly water. Frank quickly removed a panel behind the tub, reached in and closed a valve. Then he reached into the tub and removed the stopper. Mrs. Sanchez floundered to get a bath towel. Bubbly lilac scented water splashed everywhere on the tile floor. Frank held out a towel to her, averting his eyes.

Mrs. Sanchez wrapped the towel around herself and raged.

"I'm sorry," Frank responded. "It's an emergency." Frank pointed to the sign taped to the tiles under the shower head. He read it out loud, "Cape Ann has a water shortage. Please do not fill the tub." Jack had them installed in all of the second floor rooms, fearing that the floors would collapse under the additional weight.

"No puedo leer Inglés."

Then Frank felt the floor tremble; it was about to give. He reached and grabbed Mrs. Sanchez and retreated but slipped and fell back away from the tub just as the bathtub and all plummeted. Mrs. Sanchez screamed and Mr. Sanchez burst through the bathroom door and saw his wife lying on top of Frank. He froze as he gawked at the hole. Harley, paralyzed in the doorway, then staggered forward as Jack bumped him on the way in.

Mr. Sanchez helped his portly wife up from the floor and held the towel around her. Shielding her with his body, he walked her to the hallway past Jack and Harley. Frank slowly got to his feet. Soaked from head to toe in a film of bubbles, he looked down through the hole in the floor with Harley and Jack.

"Anybody down there?" Jack called.

There was no response. Then: a very nervous voice stuttered, "Jjjjjjjust mmmmmeee."

"Who is that?" Jack whispered to Harley.

"Room nine. Harold Perkins," Harley said.

"Mr. Perkins, it's Jack. Are you OK?"

"Well,ahh, y y y yes," the voice said. "I'm O O O K now. Was a little constipated but it's OK now."

"Musta scared . . . "

Jack cut Harley off. "Don't!"

Harley wiped tears from his cheeks.

Frank dripped as he stood in the office. "I'm telling you, Jack, we've got to do some serious work to this place or it's all going to fall in."

"Tell me something I don't know, Frank. We're struggling to pay the mortgage. Without some serious cash, major repairs are out of the question."

"What about investors, Jack?"

"Invest in what, Frank? It's not an investment when the goddamned place is never going to make money. Even if we're filled to capacity for the season, the mortgage payment is too much. My father paid too much for this dump and even with tax breaks, it's a huge loser."

"Why doesn't he sell?"

"Who's going to buy now? Inflation is sky rocketing. Interest rates are going through the roof. The economy sucks."

"I guess, Jack, but it's sad to see this old place just fall apart. It's a landmark. Christ, nothing like this gets built anymore."

"There's only one other hotel on the harbor and it's in the same shape. They've been trying to unload it for years. They'll be lucky to get the land value out of it. Nobody wants this place, either. The old man's talking about tearing it down and building apartments or condos. If he can get the money together, he just might."

"That's too bad, Jack. It's a great place. A lot of people like it here. They're gonna miss it."

"I'm going to miss it. This is a great job. Work all summer, get the whole winter off. Christ, Frank, where you gonna find this many available women in one place. And my asshole old man's not breathin' down my neck. Don't talk to me like I don't know how great the place is."

"Jack, I'm sorry. I don't mean to be busting your ass. I just think . . . " Frank wiped the crystal of his watch and checked the time. "Oops, gotta go. Donna's waiting for me."

"Yeah, we can start repairing the bathrooms tomorrow. Get Patrick to help you move the tubs. OK? I'll get try to get Mr. and Mrs. Sanchez and Mr. Perkins rooms out on the back shore. Make sure the water is off in both rooms before you go."

"OK. Take it easy, Jack."

Frank changed out of his wet clothes and told Donna about the floor collapsing. Donna dried him with a towel from her beach bag. She laughed at Frank's story. "It's really a shame to see this place going downhill so fast."

"It's too bad Jack can't find the money to fix it up," Frank said.

"He could if he started smuggling. Pot or cocaine, guns or anything - even swordfish. You can make money smuggling swordfish, I heard. There's a lot of money to be made in smuggling, Frank."

"What?" Frank snapped.

"Importing and exporting, Frank. Makes a lot o' money. Everybody knows it's going on. Fishing boats are bringing in bales of grass and coke all the time - illegal swordfish sometimes. I even heard guns and stuff. People make money smuggling, Frank. Always have. It's been a business here since Glosta was Glosta"

Frank looked sternly at Donna. "It's not worth it."

"I just said that that's how some people are making money around heahr. A lot of money, Frank. You don't think Jack would do it?"

"No, I don't"

Donna shrugged and finished drying Frank with the towel. Then Frank slipped a tee shirt over his head. "Let's walk out to the breakwater this morning. It's too late for the beach. It'll be packed by now," he said.

"Let's make love before we go," Donna said. "I got all hahrny drying you off."

"Christ, Donna, why don't you wait until I get all of my clothes on and tie my shoes before you tell me to get naked and get back in bed."

"OK." Donna sat on the edge of the bed and pulled her tee shirt up over her head. "Go ahead and put your shahrts on and tie your sneakahrs. I'll wait."

They walked down Eastern Point Road. When they passed the Hawthorne, Frank noticed that it was falling in on itself, too. The Fairview looked better. "I read somewhere that Kipling stayed there, once," Frank remarked as they passed the rooming house.

"Who?"

"Captains Courageous, Donna, the book. He wrote it."

"Great movie."

They passed the old stone gatehouse and took off their shoes to walk along the beach at Niles, splashing in the waves like frolicking dogs. Donna bent and scooped a handful of salt water into Frank's face and he shoved her. Donna sat, slapping the water trying to get back at Frank and called him a "royal fucking asshole." A woman standing on the beach watching her children build a sand castle, turned to Frank and said, "You let her kiss you with that mouth?" while Frank leered at Donna's breasts in a thin film of wet cotton.

Frank and Donna kept walking. They crossed a dune to get back to the road, sat, dusted the sand from their feet and put their shoes on. A security guard standing by the gate to Eastern Point Boulevard said "good morning." They walked through and Frank asked Donna why the guard. She told him that it kept the tourists from disturbing the gold coasters little universe. Frank asked if they should leave and Donna said, "No, they have to let us go out. It's a public way to the lighthouse."

Donna pointed to a house, back from the road up a hill and told Frank it was the Birdseye Mansion, built by the inventor of frozen food. "He froze fish down the Fort. Nice place. I don't know if he still lives there," Donna said. When Frank said he'd died, Donna asked if they'd frozen him and Frank laughed.

They passed a stone mansion that sat behind a high granite wall; a brass plaque on an arched oak gate read: "The Turrets," a reference, Frank assumed, to those whose scalloped roof slates he could barely see over the wall. Frank carefully traced the lines of crisply trimmed privet and hawthorns that lined a cobblestone walk leading up to a wrought iron gate through which peeked the flocks of hydrangeas. He peered through the gate but could see only the granite walls of the house. He tried to satisfy his curiosity by asking Donna about the place but Donna didn't know much except what Polly had told her: "It's owned by a family from New York. I saw them at the Galley once and Polly said the grandfather of the guy who owns it now was a bootlegger. He made a fortune during Prohibition. Johnson, I think."

"Maybe the Johnson Wax family."

"I don't know, Frank. Polly told me they were in construction or demolition or something. Polly said she knew them when she was in New York. She said she met the grandfather once. Said he was a gentleman. I guess he turned his bootlegging fortune into a legitimate business and the family is now 'quite respectable,' as Polly would say. One of the sons is a big shot in the government or something."

"I wonder if the old man ran booze in and out of Gloucester," Frank said.

"Could have," Donna said. "It's not like it didn't happen here. Just like the drug thing - a lot of money changes people overnight."

Donna talked about other homes - Henry Sleeper's House, Beauport, now a museum; A. Piatt Andrew's Red Roof. "He and Sleepahr were pals," she said. "In the ambulances in World War One. Y'know, Frank for years, people believed that Sleepahr or one of his cronies designed Rackliffe House. The guy loved fooling people with secret passageways and stuff. They said he was a genius. Maybe a little eccentric but that's not all that unusual here."

Frank told Donna about the morning he'd been lost in the basement and how long it had taken him to figure out which set of stairs led where. "It's a friggin' maze. Have you ever been in there?"

"No," Donna said flatly.

Frank told her about the time he'd seen Patrick coming out of a room and how the panel completely disguised the opening. Donna had heard stories about all kinds of secret hiding places in the basement but she seemed uninterested in them. She pointed to another cottage and started to say something, but then she hesitated and asked Frank what Patrick had been doing. Frank said he had no idea, so Donna continued with the tour. "Green Alley - Cecelia Beaux lived there. She was a fabulous portrait artist. Very famous, Frank. I like her stuff a lot. Painted a lot of famous people."

"Do you ever paint portraits?" Frank asked as they walked past.

"No. Well . . . a few but now I like landscapes and that's about it."

"Will you ever show me any of your paintings?" Frank asked.

"Get real, Frank, we've been doin' it for a month. You don't have to ask to see my etchings to get laid."

"I'm serious, Donna."

"I know. That makes me a little nervous, when you get serious. I'll show you some, if you ever come ovah to my apartment."

Closer to the Eastern Point Lighthouse, Donna pointed to a Spanish style villa that sat behind a stone wall and overlooked the outer harbor. "I love this place," Donna said. "I can just imagine what it's like to stand out on that balcony with a cold beahr, watching the sunset."

"Why not a Martini or a Mint Julip?" Frank asked.

"One step at a time, Frank. Still a beer drinker."

Frank laughed.

Donna told Frank about a guy she'd dated when she was younger. He'd lived in a mansion that had a secret room in the basement. He'd showed her the room one night when his parents weren't home and she'd been wondering about the place ever since. "It was dark and clammy and painted all red and gold," she said. "There were these big couches with leather cushions and all kinds of silk pillows. Weird looking chairs and tables. Fancy carving. He told me it was an opium den. Some banker from New York had built the place and the guy's wife used to entertain friends in that room. I wonder if any of the houses on Eastern Point have rooms like that, Frank."

"Opium," Frank said. "Pretty serious stuff. Turned a lot of heads to mush in the twenties."

"Yeah. I heard that there were some wild times with that shit all ovah the North Shore. Right here on Eastern Point, too. Remember that house I showed you? Well that guy Sleeper and a whole bunch of people used to have these wild parties. Dressed up in costumes and everything. Y'gotta wonder if they were doin' it. I know that Sleeper and Andrew were in the First World War and Polly told me Phil knew some friend of theirs, a poet, who was an ambulance driver and a real opium freak. A nut case. Do you think that's what drove 'em crazy, Frank?"

"Who, Donna?"

In a Place Like No Other

"The poet, Frank."
"What, Donna?"
"The opium, Frank."
"Or the war."

Donna and Frank walked along the granite blocks of the Dogbar Breakwater. They passed a few men with surf rods casting for blue fish and nodded greetings as Donna recited its history. When they reached its end, Donna pointed to some rocks sitting just above the tide and they sat. They watched the boats head for the open water. A few draggers were heading into the harbor, low in the water. "Good day for them," Donna said. Then she talked about some of the landmarks across the harbor on the western shore - John Hammond's Castle, Charlie Fisk's house on Dolliver's Neck, the Cushing Villa. Frank said the view from there reminded him of the Bay of Naples. Donna said she'd like to go to Italy and France to paint some day.

The granite stones were warm and Frank lay back with his eyes closed. He held his head up so that the sun drenched his face. Donna rested her head on Frank's thigh and moved a hand up, under the leg of his shorts and asked Frank if he'd made love to any other women since he'd been sleeping with her.

"When? We've been together almost every night," Frank answered.

"Yeah, but I'm not around all day, Frank and there's plenty of women around the hotel. I know that Kim comes on to you a lot."

"No, Donna, I haven't. And even if I had, I'd have to lie about it."

"Why, Frank, because you love me and you knew it was a mistake after it happened and now you don't want to lose me?"

"No, Donna, because your hand is real close to doing a lot of damage if you get really pissed and I know how you get when you get really pissed."

Donna laughed and so did Frank. Then Donna pulled Frank's shorts down to his knees and removed her own. Frank pulled her tee shirt over her head.

After, Donna lay back against the rocks next to Frank. Both closed their eyes and soaked in the sun. Their fingers were locked and resting on the granite. A boat approached and Frank opened his eyes to see a couple of men trolling in a Boston Whaler that circled twenty yards away. "Whoa," one of the men yelled. "Look at those rocks."

"Finest kind," his friend blustered.

Donna laughed but never opened her eyes. She just raised her arm, and flipped her middle finger high in the air. Frank laughed and asked her, "Do you want to get dressed or just lie here and entertain them?"

"I could care less," Donna said. "I can't move anyway, it feels too good lying here in the sun with you."

The boat left and Donna told Frank to relax. He did.

"Frank, do you remember? The night of the fireworks, you said if business was good, more businesses would come and if business was bad, someone would buy up the place at a low price and develop things. Either way it would change. That's life you said."

"I remember."

"Things are going to change here, Frank. I know it. You told me, Jack said it just this morning. Stuff keeps getting bought and sold and every time the prices get higher. People like us are not going to be able to afford it."

"I guess."

"So, Frank, that's going to change things. Right?"

"I guess, Donna. Don't worry about it. You can't control it. People run around and think they can, but they can't. Everything changes."

"Yeah, Frank, everything changes, but when I feel like this I don't want it to. I don't feel like this very often and I just want to stay here with you. It feels so friggin' great."

"Yeah, it does. But that'll change, too."

"Oh, Frank, your optimism kills me."

"Donna, I didn't say it would get worse. I said it would change. It could get better. I don't know and I won't until I get to wherever it is I'm going."

"Geeezuz, Frank, don't be so friggin' distant. I'm trying find out what's going on with us. I feel incredible and then you get into this I don't know shit of yours and you make me fuckin' nuts. Stop it. Frank, maybe people stay together through bad times because it feels so great during the good times. Did you ever think of that? Did you ever imagine that maybe it can be a good thing and not the crap you had a few years ago?"

"No."

"Me either, until now."

"What do you mean?"

"Us, Frank. It feels great when we're together, when we make love. It just gets better every time."

"Yeah, it does."

"Well?"

"Well what?"

"Oh shit, Frank, forget it. I guess I'll just take it while I can."

"That's the way we should live, Donna, take it while we can. When it changes, we just move along to a new hunting ground - like the Abenaki."

"What?"

"Like the Abenaki, Donna."

"Frank, what the fuck is an Abenaki?"

Frank didn't answer. He sat, legs crossed, staring out at the harbor. Donna shook her head, lay back against a rock and closed her eyes. Frank looked at her. Her brown skin with the white tan lines, hair glistening in the sun. The briney fishy smell turned Frank's gaze into the water. Lucas' reflection undulated in the waves.

Frank, under the rocks and logs. Under the lily pads. The fish hide there to stay cool and wait for food. Frank, don't call the ducks when they're closing in. You'll scare 'em. They'll see the decoys and come anyway. Don't call when you don't have to.

Lucas dove into the pond from the big rock. Come on, Frank, Lucas yelled. He swam ashore.

Bent at the waist, wanting to dive but waffling. Lucas' hand touched his back.

Foundering. Gasping for air. Lucas' thundering laugh. You've got to just do it sometimes, Frank. Lucas pulling him out of the water.

Don't be mad, Frank. Don't be mad. I had to push you. You would never have done it.

I'll kill you, you god damned redskin.

Frank grinned and laughed out loud, remembering swinging the maple branch over his head as he chased Lucas through the trees. "Bare assed Indians in the woods," Frank muttered.

"What?" Donna asked.

Frank smiled but said nothing.

A dragger approached and as it passed close to the breakwater on it's way into Gloucester, a fisherman standing on the bow raised a pair of binoculars toward them. Frank watched as the fisherman walked to the pilot house. "Hey, Donna," Frank heard a voice shouting through a loud speaker, "I tinks Ima t' only guy you gets a naked wit."

"Oh, shit, that's my neighbor Sal," Donna said to Frank. "I'll never hear the end of this."

Then Donna cupped her hands around her mouth and yelled back at the fisherman, "Not a chance, pencil dick. You better call before you go home, I saw your wife on the Neck last night." The man on the boat waved and the boat sounded its horn a few times. Frank laughed.

"You gotta hold your own around these guys, Frank. Otherwise they'll trample you down and you'll never get up."

By the time they got back to the cottage, the sunset crowd was already starting to gather on the deck. Frank asked Donna if she wanted to join them and she punched him in the arm.

"It's been a great day, Frank. Don't screw it up."

"OK, let's take a shower and go to the Galley for dinner."

"Great," Donna said. "Together?"

"What, shower together or dinner together?"

"Both, Frank. Why stop now? It's just getting better and better."

They walked into the Galley and there were only a couple of seats at the bar. The dining room had a wait of 30 minutes and the deck was packed so they took those seats. While they waited for the bartender to deliver, Donna started telling Frank about some of the people she knew in the bar. Her descriptions had Frank laughing out of control. Polly came over to say hello and asked them if they wanted a table. She offered to move some people so they could enjoy the deck.

"Great," Donna said. "We'd like that." Frank wiped tears from his eyes and nodded.

Donna started on a story about the houses on the hill before Frank had pulled out his chair. "They call that one the Aviary, Frank, 'cause she loved song birds. Photographed 'em all the time. Put out birdseed all over the place. Said she had a pistol with a silencer to shoot at the cats that chased the birds. They say she got addicted to chocolate. Bon bons, I heard, Frank. It's addictive you know, Frank. Chocolate. D'you know that Glosta fishermen traded a load of fish for cocoa beans once. It's in the history books, Frank. Now they're tradin' fishin' for coca and makin' money doin' that, too. Hey look Frank, Moonies. There. Over there!" Donna pointed to a wharf across the cove.

"I think." Frank said. "The blue boat?"

"Yeah, Frank, the Moonies," Donna said and gesticulated wildly as she told Frank about a religious group that had set up a fishing business in Gloucester and exported tuna to the Far East. She said a lot of people in Gloucester didn't like the idea that the Moonies worked for free and the church didn't pay taxes. "They make a shit load of money selling fish, Frank," she grumbled. "It's not fair. I know a lot of fishermen who'd like to see them gone. You know, Frank, you gotta love a guy who can convince a whole bunch of people that living a spiritual life for God is all that matters and then turns around and makes a shit load of money. I wonder how you do that, Frank?"

"Religion, Donna, works every time."

"Think they're brain washed, Frank? I heard they get a lot of kids that run away from home and have nowhere to go. They pick 'em up off the streets and at bus stations and stuff and convince 'em the church'll care of 'em. I heard a lot of 'em are ex addicts and shit like that. I don't know but a lot of people around here are talking about the Moonies. Bunch of wackos."

"Maybe they're just looking for something else because what they had really sucked."

Polly strolled over and asked Frank how he was enjoying Rocky Neck. Frank hesitated, then said he thought it was interesting but a little bizarre at times. Donna tittered and so did Polly. Then Polly bent over and whispered something in Donna's ear and Donna checked out the bar. "It's OK," Donna said to Polly. Polly bade them well and walked off.

"What's OK?" Frank asked.

"Polly was just telling me that Tony Parker's sitting at the bar."

"Who?"

"I went out with him for a while, Frank. We broke up about six months ago. He still calls but I don't want to see him anymore. That ahsole was married and I didn't know it."

"Which one is he?"

Donna glanced over at the bar. "The guy with the luau shirt and the beard. That's him. I quit working at the diner for a while and went to work for Tony. I was his secretary. He started hitting on me the first day I got there. Went out with him a few times. A real prick, though. Always stoned. I haven't seen him for months. Heard he's got a bad coke habit now."

"Christ, Donna, how much do you know about drugs and booze, bootleggers and smugglers?"

"I don't know, Frank. Most of it's just talk but stuff goes on here. I don't know why. Maybe it's because we're at the end of the line and people feel stuck. I don't know."

"What's he do?" Frank asked.

"He's a fish dealer. He buys from the fishermen at a low price and sells it to somebody else for a high price. I thought he was a little slimy but I went to work for him anyway. I thought it might be a way out. When I realized it was a dead end, I quit."

"Out of what?"

"Out of where I was, Frank. I'm not really hot on spending the rest of my life waitressing at a diner. Maybe you find that hard to believe but it's true. Yea, I like to screw around and have fun, but I am serious about my painting and I'd like to do that all the time. I thought if I got a better job and made some money, I could get out of here and go to Boston or New York or even San Francisco, get my stuff into a gallery or find a dealer or an agent or something."

Frank said, "I meant it earlier, Donna, y'know. About seeing your paintings. I want to."

"OK, Frank. I'll show you sometime - when we stay at my place."

"OK. When?"

"When I'm sure."

"Sure of what?"

"You."

"Me? Christ, Donna that could be years away. I'm not sure of me. Whoa. We could be ancient by the time I get to see your paintings."

"Well, maybe, but there'll be more to look at."

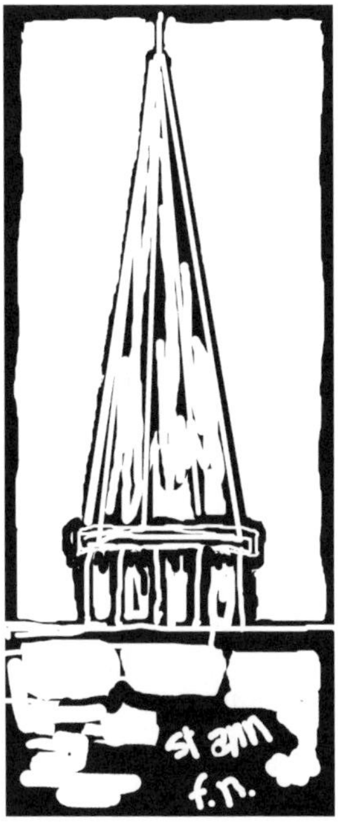
st ann
f.n.

Chapter 8

Codfish, blowfish, redfish. No fish.
Dogfish, Dogbar, Dogtown. Fishtown.
Words. Names. Fame. Fortune.
There's gold in them there hills.

Fishin' fer Gold
Bobby Crosby
1971 The Aviary Papers Publishers

Tommy 'The Big G' Lozano and Owen Chase, Gloucester fishermen and early evening regulars, sat at the bar. They stopped by a few nights a week for a beer or two on their way home after a day out on the bay. Frank had gotten to know them over the last months and enjoyed sparring with them about the Red Sox and Yankees almost as much as he liked hearing them talk about politics and fishing and 'Glosta girls.' Tommy was the grandson of a schooner captain and Owen had started fishing a few years ago. He'd gone to work for Tommy Lozano when his tie dyed tee shirt business folded.

Tommy knew Gloucester fishing from top to bottom. He'd learned from his father and grandfather. At ten Tommy could handle a boat and by the time he'd graduated from high school, he had his own and was making a living catching cod and flounder.

Tommy, now twenty eight years old, had a face scored by forty years of weather. At times, Frank would wonder why his tee shirts didn't split at the seams when Tommy grabbed a beer bottle and his biceps flexed. His forearms were immense and his thick fingered, well calloused hands were as big as the paws of a lion . His soft spoken understated style belied the immense power in his physique. Frank had asked Tommy, once, what 'The Big G' stood for and Tommy had said, "Don't ask." So Frank had changed the subject quickly to the price of diesel fuel.

Owen Chase had a different story. He'd banged around the Midwest for a few years and had ended up in Western Massachusetts selling tie dyed tee shirts out of the back of his Volkswagen bus. He'd been arrested in Chicopee for peddling without a license so he'd headed for Gloucester with ten bucks in his pocket to find a job. He'd said he always thought fishing would be an interesting life.

Owen wore his thinning tawny hair tied back in a ponytail looped through the adjustable strap of his omnipresent baseball cap. Much slimmer than Tommy Lozano with noticeably long, thin fingers, he hardly looked like he could work the kind of hours these guys did, but Tommy said Owen held his own. Owen always wiped the beer foam from his bushy moustache and then plucked at the curls at either end. Frequently he'd finger the gold ring he'd inserted in his left ear lobe and his shirt sleeves were always rolled high enough to show off the heart tattoo on his right forearm. Frank had asked who Cynthia was, once; Owen hadn't offered more than to point to a scar over his right eyebrow, saying he'd bumped into her while rolling around in the mud at Woodstock. Owen hyper-animated his words - always; false bravado, Frank thought.

Tommy ordered a bourbon and coke and Owen drank a Budweiser. Frank asked Tommy what happened to his appetite for beer. Tommy complained about a paucity of fish and wanted something stronger. Frank said they smelled like the fishing had been good and they both told Frank to fuck off.

"We worked our asses off for about a pound and a half of dabs," Owen complained, punctuating his sarcasm by tossing a handful of change on the bar. Tommy kept grousing about boat payments and house payments, and tossed in a few other monthly bills for good measure.

Frank wiped the bar and listened. Owen kept on Tommy. "Geezuz, I wish you'd listen to me sometimes. I told ya not to buy the house. Rates are too high. Rent. Put the cash into somethin' else. That's what I've done. Then I'll buy real estate."

"Fuck you, Owen, What do I want to invest in real estate foahr? I'm a fishahrman. I've been fishin' all my life. It's all I know. I don't know shit about real estate or the stock mahrket." Tommy twisted the tumbler in his fingers but never lifted his head when he answered Owen.

"Fishin's gone, Tommy. You can't compete with the Russians and the Japs. They're floating factories out there. They're using boats like yours to ferry crews to shore."

"Look, Owen, if I can just get through the next few yeahrs it'll be finest kind. We just gotta stahrt findin' fish - that's all."

"Yeah. That's all," Owen snickered "There ain't any fuckin' fish to find, Tommy. That's the point. It's fished out."

"Then I'll stahrt lobstahin'."

"Do that, Tommy, and in a couple of years, when the interest rates start falling and I own about half of this friggin' city, then you can sell everything and come to work for me. Screw this fishin' shit, Tommy. I'm going to start buying up some of these old houses and make 'em into three and four apartments. Maybe condos. The money'll start pourin' in and I'll be sittin' here talkin' to Frank while you're out burnin' a hundred bucks worth of a diesel tryin' to find a mackerel to roast."

"Fuck you, Owen. You don't know fishin' the way I do. It'll come back. Always does. Christ when the cod went bust, we found redfish. We're just in between right now. No big deal. Somethin'll happen and it'll be finest kind again. Maybe I'll get Patrick to work for me and stahrt chasin' tunah."

"Yeah," Owen said. "I wouldn't count on it. Even if he did, what about the Moonies. Ya gonna compete with them? They don't pay taxes, Tommy. They'll hang your ass out to dry."

"I could make it if I had a guy like Patrick throwin' spears for me."

"What's the story with him?" Frank asked.

"Who?" Tommy said.

"Patrick, Tommy. What do you know?"

"He's an Indian, Frank - at least that's what I've heahrd. Used to throw speahrs for Nicky Rowe. One of the best evehr, Nicky said. Worth a fortune. They always got a fish. Fuckahr nevahr missed."

"I'm not following you, Tommy."

"Yeah, I figured that, Frank. Patrick was the harpoonahr. He'd stand up on the bow sprit and chuck spears, y'know, harpoons." Frank still looked puzzled as he rubbed the back of his neck. "At the fish, Frank. He never missed. Made a shit load of money."

"I get it, Tommy. I get it. What happened?"

"Do you mean why's he living in the basement, Frank?"

"Yeah. And he never talks."

"I heahrd he was a vet. Came back with a bad habit. Made a lot of money fishing. Blew it on drugs. Quit and built a shack out on Ten Pound and then moved in heahr when they threw him off. That's all I know."

"Is he Abenaki?" Frank asked.

Tommy looked at Owen and Owen looked at Frank. "What the fuck's an Abenaki, Frank?" Tommy asked.

"Never mind," Frank said.

Tommy ordered another drink. "Gimme a Kamikaze, Frank."

"What's that?" Frank asked.

"Oh fuck it," Tommy said. "Fishin' sucks and the fuckin' bartendahr doesn't know how to make a fuckin' Kami fuckin' kaze. Fucken A! The next thing you know, the Red Sox'll trade Fisk for Yoggi fuckin' Berra."

Owen choked and spat beer. "Yogi Berra's retired, Tommy." He shook his head and laughed into the bar.

"Yeah, well, they sold Babe Ruth for nothing," Frank offered as he wiped the bar in front of Owen. "Why not trade Fisk for Berra? Sounds like the Red Sox to me."

Owen's head snapped up. Tommy glared at Frank. "Watch it, Frank," Tommy said. "You're a nice guy but that'll only get you so fahr around heahr." Owen laughed and plucked at the ends of his moustache.

"How about a grasshopper?" Frank chortled.

"Geezuz, Frank, I ain't no friggin' broad. Keeerist! Gimme a beahr."

Frank placed a Budweiser on the bar. Tommy and Owen sipped at their beers. Tommy scratched at the label on his bottle. "Ya know, Owen, you might be right but I like fishing. I like being out on the water. It's like fahrming, Owen, ya do it 'cause ya love it and ya make it work."

"I suppose," Owen said, "but I just don't have it in my blood like you, Tommy. I just want to make a lot of money and have all the toys that money can buy. Great looking broads, a few trips a year to Vegas, probably a big boat so I can cruise down to the Bahamas. Don't worry, Tommy, I'll wave as I pass you out in the bay. What do you think, Frank?"

"I don't know," Frank said, "I'm not that big on the ocean."

"Then what're you doing in Glosta, Frank?" Tommy asked.

"Sometimes I wonder," Frank said.

Tommy and Owen laughed.

"I know what you're doin' here," Owen said. "You're like me. Something somewhere else turned to shit and you ended up here because it's an easy place to live. There's always a job and a cheap room."

"Yeah, that's part of it," Frank said.

"That's gonna change, though," Tommy said. "As soon as Owen starts buying up all the property and raisin' rents."

Frank laughed. Owen smiled.

"Frank'll do fine," Owen said. "I saw the gazebo. Frank, you could find a lot of work around here as a carpenter. Hell, I'll be glad to have you on the crew when we get up and running. Let me know."

Frank laughed. Tommy looked at Owen. "You're really serious."

"Yeah," Owen said. "Look at downtown. It's already happening there. Look at the places on Middle Street. All offices and apartments."

"Not Pike's." Tommy said.

Owen chuckled. "It's a funeral home you dork. That's steady business anytime anywhere. That's what y'gotta have, Tommy - a regular supply like the undertakers."

Tommy didn't answer. He stared at his beer bottle and traced the lettering with his finger. He looked up at Frank and said, "What do you think, Frank?"

"I don't know, Tommy. Owen might have something, but it's gotta be hard thinking about giving up on fishing if it's been in your family for so long."

"Yeah." Tommy twisted his bottle as he stared into the mirror.

"Yeah," Owen added. "I'm glad sometimes I don't have all that family shit hanging around my neck like a friggin' mooring stone."

"Where's your family, Owen?" Frank asked.

"Who friggin' knows. The last I heard from my old man was a post card from some place called the Kalani Hotel. Stop by if you're in the area, he wrote. What a dipshit. Told us he was going to a convention and never came home. The old lady died a couple of years ago. I got a brother somewhere - New Mexico, I think."

Frank drifted off.

Lucas stood at the front door. Tears. Red eyes. Mumbling.

What, Lucas? What is it? I can't hear you.

He's dead, Frank. In his truck, Frank. I found him, Frank. I threw the bottles out the window. What are barbiturates, Frank? He left a note on the dashboard. Good luck Lucas. Love, Dad. Slumped, shaken - Lucas walked toward the street.

The knife prick. The blood dripped. Lucas rubbed his finger on it.

Where'd your father go Frank? Is he coming back? You're Abenaki now, Frank.

You're French now, Lucas.

Aw fuck, Frank. I hate cooking.

"What're you grinning about, Frank?" Owen said as he shook his empty bottle. Frank said, "History," and plopped a full one on the bar. Then he rubbed the end of his finger. Owen kept arguing with Tommy Lozano. "Bullshit!"

"Yeah, Owen but let me tell you somethin'." Tommy stiffened. "All of those big houses you're eying to turn into apahrtments and stuff were about families."

"No they weren't, Tommy," Owen replied. "They were all about money - put up by men who got rich taking advantage of what this place had to offer. Fishin's gone so now y'gotta to ask yourself what has this place got to offer. Beautiful weather, beautiful harbor. Sell the view, Tommy. All those big houses sitting around waitin' for me. Look upstairs some night, Tommy. Jack's makin' a shit load o' money sellin' the view. Look at the Back Shore. Ripe for the pickin'."

"That's criminal," Tommy said. "That's one of the last natural places."

"Bullshit," Owen said. "Look at what's there already. A couple of cinder block motels with pools and TV in every room. Come on Tommy, get off your high fuckin' horse. The view's only going to get better when you make a fortune and build a big house out on Eastern Point."

"What's the story with that place?" Frank asked.

"Eastern Point?" Owen said.

"Yeah," Frank said. "Those places seem to survive."

"Different money," Owen said. "That's really old money. Money that was made elsewhere. Not here. Those families weren't in the fish business. They're bankers from all over. Downtown is Gloucester money."

"Naw," Tommy said, "that's bullshit, Owen. You don't know what the fuck you're talking about. Those people are Glosta people, too. They just put up a gate and kept all the riff raff like you outta theahr."

Frank saw Owen wince. So did Tommy.

"Hey," Tommy said. "I was just jokin'. Don't get your shahrts in a tight knot. OK?"

"Yeah, sure," Owen said. "No problem."

Tommy tried to reignite the conversation. "The people who built all those big houses downtown were successful because they had big families. Committed to the family thing, Owen, not some business idea. They died out 'cause the kids moved elsewheahr. There was nothing for 'em to come back to heahr. Went off to college and stuff. Found jobs othahr places. Wasn't theahr fault that fishin' 's up and down."

"Yeah, sure," Owen said. "What ever you say, Tommy, but when the shit hits the fan, don't say I didn't tell you."

Tommy and Owen sipped their beers and Frank cleaned ashtrays. Then Frank asked Owen what he knew about the houses on Banner Hill. "Why doesn't somebody buy those and do what you're talking about?" Frank asked.

"I told you, Frank," Owen said. "money's expensive now. When it's time, somebody will. Maybe I'll buy the Rookery and make condos."

Tommy moaned. "Owen, it's called the Aviary. The guy who owned it raised carrier pigeons durin' the war."

"Yeah, whatever," Owen said.

"No mattah," Tommy said. "That old lady, Emma Wilkins isn't about to sell to anybody who's going to turn that thing into apahrtments and you know it, Owen. Besides, all those stories about the poet jumping to his death have scahred buyahrs away."

"That's a crock, Tommy." Owen retorted.

Frank told them about finding the book of poetry up in the cupola. When he finished, he said, "Maybe there's something to the poet story, Owen."

Owen said, "If it's anything, Frank, it's that crazy Wilkins lady making it up."

Donna walked in and sat a few seats away from Tommy and Owen, complaining about the smell. They both told Donna to fuck off. Donna flipped them the finger and ordered a beer. Then she said, "Hi, Frank. What's happenin'?"

"Pretty quiet. Maybe things are slowing down a little."

"Don't count on it, Frank. The Beaux Artes Ball's tonight. Big costume party and drunk down The Neck. Annual thing for the ahrtists. Wait'll you see that crowd."

"You gonna stay?"

"No chance, Frank. The sunset crowd'll be here in no time. I'll finish this and take off."

Tommy and Owen yelled "Good night," to Frank and left. Frank and Donna talked for a while and Frank tried to convince her to stay. "At least

I'd get to say hi to you once in a while, Donna."

Donna said she'd try and then the crowd from the sundeck swooped in. Their chatter filled the room but when the band started a set, they rushed to dance. Donna grimaced through the first song, and breathed relief when the band stopped. Then the singer announced the next song, *Cherish*. Donna looked at Frank, stuck her index finger down her throat, screamed "Sorry, Frank. Can't do it," and bolted.

That night turned into the busiest Frank had seen all summer. The usual banter washed over the Neil Diamond medley when, suddenly, the door flew open and a wild parade of exotic costumes, led by Bobby Crosby wrapped from neck to toe in tin foil, capered through the crowd.

"Geezuz," Frank shouted to Jack who was standing at the other end of the bar. "Help me out."

Jack, laughed, grabbed a rack of glasses and walked behind the bar. "OK. Frank. It's the overflow from the Beaux Artes Ball. Could get nuts."

"Right," Frank said grabbing bottles from the speed rack and pouring as fast as his hands could move. "Like this place has ever been anything but friggin' crazy." They kept coming and Frank counted at least thirty costumes.

Polly Perry strutted in, heavily corsetted in a garish sequined gown. Her breasts, pushed up, were within millimeters of erupting from the low cut neckline. Her cherry red lips encircled a gaudy cigarette holder - dangling dissolutely from clenched pearly white teeth. Long fake eyelashes fluttered in wells of deep violet shading. Mae West would have envied the golden curls that danced like little slinkies on her bare shoulders. "All mine," she sang at Frank, lifting her eyebrows and sprucing her locks. Frank glimpsed long red fingernails as Polly clasped the cigarette holder and thrust her chest over the bar, purring, "Why don't you come on up and see 'em some time." A thick redolence drifted across the bar and tickled Frank's nose. He sneezed violently.

Frank grabbed for a cocktail napkin to wipe his nose. Then, peering into her gown, said, "Well, Polly, the view's pretty good right here."

Polly reached across the bar and grabbed Frank by the back of the head. She pulled him to her and kissed him brazenly. When she let go, Frank teetered and sneezed again. Polly smirked. "Y'look like ya been eatin' a pomegranate, Frank. How 'bout a Manhattan?" Frank nodded and sneezed again.

"What the hell's the matter with you, Frank?" Polly asked.

"Chanel?" Frank asked in a nasal drawl.

"Yeah," Polly answered. "Hey, Frank. Lose the cherry."

Frank automatically mixed her drink while watching costumes wriggle and traipse through the door. Wiping his lips with a cocktail napkin and pinching his nostrils to stifle another sneeze, he counted seven Carmen Mirandas, fruit bowls strapped precariously to their heads, swaggering through the yellow haze. Colorful sarongs draped their hips and all but three wore flowery blouses, unbuttoned, then knotted above their navels. The others wore only bras or bikini tops. Frank watched, flabbergasted, as a hand reached out and untied the string of one of the bikini tops. It wafted to the floor, the crowd cheered wildly as the bare breasted Carmen bounced gaily to *Coming to America*. Polly sipped her Manhattan and remarked to Frank that the Carmen's breasts were minuscule compared to hers. Frank nodded.

Jack hollered, "No nudity, please." The crowd jeered.

Frank walked over to serve Bobby Crosby and his crew of six cowboys, three Lawrences of Arabia and five Marilyn Monroes. A James Dean look alike stood talking with two of the cowboys. "One of Harley's boys," Bobby whispered to Frank.

"Oh yeah," Frank said. "Who are you supposed to be Bobby?"

"A satellite from 2001 a Space Odyssey. The theme was movie stars."

"I kind of gathered that, Bobby," Frank said. "What can I get you?"

"I need some comfort, Frank. Surprise me."

"Just a shot away," Frank called out as he poured a tumbler full of booze. The band had just stopped playing, and Bobby's entourage, hearing Frank, belted out *Gimme Shelter*. One chorus and the rest of the bar joined in, a hundred frenzied voices screaming "it's just a shot away. Just a shot away." Bottles and glasses banged on the table. A fisherman Frank recognized led the chorus from atop a table. Missy Dahlgren dashed from her bar stool to dance and collided with Kim Bristol. They watched as an entire tray of beers and mixed drinks floated upward, exploding as they kissed the ceiling. In the hullaballoo, the noise of the impact was lost but Kim's shrieks scattered those in close proximity.

Jack was laughing and so was Frank. They couldn't work fast enough. Every time somebody poured a drink into Bobby Crosby's mouth, he shuddered, flickering in aluminum. One of the Marilyn's walked over to Bobby and purred, "Hi, Bobby. Polly said you're supposed to be somethin' from Midnight Cowboy. Is that true?"

"Yessss sireeee," Bobby screamed. "A Nathan's hot dog."

"Can I have a bite, Bobby?"

"Marilyn, by all means!"

Frank guffawed as the Marilyn peeled the aluminum foil from Bobby and tossed the tiny strips into the crowd. Blustery cheers filled the bar. Frank called to Jack and Jack looked up and caught a glimpse, squalling. "No! Don't . . . "

Too late. Bobby posed bare but for his cast and his stainless steel halo. Three Carmen Mirandas screeched and ran through the door. One of the Lawrences of Arabia had a roach between his thumb and index finger. Frank saw him gasping at the sight of Bobby then watched as he clutched his throat and scrambled for a beer. "Must have inhaled," Frank thought.

Four of the Marilyns sashayed across the room with Bobby as Jack screamed, "Get something to cover him or he's banned for life."

"Way to go, Jack," Polly Perry whooped.

One of the Marilyns promptly offered Bobby her dress. Bobby refused to take it and shouted, "You're jealous, Jack. If you think I'm getting dressed now, you're crazier than I am. Send the bill to my room." The naked Marilyn linked arms with Bobby. Frank, numb with shock, mouth agape, watched their bare bottoms sally out the door.

Ruthie'd walked in just as they'd left. Bellying up to the bar, she ordered a shot of bourbon and when Jack asked if she'd seen two bare assed people, Ruthie piped, "Ayuh. Headin' for the gazebo."

"Thank god," Jack said. "they're not going out in public."

Ruthie belted down the bourbon and left.

After locking up for the night, Frank walked back to the cottage and nuzzled Donna awake as he crawled into bed. He mentioned the scene in the bar and she bolted upright and insisted he tell her everything.

"The winters around here are long, Frank. These stories keep people from getting crazy."

"Getting?"

Chapter 9

God is irreverent.

War - a Morality Play
Bobby Crosby
1971 The Aviary Papers Publishers

In mid August, Jack asked Frank about his plans for the winter. Frank said he hadn't given it much thought and Jack suggested he consider his options. Jack also hinted Frank might be spending too much time with Donna. "You're doing it again. Getting too involved with one woman, Frank."

"Nah," Frank said, "Donna's great. I like her stories. She's a lot of fun and a lot better looking than you, Jack."

"Get serious." Jack glared. "Haven't you noticed how many woman are hanging around the bar? A couple guests even stopped to ask what your story was, Frank. Hey, it's great for business that you attract so many woman. Show a little interest, I'll be happy."

"Christ, Jack. What do you want me to do, hustle the clientele to boost the bar business?"

"No, Frank. I just wish you wouldn't spend so much time with Donna. Keep the guests happy. That's all I ask."

That afternoon, Frank worked in the basement repairing a couple of bar stools damaged during the Beaux Arts brouhaha. He kept flashing back to the night Jack sent Willy Hall for pizza and then ransacked his room thinking Willy had the answers to a sociology quiz. Frank paused while inserting a screw to refasten a leg brace, envisioning Jack's frustration and how it got the better of him when he didn't find them so he torched Willy's treatise on *Hamlet* by lighting off the spray from a can of Right Guard.

The next morning, by the pool, Frank asked Donna about the winters around Gloucester.

"The Neck's a tomb, Frank," Donna said. "You could probably get a job in a restaurant downtown, but it's pretty slow."

"I guess I could go back to the mill for the winter," Frank said.

"Back to New York?"

"Yeah."

"What about living with your folks? Isn't that going to be the same old shit - fighting and stuff?"

"Probably. I guess."

Donna stood up and told Frank she had to get to work. She bent to kiss him. "I'll see you tonight. We can talk about it then."

Driving to Rowley, Donna sang along unabashedly with every song on the radio, waving indiscriminately at drivers she passed. Before she got through Ipswich, she'd decided to talk to Frank about living together over the winter. She imagined an apartment out on the Back Shore and watching the sunrise, sipping coffee in bed with Frank. Then she thought about Andy Pratt and how he'd proposed the night before he'd shipped out and the letter from Manila saying he'd married a Japanese woman. She turned the volume up and pounded her palm on the steering wheel. "What a bozo!" she thought and she cringed, remembering how the cop in Beverly scolded her for setting fire to the dumpster. When she told him why she'd burned Andy's stuff, he laughed but told her she'd better not do it again. Then she thought about Frank and sang louder.

Frank spent the early afternoon considering his future while he polished the brass fixtures in the lobby. Harley walked by. "Want to have coffee, Frank?"

Frank hesitated, then said, "Sure," as he wiped his hands on a rag.

Out on the deck, the August sun was warm but it sat lower in the sky than a month ago. "The season's too short, Harley. I'm just getting used to the place."

Harley enjoyed the off season. "It's just different, Frank. It's quiet. I have time to read and listen to music and I visit friends. I enjoy fall and winter as much as summer."

Frank asked Harley where he lived and Harley smiled. "Shall I show you sometime?"

Frank shook his head, slowly.

Harley rented a room from a retired couple that had moved here a few years ago to their family home on the Moors. It was big, uninsulated and expensive to heat. "Grand old fireplace," Harley said. "It really takes the chill off. You need warm blankets at night." Then Harley reached over and squeezed Frank's knee. "Or a warm body."

Frank smiled. "Harl, give it a rest."

Harley laughed. "Of course, Frank. I'm just teasing. You're a nice guy, Frank, and I hope something works out for you. I won't pry, but if you want to tell me, it's OK."

Frank shrugged and went back to work.

That night, when Frank unlocked the door to the bar, a hand came from behind and covered his eyes and another grabbed his crotch. "Donna," Frank said.

Donna laughed and kissed him on the back of the neck. As he opened the door to the bar, she said, "Frank, I've been thinking all day about this. We should get a place together. For the winter. Two can live cheaper than one. See how it goes. What do you think?"

"See how what goes?" Frank asked.

"Us, Frank. We'd have fun. Why not? Share expenses. Spend time together. I'll work at the diner and you'll find a job. Go out sometimes."

Frank fumbled with his key ring and dropped it. "Shit," he groused as he bent over to retrieve it. He opened the door and walked into the bar - never turning to recognize Donna. He hurried to stock the coolers and line up glasses. He wiped the bar several times and kept repositioning the bottles in the speed rack. He walked over and cranked open the jalousie windows to clear the smell of stale beer and cigarettes, never speaking to Donna, who'd noted his disquiet.

"Geezuz, Frank, I guess I scared you. You're sweating bullets. Your shirt is soaked. Forget it. I didn't mean to give you a heart attack."

"You didn't scare me. I'm just late getting this place open."

"Bullshit!"

Donna nursed a beer at the bar until nine. The only time Frank spoke to her, he asked if she enjoyed the Beach Boys. He'd reached for a bottle on the shelf behind him before she'd answered, but her response flashed in the mirror as she mouthed "Fuck you, Frank," and flipped the finger.

Jack stood at the end of the bar and watched. When Donna left, slamming the door, Jack shouted over the music, "Looks a little pissed. Frankie boy finally getting with the program?"

Frank strode to the end of the bar. "No, Jack. Just taking a break.

She's talking about living together this winter. A little surprised."

"Geeezuz! Never told her about Allie. Did you?"

"She knows."

"You still in love with her, Frank?"

"Allie? No."

"Hey, look, Frank, wouldn't blame ya. She was somethin' else. What a body! Too bad she split."

"Best thing that ever happened to me, Jack."

"Yeah, right, Frank, only three years and a friggin' truck load of bourbon to get you over it."

Frank hesitated.

"So why get involved again, Frank? And with Donna Pearce? Great sex, Frank? You can get that anywhere?"

"I'm not that involved, Jack. Back off will ya."

"Every night is pretty involved. Face it, Frank. Like I said. You don't get it. Give it up. Screw around a little. See those two?" Jack pointed to a couple of women sitting at a table. "Either one would spend the night with you in a second. Come on I'll set it up."

"No!"

Jack leaned on the bar and motioned Frank closer. Frank stared into an empty tumbler but heard: "Look, Frank, those two woman at the table are a couple of old friends of Rackliffe House and I need a favor. They've been coming here for more than twenty years. They used to come with their father, Preston Walters."

"The writer?" Frank asked.

"Yup. Came every summer. Brought his entire family. Took three rooms for a month. Now it's just them." Jack nodded toward the table. A brunette with her back to Jack turned and looked toward Frank when the blonde, opposite her, winked at Jack. "They're important customers. Those two babes are sitting on a fortune. When Walters died, they got it all. They're talking about investing in this place because they love it and they don't care if it makes money or not. They just want it to be here so they can come for a month every summer and have fun. Besides, Frank, they love a good party and they're wild."

"So." Frank noticed the innocence Jack always managed when he needed a favor.

"So? So let's close the bar and show 'em some fun. Come on, Frank.

We'll go to the cottage, play some music, drink some beer, have a laugh or two. That's all. Cindy, the brunette, told me this morning she thought you were kinda cute. Remember, Frank, you're the one who was talking about fixing up the place. With a chunk of cash, we just might be able to do it. Come on."

The morning after, Harley basked in the sun on the deck when Frank sat down at the table with a cup of coffee. He said good morning to Harley and asked what the news was, pointing to the copy of the *Globe* on the table. Harley ignored the question and asked where Donna was and Frank said, "Just needed a break, Harley."

"You or her, Frank? And why are you so tired if you spent the night alone?"

"I did sort of but Jack and I entertained the Walters sisters until about four."

"The Walters sisters? Don't know 'em."

"Preston Walters' daughters. They were in the bar last night. Jack said they're here every summer. You should know them by now, Harley."

"Oh, yesss." Harley tapped his finger on the table and grinned. "Is one a tall, beautiful blonde with legs, legs and more legs, and the other a shorter brunette, kinda frumpy?"

"Yeah, the Walters sisters. Big bucks. Jack says they want to invest in the hotel."

"Oh boy, Frank, you've been had - literally and figuratively. Not that that's anything new around this place."

"What do you mean, Harley?"

Harley told Frank about the blonde. "She's Jack's old girlfriend from high school. She's married but shows up with a friend and spends a night or two with Jack." He added that the brunette was just a cover but admitted that Jack had been known to entertain several ladies at once.

"I've known Jack for a while, Harley," Frank said. "He's never mentioned that."

Harley said he'd heard that when Jack went off to college, she'd married the first guy that asked her and Jack begged her to get a divorce until he found out she was pregnant. Harley didn't think it was as much a love affair as a break from married life. " . . . for her anyway," Harley whispered. "My guess is that the husband's away and she dumps the kid and comes up for a night or two. This is her third time this summer. She cruised in yesterday afternoon and asked for Jack. I asked her if she would be taking a room and she said no, so I guess she and her friend have left. You'll always know if she's been around. If Jack's wearing sandals, check it out, Frank."

"What?"

"You'll see, Frank."

Stunned, Frank mulled then he thought he smelled pizza. Chuckling inwardly, he sipped his coffee and mused, staring at the harbor. But for the putter of boats in the harbor and the racket of gulls overhead, he and Harely sat in silence. Then Harley asked Frank if he'd thought any more about his plans for the winter and Frank said he was thinking about Donna and the idea of them living together but it made him nervous. Harley said he thought he understood because Jack had mentioned something about Frank's old girlfriend and Frank's drinking. "Is that the problem, Frank?"

"Maybe," Frank said.

"Well," Harley offered, "there's no maybe about it. Either it is or it isn't. You know. I don't. It's yours to deal with but let me tell you something. It's not advice, just a story. Take it for what it's worth."

Frank listened as Harley talked about his career as an English teacher at a private school in Vermont and about the drinking problem he'd developed because he couldn't come to terms with his homosexuality. Harley said he'd known he was gay since he was fifteen but he'd never confronted it, so he'd spent a lot of time drinking alone. After a faculty Christmas party, Harley was driving home and turned onto what he thought was a street but it was a driveway that led to the overhead door of his headmaster's garage. His car entered the garage and the headmaster's beloved riding mower exited through the back wall. The plow attachment uprooted a couple of prize winning rose bushes from the gardens. Harley moaned, "The antlered behemoth tore through the glass wall of their sun porch and demolished their antique dining room set."

Frank laughed. "Sorry, Harley, the part about the mower's funny."

Harley frowned and told Frank how much he'd loved teaching and how much he missed it. Frank said he thought Harley was better off knowing who he really was. Harley said he'd always known who he really was but didn't admit it and if he had he could have had it all.

Frank said, "But you seem happy, Harley."

"I'm as happy as I'm going to be, Frank. That doesn't mean as happy as I could be."

"I guess I get you, Harley, but I don't have a clue about where I'm going. No idea what I want to do."

"Maybe you should just travel a little. Go to Europe. Spend some time in Tuscany. It's warm and wonderful. The people are friendly and the food and wine are divine. I love it there. You don't have to stay long. Just long enough to get away from here for a while."

"I just got here, Harley," Frank complained. "Now, I should go there to get away from here which is where I am because I came here to get away from where I was. I was there to get away from where I was before that and before that I was there to get away from the place I ended up going back to. Something isn't working, Harley."

"Good point, Frank. Maybe it's the getting away that isn't working, then. You got to start getting to. Move toward something. You haven't found a passion in life. You banged around in college doing something you thought might lead somewhere but didn't. You left it behind to try to find something else. Now, you're doubting yourself when you should be excited because if nothing else you're on the way to finding it - I hope. Some people look and never find it, but at least they've looked. A lot of people die everyday from boredom, Frank. You've got a shot at avoiding that painful death. Don't blow it."

Frank smiled and said, "Great choice of words, Harley. Thanks for the conversation."

Donna came in that evening and sat on her usual stool. She seemed more tentative when Frank walked over to say hello. Then, instead of speaking Frank found himself leaning over the bar and kissing her passionately. "OK," he said, "let's try it."

"OK what, Frank? The apartment? Living together? Is that it?"

"No, I kiss every woman like that when I'm trying to get them up on the bar for a quickie." Frank's sarcasm did not go unrewarded - Donna's eyes lit up and she yanked her tee shirt out of her jeans.

"Aw shit. No. Come on, Donna. Come on. Don't do that now. You know what I'm talking about."

"Yeah, Frank, I do. Living together. Great! But a quickie on the bar is great, too."

"Donna, when we close. We can't now. There's no telling who's gonna walk in."

"OK, Frank, but at one I'm bare ahsed and on that bar."

They talked for a while and when Donna finished her beer, Frank asked if she wanted another. Donna said, "I gotta go, Frank. I'm wild about you. You're a fabulous fuck and you know I'm excited about this living together thing. But the band sucks. I mean a girl can only go so far, Frank. I'll be back around midnight. I'm going down to the Galley. I'm really in the mood." At the door, Donna paused and spun quickly to wave good-bye, grinning broadly. "I might have something to eat, too. Thinking about making love to you all wintahr is making me hungry. Gee, maybe I'm pregnant."

The glass Frank was wiping crashed to the floor. Donna laughed and walked out.

It was almost one when Donna returned. Frank was starting to break down the bar. When he brought a beer over to Donna, he asked her if she'd had fun at the Galley. She told him how busy it was. Then she brandished a walking stick she'd just bought from Ruthie and said, "A little impulse I had, Frank. Thought it would look great in our new apartment."

Frank grinned painfully. "It was pretty crazy here, too. I'm fried."

"What! Don't try to back out, Frank." Donna slapped the bar with the stick.

Frank yelled, "Last call." By 1:30 the bar had cleared and Frank locked the door. When he turned to walk back, Donna sat on the bar, legs crossed under her, her clothes folded neatly on a stool, the walking stick leaning across the bar. "You don't forget a thing, do you?" he said.

"Not when it comes to you, Frankie boy, and this is all new." She sighed dramatically as Frank walked over and caressed her.

"What's new, Donna? We've been doing this for a month." Frank began unbuttoning his shirt but Donna took over saying:

"This is different, Frank, not just doing it on the bar . . . Never mind."

"Never mind what? What's different?"

"Well, Frank." Donna wrapped her legs around Frank's waist and kneaded his chest. "We're sort of more, ummm, committed. Like we're really making love."

"Donna, we've been making love all along; at least I have."

Ed Touchette

"Yeah, Frank, but now it really means something. It's different because we'll have a future. You're not going to just run off in a few weeks. You're going to be here and we can make plans and things."

"Future is a tricky word, Donna." Frank grabbed a towel and wiped a smudge from the bar rail. "We talk about it but that doesn't mean it's there. We don't know if it is until we get there and that's as close as we get to it because then the future is something beyond." Frank fidgeted with the towel. "It's always somewhere out there. I'll take what's here right now. I like that."

"Frank, you're a little scary sometimes. I thought we were going to make plans and stuff. You know, see how living together went, get more involved, even . . . married . . . or something."

"Donna, you're getting way ahead of me. Now you sound like somebody else."

"Who?"

"Allie. Don't you remember how you told me she went off with Chuck because I scared the shit out of her because she wanted to get married and I didn't know what I wanted. You sound just like her. Are you getting into the pattern?"

Donna recoiled. "Well, fuck you, Frank. If you're going to stahrt talking about your old girlfriend while you're screwing me, forget it."

"I'm not talking about her, Donna. I'm talking about you. You sound like what you said she sounded like."

"Frank, I'm getting pissed. Either apologize or hand me my clothes."

"OK." Frank reached over and picked up Donna's clothes. She snatched them, dressed and stooped to tie her work boots. Frank buttoned his shirt and walked behind the bar.

"I need time to think about this, Frank." Donna stomped to the door.

"OK." Frank didn't look at her.

"OK. OK. OK. Fuck you, Frank, everything is not OK. I'm in love with you and all you say is OK. OK. OK. Damn you Frank. You do scare the shit out of me. You can be such a friggin' asshole."

"I guess." Frank, impenitent, grabbed the towel and wiped the bar.

Donna unlocked the door and started to leave. Then, she turned. "Damn it Frank, at least you could lie a little sometimes. It would have been nice to make love to you tonight. It would have been nice to make love with you all winter long." She bit her lip.

Frank didn't respond. He stood behind the bar staring at a bottle of bourbon that he'd just set next to a glass of ice cubes. Then he said, "Hey, you forgot something," picking up the walking stick and waving it.

"Sit on it, Frank."

Jack found Frank the next morning sitting on the deck with Harley. Harley drank coffee and Frank clutched the neck of a bourbon bottle.

"A little early for that, Frank," Jack said. "What happened?"

"Same old shit," Frank said.

"Shit!" Jack whined. "You're doing it again. Goddamn, there're only a few weeks left and you can't work if you're stoned all the time."

"Jack, I haven't touched it. I'm just carrying it around. It feels good."

Jack looked at Harley who shrugged and said, "He seems fine to me, Jack. I haven't seen him touch it." Harley went to the kitchen and got Frank a cup of coffee and when he got back he heard Jack say:

"Christ, Frank, you're the most bizarre son-of-a-bitch I know. Let me guess. Donna?" Jack sat down. Kicking off his Docksiders, he put his feet up on a chair and hugged his knees. Then he quickly put his feet down and back into his shoes but not before Harley and Frank caught a glimpse of his crimson toe nails.

"I think so," Harley said, pushing the mug of coffee toward Frank. As he sat down, Harley caught the smirk on Frank's face.

"Frank?" Jack insisted.

Frank hesitated then reluctantly mumbled, "Yeah, Jack, Donna. She got pissed because I mentioned Allie last night when we were going to do it on the bar."

"Downstairs?" Jack screamed, jumping to his feet. "Goddamn, Frank, don't pull that shit in the hotel. I don't care what you do in the cottage but don't screw around over here. OK?"

"After the last few nights, you're worried about me and Donna doing it on the bar?"

"They're paying customers," Jack griped.

"Fuck off, Jack. Nothing happened. She's just like the rest. Guarantee tomorrow . . . or they freak out."

"I've been telling you that, Frank. Listen to me and stop trying to have a relationship. Screw around." Jack paced along the deck, hands locked behind his back.

"I would, Jack, but the only other woman I had the hots for this summer was that short fat brunette. You know - one of the Walters sisters."

Harley tittered. Frank slurped coffee.

Jack furrowed his brow and almost asked, "Who?" when his eyes widened, and he snapped a look squarely at Harley. He threw his hands upward in frustration. "Shit, Harley, I should have known you'd figure it out. Christ, there's nothing worse than a busy body fag getting into your personal life. Couldn't you just keep your mouth shut for once?"

"Well, Jack," Harley said. "If I kept my mouth shut, I wouldn't be much of a fag would I."

"Fuck you, Harley," Jack said.

"Oh boy," Harley snapped back. "On the bar downstairs?"

Jack stomped into the lobby. Frank grinned broadly as he looked at Harley and nodded toward Jack's feet. Harley smothered a guffaw.

"What the hell?" Frank's nose wrinkled.

"I don't know. Some kind of fetish. I see it when she shows up."

Frank grimaced and shook his head. "Man, Harley, I'm not sure how much more of this friggin' insanity I can take."

Harley smiled. "Frank, come on. The sun's bright, it's warm and you just nailed Jack's ass to the wall."

They both laughed but Frank's glee quickly dissipated. "I feel like shit, Harley."

"You look like shit - if I may say so, Frank."

"I'm tired."

"You should be. You've been awake all night staring at that bottle."

"No, Harley, tired of everything. This sucks. Bad Karma, y' know. The country's a mess. Nobody knows if we're comin' or goin'. We're all friggin' insane." Frank shook his head in disgust. "Geeezuz. All you had to do was be in the bar this summer to see it. We're gonzo, Harley. You, me, Donna, Bobby Crosby. All of us. Damn. We're refugees."

Harley stared out at the water. Beads of moisture speckled his brow as he squirmed in his seat. Frank caught it and said quickly, "Sorry, Harl. Didn't mean to upset you."

"You didn't, Frank. Just reminded me of something."

Frank did not pursue the topic. He sat mute and immobile until Harley asked: "Were you in Viet Nam, Frank? I mean you, ahhh . . . sometimes you seem shell shocked."

In a Place Like No Other

Frank glared at Harley then fired, "Weren't we all, Harl? Television every night. Body counts. Game winning statistics. Every night. A lot of friends came home in body bags. I still get sick thinking about it. It was a horror show. Riots and protests. Remember the friggin' sixties, Harley? Dead presidents, dead everything. I sure as shit do. A friggin' nightmare." Frank looked away and his voice softened. "My best friend. Gone. Poof - just like that. Vaporized."

"Sorry, Frank. A lot of good people died there. I lost . . . "

Frank looked up at the gulls gliding overhead. "That's the ridiculous part, Harley. Lucas made it through two tours. When he came back, he went back to college, got a degree and was on his way to becoming a great sculptor. Had sell out shows." Frank stood and flung the coffee from his cup. "Bang! Drives his friggin' Chevy off a bridge. Thirty yards out in the lake there's a wreath of Genesee bottles frozen in the skim ice. That's how they found him."

Harley shook his head sympathetically.

Frank, standing with his back to Harley, raged: "Can it get worse, Harl? Sure. His mother got religion and drove a truck into his studio. Demolished the place. Carvings, sculptures, everything, his whole life friggin' smashed. Then she burned it to the ground. Told the cops she'd destroyed all his stuff because Lucas' work was evil. Some of the statues showed sex parts. The work of Satan. She was proud her son had killed himself because he was destroying the devil inside of him. You want friggin' nuts, Harley? There y' go."

"Nothing left, Frank?"

"Nothin' I know of, Harley. What a joke. Huh?"

"At least he got the chance to do it, Frank."

"So."

"Well, Frank, to him that could have been everything. At least he had a passion for . . . "

"What?" Frank whipped around, glowering with such intensity that Harely balked. Then: "Passion. Frank, he was alive when he worked. It felt good. At least that was something. For him it could have been everything. Anything worthwhile comes from passion, Frank." Harley exuded joy as his arms swept in great circles in the salty air. "Great art, great music, inventions, discoveries, everything great. Somebody just has to do what they do. They do it and they do it and they do it because it's them.

They found themselves and they couldn't ignore it and so they do this thing that makes them whole. They're passionate, Frank. I told you yesterday, you just haven't found it yet."

Frank returned to his chair and placed the mug and the bottle on the table, then resting his palms on his knees, he said softly, "I'm not looking, Harley. I told you, I'm not going down that road again. It's a dead end. I just want to live."

"You won't live, Frank, until you're passionate about something. You're just going to exist. Your passion is you, Frank. You find it, you find you. I see you sitting around out on the rocks some afternoons with your legs crossed - just staring out at the water. You're thinking. Trying to figure it all out. I can tell."

"Trying to clean it all out, Harley. Big difference."

"What then, Frank?"

"Live day to day. Take it as it comes. No big plans. No big deal."

"I doubt it, Frank. Be careful, you could end up like Patrick. Never saying a word. Just popping up here and there. That worries me a little."

"What's so bad about that, Harley? Patrick's OK."

"I suppose."

Frank grabbed the bourbon bottle by the neck and contemplated the label. He twirled the bottle a couple of times then offered Harley a puzzled grin. "Is he Abenaki, Harley?"

"What?" Harley was baffled.

"An Abenaki, Harley? Patrick. Is he an Abenaki?"

"Frank, what the fuck is an Abenaki?"

Frank's grin broadened and he spoke with new vigor. "Indians, Harley. Lucas' people. He told me all about 'em."

"Yeah, what about 'em?"

"First tribes to see the white men, Harl. Kept pretty much to themselves. On the move. Here in the summer and inland in the winter. Interesting people. They didn't live in big groups so it was hard to hunt 'em down and it's probably why they weren't wiped out by disease like some other tribes. They survived. Could be why. Y'know?"

Harley queried Frank silently with a doubtful look.

Frank straightened his back. "It's true, Harley. Lucas told me. They were story tellers. That's how they taught their kids. Passed it down. Inherited - like the hunting grounds they got from their fathers. Otherwise they had nothing. Stories, Harl. They told stories to keep it going. Lucas was the funniest bastard I ever knew. If he didn't know a good story, he'd make one up to make a point. He'd get you listening then add something so off the wall that you'd end up choked or you pissed your pants. He was a riot, Harley."

Harley smiled at Frank's buoyancy but said cautiously, "Boy, Frank, that doesn't sound like Patrick."

"I know, Harley."

"Frank, think about it." Harley reached across the table and touched Frank's hand. "There is something left."

"What, Harley?"

"The stories, Frank. The stories. Do you remember them?"

"Some, Harl. I didn't write 'em down or anything. I just liked listening. Like Donna, Harley. She tells great stories."

"Hmmm," Harley mumbled.

Frank still held the bottle as he walked down to the basement. He'd packed up some tools and was about to leave to repair a bench he'd found in the furniture storage when Patrick walked up behind him and tapped his shoulder. Frank looked up at the Indian. A shaft of light from the clerestory underscored the vehemence on Patrick's face and in his coal black eyes as he pointed to the bottle and said, "No."

Frank reeled at the first word he'd ever heard Patrick speak. Then he recovered and said, "Yeah, I'm not drinking it. It's just there."

Silent, Patrick twisted his enormous frame, and with a sweeping motion of his brawny arm, commanded Frank to follow as he stepped off swiftly toward the stairs leading up to the lobby. Powerless in the vortex of Patrick's fervour, Frank stayed close behind, taking stairs two at a time to keep pace. They soared past the lobby and up to the top floor where Patrick unlocked the door to the observation decks with his jackknife blade. Deftly, Patrick climbed the ladder and, opening the door to the widow's walk, called back down, "Come on, Frank. I want to show you."

"Look," he said, when Frank, gasping for air, climbed out onto the walk. "I lived out there in a shack I built from drift wood."

"I know," Frank heaved.

"I was tired, Frank. Like you."

Frank's puzzled but silent query educed more from Patrick and Frank listened closely as the Indian spoke calmly about his experiences during the war and how, when he came home after the army, he'd started fishing for Nicky Rowe. Patrick said that he was bothered by all of the killing he'd done. "Not in the war, Frank," Patrick said stridently. "That was my duty. The fish, Frank. That bothered me a lot. They're beautiful creatures. I was gettin' greedy. Killin' for money not food. I'd dishonored what I was given. That bothered me. So I quit and moved there." Patrick pointed again to the island.

"Ya gotta eat, Patrick. Lucas told me that."

"Who's Lucas, Frank?"

Frank gazed at the island, shaking his head, telling Patrick about his boyhood friend and how they'd become blood brothers after Lucas' father killed himself and Frank's father left home. Patrick laughed benignly at the story but when Frank told him how Lucas had died, Patrick frowned and launched a tirade about the evils of drugs and booze.

"How'd you get addicted, Patrick?" Frank asked when Patrick finished his speech.

Patrick whooped. "Why'd you ask that, Frank? Somebody say I was?"

Frank nodded and Patrick whooped again.

"Y'know, Frank. I don't say much. I've said more to you just now than to most people I've known for years. Unless I have a reason to talk, I keep quiet. That makes people nervous so they make up their own reasons for why I don't talk. I don't drink and I never took drugs in my life, Frank. That's the truth. I had a beer when I turned eighteen and joined the army. I got so sick I couldn't get outta bed for a day and almost missed the bus to bootcamp. Never touched it again. Somethin' about my body just can't take it. Drugs? Never saw the point. I sit and watch the world. That gets me pretty high. I like that."

"What about Viet Nam, Patrick?"

Patrick scowled. "What, Frank? Because I was there I did drugs?"

"No, I guess not." Frank paused, then added, "Lucas hated it. He wrote to me once and told me to tell people not to go."

"It wasn't good, Frank. Things like that never are."

"Yeah, Lucas said that. But something happened. Lucas changed. I never knew what."

"Could a been drugs, Frank."

Sullen, Frank stared out at the harbor and Patrick said, "Sorry about

Lucas, Frank. It happens."

Frank responded with a slight shrug and closed his eyes as he rubbed his temples. Addled by the digging of Lucas' voice deep in gray matter, he rocked back and forth from his heels to the balls of his feet and, dropping his gaze to the street below, tracked figures fading in and out of the shadows of the trees.

Y' gotta help 'em out, Frank.
Why, Lucas?
They're kids. What the fuck has anybody done for them?
Why me, Lucas?
You owe me, Frank. Get'em to Canada.

Patrick muckled onto the back of Frank's tee shirt, saying "You OK?" and as Frank shook away the cobwebs and nodded "Yes," Patrick let go and pointed to a couple of Black Ducks setting their wings to land near the island. A deep breath recharged Frank and he darted into more stories about how Lucas had taught him to hunt and fish and about the big rock at the pond where Lucas taught him to swim.

Patrick chuckled frequently and when Frank finished, he said, "Lucas was a good friend, Frank."

"He was a great friend, Patrick. He taught me everything. I owed him everything."

"I can teach you things about living on the water, Frank."

"I don't like the water that much, Patrick."

Patrick cast a quizzical glance at Frank.

Frank shrugged.

"The water's good, Frank. You just don't know it yet. Maybe it will wake you up someday - like me. I swam every day for two years when I lived out there. It helped me get my head straight."

Frank shrugged again. They laughed and joked for a while longer and after Patrick told a funny story about his childhood, Frank asked him if he was an Abenaki. Patrick's face slackened as he spoke about his childhood. He'd never known his real family. His mother'd died when he was a baby and a family over on Staten Street had raised him. "They were really kind to me. They knew my mother when they all worked together. Here at the hotel. After the Senator bought the place, they managed it for a couple of years. He took good care of them, Frank. Good man. He even offered to send me to college but I joined the army instead." Patrick went on about how the Senator offered him the room in the basement when the city threw him off the island. "I do odd jobs to pay my rent. In the kitchen. Deliveries. Keep track of the Senator's papers and stuff like that."

"In that secret room?" Frank asked.

"What room, Frank?"

"You know, Patrick. The one I saw you coming out of."

"Oh, yeah," Patrick said. "It's a big vault. Nobody knows it's there but me and the Senator. He stores all his important papers there."

"I know it's there, Patrick."

"No, you don't, Frank. Can you find it again?"

"No."

"Then you don't know it's there."

"No, Patrick, I just can't find it. I know it's there."

"Same difference." Patrick smiled.

Frank laughed.

As the sun neared the Magnolia hills, Frank complained about having done nothing but sit and talk all day. Then, commenting on the majesty of the sunsets, he sniggered as he remembered a story Lucas had made up.

"What's funny, Frank?" Patrick asked.

"Lucas had a great story about the sunrise and sunset."

"Tell me," Patrick said.

Lucas' voice echoed as Frank iterated: "There was this great warrior, Dog of Many Colors, who pulled the sun from the shore to the mountain. Bound by his word, he labored every day, hauling the sun across the sky. You see, Dog of Many Colors had fought with the French on Lake Champlain and had been weakened by their wines and roasted ducks. When the Redcoats drove the French and Dog of Many Colors and his people back to Quebec, Dog of Many Colors promised the great god of the north that he would drink no more alcohol and regain his wits and fight the whites again in the great battle and save his people, reclaim their lands and hunting grounds. Until then, he would strengthen his body by pulling the sun from the shores to the mountains. The great god of the north told Dog of Many Colors, "The red people have to make lots more red people before the great battle can begin. The great battle could be many, many moons away."

"That could be a long fucking time," Dog of Many Colors told the great god.

And the great god said, "That's exactly what we'll call it - the long fucking time."

Patrick laughed so hard he started to cough and choke. When he caught his breath, he wheezed, "Damn, Frank, that's funny."

"Harley thinks I should write Lucas' stories down. He thinks it's important, Patrick. I just like the stories. That's all."

"Either way. It's good to have a history like your friend and you, Frank." Patrick looked longingly at the harbor, then laughed and said, "Gotta go, Frank," as he reached out his hand. Frank shook it, noticing Patrick's chafed wrist. As he ducked his head to clear the cupola door, he glimpsed the red paint on Patrick's toe nails and asked what it was about.

"Oh, just some Indian, thing, Frank - I guess."

Chapter 10

Misspelled Carillon.
Missed smell Ticonderoga.

History's Only What You Make It.
Bobby Crosby
1971 The Aviary Papers Publishers

Just before Labor Day, Frank strolled off Rocky Neck, crossed the causeway and walked up the hill along Mt. Pleasant Avenue. He wanted to say good-bye to Emma Wilkins. Geraniums still glowed in pots and the window boxes dripped ivies. Through the side porch of a Queen Anne style cottage, Frank could see City Hall and St. Ann's in the distance. Almost to the drive, he smiled when he saw Euripedes sunning himself on the grass. Emma weeded along a row of rosa rugosa. Up the drive, the bouquet of roses blended with lavender and the slightly bitter essence of arborvitae into a pleasant potpourri that made Frank smile as he marked the remnants of color in a bed of zinnias, cosmos and snapdragons. A pair of cardinals whistled and a flock of finches nibbled at the sunflowers bordering a small vegetable garden. Euripedes had already tried to warn Emma Frank was coming but she'd not paid attention to his bark.

"Hello, Emma," Frank called.

"Henry?" Emma jolted upright.

Startled, Frank grew more uncomfortable as she squinted her eyes and asked who he was and how he'd known she'd be there. He pointed to the top of the Aviary and asked if she remembered how he'd helped her with the plastic in the cupola. Then he mentioned talking with her and Haddie Baker at the hotel.

Emma said, "How'd y'know Haddie?"

"Emma, I rearranged furn . . . "

"How'd you know my name, smart alec?"

"Oh, boy," Frank whispered down at Euripedes. He thought; then said, "Emma, I dropped by to say hello. I'm heading back now. Enjoy the day. It was nice meeting you." Frank turned to walk down the drive, the

Labrador following, tail wagging.

"Euripedes," Emma squawked. "Where you going, you dumb old dog? Get back here. Henry'll be home soon and he'll be asking where you are."

Frank and the dog turned back to her. She wagged her finger at Euripedes, who lay down again on the grassy side of the drive. Frank came back and said, "Emma, are you OK?"

"Well, of course, I'm OK, you young fool. Otherwise I wouldn't be out here tidyin' up for when Henry comes in. They'll hit the whahrf at six tonight. Henry'll run up the hill and we'll be sitting right there waiting for him." Emma pointed to the crest of the hill. "And if I know Henry, he'll have a nice big halibut. He'll steak it out and we'll be bakin' it before you can say . . . Oh damn, I can't remembahr. Damn! What is that Henry used to say? Before you can say . . . "

"Geee willickers," Frank offered.

"Yes, that's it. Geee willickers. Say, how'd you know that?"

"I don't know. I just did."

"Well that's nice, that a young man'd know these things." Emma bent back to her weeding.

"Emma, would you mind if I went over and sat on the ledge for a while. I'm going to be leaving soon . . . "

"I don't know, son. You seem nice enough but she . . . she's a little finicky about people being around the house. Well . . ." She rubbed her brow. "Might be. Just stay away from the house. The poet may be up theahr reading to her."

"I won't make a sound. Thank you."

"Say, young fella, my name's Emma."

Frank headed for the ledge. He could hear Emma talking: "Euripedes, you go along with that boy and keep an eye out for Henry. Give a bahhrk if you see the boat coming. Good boy, now. Get going."

Frank glanced to his side. "Are you a good dog Euripedes?" Frank said. The Labrador wagged his powerful tail.

Looking over at Portugei Hill, Frank wondered which house was Donna's. He studied the intoxicating colors on the western shore. "In June, that sun would have been over by City Hall."

"Is he heahr yet, Euripedes?" Emma walked up behind them and sat next to Frank on the ledge.

"It's a beautiful sunset," Frank said.

"Always is."

"You see this every day and never get tired of it?"

"Nevahr," Emma said. "Always different. Nevahr the same colors twice. Nothin' is, y'know. You just have to look to see it."

"I guess."

They sat for some time. Emma peered into the harbor shading her eyes with her left hand. Frank tried a few times to start a conversation, then fell silent. Suddenly, Emma peppered Frank with remarks about the boats she saw. Frank couldn't see any of the masts and sails she described. Her face lit up. "There she is. I better get the stove lit. Stay heahr, Euripedes. Wait for him." Emma got up and walked back to her house. Frank stayed.

He thought of the story of the sunsets and smiled. He was glad the stories made Patrick laugh. He himself laughed out loud as Lucas' voice filled his head again.

I take that story very seriously, Frank. I do my duty to my people as often as I can so we can come back and murder Frenchmen.

Lucas' Chevy careened down Maple Street - top down, Lucas at the wheel caterwauling; his girlfriends wielding beer bottles, hanging over the sides.

Frank watched draggers plowing toward the wharves over by the ice house. The putter of their diesels reverberated across the harbor. Just below, in Smith's Cove, two people rowed a dory, their rhythmic strokes gliding the dory over the water.

The afterglow waned when Frank got up to leave. He walked toward Emma's. Euripedes followed. Nearer the porch, Frank looked up. Emma swayed in a white, wicker rocker. "There you are you dumb old dog. Euripedes, I told you not to leave the yahrd. Hello, Frank."

Frank managed a tentative "Hello."

Emma rubbed the dog's chin and told him she'd missed him. Then she said to Frank, "Nice to see you again. Sit and talk a while, Frank. I'm just relaxing in the twilight before I make my dinnahr. Ice tea?"

Frank sat down in another wicker chair, declining the tea. They sat quietly for a while and Frank scratched the dog's ears.

"You know," Emma said, "the sky stays light for an hour after the sun goes down - this time of yeahr, anyway. Toward wintahr, it'll blacken right up. I love to sit heahr and watch the lights ovahtown through the trees. My own little stahrs. Henry used to talk 'bout bein' out on the banks at night. The stahrs just set theahr. Everywheahr he looked was stahrs. They'd come right down to the edge of the ocean and go right back up to the top. He wrote a poem once. He called it "Emma." Said it was for me." Then Emma laid her head back against the wicker and rocked with her eyes closed.

Frank peered out through the trees as incandescent lights broke through the dusk. He thought about Owen Chase buying houses and selling the view. A rich knelling wafted from across the water.

Emma shot forward, eyes wide open. She leaned as though she could see the sounds. "Listen. The carillon at the Portugei Church, Henry." Then Emma glimpsed Frank. "Oh, my. For a second theahr, Frank, I thought you weahr Henry. Why, coming up over the hill with the dog'n all. But Henry was much talleahr and lots more handsome." Emma closed her eyes and rocked.

Frank closed his eyes and listened to the creaking of Emma's rocker. The carillon sang.

Lucas drifted by on the lake paddling his canoe.

Acrid. Stinging. Sulphureous.

Frank sniffed, "Salty," pushed Lucas aside and spoke to Emma. "Was Henry a fisherman?"

Sublime, Emma rocked and spoke softly with her eyes still closed. "Almost sixty yeahrs. All those yeahrs and neveahr got a scratch from a hook. Wintehr storms, fog as thick as a mountain, everything a man could have to outlive, he did. Almost got torpedoed by a German sub one time, but Henry turned her bow to and they missed him clean. You had to get up pretty early to beat Henry on the watahr, you know." She paused then murmured, "Emma, I sit beneath all of the stahrs in God's creation. I watch them. They fall to the weateahr and sparkle on the crest of the waves. I gathehr them up into my bucket and count them. Not enough, I say. Not nearly enough. I toss them back to the ocean and ponder my dilemma. I'll need another sky full to match the light of Emma."

"Oh, that's Henry's poem," Frank blurted.

"Ayuh," Emma said. "Thank God he could fish. We might have stahrved otherwise."

Frank winced.

Emma opened her eyes slowly. "Come on, Frank. It's an awful poem."

Frank laughed. "Well, you can't have everything."

"Oh, but I did." Emma closed her eyes tight and continued rocking. "I lost most of it when Henry died."

"I'm so sorry," Frank said.

"Don't be, Frank. We had a wonderful time. Still is, some days. I remember him like it was yesteahday. It's been ten yeahrs since the truck ran him over. Killed him dead as the halibut he was carrying. Right down at the bottom of the hill when he was crossing ovahr from the boat. Must've been looking up the hill for me and the dog. Nevahr saw it coming."

"Oh," Frank exclaimed, "well, I'm glad to hear that. No, I mean I'm glad that Henry wasn't the poet who jumped from the cupola. Oh, ahh, I'm sorry. I didn't mean . . . "

Emma broke into fitful laughter and wiped her tears with a lace hanky as she spoke. "Oh, my gosh, Frank, you've heard the story. Oh, goodness me. This place loves its stories. The poet that jumped from the cupola. That was just a prank the Wells boy pulled. He went up to the widow's walk with a bag full of acorn squashes. He tossed the bag and the cape oveahr the side and it made a godawful sound like a body smashing to bits on the rocks. She was sittin' on the porch with his folks. They saw the whole thing. She got hysterical. In a panic. In bed a week. When the boy came down the staihrs laughin', his fatheahr whooped him good."

"You did know about the poet and the cape."

"Sure, Frank, knew all about it. I used that story for yeahrs to keep the kids from harassin' the place. Scahred the dickens out of 'em. I tried to scahre you with it. You weahr just a little too curious about the house. Can't be too cahreful. Well I've got to have my dinneahr now. If you stay around heahr, come by and say hello again. If not, good luck."

Walking back to the hotel, Frank glimpsed the lights of the city beyond the trees lining the crest of the hill. Frank thought of Emma and hoped she'd live happily on the hill for a long time. The carillon pealed and Lucas, silhouetted by the orange yellow glow from a window, rocked on the porch of the Queen Anne cottage nestled among tall maples.

History, Frank. Remember: The fort controlled the lake but they took it without a shot when they captured the hill above it.

Chapter 11

Get down
comfort 'er
Stay warm
lay 'er

November
Bobby Crosby
1970 The Aviary Papers Publishers

Jack decided to close down the hotel after Labor Day weekend but keep the bar open weekends until the end of September. He told Frank to use up the inventory and order only the staples, beer, gin and vodka and a couple of extra kegs for the employees' party the Saturday after they closed.

Frank noticed how quickly things quieted down after the Labor Day onslaught. He wondered if Donna'd show up before they closed. He'd seen her car parked down by the Galley a couple of times since their last argument, but he'd not gone in: best to just let it go for now.

Jack was probing Frank's plans for the off season. He offered to let Frank stay in the cottage until the water was shut off in November because it'd take a few weeks to close the hotel. They'd start the Monday after the employees' party - turning off water, cleaning the kitchen, covering windows and putting furniture in the storage rooms.

Frank liked the new schedule. One Tuesday afternoon when his maintenance work was done, he wandered into the lobby to talk to Harley who was behind the desk cleaning up paper work and caressing a snifter of brandy. When Frank asked to talk, Harley motioned to the wing chairs by the fireplace.

To Frank, the place seemed dead and he thought it must be downright gruesome in the middle of winter. Harley agreed but told him it had its moments. Then Harley looked away and told Frank stories about the waiter from the Loft who'd lived in San Francisco and had driven his

Triumph across country to visit Rocky Neck; the gay chef from Rockport who went to New York to become an actor. Harley paused and gazed out at the harbor.

Then Harley asked Frank if he'd talked with Donna. The crackling fire mesmerized Frank. Harley had to repeat that question several times. Finally, Frank said he hadn't. Harley quietly suggested that the winter could be absolutely disheartening if he ended up living in squalor in some rookery or in the basement with no heat and water like Patrick. Frank grimaced and Harley said cheerily, "I know, Frank, let's go downtown for dinner tonight. We need a change. We'll go to Captain Jerry's - a really funky place. You'll love it. We can talk and have a few drinks and get away from the Neck for a few hours. It'll do you good. What do you say?"

"I guess so, Harley. OK."

"This is bizarre," Frank said as they walked through the door of Captain Jerry's Kitchen in Gloucester's West End. Pleated turquoise naugahyde covered the seats in the round booths. Tiny plastic grass skirted dancers jiggled on the bar. The place seemed coated with fried fish grease. Harley nudged him to an empty booth and suggested a fisherman's platter as they sat. "It's enough for two and it's only five bucks, Frank."

"I bet, Harley." Frank couldn't believe the decor. A ship's wheel and a binnacle stood on the floor. A marlin and a miniature sailfish leaped over the mirror mounted behind the bar. Over the swinging doors to the kitchen, driftwood stenciled "GALLEY" hung crookedly, and more driftwood over the bathroom doors read "HEADS" - "TAILS." In another corner potted palms drooped lazily over wicker chairs. The ceiling fan was idle. Busy chatter and tinkling glass filled in the background.

"The only thing missing is Hemingway." Frank pointed to the palms. Harley laughed.

Frank admired another gaping mounted fish on the wall behind a fern when a familiar voice spun him around.

"What can I get you guys?" Donna said, snapping gum and tapping a pen impatiently on an order pad. She bounced her weight from one leg to the other.

"DDDonna." Frank stammered. "What are you doing . . . "

"Taking notes for the social register." The sugary voice modulated sharply into a growl. "I work here, Frank. What would you like?"

"It's great to see you, Donna. How've you been?"

Donna sneered and turned to leave saying that she didn't have time to "shoot the shit." Harley timidly asked for a couple of beers.

"Sure, Harley," Donna said. "Right back."

Frank looked at Harley. "Did you know she was here, Harley?"

"I swear I didn't," Harley said. "I thought she worked days at a diner."

Donna walked back to the booth and placed two Budweiser bottles on the table. "Ready to ordah, boys?"

"What are the specials?" Harley asked.

Donna fixed her eyes well above Frank's head. "Gentlemen, for your dining pleasure, we have your basic fried seafood plattahr at four ninety five. This tastefully prepahred dish is a wealth of fried shrimp, fried scahllops, fried clams and fried scrawd on a bed of french fried potatoes. We have the house special, the famed fishahrman's seafood plattahr: fried shrimp, fried scahllops, fried clams and fried scrawd on a bed of french fried potatoes for four ninety five. And, today only, at four ninety five this special - a deep fried seafood plattahr with fried shrimp, fried scahllops, fried clams and fried scrawd on a bed of french fried potatoes. No substitutions, please."

"I like the first one," Harley said. "What do you think, Frank?"

"OK."

"But of course," Donna said. "Everything's OK with Frank. I'll be right back."

"Geezuz, Harley," Frank whispered, "this is going to get tricky. She's nasty when she's pissed and she's still pissed."

"Relax. She still cares for you, I can tell."

"Oh yeah. How, Harley?"

"Well, she didn't dump a beer in your lap."

"Oh, great. That's a sign."

Harley rambled on about his love of fried clams and how that guy Woodman in Essex had a real passion for cooking them. Frank looked over at the waitress station and answered "I guess," when Harley asked if he agreed. They chatted briefly then Donna clunked a large platter of fried seafood in front of them. "Knock yourselves out," she said. "And if this doesn't do it for ya, we have rawr oystahrs."

Frank was still laughing at a story that Harley had told about one of his old boyfriends as they finished. Harley swigged the last of his beer. Donna came over to the booth and asked if they wanted anything else.

"We're fine," Frank said.

"Says who?" Donna scowled.

"Just the check," Harley said.

After they paid the bill and Harley said he'd get a cab if Frank wanted to stay and talk to Donna. Frank pondered, then looked over at the bar. Frank said, "OK, Harley, see you tomorrow," and went to sit at the bar by the waitress station.

Donna came to pick up a couple of drinks. She sniped at Frank, "What happened to your boyfriend?"

"Come on, Donna, you know I'm not gay. Harley and I just . . . "

"I wonder," Donna said.

"Come on. After this summer, how can you say that?"

"Frank, when it gets beyond holding hands, you friggin' panic."

"That's bullshit, Donna. We had a great time together." Frank stared at the label on his bottle.

"Yeah, we did, Frank, but it's ovahr. Y'made that pretty cleahr."

Frank didn't get a chance to answer. He wrinkled his nose as the scent of English Leather mixed with the stench of fried fish. When he looked up, the bartender hulked before him, growling, "Everything OK here, Donna?"

"Yeah, Jerry, we're fine. Just rememberin' old times. That's all."

"New boyfriend, Donna?" Frank said after the bartender left shaking his head.

"Watch it, Frank. Jerry loves my ass. One word from me and you're swimmin' in shahrk shit."

"Judging from the size of him," Frank said, "I guess you're right. He must weigh 300 pounds. His arms are bigger than my thighs. Sure fills out that luau shirt."

"Yeah," Donna said, "and he's fantastic in bed."

After she served her customers, Donna barreled through the swinging doors into the galley. Frank stared at himself in the mirror behind the bar. He was wondering whether to stay or leave when Jerry came back. The bartender, arms crossed over his barrel chest, glared at Frank. He reached up and stroked his full black beard as he spoke. "You Frank?"

"Yeah."

"Donna talks a lot about you. She's the best. Finest kind. Don't mess with her, man. You hurt her again, yahr ahs goes to the top of my list of things to do."

Frank gulped his beer and nodded his understanding. "Hey, look, I'm just here to say hello. If something's going on with you two, it's cool."

"I wish." Jerry hitched up his jeans, laced his fingers and cracked his knuckles as he stepped off to service another customer.

Donna came back. Frank glanced at her reflection in the mirror. "You look great, Donna."

"Yeah."

"What are you doing here anyway?" Frank asked.

"I'm working heahr a few nights a week for extra money. I'm going to get out of this place and go to New Yawhrk or San Francisco, rent a place and paint."

"When did you decide this?"

"Oh, geee, let me think." Donna placed an index finger on her right temple and chewed the eraser on her pencil. "Oh, yeah, Now I remembahr. It was about a minute and a half aftahr this ahhshole I was screwing all summeahr stahhrted talking about his old girlfriend while he was tearing my clothes off."

"You didn't need any help getting your clothes off."

"Or on," Donna shot back. Then her face softened as she said, "But you know Frank, that was a long time ago. I ahh, just . . . "

Frank stared into his bottle and took a deep breath. "Look, Donna, this is going nowhere. Could you have overreacted? I mean, I thought about it. I wish I hadn't said what I did, but we could've talked about it? You just got pissed and left."

"Yeah, I wish I hadn't, Frank. I kinda knew what you meant but I still thought you were hedging and I've had enough bullshit thrown at me to know what it smells like."

"Donna, I never bullshitted you. That's why you're so friggin' mad."

"Like I said that night, Frank, you could have lied a little. Woulda been worth it." Donna looked down at the drinks Jerry had placed on her tray. She shuffled the glasses and placed mixing straws in a couple of them. She realigned the pile of napkins, then moved the glasses around again. She looked Frank in the eye. "Look, Frank, I can't keep talking to

Ed Touchette

you heahr. I've still got customeahrs. Come back tomorrow night - early. It's not as busy. I'd like to talk to you but I can't now."

Frank stood to leave. Donna picked up a tray of drinks and turned to walk over to a booth.

"Hey, Donna," Frank said, "do you remember the story? The Greek fishermen's hats."

Donna looked back over her shoulder and said, "Yeah. Shoer. The ahhrtists from Jersey."

"What's Jerry wearing?" Frank jerked his head toward the bar.

"You got a problem with it, Frank, you tell 'im."

Frank waved good-bye as he walked to the door.

Donna followed him with her eyes. When he reached the door, Frank turned to look at her. "Tomorrow night. I'm here by six thirty," Donna said. "Don't be late." She smiled.

Frank smiled back.

Frank already sat at the bar talking to Jerry and nursing a beer. when Donna walked in the next night. She walked over and kissed Frank on the back of the neck while she tied her apron and waved at Jerry. Jerry winked then turned back to Frank. Palms resting on the bar, Jerry leaned toward Frank and whispered, "Yeah, Frank, a lot of guys around heahr smahhrtn up in Septembahr." Frank smiled.

Donna shuttled back and forth to her tables but it wasn't too busy so she and Frank got to know each other again. But Frank got frustrated when they tried to work out a time they could have dinner and talk more. Donna said, "Wait. It's slow. Let's go somewheahr now. What time is it?"

Frank said, "Seven, but let's not upset Jerry . . . "

Donna laughed, "Look around." Then she beckoned to Jerry. He swaggered over and leaning on the bar with his elbow, gazed toward the kitchen with his head tilted toward Donna.

"Jerry, darlin'," Donna cooed in his ear as she fingered the gold cross hanging from his neck. "Do you think I could leave a little early tonight so's I can be sure little Frankie, heahr, doesn't get lost goin' home?" Donna squeezed his bicep.

Jerry mulled, stroking his beard with his left hand. "How early?"

"Oh, I don't know, Jerry, honey. Let's say, ahhh . . . about now."

Jerry jolted upright and folded his massive forearms across his chest.

"Christ Donna, it's just seven."

"Aw come on, Jer. It's clammy as hell outside and it's Tuesday. This place'll be dead as a mackerel and you know it."

Jerry shrugged. "Yeah, go on. I can handle it. If it gets any busier, I'll let Isabelle out of the kitchen."

"Thanks, Jerry, I'll owe you."

"Yeah, and what'll I get?" Jerry put his palms on the bar, raised his eyebrows and smiled. He leaned toward Donna with his lips puckered and closed his eyes.

"Well, Jerry, let's talk. How about - yeah, I got it. How about a kick in the balls if I tell Isabelle you're coming on to me. Watch what you ask for, Jer, you just might get it."

Frank and Donna could still hear Jerry's booming laughter as they walked out and turned up Main Street. Donna pulled up the collar on her coat telling Frank she was cold. She slipped an arm through Frank's and spoke in a raspy whisper: "I've missed you, Frank, like even I can't believe. I loved spending time with you. I've been hoping for almost a month to bump into you but I just didn't have the balls to walk back into the bahr when you were working."

"It's probably good that you didn't, Donna. A few weeks off was a good thing."

"I think it sucked."

"I had time to think," Frank said.

"And what were you thinking about, Frankie boy? All of those hot nights we spent togethahr at the cottage? That afternoon out at the breakwatahr? The quickie you never got on the bahr?"

"Actually, Donna, I was thinking a lot about something you said out at the breakwater."

"What was that, Frank? Wanna fuck?"

"No, Donna. I was thinking about when you said - maybe people hang on to each other through the bad times because the good times keep getting better."

"Yeah, I remembahr that, Frank."

"Yeah, Donna and I've been - well it crossed my mind sort of."

"What crossed your mind, Frank? Spit it out."

"I was ahhh thinking of hanging on to you for a while to see just how much better it could get."

Ed Touchette

Donna drew closer and buried her face in his jacket. "I thought about how your voice got me really hahrny, Frank, and how all I wanted to do was take my clothes off when you talked."

Frank laughed and they walked. Donna talked about the West End. Pointing to the St. Peter's Club, she mentioned the fishermen's parties, fiesta and wild dances with great bands. When Frank asked about a store where a red white and green flag hung limp over the doorway in the dank air, Donna said they had the best Italian sandwiches because they baked their own bread and used great oil. They stopped to look at older brick buildings that were being restored because they were listed on the historical register. Frank wondered why Jack couldn't get a grant to restore Rackliffe House.

Frank told Donna how much he liked walking on streets with buildings that were only a few stories high. He felt more human, less intimidated. He told her how much he enjoyed looking at downtown from the ledge at the Aviary. At Center Street, they walked up the hill to a small French restaurant called C'est Bon - a favorite of Donna's: "Fabulous omelettes and onion soup. Roger's pastries are killah."

Inside the café, Donna waved hello to a small man with heavy beard stubble who strolled from table to table. He had an apron tied at his waist and a towel hung from his right arm. His head, covered with a blue wool watch cap, dark hair curled up around it, bobbed gaily as he spoke to his clientele. He wore white Converse high-cuts with red laces and the two inch rolled cuffs of his jeans sat just above the tops of the sneakers. The buttons on his red checked flannel shirt were fastened tight up to his neck where the tips of the raised collar brushed his thick mutton chop sideburns. A square tipped solid black wool tie, loosely knotted, dangled from around his neck.

The room held no more than twelve small tables, draped with white and red checked linen, each with only two wire back chairs. Frosted glass, flower petal wall sconces preserved the intimacy, casting a dim but warm yellow glow to the ceiling. Several couples sat, hands entwined across the table cloth, eyes glazed, mouths wanting.

"Dohna, Dohna, ça va." Guttural tones filled the dining room.

Donna smiled and waved again. She cast a puzzled grin at Frank. "Every time I come in, he says that. What does it mean?"

"How's it going?" Frank said.

"Thanks. Now what do I say?"

"Très bien."

"Très bien," Donna said and she waved again.

The short Frenchman hugged her. "Voila." He pointed to a small table in a dark corner then offered his hand to Frank. "Je suis Roger."

"Heureux à moi vous. Je m'appelle, François."

"Bon," Roger said and turned to walk into the back.

"Hey, Frank," Donna said as she sat down. "Knock it off with the French. It's a little too sexy before supper."

"Oui," Frank said.

"I mean it, Frank," Donna whispered.

"OK," Frank said.

"OK. Oh, man, I hate that phrase. I think I liked the French, better." Donna picked up her menu, then lowered it. "Where'd you learn French?"

"My father taught me a little before he left. He was part French."

"What do you mean left?"

"My father left when I was thirteen, Donna. I told you that."

"No, Frank, you never did. You told me you'd lived with your parents and that they might be coming for a visit in August."

"He came back when I went to college. We're not very close."

"Did they come out in August when I wasn't around?"

"No. I told them the hotel was full. What are you going to have?"

"An omelette. Onion soup first."

"Me too."

Roger took their orders, brought onion soup to the table and talked a little. Frank enjoyed his story: He'd joined the Foreign Legion to avoid jail. He'd spent time in the Congo and Viet Nam and the he'd moved to Montreal where he'd married a Japanese woman, who'd left him for a jazz drummer, so he moved to Gloucester thinking he'd buy a boat and sail back to France, but decided to stay. "Oui," Roger said. "It very much, ahhhh, how to say, il me rappelle?"

"Reminds me," Frank said.

"Merci. Reminds me of France. J'ai plaisir à peindre ici."

Frank liked the sound of Roger's voice and the way he weaved his French and English to tell his story. They talked painting and books and even Montreal. Frank had been there once when he was young. Roger complimented him on his French.

Ed Touchette

Donna removed a foot from her shoe and walked her toes gently up Frank's leg. "Frank, darling, knock it off," she murmured through clenched teeth when Roger left.

"C'est marveilleux." Frank grinned as he tasted his soup.

"You bahhstard, Frank. Knock off the French. You're doing it on purpose. You don't think I'd dahre jump your bones in a public place. Well, you're wrong, suckahr. I'm so hahrny now I don't care."

Frank laughed. He reached under the table and squeezed Donna's foot. They talked, finished their soup and nibbled at the mushroom omelettes Roger had quietly delivered. Donna rubbed her toes along the inside of Frank's thighs. She asked Frank if he'd missed her and he said he had. Donna asked if he'd seen any other women and Frank said he hadn't. Donna laughed and said, "Really, Frank, or are you thinking about how close my foot is to doing some serious damage if I get really pissed - and you know what I'm like when I'm really pissed."

Frank smiled as Donna reached across the table and stroked his hand. "Frank, that day at the breakwatahr was the best day of my life. Making love to you in the hot sun, sleeping naked on the rocks, dinner at Polly's. I could get used to that."

They'd finished and Roger cleared the table. He asked if they would like to try his chocolate mousse. "Incroyable. Magnifique," Roger said as he twisted his head up and blinked.

"Would you like to split one, Donna?" Frank asked.

"Ou lala la! Le chocolat, c'est un aphrodisiaque," Roger said. He winked at Frank.

"What did he say, now?" Donna asked.

"Chocolate's an aphrodisiac."

"Right! Like I friggin' need that listening to your French. Pay the tab and let's get out of here."

"Merci beaucoup. Au revoir." Frank said and paid the bill.

"Au revoir." Roger said.

Frank and Donna wandered down the hill toward Main Street then, suddenly, Donna shoved Frank sideways and pinned him against the wall of an entry way, both of her hands planted firmly against the bricks. Frank laughed and Donna kissed him.

"Frank, did you mean what you said earlier about hanging on to me because it would get bettahr?"

"Yes, I did. Should I repeat it?"

"No. I won't forget it."

"I could say it in French if you like."

Donna grabbed his head and glued her mouth to his. "Let's go to my apahrtment, Frank." She bit his lip.

"Won't I see your paintings, if we go there?"

"Yeah."

Frank drove and Donna directed him to her apartment building on Portugei Hill. Frank turned up Pleasant Street and commented on the Mediterranean feel of the church with two blue steeples. Donna reminded him of all of the Portugese and Sicilians that lived there. When Frank said, "Oh. Right!" Donna raised her eyebrows and shook her head. At the top of Friend Street, Donna told Frank to park wherever he could find a space.

"I'm going to run into the mahrket to get milk," she said. "I've got coffee but no milk. Do you want anything for breakfast?"

"No. What makes you so sure I'll stay, anyway? What if I don't like your paintings and decide to leave?"

"Yeah, real funny, Frank. You think that hasn't crossed my mind? I'm a little nervous so lighten up. OK?"

"Sure. Sorry. I won't say a word even if I hate them."

"Oh, Frank. You're too kind."

Then Donna pointed to a three story apartment house painted bright yellow with lime green trim and said, "Theahr. Second floor. Heahr's the key. If you're not theahr when I come up, I'll know what you think."

"Great colors." Frank nodded toward her building.

"Yeah, maybe on a draggahr, not on a house."

Frank let himself in. Dozens of canvases stacked along the walls, resting against chair backs and sitting on table tops arrested his eyes. A flowerless vase on an end table propped a small canvas; another leaned against a Mateuse bottle. Frank ducked to keep from bumping a canvas that swung in a macramè plant hanger in the hall. He walked around the sparsely furnished apartment, awestruck by rows of paintings full of energy, color, expressive brush strokes. Raw. Mountains of pigment. In the bathroom, two paintings rested against the pedestal of the sink. Oil paint and turpentine odors stung his nostrils.

The kitchen, the only room not cluttered with canvases, sparkled. Utensils ordered by size hung neatly from hooks. Pots and pans and dinner ware sat perfectly aligned in open shelving. He could see his reflection in the white porcelain sink. A photograph of Amelia Earhardt taped to the wall above the sink overlapped another of Bobby Kennedy. A calendar from a garage named Whitey's featured a busty blonde. Frank did a double take when he realized the evening gown she wore had been painted on.

A small radio on the counter played a Bach concerto at a low volume as Frank cracked the door, then decided not to peek into Donna's bedroom. But he glimpsed a painting hanging at the head of her bed, and even in the dim ambient light, the canvas demanded his attention. He flipped the light switch and slashes of brilliant: oranges, yellows, reds, deep blues and greens vibrated. A massive chunk of white pigment curled over under its own weight where the canvas had been torn. "Geeeezuz!" he blurted, "Incredible," as Donna walked through the door.

"Oh good. You're staying. Great, I'll make coffee and we can look at the view from my front room."

"Forget that. I want to look at paintings. Exciting. Better than I could have imagined. Some serious shit."

"What does that mean, Frank?"

"They're great. Direct, honest. You paint like you talk - no bullshit."

"I love to paint, Frank. I get lost for hours in these paintings."

"I can see it. But you never talk about it. You're always telling stories about everybody else. I never would have known if you hadn't dragged me over here."

"I don't think I had to drag you, Frank."

"You know what I meant, Donna."

"Yeah, I do. I'm going to make coffee while you look. OK?"

"Sure. "

Donna called from the kitchen. "The painting over the bed is my favorite."

"Did you tear the canvas on purpose?" Frank asked.

"No. I got so excited that I drove the brush right through it and when it curled over I said, Wow that looks great. I guess I'll leave it. Looks like a wave."

Frank studied the painting a while longer and Donna came back with coffee. Frank asked Donna if she'd ever had a show.

"You're one of the few people who's ever seen them, Frank. I send slides to galleries sometimes but nothing ever happens. My folks? They're so disappointed I left school that they just don't cahre. Now all my mother talks about is find a guy, settle down, get pregnant. She's obsessed with grandchildren. That's why I moved back. Can't listen to that shit all the time. I don't like arguing with them, so it's bettahr if I stay heahr."

They looked at the painting a while longer, then Donna led Frank to a sofa in the living area. She asked Frank to help her turn it so they could sit and look at the harbor. Frank told Donna that her paintings reminded him of Lucas and he tried to explain telling her about their adventures in the mountains and the time they pricked their fingers with a knife and became blood brothers. Then Frank talked about Lucas' sculpture and his death and the bizarre behavior of Lucas' mother.

Frank's story trailed off, Donna stared out at the harbor and whispered, "You know, Frank, that's not a sad story, it's friggin' sick. People can be so friggin' stupid it boggles the mind." Then Donna put a hand on Frank's neck and rubbed. "The fog's lifting," she said. "You can see the breakwatahr, Frank. That flashing red light is at the end. Remembahr that Sunday afternoon, Frank?"

"I remember," Frank said.

"So now I know what Abenaki means. Tell me one of his stories." Donna curled her legs under and rested her head against Frank's arm, listening to the story of the sunsets. When he finished, Donna hooted, "Frank, it's an omen."

Frank laughed as Donna pointed out the window to a house across the street and down the hill. "There. That's Sal's house. Remembahr at the breakwatahr when I yelled back at him?"

"Yeah."

"He's a great neighbor, Frank. He keeps an eye on things when he's in. Everybody heahr's like that. They're all great neighbors. They take care of each other. It's a great place, Frank. Safe. No ahshole thieves stealing your fifty dollar stereo. No muggahrs. At least not yet, anyway. But I've been hearin' stories about more junkies stealin' stuff. I hope this place isn't gettin' into heroin. Could be. That sucks. Nick, the guy who runs the mahrket, told me that a guy held him up not too long ago. Two days later the cops came by and showed Nick a photo of a body they found washed

Ed Touchette

up at Niles Beach. Nick said it was the guy who'd robbed him. The cops asked Nick if he knew the guy and Nick said he didn't. The cops told Nick the guy had a bullet hole in the back of his head and they asked Nick if he knew who killed the guy. You know what Nick said, Frank? It coulda been a suicide."

Frank roared.

The red and green running lights on the draggers flickered. The fog horn bellowed at Eastern Point and the light painted a white stripe across the horizon. Gulls flew - ghostly against the night. Frank looked along the ridge of Banner Hill until he spotted the house. The light from below cast a death-like pall. "The Aviary," Frank said. "Still haunted by the ghost of the poet, Donna. I guess that's why no one lives there. Right?"

"Probably isn't heated, Frank. That's why no one lives there. Freeze your ahs, *ass*, off in the winter. That northwest wind comes across the hahrbor and you're gonna look like somethin' out o' Birdseye's cookbook."

Frank laughed. "Yeah, but what a . . . Hey what was that?"

"What?" Donna asked.

"Christ, it looked like something just flew off the cupola."

"Probably a gull gliding by, Frank."

"Yeah, I guess. Maybe that's why people keep seeing the poet jump."

"Could be."

"We should walk over there someday and visit Emma - unless you're still going to New York or San Francisco."

"What does that mean, Frank?"

"It means I was hoping we'd live together. For the winter. Find out."

"Find out what?"

"If we should keep living together next summer."

"And then what, Frank?"

"Donna, I don't know. Besides, you're going to the big city to make a name for yourself."

"I have a name, Frank. Donna Pearce."

The next morning Donna dressed for work and Frank walked around the apartment rifling through the stacked canvases. Donna told him he was obsessed with the paintings and he agreed. Then they walked down to the street to Frank's car. A couple of men sat on a stone wall that bordered a basketball court across the street. One waved and the other asked, "Cool?"

Donna waved back and yelled, "Finest kind, Vincie. Thanks." Then she turned to Frank and said, "What are you doing after work tonight? You got ten seconds to come up with the right answer or it'll take more than those guys to pull me off you."

"I'll be here a little after one."

Donna put her hand on the back of his head and pulled him toward her. "Frank," she said. "here's an extra key. It'll be two before Jerry and I can lock up. We'll have to clean the kitchen. Be here and be naked when I get home. Luv ya."

Frank cleaned empty guest rooms at the hotel that afternoon. Harley had put the three off season visitors on the second floor. Frank turned the mattresses on their sides and leaned them against the walls. He'd piled the linens in the hallway and vacuumed the rugs. In the bathrooms, he shut off the water mains and drained pipes. Most of the first floor rooms had working shutters so he closed and secured those to protect the glass against winter storms. When he'd finished, he carried the linens he'd gathered down the stairs to the laundry room in the basement. Over the clatter of the washing machine, he heard voices reverberating. One was Jack's. He looked up at the vent in a duct overhead.

"We'll leave it here. The season's over. No one'll open this. The walk-in's cleaned out. It'll last in there until we turn off the power in October. I'll lock it."

Frank walked back up the stairs to the kitchen for coffee. He was pointed toward a fresh pot, grabbed a cup and walked out to the lobby. Harley was writing in a book and Frank asked what it was.

"Oh," Harley said. "This is the wish book. People put their names and important information on a file card we leave in the rooms. We ask them if they'll be returning and if they say yes, we ask them for a tentative date and what room they'd like. Like this." Harley flipped a card to Frank.

Frank read the card and laughed. "Understandable." He handed the card back to Harley.

Harley spoke out loud as he pretended to enter the information in the book. "Mr. and Mrs. Sanchez. Dates desired, August eight through fifteen. Room request - anywhere on the back shore." Harley laughed, tore up the card and tossed it in the wastebasket.

"When are you going to drain the pool, Frank?" Harley asked.

"Jack said not to do it until after the employees' party, Harley."

"Why, Frank. Nobody's going to be swimming before next summer. It's too cold."

"Well, ahh, I guess, Harley, but Jack figured that if somebody gets loaded and falls in, it's a lot better if there's water in it."

"Good point. Hey, Frank, I was down at the Loft last night singing and drinking with a couple of friends. When I walked home, I couldn't help but notice your car wasn't in the lot. Anything I should know about?"

"I was ahh, out."

"Yeah, Frank. And?"

"I spent the night at Donna's, Harley. Geezuz, Jack was right. You are a busy body old fag, but a hell of a nice guy, so what the hell. Yeah, I went back to that place . . ."

"Captain Jerry's."

"Yeah. Right. I talked to Donna and well . . . "

" Great, Frank. I'd love to see you happy and she makes you happy."

"She does, Harley. She makes me laugh and she really has balls. Well, ahhh . . . You know, Harley."

"Yeah, Frank. I know."

"She makes me smile. I really missed her."

"Christ, Frank, you've fallen in love."

"Nahh, Harley. Shit, I don't know but I saw some of her paintings last night. For the first time in a long time I saw something that matters. Her paintings, Harley. Powerful." Frank became animated. "You've got to see them, Harley. They're her." Frank gestured wildly as he described the paintings. He swept a hand from left to right and said, "Colors slash at your eyes. And every once in a while, Harley, you see that sense of humor of hers. Unreal."

"She's found her passion, Frank. She's found Donna."

"I guess. If that's what it means, she certainly has. Have you ever seen her work, Harley?"

Harley dropped his eyes and wrote.

Frank enjoyed a quiet night chatting with a couple of the waitresses from the Galley. They sat at the bar sipping vodka and tonics and Frank asked them what they did during the winter months. One of the women told Frank that she hated the cold, so she drove to Key West in January and came back in May. The other said, "I just hunker down for the winter and cook for the old man. He likes having me home and believe me, I like bein' there when he gets in from a two or three day trip."

Frank laughed. Then he asked if they knew of any apartments that might be available for the winter. They didn't.

"What about work?" Frank asked. "Know of anything around?"

"Why don't you talk to Jack?" one said. "I heard him talking to Polly a couple of nights ago. He said he's going to do some importing this winter. He wants to get some kind of business going in case the hotel folds."

"I didn't know anything about that," Frank said. "Christ, Jack told me to come back and work here next season if I was around. I didn't know things were that bad."

"Probably not, yet, but a few bad weeks of weather next year and this whole friggin' Neck could go into collection. It's season to season around here, Frank. That's the truth."

Frank was sitting on the sofa in the apartment looking at a couple of paintings he'd leaned against the wall when he heard the lock turn and Donna walked into the apartment. She looked at the paintings and, affecting a glare at Frank, pointed to the bedroom. "Now," she said.

Over coffee the next morning, Donna and Frank discussed living arrangements. Donna said that she'd miss watching the sunrise from Portugei Hill. Pointing to the window, she told Frank it came up over Good Harbor Beach and flooded the room with warm light. Frank mentioned he'd heard apartments weren't easy to find. Donna said that they could look around but live here until they found something. "I already said something to Lou and he said OK."

"Lou's your landlord, Donna?"

"Yeah, Frank. He said he's already checked you out and you're cool - or as Lou said, "S'OK, butta no biga party a' no drug.'"

"How does he know?" Frank asked.

"Those guys sitting on the wall yesterday morning, Frank?"

"Yeah."

"They know everybody in Gloucester."

"Donna, you just said, Gloucester not Glosta. What's with that?"

"Been working on changing my life, Frank. Impressed?"

Ed Touchette

"I already was, Donna. Either way is fine with me."

"Well, Frankie boy, it's not fine with me and I'm thinking about taking French lessons so I can talk right along with you and Rojahr, *Roger*, when we go to C'est Bon." Frank told her he was impressed with her beautiful French.

"You see," Donna said. "Pretty soon you'll be tearing your clothes off when I speak in French. Ha."

Frank laughed.

"Hey, Frank, what were you dreaming about last night? Your moaning woke me but I couldn't figure out what you were talking about."

"I don't remember, Donna."

"It sounded a little scary, Frank."

Frank pensively rubbed his neck then mentioned Jack's import-export business. Donna chuckled.

"Are you for real, Frank? If you don't smahrten up, I'm gonna have to hire Lou's boys to make sure you stay in the apahrtment all day otherwise they'll find you living in some dumpstahr somewhere. Importing business? Jack doesn't know shit. That's a tricky business. I know. Tony Parker tried. He got his clock cleaned buying stuff he thought would sell big time like the next pet rock or something. Lost a shit load of money. It's not easy. There are a ton of guys in Glosta -I mean Gloucester - who've been cleaned out. Don't do it, Frank. You'll lose." Donna looked away then turned back to Frank. "Besides, Frank, I don't like Jack. The way he looks at me or something. I don't know. I don't like it."

"He doesn't know you, Donna. Jack's OK. If he knew you better, he'd be a lot friendlier. Maybe we should all go out to dinner. You'll get to know each other."

"No fucking way, Frank!" Donna slammed the table rattling cups and dishes. "No way! My instincts are good. I know enough about Jack."

Frank eased back in his chair. "Whoa. OK. Forget I mentioned it. Man, you can get down on people but this is adamant."

"What do you mean, Frank?"

"Adamant, Donna. Dead set - no fucking around."

"You're right, Frank. I am fucking adamant about this one. I do not want to get too close to Jack."

Chapter 12

Uncle Albert said rock'n roll would make me a juvenile delinquent. Aunt Mary said touching it would make me insane. They were right.

Years from Then
Bobby Crosby
1970 The Aviary Papers Publishers

Tommy Lozano and Owen were the first regulars in the bar on the last night. Frank gave them a couple of beers on the house. Tommy seemed happy and when Frank asked how he felt, Owen told him that they'd had a great day and the Sox had won again. Frank congratulated them and asked if he should charge double for the next drinks. Tommy flipped Frank the finger. Then Tommy and Owen speculated about the World Series betting beers on whether the Red Sox would win the Series in 5 or 6 games. Frank said they'd lose in seven and both told Frank to go fuck himself. Frank laughed and said, "Just kidding." Tommy didn't laugh.

Owen said something about the Aviary but the only words Frank caught were, "another poet took a dive," because Jack rushed through the door and slammed it against the wall, tearing the chart of St. John's Harbor.

"Last night, Frank," Jack said. Frank asked what had happened.

Jack's shirt was soaked with perspiration and he was wiping his forehead with a bar napkin. "Oh nothing. I rushed to get down and see what's going on. Last night. Always big." He glanced furtively around the room then took an envelope from his jacket pocket and tossed it on the bar in front of Frank. "You made it through a whole summer in Gloucester. Congratulations. I hope we open up next year and you come back to work. It's been a good summer. You've been terrific, Frank."

"What's this?"

"Well, ahhh, let's call it a bonus,"

"A bonus? For what, Jack?" Frank paused and mulled. He caught a glimpse of a grin he knew and pushed it back at him. Jack held his hands

Ed Touchette

above his head.

"OK. Fine, but don't come back at me and say I owe you. Remember, Willy Hall, Jack?" Jack cringed as Frank recalled the weekend Jack loaned his car to Willy Hall so Willy could visit his girlfriend at Green Mountain. The following Monday, Jack had demanded Willy's assistance with a research paper saying he couldn't get to the library because it had been too cold to walk and Willy ended up writing the paper.

"Nah. Come on, Frank. Willy was a quiff. Look, you worked your ass off this summer. Every night. You did more work on this place than got done in two summers."

Frank opened the envelope and pulled out twenty crisp one hundred dollar bills. "Geeezuz, Jack, two grand."

Jack looked around the room and whispered, "Keep it down. This is between me and you."

"Thanks, Jack. I had no idea the season was that good."

"Great season, Frank. Thanks."

Frank was stuffing the bills into his pocket when Donna walked through the door. She called out, "Hey bahrtendahr! Gimme a beeeeeaaaahhh," sashayed blithely twirling her car keys around her index finger and leaned against the bar.

Frank laughed. Jack looked at Frank and said. "I hope you haven't pissed away a whole summer for nothing, Frank," as Frank popped the top off the bottle and slid it down the bar to Donna. He followed along and when he got there he leaned to her and said, "Hey, lady, you're new around here. Wanna screw?"

Donna reached out, grabbed his head with both hands and pulled him to her. She kissed him then lightly bit his lip. "Not bad, pal, but there's only one guy for me and he's busy 'til one. I'm just gonna sit here and watch all the men that come 'n go and think of a million reasons they can't do it for me like him."

"Gimme one, lady."

"I love him."

"Can't argue with that, lady. Enjoy your beeeeaaaahhh - rrrrr." Frank leaned over and kissed Donna then whispered, "Wait'll I tell you . . ."

Donna cut him off.

"Hey, Frank, come here." She beckoned him closer and whispered, "I just pulled into the lot 'n almost hit a couple of guys running out to the street. Christ, I'd had a few beahrs at Jerry's. Scared the shit out a me."

Frank looked at her and said, "Geezuz, Donna, smarten up. Don't drive when you've been drinking," then went to get a drink for another customer. He turned suddenly. "What are you doing here? Why aren't you working for Jerry?"

"Frank, I gave Jerry my notice so I can spend time with you. He let me out tonight so I could come over. I figured I was here on your first night and I wanted to be here on your last night at Rackliffe House. Sweet of me, huh?"

"That's kinda what I like about you. You surprise me - all the time."

"Yeah, well get the hook outta yer mouth, Frankie boy. I only came here to be sure none these desperate Glosta broads - I mean Gloucester girls - come in here tryin' to score the best piece of ass that ever walked the Neck before he disappears for the winter. Besides, Jack canned the oldies group so I won't have to listen to the Moody fuckin' Blues."

Harley waved at Frank as he walked in and sat with Donna. He gave her a hug and she kissed him on the cheek. Harley ordered a Bud.

"Here you go, Harl." Frank plopped Harley's bottle on the bar.

"A glass, if I may be so bold," Harley said.

"Sure," Frank answered. Then as Frank walked down the bar refilling glasses. Harley asked gently, "Donna, how's the painting? Frank's blown away by your stuff, you know."

"Yeah, I know, Harley." Donna spoke to Harley but watched Frank's every move.

"Wow," Harley said, "you've got it bad."

"Yeah, Harley and ain't it great?"

"Donna, again, are you painting?"

"Not really, Harley. I haven't had time."

"Oh. Don't blow it, Donna."

"Not a chance. I'm nuts about him, Harley."

"I meant the painting, Donna."

"What? Huh? I didn't heahr you, Harley."

Someone put a quarter in the juke box. A pounding bass guitar. Donna rocked her beer bottle back and forth on the bar and swayed in her seat. She cupped her hands. "*Crossroads*, Harl. Cream. Best band evahr," then turned to ogle Frank some more.

Ed Touchette

The employees' end of the season party rocked when Frank arrived at three o'clock at Rackliffe House. Around the pool, the whole crew danced and sang to blaring, pounding music. Frank pumped a plastic cup full from one of the two kegs sitting on ice in the battered bathtub from seventeen. Harley chatted up one of the waiters over by the pool.

Frank looked around to find Jack but he didn't see him so he surveyed the hotel. She looked a lot better than the first time he'd seen her. The shutters were closed and seemed straighter. The railings glistened with fresh white paint. He groaned audibly when he looked over the translucent awning casting its diffuse pea green pall on the sundeck. As he turned to check the glass he'd replaced in the office window, he glimpsed one of the chambermaids walking down the steps from the sundeck, gathering her hair into a pony tail. She stopped at the bottom step, shifted her skirt and fastened two buttons on her blouse. Behind her, Jack closed the door that led to the passageway from the lobby. "Geeezuz," Frank thought, "I hope he's not that stupid. She's young."

Jack filled a cup at the keg, then circulated through the crowd thanking them for their efforts. To Frank, he said, "Man, I just had the best sex of my life. Off and on all summer, but this was the best."

"Jack, Molly's a friggin' kid. She's not even eighteen. You'll go to jail if she tells her parents?"

"She won't."

"How do you know, Jack?"

"Because I've been bangin' her all summer, Frank. She loves the candy." Jack waved a small plastic bag of white powder. "Couple o' lines before, a little after. Loves the stuff."

Stunned, Frank walked away. He still heard Jack: "Come on, Frank, lighten up. Get loose, for Chrise sake."

Frank drifted through the party and stared at the harbor, sipping his beer. He walked down the path to the gazebo and watched a couple of draggers plowing through and then focused on the hypnotic slapping of water on rocks. A freighter glided by on its way out, and a couple of cat boats hoisted their sails and cruised in the cool breezes. He glimpsed the castle on the other side and laughed as he remembered Donna's story about a ghost boat. Then he winced remembering Katy Griffin, Allie's roommate freshman year. Jack swore he hadn't laced the Kool-Aid. Katy couldn't swim but walked into the river anyway convinced the water would part.

Donna got to the party later in the afternoon. When she couldn't find Frank, she got herself a beer and perched on a red plastic chair. Finally she spied Harley, walked over and asked if he'd seen Frank.

Harley unglued his eyes from the young waiter beside him. "Not for a while, Donna. He might be with Jack. I saw them talking."

"Where's Jack?"

"One guess." Harley looked up at the hotel. Kim entered the lobby.

"With Kim? He wouldn't, Harley."

"I doubt it," Harley offered. "Unless. . ."

"Unless what, Harley?"

"You know, Jack, Donna. But Frank? I doubt it."

Donna couldn't see Frank on the sundeck or at the pool, so she walked up the stairs into the lobby murmuring to herself, "If he's up there, I'll fuckin' kill him. That no good son of a bitch."

She took the stairs to the second floor two at a time. Chest heaving, she banged on a couple of doors with her fist. Three doors down, she caught a glimpse of Jack quickly retreating into a room. She ran to the door and banged furiously with her fist.

"I saw you, Jack. Is he in there? I'll fuckin' kill you both. Let me in. Open that friggin' door, Jack, or I'll kick it in."

The door opened and Jack stood in front of Donna - naked, grinning.

"Geez. I know we had a few good times, Donna, but can't you wait? We're a little busy right now."

"Fuck you, Jack. We who? Where's Frank?"

Jack turned his head as if to look into the room and said, "Like I said, we're busy. Can you come back. Ahh unless you'd like to ahhhh . . ."

Donna burst past Jack and looked. Kim was in the bed. Frank wasn't. She checked the bathroom and closet.

"What's the matter, Donna, losing your grip?" Kim said.

"Real funny shit, Kim."

"Donna, you're still hot for me. I can tell," Jack said. "Come on. Join us. Three's fun sometimes." Jack put his finger to his chin and wrinkled his brow. His sardonic grin slashed at Donna. "Oh, I forgot. Of course. You already know that. Don't you?"

"Fuck you, Jack." Donna stomped out.

"Should I call Chris?" Jack called after her.

Donna turned back, tempted to knee Jack in the groin. If Jack hadn't jumped aside quickly, she'd have bashed him as she slammed the door in his face and screamed, "Jack, you're a fucking pig. Leave me the fuck alone. I told you once, if you evahr tell anybody, I'll kill you. Now I'm tellin' you again and if Frank ever finds out, I'll have some of my friends drop you off on their way out to Georges."

Donna was almost to the first floor landing when she sat on the steps and sobbed. "Fuck," she said out loud then she whispered to herself. "Why'm I so friggin' stupid . . . Oh fuck! Double fuck!" She took a deep breath, wiped tears from her cheeks with the sleeve of her tee shirt and went back to the party. "Where's that asshole anyway?" she asked herself. "God, Frank, I want to see you right friggin' now. Where are you?"

Harley knew Donna'd been crying. "Oh, no," Harley said, "tell me he wasn't up there. Oh, that asshole Jack."

"He wasn't, Harley," Donna said. "God, now I almost wish he was."

"Now, there," Harley said softly. "No, you don't." He put his arm around her and led her toward the gazebo comforting her. Then: "Look, Donna, there's Frank."

Donna saw Frank and ran to him, threw her arms around him and buried her head against his broad back. "Frank, you shithead. I've gone nuts tryin' to find you. What are you doing out heahr by yourself?" She came around the bench, cuddled close to him.

"Sitting by myself. Pretty obvious, isn't it?"

Donna punched his arm. "Damn, Frank. Don't tell me you'll meet me somewhere and not show up. Don't."

"Why're you so shithouse, Donna? I'm here. Christ, I told you I'd meet you at the party and I'm here. Where were you all day, anyway?"

"On my way here, don't change the subject, Frank. You said the party and you're not there, you're here." She punched him again.

Harley sat down, too. "I'm not leaving," he said. "I want to sit here with you two and enjoy this. All of this love and affection. It makes me kind of, ahhh, dreamy, I guess."

"Christ," Frank said, rubbing his arm. "That hurt. What's with you?"

"Oh, it's my fault, Frank. A little misunderstanding," Harley said.

"Shut up, Harley," Donna said.

"The more you tell him to shut up, the more I want to know," Frank said. "So tell me, Harley. What happened?"

"A misunderstanding, Frank. When Donna asked where you were, I said I saw you with Jack but I meant before and she thought I meant then, and she said, where's Jack, and I looked up at the hotel and . . ."

"Why would I be with Jack there? What was he doing?"

"Screwing a waitress," Donna said.

"How do you know?" Frank asked.

"She went up there," Harley said.

"Shut up, Harley," Donna said.

"Why?" Frank said.

"Because she thought you were in there with Jack," Harley said.

"Shut up, Harley," Donna said.

"But I'm not gay," Frank said.

"I know," Harley said.

"Me, too," Donna said.

"What did you think I was doing?" Frank asked.

Donna said. "Don't ask."

"A three way," Harley said.

"Shut up, Harley," Donna said.

"Could be fun," Harley said.

"I don't think so," Frank said.

"What about two women?" Harley asked.

"Shut up, Harley," Donna said.

"Hmmmm," Frank said.

"Fuck you, Frank," Donna said and punched him in the arm.

"Ouch," Harley said.

"Shut up, Harley," Donna said and punched Harley in the arm.

"Ouch," Harley said.

"Would you?" Frank said.

"What?" Donna said.

"Two women?" Frank asked.

"I think I'd better go," Harley said.

"Sit down, Harley, and shut up" Donna screamed.

"I'm exhausted," Harley said.

"Me too," Frank said.

"I have an idea," Donna said. "The three of us should go to C'est Bon for dinner to celebrate the end of the season."

Frank and Harley agreed.

"I need to go home and take a shower," Donna said.

"We can take one here, at the cottage," Frank said.

"Together?" Donna asked.

"Oh boy," Harley said.

"Don't, Harley," Donna said.

Frank laughed.

"I need to get some clothes," Donna said.

"OK," Frank said. "We'll pick you up at seven. Is that good?"

"Good for me," Donna said.

"Good for me," Harley said.

"Good," Frank said. "We'll have a ball."

"Yey," Harley said.

Donna punched Harley in the arm. Frank laughed. They stared out at the harbor, listened to the slapping water then went back to the party. They saw Jack talking to Pam and Kim. Frank laughed as Jack and the waitresses left the party and walked into the hotel. "The guy's gonna kill himself at this rate," Frank said.

"If somethin' else doesn't get him first," Donna said grimly.

Part 2

Backlogue

Chapter 13

Fall colors add excitement to Gloucester's beauty as the rolling hills surrounding the port feature threads of yellows and oranges stitched into the patchwork of masonry and wood. Deep violet shadows crisp their edges and, like a rich thick paste, hold it firmly against the cerulean backdrop.

A Beautiful Find
Les Moor
1968 The Aviary Papers Publishers

Frank picked up the telephone. "Hi, Mom. Yeah, I'm fine.__Very, Mom. Donna is terrific. We get along great.__ Well, sure I am. There's only one bed.__I haven't met them, yet, Mom. __Yeah, I'm sure she's told them.__No, Mom, we haven't talked about that. __No, Mom, Donna's on the pill.__No, Mom, I'm working a couple of part time jobs.__No, Mom, I'm not thinking about doing that again.__Yes, Mom, I'll see if there's a room.__When?__I doubt it, Mom. That's Fiesta. The place is packed.__ Sure, Mom, I'll try.__No, Mom, I won't._____

Oh, yeah, how is she?__What?__When?__No shit, Mom, I didn't know. I haven't talked to her since I left.__Oh, no! Why'd you do that?__I wish you hadn't. I don't want to talk to her.__No, Mom, I really don't.__Yeah, Mom I will.__Goodbye.__Yeah, sure, love ya, Mom."

Chapter 13a

Details. Details. Details.
Handrails. Chair rails. CUUUUUpola la la la.

Our House
Les Moor
1969 The Aviary Papers Publishers

By the second week of October, Frank and Donna had had no luck finding a new place so they decided to stay in Donna's apartment for the rest of the winter. They'd found a cottage out on the Back Shore, but when Frank, as Donna put it, "just couldn't tell a lie" and the landlady found out they're weren't married, she gave back Frank's check and Donna quit packing boxes.

Frank got to know the neighborhood around the Friend Street apartment. He spent time talking to Nick at the market because Nick told great stories. Sal had offered Frank a site for the winter but Frank had turned it down. "I don't like the ocean all that much," he'd told Sal. "I'm not a good swimmer." He did accept Jerry's offer to tend bar at Captain Jerry's Kitchen from time to time.

Harley visited frequently. He stopped by for dinner at least once a week and they always enjoyed his company. Harley'd bring an expensive bottle of wine and tell Frank and Donna, "The cheap ones make you sick."

Donna was "over the edge" as Frank had put it, "making the apartment comfortable - kinda homey, like." She'd hung new curtains in the living room and had recovered the sofa with matching fabric. She'd bought a Swedish ivy for the macramé plant hanger and the two paintings, once in the bathroom, now occupied wall space. She'd framed Frank's favorites and hung them throughout. She even burned incense and candles to mask the pungent smell of paints. The walking stick she'd bought from Ruthie hung above the door to the kitchen.

Some nights while Donna cooked, Frank and Harley would drink wine, sitting in the living room talking about the paintings. If they got really excited, they'd walk from room to room conducting a moveable critique and Donna would sometimes chime in with "You guys are so full of it, it's unbelievable," or "Are you guys for friggin' real? I couldn't have thought about all of that and finished that painting." Harley and Frank would laugh and she would blush and say something like, "Thank you guys. It's flattering."

Harley would sit on the sofa or in one of the over stuffed chairs and sip his wine. He'd lay his head back, close his eyes and herald Donna's future: 'You, Donna, will be infinitely collectible as an artist among the rich and famous.' Donna often pooh-poohed Harley and then served food. Some nights Harley would finish dessert and leave, quickly. Donna thought he was meeting a secret lover. If Harley stayed until 3 or 4 in the morning, the conversations ranged boundlessly.

"If you do become rich and famous," Harley'd said one night, "I'd like you to remember who your biggest fan was."

"Not to worry, Harley" Donna had said. "I could nevahr, *never*, forget, Frank."

"Bitch," Harley'd replied with mock disdain and then he'd jumped off the sofa to hug Donna.

Frank recuperated from the summer madness by walking a few hours at a time and finding new ways to get from the apartment to somewhere else and back. He became infatuated with, downright awed, by the variety of the city's architecture. Quickly he developed an affinity for the built record of Gloucester. He'd stand in front of a house for hours, noting details in his wire bound notebook, and surmising the lives of its inhabitants, present and past. Over the course of a few weeks he'd examined almost every building on Middle Street. From Pleasant to Washington, he walked and admired the craftsmanship of some of the first homes built by Gloucester's successful people. He spent hours at the library on the corner of Dale Avenue reading architectural design and history books.

His favorite building was the brick three story Garland Building at the intersection of Pleasant next to the Cooperative bank. "Fabulous," he'd told Donna. He'd stop to analyze it each time he journeyed downtown. The eclectic mix of features confounded him as he tried to place it in a period; at the same time, their diversity and abundance mollified him.

In his notebook he'd scribbled: "Steep, hipped roofs like a French chateau but the front-facing gable with the diamond decorative motif says Victorian - Queen Anne. The side nearest the bank, two gables, side by side, and later the valley between the two was bricked and covered. Different. The chimneys may be Queen Anne and the ornate rounded brick corbeling under the cornice. And differing wall textures. Simulated overhangs. Anything to avoid a flat surface. Something about the windows and doors - flowered decorative blocks. Italianate? No. Who dreamed this together?" Once he'd wondered if Gothic Revival might be an explanation.

He'd noted a consideration of the masons: "Immigrants who'd opted out of fishing? Maybe!" Then back to details: "The chimneys have a finely detailed crest. Hipped roof, walled dormers along the roof line - French chateau again; the rust on their metal cladding drips age onto the charcoal grey slates, the weathered edges carry their own declaration of era, black marble panels below the glass front? Added later - more modern. Deco?"

The Garland Building housed a barber shop and a card shop on the first floor; the rest of it seemed deserted. The barber was alive and well; Frank had seen the red, white and blue stripes spiraling. He'd wondered if at some time past this might have been a single family residence. "Certainly possible," he'd judged. He'd made a note to check out a few books at the Sawyer Free Library for more information. When he'd found a story about a barber who had taught his daughter the trade and she'd passed it on to her daughter, he wondered if they might have lived in the brick house.

The widow's walks and cupolas atop a number of Gloucester's homes enthralled Frank. He'd read enough sea stories to make him sick so he understood their alleged purpose, but he'd asked Donna anyway, "Were all built by sea captains? Or was it stylish . . . a symbol of wealth?" He remembered being up in the Aviary and the commanding view of the world it offered. He'd thought of Emma watching out for Henry.

Donna'd shown him a Hopper painting of a home on Rocky Neck. It had a mansard with dormers and an incredible cupola, ornate balustrades, massive brackets with pendants, dentils. Frank had asked her, how he could have missed it and Donna told him, "You're just getting to know the place, Frank. Check it out more closely next summer."

Frank insisted they walk the length of Middle Street at night whenever they went off to Roger's for a bite or to Jerry's for a beer. He'd look into the lighted rooms of houses to view the inhabitants' tastes for art and furnishings. Unfortunately, many of buildings had been converted to offices and apartments so traces of their original residents had disappeared.

Still Frank would fabricate a vision and speak it as they strolled.

One night in front of a two story Colonial, they'd been considering what they could see from the street. "That watercolor looks like a Marsden Hartley," Donna'd noted and she'd pointed to a drawing she thought was a Stuart Davis pen and ink. Frank had noted a Chippendale highboy and what appeared to be a tiger maple desk. "It's warm, don't you think?" he'd asked Donna. She'd nodded in agreement as she'd studied an ornate carving that capped the newel post of the handrail, its bald eagle gold leafed. Frank had compared it to Ruthie's walking stick and Donna'd flipped out. "Geezuz, Frank this is hand-carved. Ruthie's are mostly done on a lathe. Phil turns 'em and she adds a few details with her jackknife. Are you jokin', Frank? There's no comparison."

Whenever they passed the Sargent House, Donna mentioned John Singer Sargent's portraits asking Frank if he'd ever seen any. Sargent was one of her favorites and she knew he was a distant cousin of the original owners. Frank had said he was familiar with the painter and wondered if there were any of his works inside. Donna'd told him there was a very sensitive portrait of Sargent's father. "It's small, but it's really a great little painting. A little dab of white paint on the forehead. Reflected light. It's so sensitive, though. It seems like he placed it with such care. Oh, I don't know, Frank. I love his work."

Frank talked about the roof style, the shutters, the cornices, the doors and windows. Occasionally, he'd repeat detailed appraisals several times. "OK," Donna would say, "Frank, geeezuz, I get the picture."

When they'd reach Washington Street, they'd walk down the hill and say "Hi" to Jerry, go on to C'est Bon or turn and walk home along the opposite side of the street. Whichever, they always stopped and admired the statue in front of the American Legion Hall.

"Joan of Arc," Donna'd told Frank the first night they'd stopped to view the bronze. "The French gave it to us, to show their appreciation. Y' know, the ambulance drivers, the First World War. They sent it here. It's great to see in the middle of town. It's like our own little Statue of Liberty. Remember? I showed you the houses on Eastern Point, Frank? Sleepahr, I mean Sleeper, and A. Piatt Andrew, those guys were the ones who did it. Pretty cool, huh?"

"Cool," Frank had said, staring blankly at the horse. Lucas had taken him away.

Come on Frank you gotta meet Antoine. He's neat. The small log cabin over by the lake. Wood smoke. The guns: Mausers, Enfields, a BAR. The water cooled Maxim. Helmets and canteens and gas masks.The photograph, framed in gold, dead soldiers piled high over barbed wire, legs without bodies in mud holes. Underneath, the Ross Rifle. Antoine's calm soft voice. Joined the CFS in Quebec at seventeen. Wanted to get off the reservation. I was a sniper. The Ross was the best for that. More stories. Glued to his words. Star shells and whistles and screams. Deafening artillery barrages. Explosions from mines shook the earth. The rattle of machine guns. I raised the rifle and the German's head filled the sights. He fell back. I could see the others in the foxhole. Bewildered. Scared. Scrambling. Lucas bewildered, scared. I found Antoine, Frank, in a pool of blood with the Ross lying across his chest. Poor Antoine, Frank.

Frank's face had tightened; his breathing had gotten deep and sharp. Donna had touched his hand and asked, "What's the matter, Frank?"

Frank had shook his head. "History."

At C'est Bon, once, Frank had mentioned the Germans and France to Roger. "Mauvais." Roger had spat with an angry glare. Frank quickly mentioned the paintings of Degas. After Roger had returned to the kitchen, Donna'd told Frank that one night when she'd stayed after he'd closed, Roger had told her about his father being killed at the front and his mother being raped and murdered by the Nazis during the Occupation. They'd drunk a couple of bottles of wine together.

One Friday night when they were headed for C'est Bon and passed the Sargent House, Frank told Donna that he'd been looking at some books about Sargent's paintings at the library. "There was some unbelievable stuff that he'd painted during the First World War. One showed a line of soldiers blinded by a gas attack, groping their way along a muddy hill. Horrifying." Frank shuddered.

"I know that painting, Frank. *Gassed*. It's gruesome."

"I wonder if Roger's father fought in that war, too."

"I don't think you should ask him."

"God all mighty. Can you just imagine the nightmares that man must have about the Nazis and Viet Nam. Good lord."

"What're your nightmares about, Frank?"

Frank didn't answer. They walked down Middle Street to say good evening to Joan then headed to Roger's.

Chapter 14

Read a book. Write a poem.
Paint like you did when you were in kindergarten.

Well Hung: Poems about Gloucester Painters
Bobby Crosby
1971 The Aviary Papers Publishers

Their Sundays now consumed with passions, Frank and Donna: took painting trips so that Donna could express her feelings about the changes that were creeping over Gloucester's vistas; walked the streets to peek at the historic homes so that Frank could gather information for his records; and made love until the cows came home and there weren't a lot of cows around. Like squirrels scampering to store food for the winter, Donna seemed to be soaking in as much color as possible to carry her through what she called "the bleaks of November and December. It's miserable, drab until the first snow falls, Frank. Don't get depressed, though, we'll have fun." She painted constantly, it seemed to Frank.

Bright sunlight washed over the last Sunday in October as Donna and Frank drove along East Main Street toward Eastern Point. Donna peered through the gaps between buildings at the water in Smith's Cove. Frank noticed the bright yellow that now wreathed the Aviary and suggested they visit Emma Wilkins so Donna could paint from Banner Hill. Then Frank furrowed his brow. "If she remembers me." Donna agreed so they drove up Mt. Pleasant Avenue and turned into Emma's. Euripedes sunned himself on the grass. He barked as they pulled to the side and parked the car. Frank said, "Hello, Euripedes." Donna stuck her head out the window and woofed at the dog. Emma rounded the corner of her house, saw them and waved. Frank waved back.

"Emma," Frank chimed, "just stopped by to say hello."

"Hi, Frank," Emma said as Frank and Donna walked over to the fence. Frank introduced Donna, explaining to Emma that he was staying for the winter. Emma said "terrific." Frank told her that Donna was an artist and would like to paint the view from Banner Hill.

Emma was delighted. "Grand! A paintahr come to paint on Bannahr Hill. Just like the old days." Emma positively glowed as she chronicled the dozens of painters she'd known who'd painted here. Donna, impressed, told her it was like an art history lesson.

Frank and Emma laughed. "I wondered when you'd be back, Frank," Emma said. "I kind of get to know people and something told me you'd be around for a while. Frank, are you going to paint, too?"

"No. I'll just sun myself and watch. Maybe I'll work on some notes on the Aviary. Come sit with us for a while, Emma, and tell me more stories from Banner Hill." Frank beckoned with a circular motion of his arm.

"Oh, that would be just grand," Emma said, "Say, how about if I make some sandwiches and coffee. We'll have a little picnic on the lawn. We used to do that a lot, you know." Again, Emma iterated the names of artists who'd painted here. Donna smiled sweetly.

Frank offered to help Emma with the picnic while Donna painted. Emma said that she could manage easily, but since it was Frank and he was such a nice boy, she'd humor him. Frank laughed.

Donna walked over to the crest of the hill and set her easel. She placed the canvas and secured it and then took out a palette and started squeezing globs of red and yellow, blue and green. She poured some turpentine into a small can, added a little Damar varnish, grabbed a rag and a brush and started slashing at the canvas. Euripedes curled up at the base of the easel.

She scooped up a brushload of cerulean and scrubbed it into the top of the canvas. She wiped some of it off with a rag and scooped up a mixture of orange and yellow and brushed it on below the blue. She drew a strong red line to separate that from the white that was left below. An ultramarine with a touch of alizarin crimson got washed over the white at the base of the canvas and then she peppered the mid ground with greens and yellows and some cadmium red.

She worked back up to the top of the canvas and the Damar varnish she'd dropped in the can of turpentine, sticky, grabbed the pinkish white that she laid over the cerulean. She dropped her arm stepped back and looked at it, cocked her head to the right and said, "Euripedes, you're an awfully good, dog."

She stepped back to the canvas. Dabbing at the green and mixing it with a touch of cadmium red, she then swept it over and along the red line. With the handle of her brush, she scratched in squares and triangles, then grabbed a palette knife and scraped at some of the green. She dabbed at these areas with an index finger covered with a turpentine soaked rag. Canvas reappeared. She mixed a white and blue and slapped it over the squares and triangles she'd just drawn with the brush handle.

For forty minutes she scraped and scumbled, drew and scrubbed then glopped chunks of paint onto the canvas. Big washes of color were painted and repainted and covered with more vibrant layers. Lines dragged here and there. The array of colors that peaked through edges of layers produced a staccato that reverberated throughout the canvas.

She squeezed paint directly from the tubes and smeared it around the canvas. Rhythmic swirls faded in and out. Scraped more paint. Exposed more canvas. She wiped the palette knife on her jeans and applied a different pigment. Grabbed a large brush and wiped that on her jeans then loaded it with yellow and plastered. Wiped her face with the rag . . . Grabbed the tube of white paint and, like a cake decorator, added huge mounds of titanium white to the deep cerulean at the top of the canvas; took a brush and dragged some of it into the ultramarine at the base. A swath of orange was wedged into the ultramarine and then she added a few swirls of cadmium red and tipped these with white, cerulean, orange and yellow.

Stepping back to look again, she smiled and sat on the grass next to Euripedes. She looked up at the painting as she scratched the dog's ears, breathing heavily.

Emma and Frank walked up behind her and Emma spoke softly when she said, "May we look?"

"Oh, sure," Donna said.

Frank and Emma stared at the painting. Emma looked down at Donna and Euripedes.

Frank said, "Powerful."

Emma said, "Well! I mighta knowed. You paint like a man."

Donna smiled.

"Oh, my." Emma winced. "Didn't mean an offense, Donna. But when I was a girl that's what they'd say if a woman was really good. Y'know like Cecelia or Theresa"

Donna laughed.

Frank looked at Donna. He grabbed her paint rag and walked over to her and started to wipe the paint from her face. "Two for the price of one," he said. Then he held her hands and wiped her fingers.

"What do you mean, Frank?" Donna asked.

Frank pointed to Euripedes.

"You and Euripedes look like a couple a 'paches goin' to wahr," Emma said, grinning and shaking her head.

Donna looked at the dog and bellowed. "Sorry, boy." Frank wiped a glob of red paint from the dog's silky ear.

"Can you take a break and come have a sandwich with us, Donna?"

"Oh sure, Emma. I'm finished with it."

"Oh?" Emma said.

Donna smiled.

They spread a blanket on the grass and took out a thermos of coffee. Emma laid the sandwiches on paper plates and Euripedes bolted to his feet and cozied over. He nuzzled Donna's arm and she broke off a piece of her sandwich and gave it to him.

"Be cahreful," Emma said. "He nevahr says no."

When the dog walked over and nudged his arm, Frank laughed and scratched Euripedes behind the ears. Emma reveled in memories of the artists who'd painted here and all of the paintings she'd seen going down the drive. Some she liked and some she didn't. Then: she asked Frank what he thought of Donna's painting.

"I like it. It's Donna, that's for sure."

"Sure is," Emma said. "You see all that color jumpin' up and down and it kinda makes you want to dance."

"I like that," Donna said. "I wish I'd thought of it. It's true. When I have a great time painting, I kind of feel like I'm dancing."

"You know, Henry wrote me a poem like that one time. He said when he thought of me and he was out there having a good day haulin' he just kind of felt like dancing."

"Did you and Henry ever go dancing, Emma?" Donna asked.

"Sure we did," Emma said. "Danced all night when we got married. We danced the day they ended the wahr. Right down theahr." Emma pointed over to the rose garden in front of her cottage. "Henry picked the biggest red rose from that bush and held it in his teeth and we danced around the gahrden hummin' and laughing. Then Henry made up a poem - Emma, my Emma. Rose of the hill, everything wondahrful blooms in hehr still."

"That's great," Frank said.

"I love it," Donna said.

"Good thing Henry wrote it," Emma said.

They all laughed.

After they'd eaten, they lay back in the grass and watched the gulls drifting above. Euripedes scarfed up crumbs from the blanket. Emma fell asleep and started to snore. Donna looked over at Frank and smiled and Frank wiped a smudge of paint from her cheek. Euripedes walked over to Emma and sniffed her cheek. "Henry, stop it now, y' old fool," Emma said as she rolled to her other side. Euripedes nestled next to her.

Donna's eyes were closed and her hand rested on Frank's leg. Frank took out his wire bound book and made notes about the Aviary, sketched a couple of details, and filled two pages with notes about the detailing. He noted the lightning rod and wrote a reminder to check old mail order catalogs the next time he visited the library.

When Emma awoke, Frank asked her if she knew who'd built the house. She thought it was built after the Civil War by a man who owned a lumber yard at the bottom of the hill. He'd imported a lot of the wood from South America. "Henry told me," she said. "Henry was like you, Frank. Loved the hist'ry o' stuff. Boats mostly. Kept a journal but he nevahr told me where it was befohre he died. Nevahr found it. Wished I could."

Donna lifted herself to rest on her elbows, raising an eyebrow to query Frank.

"I just asked about the history of the house, Donna."

"Oh." Donna rolled over.

Frank made more notes in his book then closed it. He wondered: "Civil wars?" Then Frank noticed the shades on the third floor were open. He asked Emma if she'd been going up to look at the view.

"No," Emma said, surveying the house. "Those damned kids must be getting in. I'll fix 'em, Frank. Come over on Halloween and see." Emma snickered. Then: "Frank, why are you so int'rested in that old house anyway? You been perusin' it ever since I met you."

"It fascinates me, Emma. All of these old houses do. I've been studying them for a while now. I've been walking and looking, and I'd like to know more about them and who lived in them. Maybe if I knew why people did what they did, I'd have a better idea of why people do what they do." Frank sighed and rubbed his neck. "Then again, sometimes I just think it doesn't matter. We're all crazy anyway." Frank glimpsed Donna.

Donna laughed and squeezed Frank's leg. Emma said, "Ayeah." Euripedes lay with his head on his paws. His eyes were glued to a squirrel bounding across the lawn toward an oak tree.

Donna packed up, so Frank helped her carry everything back to the car. Emma stood in the drive with Euripedes as they left. "See you soon, I hope," she said as they waved good bye and drove away. "Come on, Euripedes, let's light a fire and read something good."

Frank drove around the Back Shore and then headed downtown to check on something, parked on Middle Street and invited Donna to join him. Donna said she'd wait in the car and Frank walked toward Washington Street. He stopped in front of a large house that sat on the corner of Short Street. He noted the stained glass in the lower story windows of a rounded tower. The front door's panels featured a relief that appeared to be hand carved. He looked up and noted the overhang of the tower's peaked roof. A lightning rod with a round glass ball sat at the top. "There it is," Frank thought.

When he got back to the car, Frank answered Donna's questions before she asked them. "The lightning rod here and the one on the Aviary are a lot alike."

"So?" Donna griped.

"I'm just interested," Frank said. "I like investigating this stuff. Where did they come from? That's what I wonder."

"Why do you care?" Donna asked.

"I don't know, Donna. I'm just curious. Think about it. Maybe some guy had a thriving business making lightning rods for these houses - like the guy who printed all those fish boxes. He came up with a machine to hot stamp the wood and made a fortune. Like Clarence Birdseye and all of his inventions. Like Hammond. What made them do what they did? Some guy came up with the idea that making lightning rods was a good way to make money or something like that. Maybe he had a small mail order catalog. Did you ever look at old newspapers? The ads. You could buy anything by mail. Those lightning rods are a lot alike. There's a connection. I'm just curious. Don't you think it's interesting?"

"Y'know what I think, Frank?"

"What, Donna?"

"I'm glad you're good in bed, Frank."

Frank laughed.

Halloween. Frank, Donna and Harley met at the Party Boat Lounge on East Main Street for dinner before going to Emma's. Donna had made paper masks and painted skeletons on sheets for costumes. Donna couldn't wait to see Emma's reaction to them as trick or treaters. Frank had called Emma and warned her they'd be stopping by "just so three adult sized ghosts don't scare you, Emma." Emma had laughed at Frank and said, "Ain't 'fraid o' no ghosts, Frank."

Emma's house was dark as they walked up the drive. A jack 'o lantern burned on the steps of the Aviary at the end. They stopped near the steps to Emma's porch. "I told her we'd be here about six," Frank whispered. "I'll knock at the door."

"Trick or treat." Frank rapped on the wood frame.

A muffled voice echoed from the side. "Frank. Frank, it's me, Emma, come help me."

Frank looked at Donna and Harley and then peered around the corner of the house. Frank heard a squeaking noise and turned as a white sheet came flying across the drive. Euripedes barked as he jumped in the air chasing it. Donna jumped up to the porch screaming and grabbed Frank. Harley screeched and jumped to the porch and grabbed Donna.

"We should have expected that," Frank guffawed. Donna punched him in the arm and said, "Damn, Frank, did you know she was going to do that?" Frank said he didn't but he'd suspected something.

Emma came around the corner of the house, stumbling, bent with laughter. "Geee willickers! I've been scaring the living daylights out of them kids and old Euripedes is sure having a lot of fun chasing that sheet. Hi, Frank, Donna. Who's your friend?"

They took off the masks and Frank introduced Emma to Harley. Emma said she remembered Harley from the hotel then she explained the contraption with the bed sheet. Then Emma asked Frank if he wanted to scare some kids and Frank said, "Sure."

"OK!" Emma said, "Let's."

Around the corner of the house, Emma showed him how to haul the rope so that the sheet pinned to the clothes line would zip across the drive. "Get ovahr theahr and sit," Emma said to Euripedes when she heard voices down the drive. "Come on, you two, we'll hide around the cornahr." Euripedes crossed the drive and sat under an arborvitae.

Trick or treaters walked onto Emma's porch and she signalled Frank to yank the rope. The sheet flew across the drive on the clothesline with Euripedes barking frantically after it. Two of the kids ran back down the drive and the one who stayed said, "Aww, come on Mrs. Wilkins, I've seen that before."

"That you, Billy?" Emma said.

"Yeah, Mrs. Wilkins. Where's my treat?"

"Grab an apple from the basket by the door, Billy." Emma walked up and lifted the youngster's mask. "Yup, it's you."

"Hi, Euripedes," Billy said as he reached down to scratch the dog's ears. "You know, Emma, I liked it better when you wore the cape and red bandana and pretended to be the crazy poet in the big house. That was really scary."

"Begone, now, Billy. I can't do that anymore. I'm too old."

"Thanks, Mrs. Wilkins."

"Emma," Donna said as Billy skipped off the porch, "what's that kid talking about?"

"Nothing," Emma replied as she glanced warily at Frank, "He's a kid. Just talk."

"You told me," Frank said.

"No I don't remembahr, Frank," Emma snipped.

"Emma, are you afraid of ghosts?" Donna asked.

"No, Donna, I am the ghost. Well, was. Too old now. I knew all those stories about the poet's ghost. Geeee willickers, just last month, Grace Perkins called and said she saw someone fly off the roof. I tell ya that Wells boy sure stahrted somethin'. Remembahr, Frank, I told you. The Wells boy. The squash."

Frank laughed. Harley and Donna looked puzzled as Emma continued. "I used to go up there once in a while, 'specially on Halloween, and walk around in the cape and the bandanna. I thought it was a good way to scahre the kids away and keep 'em from breaking the windows. Hell, 'nuff people talked about the poet so I figured I'd keep 'em believin' it. Used to howl and scream and the kids'd run. Scahred 'em good, I did. I don't talk about it much, Frank. I'm fohrgetful enough as it is, people know it was me up theahr they'd lock me up, for certain."

Frank and Donna laughed. Emma told them firmly it wasn't funny, then she smiled and invited them into the house for coffee. They sat around the kitchen table, talked and drank coffee. Emma told more Halloween stories and how she had to sit down there and guard the house because of all the kids that would climb up the granite steps from the street.

"It sounds like you enjoyed it, Emma," Donna said.

"I did. It was funny when those kids dropped their beahr cans and ran fahr home screamin' fahr theahr mothahrs"

The gleam in Donna's eyes spoke volumes. "Do you still have the cape and bandana, Emma?"

"I do" Emma jumped up and chortled. "And I like what you're thinkin'"

"What are you thinking, Donna?" Harley asked.

Emma ran to the broom closet and returned with a black cape and a red bandana. She, Donna and Euripedes were out the door before Frank and Harley got up to follow down the drive.

Emma opened the door to the Aviary and they walked in. Euripedes sniffed along the baseboard in the kitchen and Emma watched him curiously. Then she saw the door from a back room opened so she closed and locked it. "Hmmm," Emma muttered. Frank asked if she thought someone had been in there and Emma said, "Could be," as she kept watching the dog. Her lust for the prank reignited and she poked Harley with her finger, "OK, you'll do fine." She draped the cape over Harley's shoulders as Donna tied the red bandana around his head.

"What do I do?" Harley squealed nervously, and Emma barked out instructions: "Hahrley, on the first floor. When Frank and Donna whistle from down on the ledge, I'll turn some lights on and Hahrley, you'll run 'round flappin' youhr ahrms."

Frank and Donna chuckled as they headed for the ledge. Euripedes tagged along tail whirling. Emma went up to the second floor and turned on a light in the third floor hallway. She pushed the hatch open with a broom stick and the light shone up into the cupola. Awfully eerie from where Frank and Donna sat. "Upward shadows always cast a pall," Frank whispered to Donna. Donna giggled at Emma's excitement.

They sat for a few minutes, then Euripedes growled a warning. Frank heard a noise. Donna whistled and the lights went on in the front room of the first floor. Frank and Donna watched Harley run around flapping his arms like a chicken trying to fly. A group of teenagers crossed the bramble to the clearing below the house and Euripedes barked. They looked up and saw the flapping black cape.

"Oh my god," a voice shouted. "It's true. Let's get outta here."

Euripedes barked again and Frank and Donna laughed as cans clanged along the granite steps.

"How was that?" Emma called through an open window.

"Pretty good, Emma," Frank said. "But Harley should go up to the cupola and climb out to the widow's walk. That'd be really scary."

Donna nudged Frank. "He can't. He'll break his neck."

"Yeah, you're right," Frank said.

Emma hollered, "You know youhr way around up theahr, Frank. You go up."

"No," Donna grumbled. "Nobody should go up thea - there."

"Yeah," Frank said. "Emma's right. It's safe."

Frank thought for a second and then stood and walked up to the house. He met Harley and took the cape and the bandana. On his way into the house, Frank blew out the candle in the pumpkin and tucked it under his arm. Harley came down to sit with Donna and Euripedes.

"This is stupid," Donna said. "That widow's walk is decrepit."

They could see shadows dancing along the ceiling of the cupola. Then Frank's caped silhouette danced against the cupola as he walked out and stood by the railing. Frank looked out and marvelled at the view: ships on the ocean, the Boston skyline. Then he waved his arms and hollered, "How does it look?"

"Scary," Harley yelled up to Frank.

"OK," Emma shouted, "Get ready."

The house stood dark. Harley and Donna sat and Donna scratched Euripedes' ears. "Good boy," she cooed as she rubbed his chin. Then she felt a growl in his throat. Voices! Then stumbling steps and thrashing in the bushes.

"Theahr it is," someone said.

"Wow, it's really scahry."

Lights went on. "What's that?"

"I don't know."

"Look up theahr on the roof."

Donna and Harley looked up to see Frank's silhouette waving wildly, the cape flapping. "Booowwwhaaaaaa," Frank wailed, "Booowwwhaaaaaa."

"Fuckin A," somebody bawled. "It's true. The place is haunted."

Frank shrieked again. Euripedes barked. Donna and Harley laughed.

"Let's get out of heahr," a voice squealed.

Wood cracked and Donna looked up to the widow's walk. Frank screamed, "AHHHHHHHHHH," and the cape tumbled through the air. Donna heard a horrible splattering sound from the rocks below the house. She screamed, bolting down the steps. Harley screamed. Euripedes barked.

"Come on, Billy," a boy shrieked. "Run for it."

"I can't move, Sammy," another squealed, "I shit my pants."

Donna screamed, "My god, Frank," as she leaned over and picked up the cape, soaked with emulsified pumpkin. Then she unraveled it from the broom head and cracked broom stick. She groaned, "You bahhhstard, Frank Noal. You mothahhr."

Harley, winded when he got there, panted furiously. "If I were you, I'd beat him senseless. That was cruel."

Laughter erupted from two silhouettes on the crest of the hill bent in half against the light of the moon. Frank convulsed and dropped to his knees. Emma capered wildly. Euripedes' legs pawed the air as he rolled on his back. Donna ran up the granite steps and leaped on Frank's back. She grabbed a handful of his hair and yanked him backwards to the grass. Emma cried out, "Don't hurt him Donna. Was all in fun."

Frank, weak with laughter, went limp and prone as Donna put her knees on his arms and pummeled his chest with her fists. Euripedes came over to help and licked Frank's face. When Harley arrived, he walked over and kicked the bottom of Frank's foot.

Donna screamed, "Are you friggin' crazy, Frank? Are you stupid or something? We really thought you'd fallen. You can't do stuff like that, Frank, you scahhred the shh . . . crap out of us."

"Not to mention the kids," Harley added.

Frank couldn't stop laughing. Emma cried. Donna and Harley joined them. Euripedes rolled in the grass again, scratching his back, moaning.

"Y'know," Emma said when she regained her composure, "those kids'll tell everybody 'bout the poet fallin' off the Aviary. They won't dahre come back. It'll scahre 'em all again. Nobody'll want to buy it. Good." Emma snapped a right hook at an imagined figure with a loud,

"Ha! We'll get 'em."

Emma had invited Frank and Donna to Thanksgiving dinner so they spent the Wednesday afternoon trying to decide what they should bring. Donna said, "Apple pie," and Frank said, "No. Wine." They threw fingers to see who'd win and Donna threw rock but Frank covered it with paper. Donna punched him anyway and said he'd hesitated. They laughed and agreed to bring both the pie and the wine.

They walked down the hill to the market to get apples but Donna didn't like what she saw so they walked to the A&P. "There's a packy next door," she observed.

On their walk back, Donna, exhilarated by the crisp cool evening, suggested they take the steps at Herrick. "Where Rogahrs and Main Street split, right at Rose's, down a ways, past the Crow's Nest, they run up the hill to Friend Street between a couple of big old houses. I saw a painting once, at the bank, Gruppé did it from the top of the steps. A couple of old ladies walking down to the whahrf. It's really neat, Frank. It's so homey, kind o'. Just everyday stuff. I like that."

At the steps, Frank studied the houses on the hill. On the first landing, he rambled on about the style of a cupola on one of the homes they'd passed. Then he grimaced at a fire escape winding down another. It thoughtlessly effaced the geometry, dissecting arched windows where sheets of painted plywood replaced glass panes. Vertical strips of aluminum siding similarly dismissed the graceful curve of a tower. The door and window moldings fared no better.

At the top steps, they turned and looked down at the harbor. Draggers hugged wharves. Cranes swung to and fro as lumpers emptied a freighter at the State Pier. The lights of the city washed out to East Gloucester and, beyond, the lighthouse swept a welcome across the night. The red light at the end of the breakwater blinked its warning. They stood awed by the scene, listening to the joyous clamor of the waterfront.

"I love this place, Frank," Donna sighed.

Frank gazed at the water, mesmerized by reflected light. "The gift of water."

"What?" Donna asked.

"The great dry lake bed."

"Lucas?" Donna asked.

"Yeah, Donna, it's funny. Listen. When he invented the world, the great god of the north made a lake and called it Halcyon and he gave the lake to these people who lived in an arid land and had no food and no water so they could fish and swim and drink cool clear water from the lake. For years they enjoyed the bounty of the lake and a beautiful village grew up around the lake. Then one day, a maiden they called Lazy Susan saw her reflection in the water and told everybody in the village and they all ran to the shore of the lake and stared into the water and became so enamoured they spent all their time preening and gussying and forgot what the lake was really for. The great god of the north stood above them on a high rock and watched and watched. This went on for years. Finally he got really mad and pissed and a giant wave wiped out the whole place."

"Geez, Frank, that's depressing," Donna whispered.

Thanksgiving morning looked good so Donna and Frank walked to Emma's. Off to the southwest, thick grey clouds rolled toward the harbor over the Magnolia Hills. At the bottom of the steps, they turned to walk along Main Street and Donna said, "Better hurry. It's going to rain, Frank." Just below Banner Hill on East Main, the wind whipped through the buildings and it started to pour, so they waited under the awning of a row of shops until the squall passed and then Frank said, "Let's walk up the steps to Emma's. I'll carry the stuff." Donna agreed. When they got to a thicket of briars she scratched her hand trying to climb through. She cursed Frank.

"You're OK," Frank said. "We're almost there."

At the top of the granite steps, Frank swung around to look at the harbor. The sun shone again and the residue of the passing storm bedizened leafless shrubs. The wind had abated and the harbor sparkled. "God, this is beautiful," Frank hollered at the sky but Donna shushed him with a finger to her lips and they stood surrounded by a silence broken only by the squawk of a gull and the chirping of a cardinal. "Look there," Donna whispered as she pointed to a crimson flash in a crab apple tree. To the west, over Magnolia's hills a swath of yellow and pink grew between the tree tops and the last of the storm clouds. Donna thought, "The worst is over when you see that."

Frank looked across the lawn as Euripedes ambled toward them, yelping a greeting, his tail spinning joyfully. Through the tree line in front of the white mansion that sat empty beyond the Aviary, the limbs stood bare and the skeletons of oaks and maples fractured the facade into a cubist image. He cut across a lawn and walked toward the house and Donna called out asking where he was going. "Just want to see something," he said as he passed the tree line. He eyed the house from top to bottom. Donna and Euripedes walked up behind him.

He walked around the house and with Donna and the dog in tow, rendered a vision of what life might have held for the inhabitants. "That's the kitchen. A huge hearth. Can you imagine baking your pies in there, Donna? Look at that oven. Pots hanging over the counter. Yeah! Big fire roaring. Kids running around laughing. Me sitting . . ."

Donna interrupted: "Whoa, Frank. Kids. Me cooking. What's with this? Keeerist, a few months ago you got nervous when we talked about living together." Donna paused then asked, "Frank, where's my studio?"

Frank pointed to the top of the tower.

"Hmmm. Not bad." Donna walked up behind Frank, placed the pie on a granite rock, stood on another, put her arms around Frank's chest, and nuzzled his ears. She whispered something and Frank turned. When he saw Euripedes gobbling up the pie, he chortled, "Good thing we brought the pie, Donna. Euripedes was hungry."

Donna turned quickly but Euripedes had unwrapped the pie and nibbled at the crust. "Oh man, Euripedes, can't you control yourself?" Donna howled as she shooed him away. "Good thing we brought wine, Frank. We might as well let him have the rest."

Emma threw open the door. "Hello, hello!" Her voice crackled with warmth and she hugged Donna. When she saw the squeaky clean pie plate, she jiggled with laughter. "I guess Euripedes met you at the hill."

"Yeah," Frank said. "Donna wanted to bake a pie just to be sure we had something you liked. We didn't know if you liked wine." Frank held out the bottle.

"Oh my," Emma said and checked the label. "French - ayeah, one of my favorites, for certain."

Donna breathed a sigh, relieved, and Frank smiled. "We should have known," Frank whispered to Donna.

"Come on in," Emma hollered. "Let's sit by the fire and sip this beauty. It'll be a while before I can take the turkey out, so we can talk."

Frank and Donna sat in a couple of wing chairs that were placed in front of the hearth. The fire crackled under a pot hanging from a metal rod.

"What's in the pot, Emma?" Frank asked.

"Beans," Emma said. "Real baked beans. They've been cooking for a while, now. Should be perfect. Course I really should 'a dug a hole out back and buried them in a fire. That's the best way. Did you ever cook 'em that way, Donna?"

Donna said she hadn't, so Emma took her by the arm to the counter to explain the process. Frank listened for a while and then wandered into the hallway to look at the photographs on the wall. "That must be Henry," he thought as he glanced at a photograph - a man standing on a wharf holding a large fish. He moved to the right to admire the photo of a schooner under full sail but couldn't read the name. Beneath that, he saw a photograph of a group of people sitting on the ledge by the Aviary looking out at the harbor. Frank recognized the man he'd assumed was Henry with Emma next to him. The rest of the group was unfamiliar except - Frank leaned toward the photograph and peered at the image. "Christ, that's Bobby Crosby," Frank whispered.

When Donna and Emma came back to the hearth, Frank asked Emma about the photographs. Emma took them down, blowing off dust as she passed them to Frank and Donna, and described them. She verified Frank's assumption regarding Henry and noted all of the artists in the other photo. "The schooner's the *Elsie*," she said. "Now let's see. Ayeah, that's another bunch of artists: Gordon, Bill, hmmm, I don't know that one. Can't remember his name. Gettin' old. That's the trouble. Oh yeah, it's Phil and Ruthie."

"That's Bobby Crosby," Frank said, pointing to the young man holding a black book. Donna leaned over for a closer look. Her mouth dropped.

"Oh," Emma said. "I remember. The Wells boy. All grown up there."

Chapter 15

Ho ho ho.
Ha ha ha
Bah bah bah
Humbug

Christmas Spirits and Other Libations
Bobby Crosby
1971 The Aviary Papers Publishers

Before Christmas, Harley stopped by the apartment with a bottle of wine and a bag of colorfully wrapped gifts. Frank took his coat and the bottle of wine and Harley placed the packages under the tree. Donna greeted him from the kitchen and announced they'd be having tongues and cheeks for dinner. Harley remarked on the size and shape of the Christmas tree and raved about the creativity and color of Donna's paper and canvas decorations.

"Frank'll tell you all about the tree, I'm sure," Donna said.

"We carried it all the way up from the West End," Frank complained.

"Car break down?" Harley asked.

"No," Frank said, "We were at Virgilio's. She saw this tree and -" Frank raised his voice to a falsetto, "We just had to have it. It's the perfect one for us." Frank lowered his tone and said, "So I offered to walk back and get a car and she said, "Oh, no, we can't risk it. It'll be gone by the time you get back. And it would be so romantic to carry our tree home." So she grabbed the top and I grabbed the trunk and we walked up Main Street looking like Currier and Ives. Of course we had to take the long way and come up the steps at Herrick Court."

"Yeah," Donna called over the whir of the mixer, "and Frank slipped and fell on his ass. He rolled down some steps and so'd the tree. I thought he'd roll into the harbor. Sal's wife saw the whole thing and the poor woman almost had a heart attack from laughing."

"Ha, ha," Frank said.

"Luv ya, Frank," Donna chirped. "Crazy in love with me, Frank?"

"I don't know yet," Frank said as he reached around and rubbed his lower back.

Frank opened the wine and poured three glasses. Harley took his and sat on the couch while Frank took a glass to Donna. Donna was mixing a salad and Frank walked up behind her, reached around and placed her glass carefully on the counter. Donna wheeled around and kissed him. They embraced and kept kissing until Harley's voice interrupted.

"OK, kids. I'd like dinner sometime tonight."

Frank came back into the living room and sat with Harley, gazing out the window. Then he told Harley how much he enjoyed living on Friend Street. He said the closeness of the neighborhood reminded him of his grandfather.

Harley asked about where Frank had grown up and Frank described a small town in the Adirondacks - "railroaders, mill workers and farmers. Working class, Harl. Decent people. Religious. Too religious for me, though. Beautiful place on the lake. Mountains. God, what colors in the fall. Freeze in the winter. Tons of snow." Frank said he'd lived with his grandfather after his father had left to go to Memphis to work for Elvis and his mother had driven to Oregon to live with her sister.

Harley seemed dumbfounded. "Elvis?"

"Yeah," Frank said, "He was nuts about Elvis and my mother was just plain nuts so I stayed with my grandfather and finished school. Graduated and went to college. My life in a nut shell."

"Did they ever come back, Frank?"

"Yeah, Harley, when I left for college, they both did."

Harley shook his head.

After dinner, Donna made coffee while Frank washed dishes and Harley talked to them from the living room sofa. He said he liked the midair Christmas tree over by Rocky Neck. When Frank asked what that was, Donna explained that they put a tree with lights on the crane at Bickford's Marina every Christmas. They talked about the decorative lights on the houses and Donna said she hoped it would snow for the holiday.

"Too cold," Frank said. "Man, it must be twenty below."

"Probably more like forty below with the wind, Frank," Donna added. "Did you notice the sea smoke this morning?"

"Yeah," Harley said. "I was over on The Neck. It covered the cove

In a Place Like No Other

and the harbor."

"What were you doing over there on the Neck, Harl?" Donna asked.

"My usual morning jaunt," Harley said.

"Harley," Donna said. "The bars are closed until next season."

"Ha, ha, ha," Harley chuckled. "I walk down there every morning. It's so peaceful and calm. I love it. I walked up by the hotel and saw Jack's car. He must have been checking something. I looked around for him but didn't find him. The place was all locked up. The cottage, too."

"Visiting Patrick?" Frank asked.

"Never," Harley said, "Jack wouldn't do that. He doesn't like Patrick at all. The only reason Patrick's there is the Senator. Jack wants him out but the Senator said he could stay as long as he needed a place to live. I think Patrick may have done some dirty work for the Senator and the Senator owes him. Jack hates him though. I know that."

"Jack was probably up in one of the rooms screwing a prospective waitress," Donna said.

Frank laughed and so did Harley. Then Harley sighed, "There may not be any prospective waitresses this year. It was not a good season. We lost a lot of money."

"What do you mean?" Frank asked while he and Donna shot silent queries at each other in the kitchen.

When Harley explained that the hotel had lost almost sixty thousand dollars that summer, Frank threw his dish towel on the counter and bolted into the living room.

"Holy shit," Frank said. "I can't believe it. I thought it was a great summer. Jack gave me a bonus. Didn't you get one, Harley?"

"No."

"Oh, fuck! I should have kept my mouth shut."

"It's OK, Frank. Jack does stuff like that. Maybe he'll take care of me in the spring -if we open. We'll know soon enough," Harley said. "Usually around the first of the year Jack calls and asks me to start getting the mailings together."

Harley and Frank speculated on the hotel's prospects, discussing its possible sale or a rescue by investors. Both looked chagrined until Harley chortled. "Like the Walters sisters?"

"Fuck you, Harley," Frank said.

"Who're the Walters sisters?" Donna asked as she walked into the

193

room.

"Never mind," Frank said.

Harley tried to cover a wicked smile with his hand. Donna jumped to the couch where he sat and grabbed his nose. She twisted it and demanded explanation.

"Leave him alone, Donna," Frank said. "It was nothing."

Donna grabbed Harley's ear with her other hand. "Keep talking, Frank. The more you tell me it was nothing, the harder I twist. One of you better talk or Harley is hurtin'."

"Christ, why me?" Harley said. "Frank did it."

"Thanks for nothing, Harley," Frank blurted as Donna flew into his lap and twisted his ears. Then she punched him, repeatedly, in the arm. She growled, "Talk, Frankie boy, or this is going to be the first of many nights when you ain't gettin' any."

"That'll be the night," Frank quipped.

Donna reached down and grabbed Frank's crotch. "If I squeeze, Frankie boy, it ain't gonna matter how I feel about it. How you feel is going to make all the difference in the world."

"Owww," Frank howled. "OK. OK. I'll talk. Let go."

Donna let go. Frank described the night he and Jack entertained Jack's old girlfriend and her companion. "But nothing happened. I swear," Frank insisted. Harley agreed.

"You know," Donna said. "I've heard that story but with a different twist. She was Jack's old girlfriend from high school and she got married right after Jack left. Some old bastard who couldn't get it up half the time but he was worth about a hundred mil. Jerry told me. He knows. He knows Jack, too. If she got prego, it wasn't from the old guy. Jerry said she told him the geezer was shooting blanks."

"What's going on?" Frank said gawking at Harley.

"I wonder," Harley said.

In bed, Frank groaned to Donna that he'd blown it by telling Harley about the bonus. Donna told him to forget it. Frank hoped he hadn't hurt Harley's feelings and Donna said Harley would get over it.

"I don't know, Donna," Frank kept on. "I feel bad. I wish I still had it. I'd split it with him."

"What?" Donna said.

"I said I'd split it with him, Donna. Harley's a good friend. He got me to go to Captain Jerry's that night when I ran into you. If he hadn't, I probably wouldn't be here now. I owe him."

"Hey, screw him , I'm the one who told him to bring you there, asshole. Where's my cut?"

"What? Harley said he had no idea you were there."

"Forget I said that, Frank."

"Bullshit. Get up right now. You've got some explaining to do. I thought that whole thing was an accident. You set it up?"

"Frank," Donna said. "are you happy?"

"That's not the point, Donna. I've been had."

"Yeah, Frank and I'm the one doing the having. Do you like it?"

"That's not the point, Donna."

"OK, Frank. Hmm. Well then let's see." Donna reached to turn on the light and sat up in the bed then reached under the covers.

"The point is, Donna, I thought it was accidental. I thought it was ahhhh, Donna don't. Please move your hand. Donna, please I'm trying to make a point here. "

"Yeah, Frank, what's your point. Ouuu, Frankie boy."

"I, ahhh, probably would have found. . . Oh that's . . ."

"Found what, Frank?"

"I don't know. I forgot what I was talking about."

"Good night, Frank."

"Yeah, good night."

Frank had almost fallen asleep when he heard Donna ask, "Hey, Frank, what did you do with the two grand?"

"I forgot, remember. Good night."

Donna laughed.

Chapter 16

Triangulate.

                      Navigate.

Communicate.

                      Fornicate.

                    Ahab Revisited
                      Bobby Crosby
      1971 The Aviary Papers Publishers

Christmas. Harley had brought a very special Chardonnay and Donna had made a very special rib roast. Frank laughed as the two of them argued about drinking "that wine with that roast." Donna listened as Harley waxed eloquent about saving the Chardonnay for a great piece of fish or a well prepared chicken. Donna told Harley, "Open the damn bottle and enjoy Christmas dinner." Harley relented and opened the wine.

    Frank and Donna had opened a few gifts before Harley had arrived and Donna had on the sweater Frank had given her. Frank wore the tan chamois shirt Donna had given him. A set of earrings from Frank had Donna brushing back her hair every time she walked past Harley. Harley'd say, "they're just delightful, Donna. Marvellous." Frank helped in the kitchen and each time Donna returned from a trip to the table, she'd say, "Smart move, Frankie boy. You're a shoe in for gettin' laid tonight." Frank would smile and pinch her butt as she walked past him.

    Then Donna told Harley he should open his gifts that were under the tree before dinner. Harley opened the first gift, carefully placed the wrapping paper on the couch and pried open the box. "How delightful," Harley said admiring the album jacket. "Rudolph Serkin. How could you have known?"

    The second was a book - <u>Great Wines and Vineyards of France.</u> "I adore you two," Harley said. "You are wonderful people and even more wonderful friends. This is simply perfect." Harley hugged them both. "I love you, both of you," Harley said. "You two are the best." Then Harley went back to the couch to leaf through his book.

Frank sat in a chair across from Harley and laughed as Harley read the section about Chardonnays. Harley giggled as he proclaimed, "A fine Chardonnay should accompany salmon, halibut or possibly a roasted duck."

Donna walked around the corner with a beautifully prepared rib roast garnished with parsleyed potatoes and miniature ears of corn and said, "Stick it, you guys. I busted my butt over this roast and you two sit there complaining 'cause it should be salmon. I'll just toss the roast out the window and run down to the wharf and see if there's a halibut lying around. If not, I got some Gorton's fish sticks in the freezer. We'll have those."

Harley said, "Let's eat."

"Great idea," Frank said.

They'd had a rum cake from Mike's for dessert and had spent an hour talking over coffee. Then Harley'd left and Frank and Donna sat on the couch to savor a crystal clear night over the harbor. They admired the Christmas tree they could see suspended in mid air and voted for the best lights in East Gloucester and on Rocky Neck. Then Donna noticed a gray plume of smoke rising in the night sky just past the crane. At first they thought it was nothing unusual; Donna'd often commented on the stark beauty of a cold night sky and the touch of whimsy that smoke from the chimneys added. When the wisp became flames, Donna said in horror, "That's near Rackliffe House." She pointed. A siren passed below them going east on Main Street. "Must be big," Donna said.

They knew it was Rackliffe House. When the phone rang, Frank said, "Harley! Yeah, We can see it. How bad is it? _ OK. Let us know. Talk to you later." Frank hung up the phone.

"Harley said from his place it doesn't look too bad, He said the firemen almost have it out. That last blast of flame broke through a dormer on the top floor but they've knocked it down. He said he's going to walk over there. He'll call to let us know what's going on."

"Damn," Donna said. "That sucks. The place will be closed for sure."

"Maybe not," Frank said. "Jack must have insurance."

"Yeah. insurance will cover it. Won't it?"

"It should. Geezuz, I hope Patrick is all right."

The phone rang later. "Hi, Harley. What'd you find out?" Frank asked. Frank shushed at Donna but the look on his face had her whispering,

"What happened? What'd he say? What?" Finally Frank had to ask Donna to stop.

"OK. Harley. I will. Good night. Yeah, Merry Christmas."

"Harley said to be sure to thank you again for the gifts and a great dinner and he wished you a Merry Christmas."

"What did he say about the fire, Frank?"

"Not all that bad. All of the smoke was from a couple of mattresses and the rugs in two rooms on the top floor. The rest of the hotel is fine except for water damage."

"Water damage? That can be a nightmare."

"He said the coroner drove up just as he was leaving. There were a bunch of cops and a couple of detectives talking to the fire marshal. They escorted the coroner to the back of the building."

"Somebody died? Oh, man, poor Patrick. That sucks."

"No. Harley said he saw Patrick walking around."

"I'm going to try to call, Jack." Frank picked up the phone and dialed. Then: "Jack? Yeah, Frank_Good. Are you OK? _ Yeah, Jack, we could see the fire from here . _ At Donna's, Jack. _ No, Jack, Harley told me. I didn't go over there._OK, Jack, I will. See ya."

Donna looked at Frank as he hung up the phone. "He knew?"

"Yeah. The police called him."

"Frank, what's going on?"

"I don't know."

The next afternoon, when she got home from work, Donna burst through the door in a frenzy. She screamed for Frank to come and see the newspaper. "Ducky Ryan was the dead guy at the hotel."

Frank had just read about it in the police notes. "They identified the body early this morning. One of the cops knew him. It's not official, but they're pretty sure. They said he might have jumped to get out of the fire."

"What's going on, Frank?"

"How would I know, Donna?"

"Frank, I want you to start looking for another job. I don't want you around Jack anymore. I know he's tied into this somehow."

"Brilliant deduction, Donna. He runs the hotel. Of course he's tied in. That doesn't mean he was involved in this."

"My ass, Frank. I know he's your friend, but I'm telling you he's a piece of shit, scum bag, friggin' bastard. Stay away, Frank. I love you and you're a little naive. Do what I tell you, Frank."

"Donna, we both know you're too judgemental. Relax. Jack can be an asshole at times but I don't think he's a criminal."

"Oh, yeah," Donna said. "Well screwing an underaged girl is criminal - in this state anyway."

"What?" Frank said. "What are you talking about?"

"Nothing," Donna said, "Nothing. Forget it."

Frank sat on the couch thinking: He'd never said anything to Donna about Jack and the chambermaid. "Donna, how did you find out?"

"You know? How did you find out?"

"I saw him."

"What? You weren't even in . . . Never mind."

Frank looked more stunned. "Donna, what you're talking about?"

"You know, Frank, the same thing you're talking about."

"Donna, I'm talking about the dishwasher at the Loft that Jack was screwing all summer."

"Right. Right, Frank. She was underage. Jack could go to jail."

"Donna, the dishwasher at the Loft was a guy. Larry Perkins. He used to come into the bar. He's twenty two. Jack's not gay. You're so friggin' wrong it's not even funny. You're bullshitting me and that sucks. Tell me what you're talking about."

"Fuck you, Frank. I'm going to bed. If you don't believe me, shove it. If you don't like it, then get out. I told you what I thought and that's it. Go fuck yourself, Frank."

Donna slammed the door to the bedroom and Frank stayed on the sofa. He'd been staring out at the harbor for a while, when he dialed up Harley. "Yeah, Harley, Merry Christmas. _ Yeah I spoke to Jack._ Look, Harley, I need a favor. Any room at your place?"

Frank filled in behind the bar at Captain Jerry's the Saturday after New Year's. Two waitresses worked the tables and Frank had to hustle to keep drink flowing for the crowded bar. He'd run out of glasses so he hollered to Isabelle in the kitchen to have one of the bus boys bring a rack of clean ones. He'd laced beer bottles in his fingers and had placed them on a tray at the waitress station when he heard Donna's voice behind him. "Hey bartendahr! Got a beahr?" floated over the football banter at the bar.

"Sure." Frank walked over and placed a beer in front of her.

"Come with me, Frank. Right now." Donna reached for Frank's shirt sleeve with a trembling hand. She stumbled as she dragged him from behind the bar into the vestibule. They stood, visible through the glass of the swinging door, and the patrons at the bar gaped and peered as Donna, shaking, tears streaming down both cheeks, arms flailing, harangued.

Out in the vestibule, Frank stood with crossed arms as he listened: The night of her fifteenth birthday, she'd gotten dumped by her first love and she and a friend stumbled into the Rackiffe House bar drunk and brazen; Jack Carson mixed her a Martini and she gulped a few because she thought "Martini" sounded cool; and when Jack started hitting on her and her friend, they swooned. "Not from Jack, Frank," Donna screamed as she stomped on the floor and slammed her palm into the wall. "The friggin' Mahrtinis made me dizzy."

The volume of the palaver and the relentless clanging of the service bell swelled as a new customer opened the vestibule door. "Come on, Frank," a waitress screeched. "We've got people to serve. Mix drinks or get a room, will ya?" Beer bottles rapped on the bar syncopating the chant: "We want Frank." Frank turned and gave the bar both fingers through the door glass then turned back to Donna.

Unable to lift her eyes to look at Frank, Donna stammered on about waking the next morning at Jack's, naked in bed, she with Jack's arm around her and her arm around her friend. She didn't notice Frank's grin as she talked about going back to the hotel a week later, wanting to kill Jack Carson "or if nothing else," she said, "kick him in the balls." But she couldn't find Jack, so she sat in the lobby and wept. Harley had talked to her and had sent her home with a hug and some good advice and they've been great friends since.

Then Donna looked squarely at Frank and pleaded with her big brown eyes. When Frank dabbed at her cheeks, she grabbed his wrist with both hands. "Please Frank," she said, "I am crazy about you but I'm crazier without you. Please forgive me and let's . . ."

Frank said. "I'm sorry that happened. It's all in the past. Forget it."

Donna pressed Frank's hand to her mouth and Frank leaned over and kissed her and whispered, "Donna your crushing my friggin' hand and I gotta go make drinks. Go home."

Donna asked Frank if he wanted her to stay and help out and Frank thanked her but said he could handle it. Then he told her he'd see her at the apartment. When Frank walked back to the waitress station, one of the waitresses complained "Fucken A, Frank. I thought you two were going to do it right there. Jerry wouldn't like that. Y'know." Frank laughed.

Frank walked into the apartment and Donna, wearing the earrings and sweater he'd bought her for Christmas and an apron tied around her waist, greeted him with a hug and a kiss. "God," Frank said. "What are you cooking? I could smell it out on the street. I had to check the address. Thought I was at Roger's"

"Duck," Donna said as she started to unbutton Frank's shirt. "I stopped by the packy and bought a bottle of the Chardonnay Harley brought at Christmas. I went to Roger's and got some veal stock. We're having roast duck, wine and a salad. And, oh yeah, I forgot. You're the appetizer."

Frank was trying to say he realized that when his pants hit the floor.

During dinner, Frank raved about the duck and Donna told him all about the duck hunting up in Rowley and how her father'd taught her to cook. She harped about what a waste it was for a talented chef like him to be running a diner. She continued talking about him through coffee and then as they cleaned the table and stacked dishes in the sink; Frank suggested Roger's for desert. So they walked down Middle Street, arm in arm, perusing the lives of others through window glass.

After Roger's, Donna and Frank, wrapped in each other, walked home along Main Street. Donna told Frank that the chocolate tort had made her really horny. "What's new?" Frank said. Donna punched him, then she grabbed his arm with both hands. Li'l Earl's was across the street and Donna said, "Let's, for a nightcap and maybe even dance a little." Frank agreed to a beer but not the dancing.

"Oh come on, Frank," Donna said. "It'll be fun. We can look like assholes and have a great time doing it."

They walked into the nightclub and the music pounded them. Frank handed the bouncer four dollars and they sat at the bar. They sipped beers and turned to watch the dance floor. A disco ball rotated and strobe lights cast the dancers in a 16mm film. Donna hummed along with David Bowie. At the chorus, she squeezed Frank's thigh and warbled "all night, she wants the young American." Frank laughed.

Frank noticed a woman dancing wildly in the middle of the room. It was Annie Barnes. He pointed her out to Donna and said, "She's is a great dancer and she's . . . "

Donna looked at Frank and encouraged him to go on because she sure wasn't jealous. But when Frank finished his sentence with "gorgeous," Donna punched him in the arm and said, "I didn't say I wouldn't slug you if you looked at another woman." Then she kissed Frank, said, "Just kidding," and kept singing, "allll night . . ."

They'd watched the dancers a while longer when Donna shouted over the pounding bass, "Look. That guy jumping in the air and doing splits. There, Frank. Over there. That's Richie Barnes. What an asshole. He dances like a friggin' train wreck." Richie played air guitar as he lowered himself to the floor in a split. Frank laughed. Donna guffawed as Richie slinked from the dance floor with his sweater tied around his waist. "He split his pants, Frank."

The bartender asked if they wanted another but they decided to leave. Frank paid the tab and grabbed his coat. Donna said, "Shit. Frank, look who just walked in."

Frank jerked his thumb in the direction of Annie Barnes and told Donna he thought they had something going. Donna's sarcasm was obvious as she said, "her and three thousand other women."

Jack said hello and wanted to buy them a drink but Frank said they were leaving. Jack said he needed to talk to Frank about the hotel and the fire. Frank looked at Donna and she whispered, "Still adamant," so Frank made an excuse and told Jack to stop by the next day.

Lying in bed with the down quilt pulled up under her chin, Donna expressed her dismay about Frank talking to Jack and Frank said, "yeah, I know. Good night, Donna."

Donna switched the table lamp off. "Good night, Frank."

Then Frank sat upright, turned the lamp on. "What was it like the night you and your friend were with Jack?"

"I was drunk, Frank. I don't remember. I felt terrible the next day. Totally embarrassed. Ashamed. Chris and I haven't been close since."

Frank smiled. "Whoa! Christine Falco, great body. Incredible legs, nice tits, great ass! Maybe you should be friends again. It'll feel good to talk to her. Invite her over."

"Frank, you're close to death. How does that feel?"

"Then again, maybe not."

Donna disappeared under the covers but Frank, grabbed her. "Donna, I was just kidding around. I love you."

Donna gawked. "Frank, you better not be just kidding when you tell me you love me. You've never said it before and it could put me on the verge of a major fuckin' heart attack. You better mean it or they'll find two dead bodies in the morning."

"I mean it. I love you. As you would say, end of story."

"I'll let you know when it ends." Donna slipped back under the quilt.

Frank filled in at Jerry's the next afternoon. He'd told Donna he'd be back by six and to tell Jack where he was if he called. Donna had the day off so she cleaned the apartment and cooked. She walked around singing as she stirred cake batter in a mixing bowl cradled in her arm. She heard a knock at the door and when she opened it and saw Jack standing there she groaned, "What the fuck do you want?"

"Nice to see you, too, Donna," Jack answered.

"Frank's working at Jerry's place. He left an hour ago. Beat it!" Donna leaned her body against the door.

"Gee, Donna, why not invite me in," Jack said with a wry grin. "We could talk about old times. Maybe do a couple of lines together. Maybe more. What do you say?"

"Fuck off, Jack, or I'll yell to Lou and you'll be at the bottom of the hill before you know what hit you."

"Christ, Donna, why are you still angry? It happened years ago. Get the fuck over yourself, will ya?"

"It ain't that, Jack. You might like to think so but it ain't. I just think you're one piece of whale shit. I can't make Frank see it, yet, but I will. He saw enough this summer to get him thinking. It won't take much more."

"Oh, yeah, and what exactly did Frank see, Betty Crocker?"

Jack's sarcasm was met with a spoon pointed at his face. "He saw you with an underaged girl, scumbag. He knows you screwed her because you told him. And he knows you gave her drugs. He doesn't think much of that kind of shit, Jack. So just fuck the fuck off. And watch out, because Frank'll only put up with so much of that crap from you or anybody else."

Donna tried to close the door again but Jack wouldn't budge. He snickered, "You may think he's a straight shooter, Donna, but let me tell you why Frank won't say a word about the chambermaid or anything else he might not like. It's his word against mine. Besides, Frank was paid handsomely for the coke he supplied for that little party. You were there, Donna. The night we closed. He says a word and I give up Frank for selling me the coke. You might want to wise him up to that if he ever starts talking too much."

"What coke? No way! Frank nev . . ."

"The coke I gave her and a few other people around town. Frank brought it in. I unloaded some and kept a little for myself. Good shit. That kid was blown away by it - no pun intended. She's in drug rehab, now. She graduated to heroin. Quick."

"You rotten bahstard. You told him it was a bonus."

"Bonus! Ha, fucking ha. We lost sixty grand last summer. How could I give him a bonus? Harley didn't get one. I didn't get one. Why would Frank get one? It was his cut of a deal. Don't you remember, Donna? You came flying around the corner into the parking lot. Almost killed a couple of guys that were running out to the street. The dealers, asshole. You almost croaked 'em. They got spooked. So I walked into the bar and gave Frank the envelope just in case, ahh, you know. There'd been narcs around all summer. Downstairs in the bar. Pretty regular visitors. Sure, Donna, you can tell just by the way they dress. Come on, nobody around here would be caught dead in a Greek fisherman's hat. Well maybe Jerry or one of those wackos. Gettin' the picture? I made it convenient for 'em. You don't think they really want to come down on a senator's son, now. Do you? For a lousy couple a grand, I gave 'em an excuse to watch Frank."

"You scumbag pig, Jack. I'm going to tell Frank everything. He's gonna kill you and if he doesn't I will." Donna dropped the mixing bowl on a table and ran to grab the walking sticking from over the kitchen door.

Jack stepped out into the hall and shot back, "You're not going to say a thing. You're too scared I'll tell Frank about our little adventure."

Donna stomped toward the door wielding the stick. Then she paused and banged the floor with the stick. "You know what? You do that, Jack. You'll be doing me a favor. You go right down to Jerry's and you tell Frank everything."

Jack laughed as he walked away. "You're shitten yourself if you don't think I'll do it, Donna."

Donna slammed the door hard, jarring the framed canvases hanging on the wall. She sat in an overstuffed chair and slapped the arm with the palm of one hand as she tapped her foot with the walking stick. Then, she walked over and picked up the phone and dialed. "Hi, Lou. _ Yeah it's Donna. _Hey, Lou, can I come up? Gotta talk to ya. _ Yeah great. Thanks, Lou. I'll be right up."

Frank was mopping the bar when Jack walked into Captain Jerry's and ordered a Bloody Mary. They talked while Frank mixed the drink and Jack mentioned that the cops had told him Ducky Ryan had been dead for a while, from a drug overdose. "They think Patrick might have had something to do with it." Jack brandished his celery stick and griped about the basement of the hotel and how anybody could hide in there for months.

Frank insisted Patrick couldn't be involved. "He told me, Jack. He's never touched the stuff."

Jack sniggered, "And you believe it, Frank. Why? Because he's a friggin' Indian? You and the Indians, Frank. Wake up!"

Frank reeled on Jack's comment, caught himself, then asked about the fire, and Jack said the inspectors thought it was faulty wiring. They were looking at the sconces Frank had installed in the upstairs hall. Frank shook his head, then insisted he'd wired them correctly.

"Forget it," Jack said. "The insurance'll cover it."

Frank tried to change the subject to Annie Barnes but Jack didn't seem to want to talk about her, complaining she was out of control. Frank assumed he meant she wanted to get more involved with Jack but when he suggested that, Jack didn't elaborate. It reminded Frank of how Jack ignored Katy when she finally got out of the hospital.

Jack wanted to talk about the hotel and Frank working again next summer. He wanted Frank to get started repairing the damage as soon as the insurance check arrived, "In a couple of weeks. A month at the most."

Frank said, "I guess," as he wiped a smudge on the bar.

Then Jack said he wanted to get something out of the way. He started to tell Frank about his past with Donna. Frank glared and cut him off abruptly. "It's nothing I want to hear about again."

"You know?" Jack frowned and looked into his drink. "Hmmm. Well, ahhh, I guess that, ahh, changes a few things."

"Not really. Look, Jack I still think you're a friggin' scumbag for what you did to Donna and that kid at the hotel last fall. Maybe you ought to see a shrink or something. But it's your problem. Don't make it mine. OK, Jack?"

"Yeah, . . . sure . . . yeah great, Frank. Say, ahh Frank, I gotta know something, though. That thing at the employee's party. Donna know?"

"Yeah, Jack. I told her."

"What did you tell her, Frank?"

"You were screwing one of the chambermaids."

"Tell her which one?" Jack wiped his brow with a napkin.

"No. I left Molly out of it. You're the one with the problem, Jack."

"Oh, yeah, . . . well good, Frank. Yeah, I hear ya, man, well I'm done with that bullshit. Too risky. Look, just forget it." Jack swallowed the rest of his Bloody Mary, dropped a few bills on the bar and said good bye. He patted his pockets complaining that he couldn't find his car keys. Frank pushed them across the bar. "Oh, ahh, thanks, Frank. Forgot I, ahhh, put them there."

Jerry came in as Jack was leaving. Once he got behind the bar with Frank he whispered, "What's Jack's problem, Frank? He's freaked, man. Something happen?"

Frank told Jerry and Jerry fumed. "Hey, Frank, Donna's my favorite. You know that. If you want first crack at that guy, fine. I understand, man. If he's still walking around without crutches by the end of April, he's mine. I just hope I can control myself. I don't want to kill no senator's son."

Frank told Jerry he'd always been able to handle Jack and Jerry nodded, bending to organize bottles on the shelf under the bar. "But," Jerry added as he raised himself up to look at Frank, "let me tell you one more thing, man. You got your head up your ahs about that guy. He may have been your old college buddy but he smells like old fish."

"Yeah, I smell it, too. He was too quick to point to Patrick. I'm sure Patrick wouldn't have anything to do with drugs."

"No way," Jerry said. "Finest kind, that friggin' Indian. Straight shooter. No bullshit."

Donna broke up the conversation when she walked in and hollered, "Hey one of you big burly boys wanna give a Glosta girl a beeeeaaaahrr?"

Frank kissed her and Jerry brought her a beer. "Be careful, Frank, Jerry's closin' in on ya. Luv ya, but Jerry's got what I need right now."

Jerry pushed Frank aside and bellied up to the back of the bar, closed his eyes and puckered his lips as he leaned toward Donna.

"Oh, geez, Jerry," Donna said. "not now. Isabelle's looking out the porthole."

Jerry snapped to attention and wiped glasses.

"Just kidding." Donna chuckled.

Frank reached across the bar and brushed hair from Donna's eyes. "I think I'll quit for the night, Jerry. There's a babe at the bar and I want to give it a shot. Could be something in it for me."

Donna and Frank walked up Main Street to the hill after dinner at Jerry's. Frank complained that his stomach hurt from all the fried food. Donna rubbed his belly and teased him about the cake she'd baked and how he wouldn't be able to have any until tomorrow. "No sex, either," she said. Then she stopped and grabbed Frank firmly by the arm and said, "Frank, Jack came by the apartment just after you left. He was obnoxious - that's nothing new. He said something about the money he'd given you and it really bothers me." She told Frank what had transpired.

"That's bullshit, Donna. That must be why he got so nervous when I told him I knew all about you and Chris and him. I told Jerry a little about it. He noticed it too when he saw Jack leaving. Said he looked panicked. Asked me what had happened and I told him. Jerry told me to be careful. Jack's up to something."

"Yeah, Frank, about six feet of dirt. I figured out something today. The chambermaid?"

"Yeah."

"I went up to talk to Lou about Jack setting you up and asked him what I should do and Lou started complaining about one of his boy's nieces having a tough time in drug rehab someplace outside of Bahston. Damn, I meant Boston. He said she'd been a chambermaid at some hotel and somebody there had given her drugs. I didn't mention Jack but I will if that ahshole does anything else to me or you." Donna smirked, then said, "Frank, you didn't say anything about me and Jack and Chris?"

"Well . . . ahh."

"Geez, Frank, Jerry'll kill him."

"Sounds like a line is forming, Donna."

They walked a couple of blocks and stopped to look at the harbor.

"Frank," Donna said. "Something else happened today that I'm not real happy about."

"What?"

"Someone called for you today, Frank. A woman. You know what she said, Frank?"

"No."

"She said, tell him Allie called. What the fuck, Frank?"

"My mother," Frank said and he told Donna about the conversation he'd had with his mother in October.

"So," Donna said.

"Well, that's how she got my number."

"So."

"Christ, Donna, what do you want to know?"

"What do you think I want to know, Frank?"

"If I'm going to call back?"

"Good, Frank. You're gettin' theahr."

"I can't."

"Why?"

"I forgot. Remember? Last summer you said fuck your brains out and forget it. So I did."

Donna laughed. Frank looked away.

Chapter 17

A clash of titans.
Low from the south
High from the north.

Nor'easter
Les Moor
1968 The Aviary Papers Publishers

When Frank wasn't at Jerry's, he and Donna sat around the apartment at night and read. Donna's enjoyed southern writers like Faulkner, Welty and Buckingham. "I love that story about the duck hunters who'd fought each other in the Civil War," she'd told Frank. "They end up in the same cabin after the war and start drinkin' and realize they'd almost killed each other in a skirmish."

Frank read everything he could find about the history of Gloucester and its house styles. One night as he researched lightning rods, he read aloud, "and the positive charge in the earth attracts the negatively charged particles," hmmm, let's see. Yup, clouds. OK, "The heat generated sometimes reaches many thousands of degrees." Let's see, hmmm, oh yeah, "generated by hundreds of thousands of volts of electricity." Whoa, listen to this, Donna. "In Medieval times hundreds of churches were struck and damaged by lightning. Bell ringing was considered a dangerous occupation." Can you imagine that, darling? Man, can you believe it, and those little rods, remember the ones I showed you, they all came from Benjamin Franklin's experiments. They're designed to prevent disasters. Look, right . . . " Donna snored peacefully on the couch.

They had a small black and white television. Sometimes they'd watch reruns of <u>Hogan's Heroes</u>. Frank would lose control over the antics of Sergeant Schultz. Donna would say, "Frank, nobody can be that naive!" and Frank would laugh and say, "Sure, they could." Donna would shake her head and say, "Maybe you're right." Frank liked the news and Donna liked the weather, so they turned on the television at eleven nightly.

That evening, the weather lady mentioned a low front forming off the Mid-Atlantic Coast. She said it could develop into a major coastal storm and before it moved off to the Maritimes, two feet of snow north and west of Boston was a possibility. Donna said, "Great!" and told Frank she'd call in and tell her folks she couldn't make it to the diner and they'd be able to spend one or two days playing under the sheets and walking around in the snow. Frank laughed and said it would rain. Donna insisted on snow.

They woke the next morning to a blustery northeast wind and blinding snow. Frank looked out the living room window and saw several inches of new snow already covering Friend Street. He could see nothing beyond Sal's roof just two houses away. Donna started breakfast.

"Frank, over easy, OK?"

"Thanks, Donna."

"Toast or muffin?"

"Either's fine. Whatever you're having."

"OJ or tomato?"

"Prune."

"Don't be a jerk, Frank."

"Orange juice."

"OK, come and get it."

Over breakfast, the blistering winds made them shiver when they pounded the window glass and rattled the aluminum storms. They decided they'd be happier going back in bed.

They relaxed under the covers. Donna thumbed through a book of John Sargent's work and Frank read about lightning rods. He admired the sketches and asked Donna if she ever illustrated like that. Donna peeked at the book and said, "Not really."

Suddenly, Donna jumped to her feet and said, "Frank, stay right here." She ran into the other room and came back with her easel. Frank watched warily as she set it up at the foot of the bed. Then she ran out again and came back with a canvas and started to prepare her paints. Frank winced at the strong scent of turpentine and varnish. Then Donna said, "OK, Frank, throw the covers off. I'm going to paint you. Nude. I haven't done a figure in years and I'm inspired."

Frank looked puzzled as Donna directed his position. "There, right there. Try not to move too much."

"Can I read?"

"Sure." Donna started working.

An hour and a half later, she twisted the canvas around for Frank to see. "Christ! Geez, Donna, it's me. What the hell are you doing? Why'd you make it look like me?"

"Because I wanted to do a painting of you, Frank."

"Yeah, but Donna, your other stuff is so, ahhhh, shit, I mean, yeah, abstract. This is almost real. Christ, people are going to know it's me."

"So?"

"So! I don't want to be hanging in some gallery somewhere naked for everybody to see. Come on, Donna, a little decorum, here."

"Why not, Frank. I exaggerated the important parts. You won't feel embarrassed when all those ladies start raving about your pecker."

"Hmmm." Frank rubbed the back of his neck. "Yeah, OK. You might have something there, Donna. I could score a few here and there."

Donna leaned the canvas against the easel leg and then jumped into the bed and sat on top of Frank. She pinned his arms against the mattress and said, "Tell me, Frank, right now - you're mine and mine alone or I'll screw you until your brains turn to mush."

Frank said nothing.

"Do you think I'm kidding, Frank?" Donna asked after an extended silence.

"I hope not. That's why I'm not talking."

Donna kissed him. "No one'll ever see it."

"Good. I'm more modest than you think."

"Good. You'll live longer, Frankie boy."

That night, after dinner, Frank looked at the painting and commented again on how much it looked like him. Donna asked if he liked it and he nodded emphatically. They talked for a while on the sofa. The odor of oil paints and turpentine had Frank cracking the window open but a blast of cold northwest wind made him close it abruptly.

After a while, they decided to crawl into bed. Frank pulled the covers up to his chin. Donna suggested they walk around the next morning and see how beautiful Gloucester was in the snow. Frank shivered at the thought but said, "OK," and added they should walk over to Emma's and see how she was doing. Donna agreed.

Ed Touchette

After breakfast the next morning, they walked to the bottom of the steps at Herrick and headed for East Gloucester. At the liquor store they turned right up the hill onto East Main Street and walked toward Rocky Neck. They stopped and looked at the harbor. Blustery and cold, sea smoke drifted above the surface of the water.

"I never realized salt water froze," Frank said.

"Everything freezes in this cold," Donna said.

Blowing snow pelted their faces as they walked on East Main Street. They stopped just below Banner Hill to look up at the Aviary and the glistening crystals blowing up the hill swirled around the layers of the house in a celebratory sparkle.

The snow piles lining Emma's drive were almost impassable and they had to climb over a drift to get to her steps. Emma opened her door when Frank knocked and he said, "Hello, Emma. We were just out walking and wanted to stop in and see if everything's OK. Hi, Euripedes." The Labrador bounded to welcome them.

"Hi, you two. Haven't seen you since Thanksgiving. How are you both? How nice of you to think of us."

Frank and Donna stomped as much snow as they could from their boots and they brushed each other's shoulders. Emma told them not to bother and tugged her wool shawl to her shoulders. "Brrrr, it's cold. Come on in and get warm by the fire. I'll get some coffee." Frank and Donna sat in two chairs by the small fireplace in the kitchen. They watched as Emma scurried about the kitchen pouring steaming coffee into mugs. Euripedes sat and nuzzled Donna's hand. She scratched his head.

"Well, Frank," Emma said as she came in with two cups of coffee, "What do you think of youhr first winter nor'eastah?"

"It was something else, Emma. Sure is cold today."

"Well, the snow sure is pretty and the sun's bright," Emma said.

"I know," Donna said. "We want to go for a walk down by the ocean and see the swells. Wanna go?"

"Oh, my, no," Emma replied. "I'd love to but these old legs would have a hahrd time getting me back heahr. Euripedes might like to go, though. What do you think, you old dog? You want to go for a walk?"

Euripedes barked.

"Somethin' about them dogs," Emma said. "They sure like nasty weather. Ol' Euripedes loves bein' outside when it's blowin' a gale. I don't

In a Place Like No Other

know why, though. Nothin' moahr pathetic lookin' than a wet dog."

Frank and Donna laughed.

"That'll be fun," Donna said. "Frank, what do you say?"

"Let's get going," Frank said.

Frank and Donna and the black Labrador walked toward the east end of Mt. Pleasant. They passed the fire station, heading up the rise, and Frank extolled the finer qualities of the Queen Anne style house at the top of the hill. "See the way the winged gables intersect and the tower is placed right at the juncture of the two. Classic Queen Anne. The decorative trim, integral porch, cutaway bay. Look at the spindlework in that frieze suspended from the porch ceiling - all of it's just classic, Donna. Look, the lightning rod. See the glass ball. That's OK. A metal one would concentrate the energy and that's not good. Glass is OK, though."

"Geezuz, Frank, you're really getting to know about these houses. I'm impressed."

"I love it, Donna. It's really fun researching this stuff. I just need to find out more about the people who built them. A lot of records are hard to come by."

"Try City Hall, Frank."

"Yeahhhhh, City Hall, now that's an interesting . . ."

"Frank, enough. My head hurts from trying to understand all of this stuff you're talking about. Can we just enjoy the snow?"

"OK, but do you ever think about what it must have been like, you know, a big family living in these huge homes. Lots of kids running . . ."

Donna interrupted. "See, Frank, there you go again. Big house, kids, fire in the fireplace. Frank, are you proposing to me?"

"No, Donna, just wondering what it was like growing up in a big family in these houses. I bet . . ."

"Yeah, well, Frank, look, if you're getting the idea that we should get one of these houses and have a bunch of kids, well, let's talk about it. I've hardly got enough time to paint as it is. If I start poppin' out the kids, it's gonna be worse."

"I'm just talking, Donna. Who's getting nervous now?"

"What do you mean nervous, Frank? I'm not nervous. I just want to know what's going on. That's all. Every time we see one of these houses, you start talking about big families. Just want to be prepared. Should I get off the pill, Frank?"

"Not quite yet."

"Well, Frank, what does that mean? Not today but maybe tomorrow? Come on, Frank, spit it out. Does that mean you're thinking about getting married? I'd like to know, Frank. You're getting me all excited here."

Frank stood - silent, inscrutable even to himself. Donna shoved him into a snow bank.

They started to cross toward the golf course. Euripedes sauntered along with them. He tracked an occasional rabbit but managed to keep within sight. Frank had noted a Second Empire mansard at the end of Page street and muttered something to himself. Donna asked, "What?" but Frank didn't answer. He walked with his head turned toward the house and bumped into a small oak at the edge of the opening. Donna laughed and said, "Christ, Frank, be careful, will ya. Sometimes I think you're going to need full time supervision."

They reached the base of Moorland Road and stood watching the breakers crash over the seawall. Some of the water washed over the lawns and melted the snow. Dull, yellow-brown grass stuck up through a coating of seafoam.

Powerful swells rolled in and as they reached the rocky shore line, they tumbled over themselves in a cascade of foamy white. They rumbled along the shore and the clattering of cobble stones rolling over each other subsided into the next booming assault. Gulls swept along the breaking waters. Cawing, whistling wind, and salt spray filled the air. Frank and Donna had to keep wiping their faces.

Frank looked along the roadway at a crowd of people gathered around a large dark lump that rested on the rocky beach below them. Donna thought it might be a whale carcass that washed up in the storm. They walked over to look.

"What's that horrendous smell?" Frank asked as they got closer.

"The whale. Be worse if it was hotter."

Euripedes sniffed the air and nosed the ground ahead of his steps. Frank grabbed his collar. "Good thinking, Frank. Dogs love rotten smelling stuff."

They watched as people investigated, walking gingerly around the corpse and avoiding the onslaught of water. One man stood back, up the beach, holding a chain saw. The body of the whale had collapsed on itself. The waves washing in on it rolled the carcass further up onto the beach and a flipper wagged aimlessly. "Sad." Frank said.

"Huge," Donna answered. "That thing is 35 feet long. Must weigh tons."

They watched for a while and then headed back to Emma's. Euripedes would take a few steps and turn and sniff, still curious. He lagged as Frank and Donna walked up the hill toward Mt. Pleasant Avenue. "Come on," Donna would call out, "I'm frozen."

They knocked on the door and Emma knotted with laughter when she saw them. The salt spray had frozen and the matted, tangled ends of their hair started dripping. Sitting by the fire thawed the icicles, so they wiped the water from their faces and Donna wrung her hair with a towel Emma'd handed to her. Emma brought hot chocolate and laughed. "A couple of dogs in a rain storm. Boy, what fun to be young and foolish."

"Yeah," Frank said, "smell pretty bad, look like hell, but y'gotta love 'em."

Donna punched Frank and then told Emma about the whale.

"Wow!" Emma said, "That's unusual this time of year. Guess it happens though. Did they cut it up? Henry would have liked to check its belly, for sure. He always wanted to know what something was feeding on. Probably find jaw bones and all kinds of stuff in there," Emma said.

"Yuck," Donna cried.

Frank laughed. Euripedes lay on the rug in front of the fire, snoring and snorting. His paws galloped: the rabbits on the golf course must have been in front of him.

Chapter 18

*If you're drunk or tired,
don't order soup.*

A Lumper's Breakfast
The Hydeaway Poems
Bobby Crosby
1970 The Aviary Papers Publishers

At the end of February, Jack called to tell Frank that the insurance check had come but it was too cold to work in the building without any heat. Frank agreed. Jack said they would start in March and make extensive repairs to all of the rooms on the top floor.

"Does that mean people will be able to take baths this summer?" Frank asked Jack. Then he said good bye and hung up the phone.

Donna, cooking in the kitchen, heard the conversation and began grumbling about Frank working for Jack again. "Jack tried to set you. Don't be a patsy, Frank."

"OK. We've been through that a million times. It was a dumb thing for him . . ."

The telephone interrupted. Frank picked up the receiver and said, "Hello._Oh, hi, Harley. Hey! How are you? We haven't seen you for a while. _ Yeah, we're fine. _ Yeah, she's in the kitchen, Harley._ Hold on. Let me ask her."

Frank called to Donna and told her Harley wanted to stop by and introduce them to his new boyfriend and he wanted to be sure it was OK.

Donna stomped into the living room and grabbed the phone from Frank. "Harley," she said, "yeah, hi. _ Yeah, it's me, Donna. Who else would it be? _ Look you old dumb fag, you ever call here again and ask something as stupid as that and I'll come out there and kick both your butts all the way to the apartment myself. _ Of course it's OK. We've missed you. Where have you been? _ Up yours, Harley. If you can afford to go to Florida for a week then you better bring a great bottle of wine for dinner. _ Yeah, Chardonnay is fine. And . . . hey you cheap bum, get that expensive one. I've got ducks in the freezer and I'm going to blow your mind with something I learned from my father. _ Yeah, don't worry I'll impress your new friend. _ Hmmm. Oh yeah, where? _ Oh, oh, maybe . . .well ahh, I spoke too quickly. _ Yeah, we'll see. Thanks for nothing. _ Hurry up, will ya. We've missed you._Yeah, love you, too, you old fag."

Donna stared blankly at the wall as she cradled the phone. When Frank asked what had happened, she mumbled, "Fucken A! Harley's friend's a chef."

Donna scrambled around in the kitchen. Pans and pots clanked as she groused about cooking for a bonafide chef. She talked aloud to herself, fretting about cooking ducks and impressing a professional. She opened a bottle of cooking wine, poured half in a marinade and gulped the rest. Then she opened another bottle and drank more. She dislodged every package in the freezer looking for Roger's veal stock. She found it and celebrated with another glass of wine.

When Frank opened the door to greet Harley and his friend, Donna tottered behind him. Harley chimed, "Frank and Donna, I want you to meet one of the sweetest people I've ever known, Frederico Busoni - truly one of the great Northern Italian Chefs of our time." Donna erupted in a flood of tears. Frank grabbed Donna by the shoulders and turned her toward the kitchen. He told Harley and Frederico she been a little tense but everything would be fine.

"Wha de fuuk," Donna whispered to Frank in the kitchen. "Atalian. Shlit. I'm cookin duck ousing a French recipe an a fffuukin French as French cu ' be French veal sauce. You bassddurd, you di n't tell me hewuss atalian." Donna gesticulated wildly as she reached for the roasting pan, tossed it in the oven and slammed the door.

"I didn't know, Donna. Relax. He'll love it. Already smells great," Frank offered.

Then Harley announced from the living room that he'd brought two bottles of wine, but not the Chardonnay that Donna had suggested. "I thought in honor of Frederico we could drink an Italian wine with dinner."

"Great," Donna howled. Tears flooded again and she stomped on the floor. "Oh," she moaned, "now ef there's jussom shot left in the duck soee breaks a toof. We can haf a complete disaster sted a jusa mini fuuken horrah show." She kicked the cabinet baseboard and threw her hand towel at Frank. He tossed the salad, blind.

217

Frank brought in the platter of duck breasts, on a bed of lettuce, surrounded by cranberries and sauteed carrots. Donna staggered in with a bowl of green beans and almond slices and a gravy bowl with a rich, dark sauce. Frank served. They toasted the winter and the cook and began eating.

After a couple of bites, Harley said, "My god, Donna. I can't believe this. Have you spent the winter at culinary school?"

Donna paid no attention to Harley. She focused on Frederico who took small bites of the duck and then swirled the wine in his glass and sipped. He analyzed each morsel until his plate was bare, then Frederico asked if he might have more duck with the sauce. Frank obliged and Frederico ate. Then he said, "This duck is superb. You must have studied a long time to make this sauce."

Frank laughed and told Frederico and Harley that Roger's veal stock had been added. Donna reached over the table and punched Frank in the arm. Frederico smiled.

"You're an artist. You should have a restaurant," Frederico said.

Donna grinned and said, "I'm a painter."

Harley nudged Frederico and pointed to the walls. Frederico grabbed Donna's hand and kissed it. "My," he said to Harley, "what a magnificent talent she is. The paintings, the duck. Lovely." Frederico continued to kiss Donna's hand.

"Frank," Donna said, "wanna pay atteshion here."

Harley laughed and so did Frederico. Frank cleared the table.

They'd decided on Roger's for dessert but had coffee and relaxed before their walk downtown. Donna had sobered a little and got up to take care of something in the kitchen. Frederico followed her saying that he would like her to show him just how she'd prepared the duck. He turned back to Harley and said, "You know that Chardonnay would have been the perfect wine for that duck. Harley, you should know better."

Harley smiled at Frederico then affecting a sneer he mouthed, "Bitch," at Donna.

Donna laughed and flipped Harley the finger. Harley and Frank laughed.

"Harley," Frank said after Donna and Frederico were gone, "I spoke to Jack just before you called and he said we'd start repairs about the first of March. I'm kind of looking forward to getting back."

"Ahhh. Interesting. I heard from Jack this afternoon, too. He asked me to find another job for the summer."

"That sucks, Harl."

"Not really. You know, Frank, things went on in the hotel last summer that troubled me."

"Like what?"

"Some of the guests weren't quite right, Frank. Something told me they weren't who they said they were. You know, the way they dressed, or talked or something. Just didn't fit."

"Christ, Harley, you sound like Donna - sizing up people by the way they dress."

"Could be something to it, Frank."

"I suppose. So, what do you think was going on? Who were they?"

"My guess, Frank, is narcs - watching to see what's going on. They smell something and they're looking for it at Rackliffe House. Watch yourself."

"Whatever you say, Harley."

"There's something else, Frank. At the end of the season, Jack had one of the kitchen staff clean out the walk in. Everybody knows when you clean out a refrigerator and don't use it for a while, you turn off the power and leave the door open. Jack left the power on, put something in there and locked it."

"What?"

"I don't know, but they said that guy they found had been dead for a couple of months. Fits the timing, Frank."

"Harley, holy shit. Do you think Jack's dealing drugs and killed that guy Ryan?"

"Maybe Patrick. I don't know, Frank."

"I really don't believe Patrick had anything to do with it."

"Probably not."

"Come on. We should get going. Forget it. Donna said that Ryan was a real sleazy character. He was probably trying to rip off the hotel and got lost in the basement. It's happened before, Harley."

Frederico and Donna came in from the kitchen. "Ready, boys," Donna said. "Let's go for desert. It's almost ten. Roger'll be closing soon."

Ed Touchette

The cold air sobered Donna even more and she decided that Frederico should have a tour as they proceeded to C'est Bon. They walked down Friend Street to Prospect and then up toward the church. Donna walked arm and arm with Frederico and told him about the statue between the spires. Frank and Harley discussed Jack and the hotel. Donna pointed to some houses and told Frederico that Edward Hopper had painted here and that these houses were in his paintings. "He's famous, now," Donna said. Then she pointed to a small cottage with rounded windows and shutters. "That was one. Marty Welch's house."

"What an interesting place," Frederico said.

Harley whispered to Frank as they turned down Dale Avenue, "Let them get a little further ahead, Frank, I want to talk to you and I don't want Donna to hear. Tell me, Frank, is she painting?"

"Tons, Harley. Better than anything she's ever done before. She actually did a nude of me in bed."

"Can I see it?" Harley asked.

"Never," Frank said.

"Why?" Harley asked.

"Ask her," Frank said.

"OK. We'd better catch up."

Harley shuffled quickly to catch up with Donna and Frederico. Then: "Donna, darling. Say, Frank tells me your work is better than ever but I'm not allowed to see it."

"You can see it, Harley," Donna said. She looked back over Frederico's shoulder at Frank and Harley. With an exaggerated grin she quipped, "Just don't ask to see the nude of Frank," then turned back.

Harley insisted, "Come on, darling. Why not? I'm an art lover. No lewd thoughts."

"Harley," Donna said. "We've been through this too many times. He's mine. I found him and I get to keep him. I love him. He loves me. We do not share. I won't even show it to my dealer."

"What?" Harley screamed.

"See, I told you," Frank said.

"No. I mean - you have a dealer? Why didn't you tell me? Frank, you dick head, why didn't you tell me?"

"I didn't know," Frank said.

"Since when," Frank and Harley asked in unison.

"Since yesterday," Donna said. "I sent slides to the Choate Gallery and they called to say they wanted to represent me. I said sure."

Donna dropped back to walk with Frank and Harley walked with Frederico. "I was going to tell you tonight, Frank. It was a surprise, but it got all messed up."

"It's OK," Frank said. "This is exciting. We'll celebrate at Roger's with champagne."

"Frank, I'm still in shock. I never thought it would happen. Then I thought - Sure. Why not? It just keeps getting better and better." Donna reached back and pinched Frank's ass and then buried her head in his coat sleeve.

Roger's was empty when they arrived and when Roger heard the news, he locked the door, put on a Boyer tape and popped the cork on a bottle of Dom Perignon. The party got off to a raucous start. Harley and Frederico danced and Roger pushed tables into the kitchen for more room. Then Roger danced with Donna and Frank cut in on Frederico. Harley cut in on Donna so Donna cut in on Frank. Frank sat in a chair and sipped champagne. When the song ended, Donna came over and sat on his lap.

"Frank," Donna said. "thank God you stayed for the winter."

"I'm glad, too," Frank said.

The music started again and Roger came over and grabbed Donna. Frederico tasted from a table of desserts Roger had put out and Harley moved his chair over to talk to Frank.

"Frank," Harley said, "I hope this gallery works out for her but we need to be careful. Success can ruin an artist. She's a great painter, Frank. I wish her all the best, but when an artist gets too comfortable, Frank, the work turns to shit."

"Harley, she works her ass off. She deserves it."

"Be careful, Frank. Don't let her lose that passion or you'll lose Donna. Watch out for dos Passos."

Frank told Harley he had no idea what he was talking about.

Harley and Frederico took a cab to East Gloucester from Roger's. Frank and Donna walked back along Middle Street and then turned down to Main to take the steps at Herrick. Donna teased Frank about the nude painting and threatened to show it to Harley and Frederico if he made her mad. Frank laughed. Then Donna asked him to tell her a story as they walked and Frank did.

"Wow," she said when Frank finished, "that great god of the north is a prick."

"Yeah," Frank agreed.

"What do you think it means, Frank?"

"I don't know, Donna."

"What did Lucas do, Frank?"

"He made a new sculpture."

"Why?"

"All Lucas said was, 'ya gotta eat.'"

They'd reached the steps at Herrick and climbed to Friend Street.

Donna came into the apartment late the next afternoon in a flurry. She threw her coat and screamed, "Frank, where are you?"

"I'm making dinner. Thought I'd surprise you."

"Forget that, Frank, did you see the paper? Patrick, Frank, he's dead."

Frank walked in and snatched the paper from Donna's hands. He looked at the photos at the top of the front page: an ambulance parked on the road to the paint factory alongside a police cruiser; the harbor master's boat down below along the water's edge, a Coast Guard boat stood beyond it further offshore. Below was a photograph of Patrick and a short paragraph. " . . . no immediate family," it said. Frank read the headline above the other photo: "Indian Dies of Overdose."

Frank sat in a chair and read more. Donna watched the expressions on his face. Bewildered, Frank looked up. "It says he killed himself with pills and booze. I don't believe it, Donna. He told me he never touched anything."

Donna didn't respond. She walked over and looked out the window. She ran her hands up and down the curtains, apparently smoothing a few wrinkles. Then she wheeled, looked sternly at Frank. "Don't say a word. Don't argue with me. Don't do a fucking thing except what I tell you to do right now. Pick up the phone, call Jack and tell him you've got another job."

Frank started to talk but Donna cut him off. "I mean it, Frank. Do it. Do it right now or I'll friggin' beat you silly."

Frank laughed.

"I'm not joking, Frank. What do you think? You think his death was accidental? You think Patrick was runnin' buckolinos and fell in? I mean it, Frank, quit. Now." Donna punctuated her demand - throwing a book to the floor and kicking the side of the sofa.

Frank said, "Patrick swam in the harbor all the time, Donna."

"Stoned?" Donna asked.

Frank said he would think about it as he gazed out the window to stare at the harbor -

Lucas, what the fuck do I do now?

Sometimes, Frank, if you do nothing it works out the same. If you don't know what to do, do nothing.

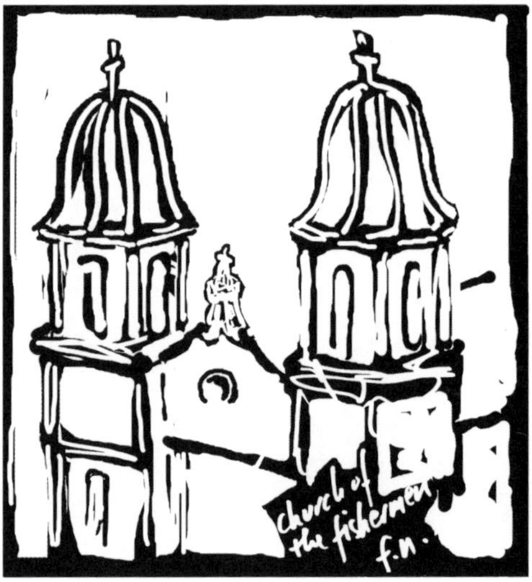
church of
the fishermen
f.n.

Chapter 19

Harry loved Dorian.
I loved Harry.
A strong geometry.

The Love Triangle
Bobby Crosby
1972 The Aviary Papers Publishers

Frank caulked the tiles in the bathroom in seventeen. The insurance money had allowed Jack to redo the entire second floor and Frank had already finished four of the nine rooms by the end of March. He took a break and when he looked out the window, he saw Jack drive into the parking lot. He walked downstairs determined to convince Jack to install lightning rods on the cupola and at the gazebo.

A plumber was testing a shut off valve in the office and Frank asked him if he'd seen Jack walk into the lobby. The plumber hadn't. Frank walked out the door and breathed deeply of the salt air to clear his head of solvents. As he crossed to the cottage, a black limousine lurked in the parking lot; the uniformed driver leaned against the fender smoking a cigarette, gazing absently at the harbor. Puzzled, Frank mulled as he bounded up the steps and rapped on the locked door. Jack opened it and invited him in, whispering, "Keep your mouth shut about last summer."

Frank's face slackened as he recognized one of the infamous Walters sisters. He couldn't see them but he knew that under the table were legs, legs and more legs. The lush blonde waves that Frank remembered were bundled on the back of her head but slight curling strands - a taste saucy - dropped in front of gold scallop shell earrings. These offset a creamy white flawless complexion surrounding perfectly lined red lips and icy blue eyes magnified by blue shadow. High cheek bones and a perfectly straight finely chiseled nose completed the exquisitely symmetrical visage blossoming from the neck high ruffles of a white silk blouse. Strands of gold and Mikkimoto pearls and one thin gold chain, hugging her neckline, caressing a two carat solitaire diamond sang in contrast to the navy blue of the wool blazer draping her shoulders. This portrait of elegance fidgeted, not nervously, more intentionally, with what had to be a six carat marquise diamond that sat in front of a diamond laced wedding band on her left ring finger.

Beside her sat a man in a grey pin stripe three piece suit, sipping coffee and caressing a long cigar with one hand as he, seeming impatient at the interruption, patted the table with the fingers of his other. The clunk of a heavy gold ring pierced the room. A mane of thick jet black hair - obviously colored as was his pencil moustache - sharply outlined his deeply tanned face. Jack introduced Frank: "Senator Maynard Carson and his wife, Stephanie." Frank nodded when Jack added, "And of course you know Owen Chase." The fisherman stood behind the table next to a window. Frank noted the hole in Owen's left earlobe and the shirt sleeves buttoned at his wrists. Frank kept his face blank as he reached out a hand to the Senator, nodded to Mrs. Carson, and said, "Pleased to meet you." He turned to Owen and said, "Hello."

Jack offered Frank a cup of coffee. Frank declined. "Jack, seventeen's done and I'm starting on fourteen tomorrow. I'm taking the afternoon off. I told Jerry I'd help him out tonight. OK?"

"Sure, Frank. We're ahead of schedule," Jack replied.

Then Frank pursued the installation of lightning rods. He told Jack the gazebo was just asking for it and the cupola needed one, too. Owen Chase asked about the cost and Frank said, "Probably minimal if I can get them and install 'em myself, Owen."

"I don't know, Frank," Jack said. "They had one up there on the cupola years ago and the place still got hammered."

"Yeah, Jack, because they stuck that metal ball on it."

"How do you know that?" Senator Carson's voice rumbled as he pushed his chair back from the table and stood. Towering over the room, he turned his head to one side, puffed on his cigar and inhaled deeply. Then he exhaled through pursed lips, releasing the smoke in short sharp bursts until he turned his head and snapped off a smoke ring that sailed across the room toward Jack. With blatant disgust, Jack waved it away when it got there. The Senator, completing his caricature, lifted a gold watch from his vest pocket, glanced at the time and replaced it. Then he fixed a glare on Frank.

"Books," Frank answered, remarking internally the Senator's height and girth. "Geezuz he's friggin' huge."

More suppliant, the Senator remarked, "Frank, Jack talks about you all of the time. He says you're the best guy we've had in years. Let me tell you, Frank, I know that hotel - every inch, from the bottom up. Gotta have people like you. I want you to know how much I appreciate your efforts. Don't worry. Owen, here, will find plenty for you to do this year. We'll talk about the lightning rods and let you know." The Senator showed Frank his back.

"Is Owen managing the hotel this summer?" Frank asked Jack.

"No. I'm still managing the hotel. Owen's a new partner. He's got some ideas about maintenance and construction. We'll talk about it."

Frank looked puzzled as he turned to head out of the cottage. He looked back at the Senator and the goddess and said, "Nice to meet you both." He nodded to Owen.

Jack interrupted Frank's reading at the apartment that afternoon. As soon as he opened the door, Frank heard: "OK. Frank, now you know who she really is. Just listen and you'll know why you gotta keep your mouth shut about this," before Jack had even removed his coat.

"Go ahead," Frank said. "This ought to be good, Jack. I've listened to a lot of your shit but this has got to be classic."

Jack's grin flowed to a scowl as he recounted the trauma of discovering his high school lover had married his father. He'd snap his head to reposition the locks of blonde hair that fell to his forehead as his arms flailed in rage. "Do you believe this shit, Frank. She marries the old man and has his kid and then when I get home for Thanksgiving, there she is. I didn't know who she'd married. She never said. Just said the guy was rich. When she told me she was pregnant, I let it go. Friggin' nightmare, Frank. Walked in the door and there she was. The old man introduced me to my new stepmother. I almost choked. "Well, Jack," the old fuck said, "Stephanie told me you weren't interested anymore and I told her I was. That's that, Jackie. I've always told you, take what you want because if you don't, somebody else will. No hard feelings, Jack," he told me." Jack paused and looked away.

"The next day, while he's at a meeting, she corners me in my room and before you know it we're screwin'. She's screamin' she still loves me and can't live like this. Man, I'm freakin'. I could never tell you before,

Frank. I could never tell anybody. It's fucking embarrassing." Jack peeked at Frank through his fingers as he rubbed his face with both hands. Frank had turned and was staring out the window.

"She's still in love with me, Frank. I know it. And I'm still in love with her. She comes up to the hotel a few times each summer and we spend time together. During the winter, I stay at the house when the old fuck's gone on business. She wants to marry me when he dies. She'd leave him now but she's afraid to lose the kid. If he ever finds out about us, he'll divorce her, disown me and with his power he'd have no trouble keeping the kid. I told her that. We decided to wait 'til the old bastard croaks and then get together for good. It's not a bad idea you know. Save a lot in legal fees. No battle over the estate then. Anyway, Frank, do me a favor. Keep this quiet. I know I'm a piece of shit when it comes to women but now you know why."

Frank walked into the kitchen, talking to Jack as he opened a cabinet door and grabbed a bottle of bourbon. He offered Jack a drink. "What a friggin' mess. Here, I think you need this." Then Frank said, "Ya know, Jack, as long as we're getting things straight, here, what about that bonus. The two grand. What's the truth about that?"

"Oh, man, Frank. Gimme a break. I'm sorry about that. Look, Stephanie brought me the cash and I was doin' her a favor. She needed some extra money so I offered to get her in on a drug deal. Yeah, I know, we're scumbags for buying drugs but she had to."

Frank winced. "So you are dealing. Why?"

"No," Jack said. "not dealing, really - just helping finance. She could get ten back for two. Y'know, we . . . she thought she could get out of this mess. Maybe get me enough to buy the hotel and fix it up. That's it. Believe me Frank, we're just bankers. We're not dealing. Not at all."

"So why'd you give me the money, Jack?"

"There were a couple of guys outside in the parking lot. I thought they were going to rob me so I dumped the money figuring if I ran into them, they wouldn't find it and they'd leave me alone. I should have just told you the truth and said hide it for me and give it back later but I figured what the fuck, the old man's got a ton of it so I'd just give you a bonus and get Stephanie to bring more. She doesn't care and neither do I so you made a score and we're all happy."

"That's not what Donna told me, Jack."

"Oh, fuck Donna. I was bustin' her ass. She's too smug, Frank. Won't let go of that ol . . ."

"Jack, enough. You let it go."

"I have, Frank. She's the one still holdin' a grudge."

"Let it go, Jack. You can screw Stephanie and anybody else. Deal drugs. Don't deal drugs. Finance the smugglers or not. Don't fuck with Donna and don't get me involved. Man, Jack, you are in a hell of a mess."

"Yeah, well it happens, Frank. That's why I'm glad I've got you on my side." Jack posed a sardonic grin.

Frank scowled and Willy Hall flashed by. "Hey, Jack, get this straight. I'm not on your side. I'm really not sure I want to work for you anymore."

"Come on, Frank. There's nothing to worry about. When they found Patrick dead from an overdose, the narcs figured he was sampling his own stuff. Y'know, back on the shit again. I told them he'd been having a rough time and probably just slipped. It happens."

"Bullshit, Jack. Patrick was clean."

"Yeah, whatever, Frank. And, look, just in case you get nervous, and want to put an end to our immoral shenanigans, think about this. All we do is finance. I don't deal the stuff. I don't even store it in the hotel - anymore. You've got nothing to worry about. One year. It'll all be over. Maybe we'll just take the money and run and you won't have a care in the world. Nobody to connect you to the Indians."

"What? Jack, you've thrown that up at me a few times. You got somethin' to say, say it."

"No big deal, Frank. Guess I'd forgotten. But, hey, since you brought it up. See, the old man keeps in touch with some old friends around Washington. Sometimes when I hire people at the hotel, he likes to do a little background check. Keep his contacts active. You know. How do you think we found out about Harley?"

"What about Harley, Jack?"

"Oh, he probably told you the story about drinking too much and driving into the headmaster's garage and shit. He did, but he got canned because he was dating half the freshman class."

"Fuck you, Jack. Harley's a decent guy."

"Frank, I'm just telling you what my father heard. Of course it ruins a lot of peoples lives now doesn't it, just telling what you heard."

"So what's that got to do with Indians, Jack?"

229

"A couple of Indians. Deserted the Army. Got a ride into Canada. Know anything?"

"They weren't deserters, Jack. They were seventeen. Dodging the draft. Nobody knew."

"Oh," Jack said, "How'd I find out?"

"So what, Jack. That friggin' war is over. Nobody gives a shit now."

"Glad you told me that, Frank. I'll tell the old man. He'll feel better. See, what he heard was that some Indian rights sympathizer gave a couple of deserters a lift into Canada. Desertion, Frank, a lot more serious. They were deserters and one was involved in a holdup. An armored car. Oh, you didn't know. Too bad. Could get a little sticky for you. I guess."

"So, what's your point, Jack? You got nothin'."

"Well, see, Frank, then, ahhh, I remembered something. Right around the night those Indians left for Canada. Yeah, I remember it. Clear picture even though it was five . . . no six years ago. That night, you were out all night. Remember? Sure you do. You borrowed my car and said you were taking Allie to dinner. I never saw you until the next afternoon. Of course you could have been with Allie at the sorority, but that was only two miles from the apartment. I kept trying to think of how I put almost four hundred miles on the odometer. Then I thought, mmmmm, Crandall to Niagara and back. Then I remembered something else. Allie called. Screamed at me about letting you take the car. Gee, Frank, you know that girl was hot for you. I had to go over to console her. Strange things happen, don't they?"

Frank stood speechless, staring out the window. As Jack got up to leave he heard: "Thanks, Frank. I knew if anybody understood, you would. You're a good friend. You'll keep this quiet. So humiliating. Can you imagine? My father screwing my high school girlfriend, getting her pregnant and marrying her. What a friggin' nightmare. God, that's bad enough. Then I find out my college buddy's a criminal. No wonder I'm so fucked up. I can't trust anybody. See ya, Frank."

"Hey, Jack," Frank shouted. "Before you go. Why's Owen Chase getting into this?"

"Simple, Frank. He's got big ideas about developing property. He scored big on a couple of late sword trips after he quit Tommy Lozano last fall. He's got cash. The old man won't dump anymore into it. Wants to sell. I want that hotel. Restore it. Owen's buying in and I can buy a load of junk and make some money. Maybe get the hotel back to where it should be. So, Frank, just keep your mouth shut and everything'll be cool."

"Yeah, Jack, real friggin' cool." Frank clenched his jaw and caught himself from slamming the door.

A late morning rain had subsided but its grey brackish residue drifted through the streets as Frank walked to Jerry's. The fog horn brayed. As night fell, the haze, pale yellow in the lights from the ghosts of buildings looming along the harbor, grew more dense, seemingly impenetrable. At eight o'clock, Captain Jerry's was empty except for Frank watching the street from the front window, hoping to see Donna walk up. When a black sedan stopped across the street, Frank watched as a woman with a black scarf over her head stepped up to the side walk. The car pulled away and she walked through the mist toward the bar. Frank laughed when he noticed her sunglasses. "Stoned," he thought.

Frank busied himself behind the bar hoping maybe the only customer he'd seen since seven wouldn't turn around and leave. She sauntered through the door and the heels of her black leather boots clicked on the floor as she walked to the bar. Her black leather jacket and matching pants creaked softly as she sat. When she took off the sunglasses and the scarf, soughing, "Bartender, Johnny Walker Black, neat, please," Frank recognized Stephanie.

She purred, "Hello, Frank," as she wriggled from her jacket. Reaching to remove a comb, she tossed her head wantonly and lush blonde hair fell to her shoulders. Blouseless, she tugged at the lapels of a black leather vest, exposing more of her chest, but Frank's eyes fixed on the stone studded leather dog collar that wrapped her graceful neck. She joked about the weather and the dearth of customers. When Frank placed a tumbler in front of her, she reached suddenly and caught Frank's hand. Frank looked down and said, "Yeah, fog's murder on business," realizing the gargantuan rings no longer adorned her left hand. Then Stephanie released her grip.

Stephanie's voice changed from soft to throaty as she told Frank what a great job Jack had done with the hotel and how much help Frank had been. Then she whispered her concern over Frank's discovery that morning and explained how the situation with Jack's father had developed. She sobbed as she recognized how she'd hurt Jack and pleaded with Frank to forego judgement because Jack respected him and needed his support. Frank clenched his jaw so tight his back teeth hurt.

"Look, Frank." Stephanie glued her eyes firmly to Frank's. "I know it sounds awful but I was devastated when Jack left for college; I screwed him like a bunny the week before he left to get pregnant and make him marry me but when he found out I was pregnant, he wouldn't speak to me. So I told the Senator the baby was his and we got married. I never told Jack." Stephanie looked into the tumbler and sighed dramatically. Then she looked at Frank with watery eyes and whispered, "I still loved Jack and I couldn't tell him I'd married his father. Then Jack came home for Thanksgiving and . . ." She looked toward the windows.

Frank coughed. "Jack doesn't know about the kid?"

"No."

"The Senator?"

"Of course not, Frank."

Frank thought for a second. "How do you know, it's Jack's?"

"Blood test, Frank."

Frank had run out of sympathy. "Get a divorce and marry Jack."

"Frank, the Senator will disown Jack and divorce me. He's powerful, Frank, and I'd lose Charlie. He's vindictive, Frank. Believe me, I know. He'd do it to hurt us. Please, Frank, don't tell anyone about this. We'll be destroyed. And please don't tell Jack I came here. He wouldn't like it. He doesn't know about the kid, Frank. He'd go completely crazy if he did."

Frank shook his head and asked Stephanie if she would like another drink and she said, "Sure, Frank, one for the road." Frank turned to grab the bottle of Scotch from the shelf and watched in the mirror as Stephanie undid another button on her vest. She took a small perfume bottle from her purse and dabbed a few drops on her cleavage and then placed some behind her ears. She opened a small vial. When Frank put the tumbler on the bar, she popped a few pills in her mouth and washed them down with the Scotch. "This weather depresses me. I know I shouldn't mix downers and alcohol but . . . Anyway, what time do you get off tonight, Frank?"

"Oh, it's a while . . . " Frank sneezed violently and excused himself.

"Bless you," Stephanie said.

"I've got to stay open even if it's . . . " Frank sneezed again.

"Bless you, Frank. Need a ride home?"

"No. I like the walk. It helps me wind down," Frank talked as he pinched his nostrils.

In a Place Like No Other

Stephanie laughed at the nasal quality of his voice as she piped, "From what? The friggin' dump is dead. Come on, Frank. Let me give you a ride. We can talk more. I'd like that."

"I'll bet. I'll pass. You've got enough going on as it is."

Stephanie gulped the Scotch, stood and dropped a fifty dollar bill on the bar. "Thanks, Frank. I know you understand. Remember, we're here to help. If you need something, let Jack know. A little bonus now and then is good for morale." She squeezed into her jacket and tugged at the sleeves. Then buttoning it slowly, cooed, "Don't you just love leather, Frank. I do. So soft, even when it's skin tight." Stephanie rubbed her hands along the curves of her hips and brought them to the front as if to smooth the leather along the insides of her thighs. "Ouuuu," she whispered, "So soft."

"I guess." Frank watched her saunter to the door and out into the street. The front window of the waiting sedan lowered and she leaned over to speak to someone inside. Frank watched from the front window as she shifted her weight from one leg to the other, the ambient light reflecting from the tight leather pants almost had Frank sympathizing with Jack. When she opened the rear door and slid into the back seat, she looked his way and blew him a kiss. Frank sneezed as the essence of Channel No. 5 tickled his nostrils again. "Allie."

Frank closed the bar early and walked home along Main Street turning up the hill to see if Roger was still open. C'est Bon was dark but a north wind had cleared the air so Frank kept on up the hill to Middle Street to enjoy some of his favorite buildings. He looked up as he passed City Hall; the clock had stopped. At Pleasant he turned up toward Prospect and admired the steeple of St. Ann's. On Prospect Street, he turned toward Portugei Hill and looked for the spires of Our Lady of Good Voyage as he walked over the crest of a hill. Lights outlined the statue sitting between the domes. He remarked the details: The Blessed Mother holding the fishing dragger, her hands protecting it from the tempest, her flowing robes. He looked up at the blue domes and wondered, "Lightning rods or faith."

Frank walked up Taylor Street and turned into Staten Street. He couldn't get Patrick off his mind. Two and three family tenements lined the narrow street - packed tightly, wall to wall. Except maybe for the uppermost floors, there could be no sight line to the harbor. Pipe railings lined steps to simple porches where mailboxes sat one on top of another, flanking the front doors. Wood posts supported flat roofs - no pendants dangled from ornate brackets, no cornices or pediments. Gabled roofs. Simple. Utilitarian. Mechanic. Wire fences enclosed the small sidewalk gardens. A tricycle dangled from the edge of a deck. A cardboard box with ragged holes for windows and doors sat limply in a small fenced yard. Below the word Frigidaire, Frank read the hand painted sign: "Devils Club House." The back seat from a car sat next to the box.

At the far end of the street, a three family house burrowed into the granite of Portugei Hill. Two small wire fenced gardens in front of the building held the remains of last summer's flowers. A bathtub Virgin humbly guarded the brown lifeless stalks to the left of the concrete walkway and St. Francis, uncovered, hands cupping a small cast songbird, loomed starkly in the pale incandescence of a street light - in the mud. "Faith," Frank thought as a grey cat bounded across the street in front of him and up the steps to the porch.

The whining of an electric motor knifed through the silence. Frank looked up. He watched as the spokes of an antenna, belted to the chimney of the three story apartment building, sparkled in reflected light as they rotated. Through a window, below the chimney, Frank could see the fluorescence of a poster. The only word he could read was "Maxx."

Donna massaged Frank's neck as he sat on the side of the bed. She asked him to tell her what went on with Jack that afternoon. Frank said he'd tell her everything but she had to keep it between them. Donna promised and Frank told her about his day. When she asked about the two Mohicans, Frank told her it was true but that they were kids and he'd not known about any robbery. "Man, to have Jack's hooks into me is not exactly my idea of fun." Donna agreed and said maybe Lou could help, but Frank didn't like the idea of Lou knowing.

As he switched the table lamp off and crawled under the covers, Frank said, "The one thing I don't get is Patrick. They must have gotten him stoned but you can't force someone to do that, Donna. And Patrick was huge. Who could overpower him?"

"She could, Frank."

"Who?"

"Stephanie, Frank. Men do crazy things . . . when it comes to women."

Chapter 20

Spring has sprung
The grass is green
Gloucester: the most beautiful
I've ever seen.

A Beautiful Find
Les Moor
1968 Aviary Papers Publishers

Spring brought the sunshine Frank'd longed for. He and Donna would sit on the living room couch and watch the sunrise as they drank coffee, then Frank would walk to the hotel. The activity in the boat yards heightened and the lilacs and forsythia bloomed full. Frank sucked in their fragrance, wallowing in the clear clean air as he meandered along East Main Street toward Rocky Neck and Rackliffe House. He left early some mornings and walked up the steps to the Aviary to enjoy the view. Euripedes barked a joyous greeting whenever he saw Frank.

Emma worked in the gardens early in the morning. She weeded around the tulips and daffodils or perfected the shapes of her rose bushes. The yards held spring soft mud so she wore the yellow boots that slapped against her shins. Her calico apron had dirt smudges and her sun hat would be wet around the sweat band. If she saw Frank sitting on the ledge, she'd come over and sit with him for a while.

This morning she brought coffee. She handed Frank a cup and complained to him that Euripedes had jumped up and stolen hot muffins from the counter so she couldn't bring breakfast. Frank laughed, looked over at Euripedes and said, "Was it good, fella?" Euripedes barked.

Emma asked about Donna and they talked awhile about the winter and how glad they were to see spring had finally arrived. Frank bemoaned his job at Rackliffe House but said he didn't have a lot of other choices. Emma clucked her tongue in empathy. Then Frank talked about the remodeling he'd done at the hotel and how he hoped it was a good summer for making tips. Emma asked about the Carson boy but Frank, staring into the harbor, didn't answer.

"Ahh," Emma said, "the curse is catchin' up. I can tell by the look on your face. Finally finding out how weird some people can be. Must be hard when he's been a friend for so long."

Frank nodded. Then he snapped a look at Emma. "What do you mean . . . the curse?"

Emma placed a hand on Frank's arm. "Come on, Frank. Give me a little credit. I been around this place longahr than most of these trees. I've heahrd all the stories, Frank. You can't fool me all that often. Besides everybody around suspects something's up at that hotel. We ain't stupid, Frank. We've known the Senator a lot of yeahrs. He's from heahr, ya know."

Frank said he thought the Senator lived in Topsfield and Emma chortled, "Senator Carson, Frank, is a good ol' Glosta boy. Grew up right ovah theah 'n Ledge Road." Emma turned and pointed. Frank looked. She told Frank his family had been in Gloucester since the city was incorporated in 1623. "Got cousins right over on Portugei Hill. Staten Street I think, Frank." Then Emma clucked her tongue again and said, "Shame that Cahrson boy got the disease."

"What disease, Emma?"

"Some people call it a blight, Frank. You know the bad seed."

Frank had no idea what she was talking about. Emma paused, then said that according to Henry, Maynard Carson had been a "crazed sexin' fool" all his life and, "cordin' t Henry, too, liked the men t' boot. We knew yeahrs ago, this would all come to no good end. So be cahreful, Frank."

Again Frank said, "What are you talking about, Emma?"

"Well, Frank as I heard it from Henry and believe me if Henry said it, it was the truth, Maynard Cahrson always had a bad reputation. They say his first wife jumped off the roof of theahr house in Washington, D.C. to escape the marriage but Henry thought she had help. Henry said she was having a little fling and got caught. The Senatahr was a bad character. Jack was just a baby. That's when they moved back heahr. They lived ovah on The Neck for a while. That's when he had another son by one of the chambahrmaids, a young Indian girl. Moved to . . ."

"Patrick?" Frank yelped.

"That's what I heard, Frank," Emma said.

"What a scandal that must've been! Is that why he left politics, Emma?"

"Politics! Oh, boy, Frank, you been bamboozled. Understandable though, you not bein' from heahr. He's no real senatahr, Frank. He was a hotel clerk in Washington. "Senatahr" was a nickname. Stuck to him like dew. His pals ribbed him when he came home to visit - called him Senatahr Carson. Used to say, "Hey Senatahr, how goes the battle in Washington?" Like Colonel Vicahrs over in the West Pahrish. They call him Colonel 'cause he likes fried chicken. Nevahr was in the Ahrmy or nothin'. Christ his feet's flat as a floundahr. Gosh, Frank, these things go on so long everybody stahrts believin' 'em, though. Like Henry always said, people love theahr stories."

"Like that place." Frank nodded toward the Aviary.

"Ayuh."

Frank couldn't shake the befuddlement from his head. Then he said, "Well, he sure has some friends in Washington, because he found out things about me no one else knows about."

Emma chuckled, "Frank, he was a hotel clerk. Could be that. Lotsa people come and go in a hotel - some of 'em too impohrtant to want anybody to know they came."

"So to speak, Emma."

"Ayeah."

Donna was curled up in a chair reading *Glamour* when Frank got home from the hotel that afternoon. Frank kissed her hello and started to tell her about his conversation with Emma. Donna stood and Frank gasped. Donna spun around several times and dipped her knees to model a bright pink and green flowered dress. She sashayed to the table, spun again and said, "A whole new look, Frank. Whatcha think?"

Frank, mouth agape, rubbed the back of his neck. Then: "Ahhh . . . geez, Donna, it's brighter than most of your paintings. I, ahhh, wellll . . ." Frank scratched his head.

"A Lilly Pulitzer original," Donna said as she bounded to the bedroom, "Wait'll you see what else I got." When she came out she tripped, stumbled, and almost twisted an ankle in a pair of platform shoes that Frank estimated had four inch heels. "The new look!" Donna said as she steadied herself with the door knob. "Well?"

Frank gaped, then walked over and glared at the shoes. He sniffed hard and asked what the smell was and Donna piped, "*Charlie*, Frank.

New. Really hot."

Frank leered a while longer then walked back to the other side of the room and eyed her more from head to toe. He stroked his chin as he sat in a chair and crossed his legs. Pensive, then: "You know something, it's you. No wonder I'm so nuts about you."

"I'm so glad you like it, Frank. I really wanted you to like it. It's important. A whole new look for the new me. The gallery called and I'm having a solo show. Can you believe it?"

Frank smiled and watched as Donna stumbled again trying to go back into the bedroom. He was getting up for coffee when he heard Donna's voice. "Frank, one more thing. Come here and tell me what you think of this."

Frank peeked slowly through the half opened door. Donna stood in front of the bed, naked but for a Boston Red Sox baseball cap, cocked playfully on her head. "I forgot, Frank, this is an important part of my new look. Do you think it goes with the dress and the shoes?"

Frank thought, rubbed the back of his neck and said, "I don't know, I can't tell until you wear them all together. Go ahead, put them on, I'll wait."

Donna put on the dress and fastened the straps of her platform shoes. She tried to spin, stumbled and fell. Frank caught her and pushed her back to a standing position. "Thanks," Donna muttered as she straightened the dress. "These'll take a little getting used to."

Frank pointed to the walking stick and said he'd get it if Donna thought it would help and Donna wobbled as she jabbed at him. Then Frank looked her over from top to bottom and said, "Nah, I liked it better without the dress and the shoes."

"Stick it, Frank."

In the kitchen, Frank smirked as he turned up the volume on the radio and rapped the side of a pot with a wooden spoon as he sang along "oh the winter's over and the summer she's comin' on strong . . ."

"Turn it up, Frank. I love Spirit," Donna hollered from the bedroom.

Frank turned up the volume, gazing at the harbor's violet glow in the setting spring sun.

Now what, Lucas?

Nothing, Frank.

Chapter 21

Everyday 5 p.m., cocktails on the veranda. When I thought of moving to Los Angeles, I realized this pleasurable event would be delayed three hours so I decided to stay on the East Coast.

Dead Beat
The Life and Times of Les Moor
Bobby Crosby
1973 The Aviary Papers

Frank's second summer at Rackliffe House started off with a bang - literally. The first night they'd opened, Billy Slidell and the crew of his newest boat had christened the onset of sun and fun season with a massive drunk. By eleven o'clock they were swimming bare assed in the pool. At one point, Frank had noticed the drinks piling up at the waitress station and he couldn't see Kim Bristol anywhere in the room. He asked the new waitress, Lisa, where Kim was and she pointed toward the pool. Frank peered through the cloud of cigarette smoke out the windows; ataxic, a conga line of naked bodies backlit by a full moon tried to navigate the pool apron. "And we're off," Frank said as he rang the bell at the end of the bar.

The clanging startled a couple of men who snored into their tumblers and one raised his head to inquire about the time. Frank answered "Wednesday," and the drunk looked into the mirror, groaned and slumped to the bar. Lisa stood at the waitress station with tears running down her face so Frank asked what had happened. She told Frank that some guy had wanted to meet her after work and she'd said "Sure," but he'd already left. Frank said he might come back, but Lisa mumbled, "I doubt it, he was with Kim." Frank made a note to talk to Kim about leaving early.

Sullen, Missy Dahlgren still sat at the bar as the band quit for the night. Frank brought her a Cape Codder and when he asked how Annie was, she started to sob. Annie'd been expelled from school for using cocaine and her grandparents wouldn't let her to come to Gloucester for the summer. "It'll be miserable here without her." Missy wept.

"A long summer for all of us," Frank thought and clanged the bell for last call. Raucous laughter still filled the bar and the dancing didn't end until Frank walked into the back room and threw a circuit breaker that cut power to the juke box. "Everybody out," Frank demanded as the angry crowd hissed, booed and stumbled out the door.

Minor by no means, these episodes paled in comparison to what Frank witnessed when he finally locked the bar at two. He crossed the drive to the cottage and noticed an old milk delivery truck parked at the edge of the lot - like the ones he'd seen when he was a kid when milkmen made their way from house to house leaving glass bottles with paper covers on every doorstep in exchange for a few coins and some empty glass bottles. "The days when cream rose to the top," Frank thought as he eyed the van painted with flowers and peace signs and names like Embarcadero, Tiberon and Sausalito. Each marked with a check. "Sausalito," Frank mumbled to himself.

A tall gaunt man walked nervously around the truck. Bare chested, wearing candy striped, bell bottom pants, and bare footed, hair almost to his shoulder blades, and a curly black beard, the sight prompted Frank to grumble, "Ahhhh, the ever popular Jesus look from the sixties." The man trembled and he kept dropping his head to one side and tapping at his ears with the palms of his hands - like a swimmer dislodging water. Then he'd shake furiously, from head to toe - like Euripedes drying his coat. In the moonlit parking lot, Frank thought it might be a Druid ritual. "Probably been in the pool," Frank mumbled to himself. "Better tell him to stay out." Frank walked toward the reeling man and said, "Hello."

"What?" the man asked. "What? I can't hear a fucking thing, man. What'd you say?"

The man lifted his right leg off the pavement and bounced on his left. He tilted his head to that side and rapped at his ear. Then he tilted to the other side and banged at his other ear with his right palm. When he stood erect again, he looked at Frank and said, "My fucking ears are ringing, man, like livin' in fucking church bells. Musta dropped a roach in that package of cherry bombs." He pointed to the van. "Scared the shit out of me, man."

Frank walked over and slid open the door of the van. An acrid cloud engulfed him, then he noticed the sweet odor of grass. He fanned a sight line with his hand. Except for the driver's seat and a thin mattress on the floor in the back, the van was bare. The metal walls were uncovered except for the fluorescent paint that danced under the rays of a black light. A pair of tweezers rested on a large smoke scar where the cherry bombs must have exploded. Frank laughed out loud and Lucas peered over his shoulder -

Remember the day we ambushed that prick Howard Dalton, Frank?

The only two hundred pound fourth grader in Washington County. Howard was always teasing Lucas about his ancestors. I snatched Howard's lunch bag and tossed it into the fifty gallon oil drum that was a trash can in front of the elementary school. Howard dove in to get it. Lucas grabbed the 2 x 4 that was holding the fire doors open and rapped the sides of the barrel.

Howard was still quivering when he took his seat in home room. Mrs. Carswell asked him if he thought he was funny. He must not have heard her; he shook his head, Yes. Mrs. Carswell sent him to the office. I laughed. Lucas did, too. Mrs. Carswell sent us to the office.

Mr. Murphy was mad. Mr. Murphy asked Howard why he shouldn't get a taste of The Great Yardstick by which all men are measured. Howard guessed wrong again. Shook his head, No. Mr. Murphy whacked Howard across the ass four times and sent him back to home room.

Mr. Murphy asked us what we were doing in his office. We told him that Mrs. Carswell had sent us to be sure Howard got there and back. Mr. Murphy told us to go.

Frank laughed harder as he stepped back from the van and looked at the guy one more time. Then he said good night and headed for the cottage. When he crawled into bed, Donna rolled over to hug him and he told her what had gone on in the bar. "Only ninety nine more days," Frank said, "hardly seems like enough."

Bobby Crosby showed up earlier than usual. He'd waltzed into the bar on the Friday night of Fiesta weekend. Frank was glad to see him, but without the head gear, he almost hadn't recognized Bobby. When Bobby'd dropped his pants and mooned the new singer in the band, Frank said, "I wasn't sure it was you, Bobby. Now I am. Glad you could make it. Martini, three olives?"

Bobby buckled his belt and sat at the bar, "Go for it, Frank. I appreciate your remembering. Got here early this year. Expecting big things with the Bicentennial coming. Should be wild, Frank, friggin' wild."

"What was last year, Bobby?"

"Pretty much the usual, Frank. Who's hot this year, Frank? I'm divorced now. No ball and chain to tie me down."

"Oh," Frank said, "is that why you were so quiet last summer?"

Bobby laughed.

Frank was back in the groove. During the days he was working on reinforcing the posts and beams that supported the sun deck and six nights a week he tended the bar in the basement. He found it difficult to satisfy his new found penchant for architectural history but the manual labor was a benign substitute. "As long as I can do it right," he'd told Owen Chase. Owen had said, "Sure, as long as it doesn't cost me more money, Frank." Owen had nixed the installation of lightning rods.

Donna came in early the Saturday night of Fiesta. She sipped her beer, talked to Frank and wondered if this summer would be crazier than usual because of the Bicentennial. Frank told her about Bobby arriving early and Donna chortled "Probably will be!" Something occurred to her and she told Frank she was going back to the apartment to paint for a while. She'd meet him at the cottage. She liked staying in the cottage during the summer, too.

Frank told her not to forget his parents were coming tomorrow so she should get ready for anything. "Yeah," Frank said. "I told you, Donna. They're a little nutty at times. They do weird things. Just preparing you, that's all."

"Who? Your parents?"

"Yeah. Who else!"

Donna laughed as she got up to leave, greeting Tommy Lozano who'd just sat down at the bar. "See ya later," Frank said. "Luv ya," Donna said.

"You guys are still getting it on," Tommy said to Frank.

"Yeah," Frank said. "we had a great time together this winter, and things are pretty good right now, too. What can I get you, Tommy?"

"Bud," Tommy said. "You gettin' married?"

"I don't know, maybe, Tommy. It works pretty good with us. We have a lot of fun and we seem OK."

"Great," Tommy said. "What are you going to do for work?"

"Same stuff," Frank said.

"Yeah, but Frank if she gets pregnant and you have kids, you're going to have to make a lot more money. Buy a house. All that shit."

"We'll see," Frank answered. "How's fishing, Tommy?"

"Sucks, Frank. Owen's gone and the new guy I've got is one lazy son of a bitch. I'll dump him when somebody else comes along."

"Do you think somebody else will?"

"Sure, Frank, This place has a crop of 'em. Guys thinkin' fishing is some sort of romantic life or some poor slob down on his luck lookin' for a job. Sure, some sucker'll be along. Sooner rather than later, too."

Bobby Crosby walked in and settled onto a stool next to Tommy Lozano. Frank placed olives in a Martini in front of Bobby. "Thanks," Bobby said as he whisked the glass to his lips and belted down the Martini. Frank had another waiting before Bobby had finished the olives.

"How are you, Tommy?" Bobby said as he stirred the Martini with the olives.

"Not bad, Bobby. Fishing sucks but it'll turn around."

"How's Owen?"

"He quit in the spring, Bobby. He's a partner in the hotel, now. Started his development company."

"Why?" Bobby asked.

"He wants to buy up old buildings and turn them into apartments and condominiums. Figures he'll make a fortune."

Bobby stirred his Martini, then gulped it down. "You know something, Tommy, I always wanted to work on a fishing boat. I've always wanted to write poetry about fishing in Gloucester. Maybe you'll take me out some time."

"Sure," Tommy said, winking at Frank. "Let me know when you want to go."

"OK," Bobby said, "I will. Let me buy you a beer, Tommy."

"Sure."

"I didn't know you wrote poetry, Bobby," Frank said as he placed a third Martini in front of Bobby.

"Yeah, I do," Bobby said. "I asked Jack, once, if I could do a poetry reading down here instead of this godawful music and he said no."

"That would be a scene," Frank said.

"Yeah, one I'd miss," Tommy said as he laughed.

"Poetry is a magnificent art form, gentlemen. I am not ashamed to admit that I write poetry. Perhaps you've heard some of my poems. I used the name Les Moor. Now I'm Bobby Crosby."

Neither Tommy nor Frank were familiar with the poems but both said they'd like to hear one. Bobby agreed to recite one of his poems but after another Martini.

Frank placed the drink in front of him and said, "Drink up, Bobby, and let's hear one."

Tommy looked at Frank quizzically.

Bobby swallowed his fourth Martini, cleared his throat and walked over to where the band's equipment was set up. He flicked the switch on one of the amplifiers and hollered, "Test, test, test," into the microphone. "How's that?" he asked his audience.

A couple, a man in a white dinner jacket and a woman in a sleeveless pink cotton dress, strolled in and sat at a table. Frank went over and took their orders. He told them they were just in time for the poetry reading. "It's a nightly event. Only at Rackliffe House."

Bobby cleared his throat. "This is a poem I wrote for my wife," he said softly. "I dedicated it to my mother." The two customers clapped their approval. "Thank you," Bobby said as he picked up a drumstick. He closed his eyes and lifted his head as if seeking divine inspiration. He took a deep breath. Lowering his head, he opened his eyes and glanced furtively around the barroom. Then he smashed a cymbal and intoned in a dramatic, mellow voice:

"Bang, my darling. Bang.

What else is there to live for

Bang. Bang bang."

Bobby smashed the cymbal again. Frank cringed and Tommy Lozano ducked as the tympanous rattle ricocheted about the room.

"Love, my darling. Love

What else is there to die for,

Love. Love, Love.

Love your country, your fellow man.

Love your fellow . . .whoa man."

Bobby rapped the drumstick on the leg of his stool. Then he got up and grabbed another drumstick and rattled a slow tattoo on a table top.

"The sky is falling.

The sky is falling.

Oh what am I to do?"

Bobby smashed the cymbal.

"Screw . . . you, Pamela.

Love L M."

Bobby lowered his head, took a deep bow. The couple applauded wildly. Frank and Tommy looked at each other and then at Bobby.

"Encore. Encore," the couple screamed, clapping wildly.

Bobby bowed again. He lifted his hand to calm the crowd and said, "OK. Here's one I wrote for my father."

Bobby sat on the stool and blew into the microphone. "Are we rollin', Bob?" he said and then he twittered. "In joke," he said to the couple. Then:

"Daddy, daddy, daddy, daddy, daddy, daddy, daddy!

Daddy, daddy, daddy, daddy, daddy, daddy, daddy!

Pop. Pop. Pop. Boom. Boom. Boom. Boom.

Love L M"

Bobby's voice trailed off. Then he shoved the microphone at the amplifier and it shrilled with deafening feedback. Jack raced down from upstairs but the bar was back to normal, except for the wild applause of the couple at the table.

"Well," Bobby said as he reclaimed his seat, "What did you think?"

"Think of what?" Jack asked.

"Interesting," Tommy said.

"Yeah," Frank said, "but I don't really know much about poetry."

"What the hell's goin' on?" Jack demanded.

The man in the dinner jacket stood behind Bobby. "Excuse me sir," he said as he tapped on Bobby's shoulder, "but I believe you owe us an apology."

"What the fuck for?" Bobby said as he turned on his stool .

"Aw, fuck," Jack said, "now what did you do, Bobby, drop your pants again?"

"I believe," the man said, "those poems are the work of Les Moor. So unless you are Les Moor, you owe us an apology for taking credit for those poems."

Bobby turned and asked Frank for another Martini. Tommy stared at Bobby. Jack demanded answers and Frank poured gin into the stainless steel shaker and looked at Bobby. "Shit," Frank said, "you're famous."

Bobby grabbed the Martini and slugged it down, ate the olives and lifted himself slowly from the bar stool. Wobbling to the door and waving back, he stumbled. "Into the night," Bobby trumpeted. "To The Neck."

Frank told Jack about Bobby's poetry reading. He thought Jack ought to consider letting Bobby do it a few nights a week before the bar got too crowded. He pointed to the table. "They loved it. Maybe a good way to get a little extra business down here, Jack."

Jack thought for a while and said, "Maybe, Frank. Ask him."

Frank said, "OK. Shit, he'll probably do it for drinks."

"Forget it," Jack said.

Frank laughed.

Typical summer Sunday for Frank and Donna - wallowing under the sheets until ten. Frank groused about having to entertain his mother for a week. Donna'd asked about his father and Frank had just laughed, "You gotta be kidding me, Donna. No matter what I do, he'll just want something else."

One of the kitchen staff knocked on the door and said, "Frank, you have visitors." Frank said, "Tell them I'm still sleeping."

"They asked me to tell you to come to the lobby. Hi, Donna."

"Hi, Bill."

Frank got out of bed, dressed and told Donna he'd be right back. "Must be them. Should we invite them to lunch?"

"I guess," Donna said. "What do you think?"

"Let me see how they are first. Then we'll decide."

"Up to you," Donna said.

Frank walked into the lobby of the hotel and saw his father looking at the photographs that lined the fireplace mantel. Even from the back, Frank could tell: hands clasped at the small of his back, the gold horseshoe with embedded diamonds strapping one of his little fingers, head twisting and turning like radar to check every possible detail as waves of Brylcream laden black hair curled above the high collar of the bell bottomed white jump suit. When he heard, "Boats. What a load of crap," Frank said, "Hey, Dad, I knew it was you."

"Hello, Frank. How are you?" His father spun. His gold medallion swung like a pendulum. Frank's nostrils filled with the scent of Aqua Velva.

"Great, Dad. Where's Mom?"

"Out there sunning her butt." He pointed to the sun deck.

Frank turned and walked out to the deck. He saw his mother leaning against the railing. She and another woman looked out at the harbor.

"Hi, Mom," Frank said.

His mother sailed up and threw her arms around him. Frank gawked over her shoulder. His past welled in deep brown eyes and curves he'd known - intimately. "Allie," Frank mumbled, "WWWhat the . . . what are you doing here?"

"Well, hello, Frank. Nice to see you, too. Can't I even get a kiss hello? I came three hundred miles just to see you. At least I should get a kiss hello, Frank." Allie's lush lips quivered.

Frank shuddered as the sonorous tones jarred years of memories and flushed them to the surface; they quickly dissipated as his mother cackled, "Yes, Francis, she should get that, at least."

Frank walked over and brushed Allie's cheeks with his. Allie grabbed Frank's neck with her hand and kissed his ear. She whispered, "God, I've missed you, Frank." Then more openly, Allie offered, "Well, Frank. I must say you look terrific. The ocean agrees with you."

"You look good, too, Allie. What's going on?" Frank said.

"Just a little vacation from the kids," she said.

"Yes," Frank's mother said, "when she called and said she needed to get away, I said she should come with us and visit you for a week. Isn't this wonderful, Francis?"

"What?" Frank asked.

"Yeah, Chuck and I split up almost a year ago. So I said what the hell. Why not?"

"Why?" Frank asked.

"I just couldn't deal with him anymore. All he cares about is his career with IBM. He never paid attention to me and the kids."

"No," Frank stammered, "I meant why here?"

"Because she wanted to see you, Francis. Don't be so strange," his mother said.

"I didn't know you had kids, Allie," Frank said.

"Oh, yes, Frank, two. Bang, bang just like that. Within a few years of getting married. Finally I'm getting back in shape." Allie threw her chest outward, struck a cheesecake pose, then she bent to touch her toes.

Gymnastics notwithstanding, she asked, "What do you think, Frank?"

"Great," Frank said. "Yeah, just terrific. Wow!"

"Well, I guess" Frank's mother said. "I wish I looked that good after I had Frank. I never recovered you know. I just couldn't get the weight off. He was such ..."

"OK, Mom, let's talk about what you want to do," Frank said.

"We're going up to our rooms and freshen up. Then we'll be ready for lunch. Where are you taking us, Frank?"

"Oh, I don't know," Frank said. "Somewhere down The Neck."

"I'm going for a swim first," Allie said, dropping her sundress to the deck. "Want to join me, Frank?"

Frank stared. Allie wore a pink bikini and from what Frank could see, two children hadn't changed much. Enticing as ever, the gestures, the face, the body - Frank's veins swelled with confusion. "Ahh, no, ummm, I better get cleaned up for lunch."

Frank's mother left the deck and walked into the lobby. Frank watched Allie swagger to the pool. She bent to undo her sandals just as Jack walked onto the deck. "Whoa," Jack said. "Who's that?"

"Allie," Frank said.

"Your Allie?" Jack said. "She's here? Oh, yeah, I remember seeing it in the guest book."

"Thanks for telling me, Jack," Frank said.

"Gee, Frank I thought you knew. Holy shit! What a scene this is gonna be. Does Donna know yet?"

"She's about to find out," Frank said. He and Jack watched as Donna crossed from the cottage. She wore one of Frank's tee shirts and a pair of nylon gym shorts. She dumped her beach towel on a chair and walked to the side of the pool. When she dove into the water, Jack said, "Maybe you can talk them into a three way, Frank."

Frank looked at Jack with a frozen face.

"Sorry," Jack said, "I forgot you're a friggin' boy scout."

Donna waved to Frank and motioned him to join her. Frank shook his head "No" and pointed to the cottage. Allie waved from the pool and Jack waved back.

"I think I'll take a swim," Jack said.

After her swim, Donna, drying her hair with a beach towel, listened attentively as Frank nervously straightened clothes in his closet, tidied up the night table and spoke about his parents. Then, as Frank explained his mother's surprise, saying, "So, you see, Donna. I didn't know. How could I? I mean ahhh . . . ," she glared, speechless. Frank knew he'd failed when Donna trudged to the bathroom and packed her cosmetics and toothbrush.

"That was her, Frank?" Donna screamed when she returned to confront him. "Fuck, she's gorgeous. Gimme a break, Frank. Do I look stupid?" Donna jabbed Frank's chest with an index finger.

"Come on, Donna, they're only here for a week. You know I love you. Don't be stu . . . upset."

"Frank, are you shitten' me? Fucken A! How could you let them bring her here? She's divorced and coming back to talk to you to see if there's anything left. And with that body, she's not going to have to do much talking. You pig, Frank Noal. You knew. You had to know. How could you not know? Fuck you, Frank. It's like I said last summer, you left without knowin'. You're gonna try to find out. If I know anything, I know men! I'm not hangin' around. You'll be stickin' it to her and then you'll be stickin' it to me. What bullshit, Frank. Total friggin' bullshit! How could you let them bring her here?"

"I told you, Donna, my mother's crazy. I didn't know."

"Well, Frankie boy, now you know. You can't have it both ways. As long as she's around, I'm not. You jerk, Frank. We had a great thing goin'. You better make up your mind real fast. You know where to find me." Donna slammed the door. Three of six glass panels cracked.

"Fuck," Frank said, "more work."

Frank met his parents in the lobby and told them they'd walk down to the Galley for lunch. Frank's father wore a ferociously loud luau shirt. A huge gold disc with a lightning bolt and the letters TCB hung from a chain around his neck. His Bermuda shorts and the black socks that barely reached the top of his ankles exposed more milky white, almost hairless legs than Frank cared to see. The sandals looked new. Frank commented on the sunglasses that sat below the white felt ten gallon Stetson. "I like those, Dad, just like the ones Elvis had on when they took his picture at the White House."

"Gotta have 'em," his father responded. "Just TCB."

Frank looked at his mother. She wore a flowery muu muu and a huge straw sun hat, its brim wobbling with every twist of her head. The fluorescent colors of the dress reminded Frank of the inside of the milk van he'd seen a few nights ago. She wore bath thongs with pink ankle socks and a pair of rhinestone-studded sunglasses that Polly Perry would kill for. A huge straw basket with painted flowers hung from her shoulders.

"Hi, darling," she said. She pursed her lips and brushed both of his cheeks with hers. Frank's father groaned and walked impatiently around the lobby trying to focus on anything. "Allie'll be right down, Frank. I know she wants to look ravishing for you - not that she has to try that hard." Frank's mother giggled, nudging Frank with her shoulder. The basket slipped down her arm and now dangled from her wrist. "Francis, I mean really. It's silly for someone your age to be getting involved with a waitress. Does she have any education, Francis? Allie does. She's a very bright woman, Francis. Really you . . . "

"Oh boy," Frank muttered under his breath as Allie walked into the lobby. Frank swallowed hard, stunned. His mother beamed.

Allie's short auburn hair curled back behind her ears revealing jade earrings Frank had given her their first Christmas together. Her brown eyes sparkled, deep, under sumptuous green shadows that sat softly on the lids and washed into a crisp curve of black liner at the outside corners. Thick mascara on her lashes fluttered as she moistened her bright red lips with a furtive swipe of the tip of her tongue. She reached into the rear pocket of her jeans and extracted a compact. She turned away from Frank as if shyly checking to see that all was perfect and Frank caught the wink she offered in the mirror as he raised his eyes from the Wrangler patch that appeared to be stitched to her ass.

"How do I look?" she asked no one as she spun and probed Frank with wide eyes. She ran her hands slowly along her breasts as if to smooth her white blouse. Her nipples, unfettered by any undergarment, poked at the shimmering silk that was unbuttoned almost to her navel. Frank didn't have to imagine much to see all of her breasts.

"Gimme a break, Allie." Frank noticed the shoes.

Allie's voice lilting through the apartment. A bra dangled from the floor lamp. A sweater limply caressed the arm of the sofa. A skirt pooled on the floor. Candies, Frank. I can get them off so fast. See. A shoe flew by his right ear as he quickly bent to unlace a boot.

"What do you think, Frank?" his mother asked.

Frank blinked, ogled Allie, then tentatively answered: "Well . . . I thought ahh, yeah, the Galley but maybe not. We should try the Loft."

"No, you ass, Francis, Allie? Doesn't she look marvellous?"

"Yes, Mom, she does."

"Don't tell me, Frank. Tell her."

Frank cringed. "Come on let's go," he said tersely.

Removing her sunglasses and stomping her left foot on the lobby carpet, Frank's mother barked, "No, Francis. Right now. You say something nice to her before we leave this building." Frank's father groaned.

Allie walked over to Frank and grabbed his arm with both of her hands. She wiggled as she rubbed her body against his and said, "Come on, Frank. It won't kill you."

"You look great, Allie. Can we . . ." Frank let go a tumultuous sneeze.

"The perfume?" Allie asked.

"Yeah."

"I thought you liked Chanel, Frank."

"That was Chuck."

"Oh, damn, I forgot, Frank. I'm mortified. I'll go wash it off now."

"Here, dear," Frank's mother chirped. "Use this." She handed Allie a wet nap from her purse. Allie rubbed at her cleavage and behind her ears.

Frank's father spoke directly to Allie's chest. "I'm starving."

"Where's your girlfriend, Frank? Didn't she want to have lunch with us? Doesn't she want to meet us, Frank? Frank, have you told her bad things about us?" His mother fired point blank as they walked toward Rocky Neck Avenue.

"We'll probably see her later, Mom," Frank said.

Allie'd recovered from her embarrassing lapse and held firmly onto Frank with both hands. "Are you madly in love with her Frank?" She nuzzled his ear.

"Yeah," Frank said, "I am in love with her."

"Madly, Frank, like you were with me?" Allie said.

"I don't think about that, Allie."

"Frank, we have to talk sometime. I've missed you terribly. I made a huge mistake in my life. I was totally in love with you. I screwed up."

"Let's talk about it some other time, Allie."

They passed Ruthie sitting on the stone wall in front of the saltbox

Ed Touchette

and whittling a walking stick. "Isn't that quaint? A real artist," Frank's mother said. "Oh, my, look at her outfit. Very nice. Just delightful." Frank's father pushed his sunglasses up to rest on his forehead and winked at Ruthie. Ruthie flipped him the bird.

"Oh, my," Frank's mother tittered.

Frank groaned.

The Loft was fairly quiet. Frank didn't know if that was good or bad. "Less of a risk than Polly's," he thought. They walked past the bar into the dining room and Frank watched as a couple of male customers dislocated their necks, gaping at Allie. The bartender mopped his brow with a towel. They sat at a booth near a row of windows that were open out to the cove. The air reeked.

"Phew," Frank's father said. "Can't eat in this place. Smells like shit. Ticonderoga smells better. Keeerist, the dairy farms in Washington County smell better even in manure season." He'd grabbed a napkin and snapped it up and down.

"It's low tide, Dad."

"Oh, great, Frank. Now that I know that, I'll probably eat a steak or two. Just knowing what it is makes it smell so much better. They probably flush their toilets in there."

"Oh, now, dear, that's not very appetizing. They wouldn't do that would they, Francis?" His mother lowered her head to peer at him over her glasses.

Frank looked up at the waitress and ordered four beers and four lobsters. "I guess you guys should at least have a lobster since you drove all the way out here to see me. Dad, you still like lobster - I hope?"

"Yeah, you oughta order us a lobster, I had to listen to those two talking for 300 miles. Nothin' sillier than a couple of broads - oh, sorry, Allie - talking nonstop while you're trying to concentrate on the road. We shoulda gone to Saratoga this summer. At least I could win some money there anyway."

Allie's foot was out of her shoe and crawling up Frank's leg. "I hope it'll be more than just lobster, Frank."

Frank didn't respond. He looked out at the cove.

"What's that, Francis?" his mother asked. "That house up there on the hill. It looks so quaint."

Frank told them all about the Aviary and his friend Emma. He said they should walk up there after lunch and look around. He told his father that he might enjoy looking at the shipyard at the end of the Neck. "It's fascinating what they do with those boats. The whole place is full of interesting people."

"Frank, I'm hungry," his father whined. "I don't really care if JFK is here, I just want to eat."

"He's dead, Dad," Frank said.

"So that would make it really interesting if he were here, wouldn't it, Frank?"

"Oh that is very funny, Donald," Frank's mother said. "Oh my, you are so quick and sharp sometimes. Just like the time you said FDR didn't die, he just got tired of Eleanor and left. Very funny."

Frank's father groaned and squinted at the cove. He snapped his napkin to move air.

Allie's foot rested in Frank's lap. Frank's voice cracked a little as he continued to talk about Gloucester and Rocky Neck. He dropped his napkin to the floor and as he leaned to retrieve it, he removed Allie's foot. The waitress delivered four beers and by the time Frank had poured his glass full, Allie's foot was working its way back up his leg.

"Do you like living here?" Allie asked Frank.

"Yes," Frank said. "It's a great place. People come here from all over the world and they're really interesting. Writers, artists, really amazing. The fishermen are a great bunch of guys."

"Is it hard?" Allie said as she wiggled her toes in his crotch.

"No," Frank answered.

"Hmm," Allie said.

The waitress brought four platters with boiled lobsters to the table. Frank's father tied his bib around his neck, viciously ripped claws from the body and mercilessly cracked them. His mother delicately picked the meat from the tail section and dropped it into her cup of butter. Allie broke off a claw and stuck the open end in her mouth. She sucked hard. "Can't get it to come - oouu- out. There it is." she said as she smiled at Frank. She continued sucking on the body parts and rolling her tongue over the edges of the shells.

Frank ate quietly. He'd removed the meat from the tail and both claws. Every time he wiped his mouth with the napkin he'd try to move

Allie's foot. She'd resist. Frank relented.

After lunch, Frank's mother and father tired quickly and decided to go back to the hotel for a nap. Allie said she wanted to keep walking and Frank's mother approved. "Go ahead, dear. We'll see you for cocktails and dinner."

Frank and Allie walked along East Main Street and Allie asked what Frank had been doing. Frank told her, "Got drunk. Worked at the mill. Moved here. Met a girl. Fell in love."

"Frank," Allie said. "I know I hurt you. I made such a terrible mistake. I've thought about you so much it hurts. I begged your mother to bring me because I knew if I showed up by myself you wouldn't have looked at me. Frank, we were together for years, we could start all over again. We were great together, Frank. You know it. You know it was. Making love in the shower. You loved it. You loved the way I made you feel and you know it. I know you haven't forgotten."

Frank didn't reply immediately. He gazed irresolutely at the cove whenever they walked past an opening between the houses. That voice - "So beautiful and inimical, all at once," he wondered. Then he said, "Allie, y'know there was something I never asked before I left. I kind of wish I had now." Frank vacillated momentarily and then girded. "I should have but I didn't."

"What?" Allie said.

"What went on with you and Chuck while we were still living together. Were you screwing him, too?"

"Never. I never made love with Chuck the way I did with you. I never really loved, Chuck. I loved you, Frank, but you were so unsure. I wanted to get married and have kids. I just picked the wrong guy."

"That's not what I asked, Allie. Let me be more direct. Allie, were you fucking him while we were still living together?"

"You ass, Frank. That's a dumb question. What does it matter?"

"Were you or weren't you, Allie?"

"Only to make you jealous, Frank. I thought you'd come and get me and bring me back home and make a commitment."

"That's the dumbest thing I ever heard, Allie. Did you really believe that? Better yet, do you really believe that I believe that?"

They'd walked as far as the granite steps leading to the Aviary. Frank looked up. He thought for a moment and said, "Let's go the other way." They walked back on East Main Street toward the causeway.

Frank rambled on about the past year and how much he liked Gloucester. He told Allie about his passions - studying old houses and the people who'd built them and Donna: "She's a great painter - one of the best I've ever seen."

Allie pouted and said she was jealous. She kept insisting she was better for him than Donna. She wanted to go back to the hotel and make love. Frank declined. He kept telling stories about Gloucester.

At the head of the causeway, Frank pointed out the historical marker that mentioned Champlain. "When I first saw it, I thought it was an omen."

"Good or bad, Frank?"

"Don't know yet. Won't til I get there."

"That's the Frank I used to know. Come on, let's go back and make love."

Frank shook his head.

Frank took a shower back at the cottage. He felt good. "Calmer than usual," he thought to himself. He washed his hair and sang *Satisfaction*. A hand grabbed him, but when he tried to open his eyes, they filled with soap. "Aw shit! Who is it?" he said. Two hands groped him. He grabbed for a towel. "Damn, Allie if that's you, I told you . . . Come on I've got soap in my eyes."

Lips on his back. Hands squeezed him gently. He relaxed. He rubbed his eyes and threw water in them, but he still couldn't open them. Then:

"Make love to me, Frank."

"Donna! I knew it was you."

"My ass, Frank. You thought it was Allie."

"No. I didn't. Well, ahhh, I thought it could be because, well, yeah, mmm, she's been acting like a god damned fool all day."

"Did you screw her, Frank?"

"Not even close, Donna. I told her I loved you."

"Did you ask her, Frank?"

"Yeah, I did. It was pathetic. Donna give me a towel, please, my eyes are killing me."

"Do you have to see me to know it's me, Frank?"

"No, Donna, but I'd like to see you."

Donna handed him the towel and Frank wiped his eyes. He looked at Donna and kissed her. "Come on."

They made love all afternoon. They were lying in bed talking and Frank asked Donna if she was coming to dinner and she said of course she was. "Great," Frank said. Then Frank asked her why she'd come back and Donna said that she was sorry she'd left so mad. "I know you love me, Frank and I'm not walking away from this - not that easily. Besides, I forgot my underwear."

Frank laughed.

They met in the lobby before dinner. The first thing Frank's father said when he saw Donna was, "You ain't half bad lookin'. Why ya hanging around with that bum?" Then he laughed and said, "Oh, just kidding."

Donna whispered in Frank's ear, "Can I say because you're a fabulous fuck?" and Frank shook his head "No."

Frank's mother commenced the interrogation immediately and dragged Donna by the arm as Allie grabbed Frank. They all headed out to the parking lot. Frank overheard the rapid fire questioning so he suggested separate cars and showed them the collection of hardware in the back of his station wagon. Allie suggested she ride with Frank so that Donna could get to know Frank's parents and Frank said, "No. We'll meet you there." Frank drove his car and he told his father to drive carefully because the streets were narrow. His father shook his head and said, "Sure, Frank, like I'm gonna get lost."

They drove through downtown, parked on Middle Street and ambled down the hill to Roger's. Donna clutched Frank and Allie walked with Frank's mother. Frank's father griped about French food and why he didn't want to eat that shit when he driven all the way to the coast for seafood.

Frank's mother continued to pepper Donna with questions. How did she like Bristol Hall for the year she was there? Was she going to go back and get a degree? Was she going to have a career?

Donna responded with short answers, "Yes," or "No," she'd say and look at Frank. Frank tried to distract his mother, but she ignored him. Allie smiled alluringly at Frank every time he glanced at her.

Roger greeted them and hugged Frank and Donna. He set a special table and brought a bottle of Bordeaux. Frank sat next to his father, Allie and Donna and his mother across from them. Roger came for their appetizer orders and Frank spoke to him in French, ordering for the table. Roger smiled and said, "Merci," as he walked away.

Frank felt a foot crawling up his leg. He looked at Donna and smiled. "Ma petite," Frank said as he poured the wine. Donna continued to smile and Frank could feel the foot getting closer to his thigh. "C'est magnifique," Frank said. The foot crept higher.

"I taught you good, Frankie," his father blurted. "Your French is still with you."

"Yeah," Frank said as he reached under the table and tickled the bottom of the foot. Allie giggled. Donna looked at Allie. Donna reached under the table and felt the leg stretching out toward Frank. She grabbed it and dug in with sturdy sharp nails.

"Owww," Allie screamed. Frank groaned. His mother asked Allie "What?" and his father said, "Who cares? I want to go somewhere for fried clams."

Donna sipped wine. "Oui," she said. "C'est magnifique."

Frank's father looked puzzled. Frank gasped, struggling for air.

Frank still couldn't talk when Roger came for their dinner orders so Donna took over. Frank's father smiled and said Donna's French made her sound sexy. Donna ignored him and spoke to Frank. "Does that sound good, Frankie, honey?" Frank nodded weakly, "Yes."

"What the hell's wrong with you, Frank?" his father asked and Frank shook his head, "No."

Roger came around with a tray of mousse, pastries and torts after dinner; he poured coffee for everyone. Everyone passed on dessert except Donna. "I'll have the double chocolate mousse," she said. "Want to share, Frank?"

Frank said, "No," but Donna insisted that he was going to need his strength.

"What for?" Frank's mother asked innocently. His father groaned. Allie sneered. When the mousse arrived, Donna fed Frank a few bites from her spoon.

After dinner they walked back up to Middle Street. Frank limped slightly but he told them he wanted them to see the statue of Joan d'arc. "That would be very nice, Frank," his mother said. "What for? I've seen plenty of statues in my life," his father said. Allie complained of a headache so they drove back to the hotel.

Frank bade them all good night in the lobby. Donna was already naked under the sheets when Frank crawled into bed. "Any idea how much I love you right now, Frank?" she said as Frank grabbed her hand.

"No," Frank said, "but I'll bet I'm about to find out."

"You bet right, Frank. And one other thing."

"Yeah, Donna, what's that?"

"She ever touches you again, I'll break her friggin' neck. I'll tell her myself if you don't, but do her a favor 'cause it might mean more coming from you. OK?"

"I guess, Donna."

"Make love to me, Frank."

"I can't Donna. It still hurts."

"Don't worry, darling, I'll fix it."

Monday night. Frank opened the bar and Allie came in for a drink. She was sipping a Cape Codder when Donna sat next to her. Frank looked at Donna; she smiled wryly at Allie, who grimaced.

"So," Donna said to Allie, "thank you."

"For what?" Allie said.

"For Frank, Allie. If you hadn't fucked up so royally, I never would have met the best thing that ever happened to me."

Allie twirled the swizzle stick between her lips, looking longingly at Frank but speaking to Donna. "You know what they say, Donna. It ain't over 'til it's over."

"It's over," Donna said. "For you, anyway. For Frank and me it's just getting good."

"Well good for you," Allie said, licking the stick. "But don't mess up, Donna, because I'll be right there waiting."

"OK," Frank said. "Can we have a nice congenial conversation about something else? Anything else. Fiesta. The 4th of July."

"Sure," Donna said. "I heard the fireworks they've got planned are the biggest ever in the history of Gloucester."

"Well," Allie said. "I'm sorry I won't be able to stay to see them."

"Too bad," Donna said.

Frank wiped out a few glasses and cleaned out a couple of ashtrays that had been left by the waitress station the night before. He checked the coolers to see if there was enough beer and then he grabbed a couple of whiskey bottles for the speed rack.

Bobby Crosby walked in and sat next to Donna. Donna introduced him to Allie, who arched an eyebrow, and Bobby ordered a round of drinks for all.

"Hey, Frank," Bobby said. "I'm going out tomorrow with Tommy Lozano. Can't wait. Should be fun. Has he been in yet?"

"Not yet, Bobby. He's usually here by now, if he's coming in."

"Going out where?" Donna asked.

"Fishing," Bobby said. "They that go down to the sea and all that stuff. I'm going to work for Tommy for a few days and get a taste of the fishing life."

"Don't fall in, Bobby," Donna said.

"So what's your story, babe," Bobby said to Allie.

"I'm Frank's old girlfriend," Allie said directly to Frank as she reached for Bobby's arm. "I came out here to see if Frank might be available but I guess he's not." Donna watched Frank's face carefully. He blandly mixed a second Martini for Bobby.

"Well," Bobby said, "No point hanging around here crying over spilt milk, so to speak, let's do The Neck tonight."

Allie said, "Sure. Why not," and they left, arm in arm.

"Into the night." Bobby's voice thundered as they walked out the door. "To The Neck."

"Does that bother you, Frank?" Donna asked after they'd left.

"Not at all, but I doubt Allie can handle Bobby Crosby."

The door to the bar flew open and Allie tore over to the bar and plopped on the stool. "That maniac had his hand down my blouse before we hit the walkway. He's crazy. He wanted me to go to the gazebo down by the water and screw. It's still light outside. My God, what kind of place is this, Frank?" Allie's hand trembled, reaching for the drink Frank had already placed on the bar.

"Wait'll the sun goes down," Donna said. "It gets better as the night goes on." Donna preened in the mirror. "See you after work, darling. Luv ya."

"Love you, too," Frank said.

Frank blew her a kiss and she grinned as she twisted the door knob. Then she flew behind the bar, threw her arms around Frank. "Be naked when I get here."

"Sure," Frank said. "Are you going to paint?"

"Yes," Donna said. "My wildest fantasies of you."

Allie frowned.

Frank and Allie talked at the bar as the crowd from the sun deck filtered in. Frank had explained the ritual. The band started playing song and a couple of guys hit on Allie to dance. She joined the party, dancing wildly, arms flying, hair bouncing to and fro. "Not bad," Frank thought. "No Annie Barnes but that body's incredible. Nice."

Making love in the waterfalls. Their special place; swimming, hot and humid days - Adirondack summers.

We're meant for each other, Frank. We should get married now. Let's not wait for graduation.

We need time, Allie.

God, she can dance, too.

I'll be back in a few hours, Allie.

You're an asshole for risking your neck for a couple of Indians, Frank.

They're scared, Allie. Kids. I owe Lucas.

You're an asshole, Frank. A fucking asshole.

Yeah, Frank, Allie called. Said she was bullshit because you'd run off to Canada. But I consoled her, Frank.

"You mother," Frank whispered as Jack's voice drifted off.

Tommy Lozano had sat at the bar directly in front of Frank and said, "Whoa, Frank. Easy."

"Oh, sorry, Tommy. Just thinking about something she said."

"Fucken A!" Tommy got a glimpse of Allie. "Who's that?"

"She's history," Frank said.

The next Saturday as his parents left with Allie, Frank thought, "I doubt that I'll see much of them again. I don't know much but I know that." He meandered toward the gazebo where a couple sat holding hands on the bench he'd repaired last summer. Their heads touched as they gazed out to the harbor. The sails on the boats snapped in the stiff breeze. A sport fishing boat blasted its way toward the breakwater as Frank stared at Ten Pound Island.

"No wonder Patrick lived out there. It would be hard for people to get to you."

Chapter 22

Prostitution: the ~~oldest~~ only profession . . . by George.

Well Hung: Poems about Gloucester's Painters
Bobby Crosby
1971 The Aviary Papers Publishers

Monday night, Bobby Crosby, in tennis whites, a white cotton sweater draping his shoulders, came into the bar early, ranting to Frank about women and the way they took up too much of his time. Frank listened attentively then mentioned some writer with a similar problem and Bobby took off on a new tangent. They spoke at length about poets and authors they liked then Frank told Bobby he was reading Moby Dick for the second time. "I don't know if I get all of the symbolic stuff, sometimes, Bobby, but I like the story."

Bobby gulped a Martini and left. Frank, startled, wiped the mahogany and wondered what had happened. Then Bobby raced back in, reached into the back pocket of his shorts and pulled out a worn paper covered book. When he handed it to Frank, he said, "Tell me what you think."

"What's this?" Frank said and smoothed the curled paper cover with his hand. He flipped it and looked at the back cover. It was bare. He turned it back to the front and read aloud: "<u>Dead Beat</u>. The Posthumous Autobiography of Les Moor. Did you write this?" Frank asked as he thumbed through the first pages. Bobby answered, "Yes."

"Can I take it and read it?" Frank asked and Bobby nodded.

Frank thanked Bobby and got him another Martini. Frank held the book and glanced through the pages as he mixed. He was still reading as he stirred the drink with three olives on a toothpick.

Bobby reached for the stem of the glass but Frank kept stirring. Bobby cried, "Hey, Frank, gimme the drink."

"Ha," Frank said as he turned a page, "That's great." He continued reading and stirring.

"Frank, my drink, please," Bobby said.

"Oh, sure. Sorry," Frank said as he let go of the toothpick and turned

Ed Touchette

another page.

Still engrossed when Bobby left, Frank waved but never lifted his eyes from the book. "Holy shit," he said aloud as he turned a page.

Donna passed Bobby on her way to her usual stool and Bobby pinched her ass. "Fuck off, Bobby," Donna snarled then whispered to Frank, "Hi, darling." Frank nodded but didn't look up from the book. By rote he reached into the beer cooler and grabbed a bottle of Schlitz, opened it and placed it in front of Donna.

"What are you reading, Frank?"

Frank didn't answer.

"Frank, I'm pregnant," Donna said.

"Hi, Donna," Frank mumbled.

"Frank, I'm totally naked," Donna said, more irritated.

Frank turned another page and said, "This is unreal."

Donna got up from her seat and walked behind the bar. She unzipped Frank's jeans and started to kneel on the floor.

"Not now, darling," Frank said. "This is an important part."

Donna snatched the book from Frank's hands. She read the cover and said, "What the hell is it, Frank?" She leafed through a few pages. "Stories about Gloucester. Who's Les Moor?"

Frank took the book back and placed it in his pocket. "Sorry, darling," he said "Bobby. Bobby Crosby. Can you believe it. He's a poet and a writer. This is his book. I'm blown away."

"Not now, Frank."

"Seriously, Donna, look." Frank reached into his pocket and pulled out the book. He turned a few pages and pointed out a couple of paragraphs. "Read this, here. From there to here. Just read that part."

Frank watched anxiously as Donna read. When she finished, she looked at Frank with amazement. "Holy shit, Frank. Out o' sight."

Frank nodded in agreement. "You remember," he said.

"Yes."

Donna gazed at her reflection in the mirror, aimlessly scratching at the label on her beer bottle. Frank stared through the jalousie windows. He'd snatch the book from his pocket, read a few lines then roll it up and tuck it away. Occasionally they looked at each other and asked with their eyes. There were no answers.

Donna broke the silence, "He must have been a kid, then, Frank."

"Bobby Wells," Frank said.

"Yeah," Donna muttered.

By the time Frank clanged the bell for last call, he'd been able to steal a few more glances at the book. He was wiping the bar when the door opened and Bobby Crosby stumbled through. Bobby ordered a Martini.

"Let me lock the door, first," Frank said.

"Sure."

"Bobby," Frank said as he poured the mix from the shaker, "what's the story. This book is great. When did you write these?"

"Sjus stuff, Frank."

"When did you write this stuff?"

"Mosly before I got killed. The last couple were after I croaked. Been dead too long, Frank. Way too long."

Bobby slugged down the Martini and Frank hoped he wouldn't ask for another. He didn't. As Bobby, stuck the olives in his mouth and tilted his head back to swallow, he fell backwards off the stool and crashed to the floor.

Frank bolted from behind the bar. "Shit, Bobby, are you OK?"

Bobby opened his eyes. "Fuck, Frank, I cracked my neck again."

Livid, Jack screamed at Frank the next morning. "Goddamn, Frank, we're gonna lose our license over this. Friggin' Bobby Crosby is gonna get this whole thing canned. Damn, why didn't you just tell him no?"

Frank said nothing. He asked Jack to call Mass General and see how Bobby was. Jack said OK and dialed the number from the phone at the front desk.

"Yeah, hi, this is Jack Carson from the Rackliffe House in Gloucester. _ Yeah, hi. Yeah, I'm glad you liked it._ Yes, we still have rooms. Say can you tell me about someone that would have been brought in last night with a cracked neck._Yeah, Bobby Crosby._ Crosby - C R O S B Y._ I'll wait."

Frank looked at Jack and Jack said, "Sexy voice. Said she's been here. Wants to come again in August. Get the book out will ya."

"Yeah, hi. Yup still here._ What do you mean? Did he check out?_ What do you mean he never checked in?._ He had to_That's where they took him._ Please check again."

"Friggin' maniac, Frank. The guy's a friggin' maniac."

"Yeah, right, a broken neck._What?_ Bobby Wells._ No. I told you it's Bobby Crosby._.Maybe that's a name he's using but we know him as Bobby Crosby._Oh thank god for that._ Yeah, sure, Thanks._Yeah. OK._OK._Sure. OK._Oh, yeah, sure. I'll put your name in the book right now._Two?_Sure._Is that Ms. or Mrs._ Great! Sure, Ms. Connie Pardy and Ms. Evelyn Tredwell._ No I don't_ She is?_ Really._ I'm Jack Carson, the owner. I'll be sure to be here when you arrive. We can have drinks on the deck and watch the sunset_. Me too._ Thanks. See you then._"

"Whoa!" Jack said. "Friggin' babes. Ms. Evelyn Tredwell, aka Bunny Tredwell, aka Bunny Divine, the porn star. I can't wait."

"Say, Jack, did she happen to mention Bobby while you were hustlin' her."

"Fuck you, Frank. Yeah, but it's a little weird that he used the name Bobby Wells and not Crosby. Why would he do that?"

"Is he OK or not?"

"He's gonna be fine. Just has to wear the halo thing again for a couple of months. It didn't break, just badly cracked and bruised. She said he could wear one of those foam collars after a week or two, maybe, but the doctor doesn't want to risk it yet. They're operating today. He'll be out in a few days."

When Bobby walked into the bar a week later wearing his stainless steel halo, a straw hat embellished the corrective gear, and Bobby flourished one of Ruthie's walking sticks. Frank chuckled and said, "You look like Moses meets the Scarecrow." Then he shook Bobby's free hand and said, "Great to see you, Bobby."

Tommy Lozano and Donna were at the bar. Donna said, "Bobby, take care of yourself, please. This place would be dead without you."

Tommy asked about the walking stick and Bobby banged it against a rafter, shouting, "I've seen the light. I have consumed my last drops of the demon alcohol and I'm on a straight and narrow road. Coke, Frank. Gimme a Coke."

"Come on, Bobby, I haven't got that shit. You want a Martini?"

"Frank I want a glass of Coke. The real thing, Frank. Coca Cola. Gimme one, please."

"Sure." Frank filled a glass cocktail shaker with ice and drained coke from the spigot. "Wow, Bobby, you're serious."

"Not to worry, Frank. I've got God on my side."

Tommy and Frank and Donna watched as Bobby sipped the coke. Then they looked at each other in wonder.

"Ahhh," Bobby said slapping the glass to the bar. "Yup. I have seen the man and it's clear as day. It's gonna take some time but I will right the wrongs I've bestowed upon the world. Born again, I'm Bobby Crosby, poet, writer and an extraordinarily new person." Then he tapped Donna with the walking stick and said, "Nice touch, don't y'think?" as he rubbed the carving with his fingers.

Donna smiled cautiously.

Later, when Frank closed the bar, Bobby stayed, drinking Cokes, talking to Frank as Frank cleaned ash trays and mopped the floor behind the bar. Animated and buoyant, a manic Bobby ranted through his story, raving about his childhood, raging about Viet Nam, ripping his wayward existence to a point where Frank said, "Whoa, Bobby, you're wired. Easy."

Bobby said, "the Coke, Frank."

Frank grimaced and Bobby laughed as he pointed to the glass on the bar with the walking stick. "Sugar, Frank," and without pause he delved more into his childhood in Gloucester and the artists and writers he'd known and how they'd turned him to poetry. "We used to stay at a house on the moors so I decided to be Les Moor - a great name for a beat poet."

Frank laughed his agreement and mentioned Emma'd told him about the poet who walked around the Aviary and that he'd found an old notebook of poems in the cupola last summer when he was helping her.

"I must've left it there. Don't worry Frank, you'll understand in a few minutes. I gotta tell somebody. Might as well be you," and he continued, telling Frank about a poet he'd heard some of the writers talk about. "Harry Crosby, Frank, a writer in Paris. Drove ambulances for the AFS in World War One. Almost got killed by an artillery shell that exploded right in front of him. He was traumatized, became addicted to opium and man, that guy screwed more women than you could imagine. Always wore black. Wild. My hero. That's when I decided to wear a black cape. Well I got the cape part from Dali. The red bandanna was my idea. Not bad, huh?"

Frank nodded and Bobby went on. "When I was almost killed in Viet Nam, I decided Harry Crosby must have saved me so I changed my name to Bobby Crosby. Least I could do, Frank. Les Moor was dead. That's when I wrote the book."

Frank shrugged.

Bobby stared at his reflection in the mirror, his eyes watered. "When I was a kid, Frank, I used to sneak up to the cupola in the Aviary to write poetry. I'd walk around the widows walk with the cape and red bandanna and recite my poems. Pretty wild, Frank." Bobby smiled and drifted deeper into his childhood. Gloucester was the most beautiful place he'd ever seen. He'd sail his cat boat around the cove and out to the breakwater and back. He recalled: the picnics up on Banner Hill with his parents and the artists; walking down to the wharves and fishermen handing him a cod or a haddock and bringing it home and his mother making chowder; the house on the moors and the theater and him writing plays about Gloucester; and how he'd stayed at Rackliffe House a few times with his parents. "Even then, Frank, it was still great. People came here from all over. They loved this place. That's why I came back here, Frank. The people. Haddie Baker was always one of my favorites. She used to tell me stories about Charleston. I caddied for her husband once and he gave me a five dollar tip. People all over the place, Frank. People! This place was always thick with diners and guests."

Frank tried to suggest they continue the conversation another time but Bobby started in on the war again. "I came home with schrapnel in my head and a bad drug habit. I had some good connections to buy the stuff so I decided to import it here, Frank. Kind of a natural, don't ya think? And with people like Jack to unload it for me, it worked out great until that idiot Ryan got involved."

Frank cringed. "Jack?" he said as he pointed upward.

"Yeah," Bobby said. "Jack was friggin' stupid, Frank. That stuff was bad. He knew, but he kept dealing it anyway. Y'know, Frank, I felt bad when they found that kid had ODed. When they found Patrick dead, I blamed myself. I can't figure out why that guy ever started. I liked him, Frank."

"Me either, Bobby. I can't believe he did. But hey, Bobby, look, yeah I suspect somethings going on but I really don't know and I don't want to know. Let's . . . "

"Well, Frank, the way it's going you're gonna have to know, because that shit's changing things. Gonna have to deal with it sooner or later. I'm making my stand, right fuckin' now." Bobby waved an envelope stuffed with bills. "This will be the start of the clean up, so to speak." Then

Bobby explained his plan. When he finished, he said, "Jack'll try to unload it and when they find out what it is, he'll be out of business. For good." Bobby grinned at his reflection in the mirror then blurted, "Y'know, Frank, maybe I can work for Nixon. Like Elvis."

Frank shook his head trying to dislodge the vision he'd conjured: Bobby in a white jump suit, gold framed sunglasses and a ten gallon Stetson. Bobby rambled: "Ducky Ryan, the imbecile started selling fishsticks. Nobody'd have caught on to frozen fish blocks. After he found out, I had to hire him. I had him picking up stuff a few miles out, off a freighter. I'd sneak up to the top of the Aviary to look for the freighter and then send him. He'd meet the guy at night and run the stuff over to the wharf. Risky, though, with a jerk like Ryan. Got real hairy when his boat blew an engine and he had to row in a dory. He sampled the wares on the way in. The dumb bastard got so stoned, once, he rowed up the cut to Annisquam before he realized something was wrong. I couldn't trust him anymore so I'd started sendin' him up to the Aviary. Last fall, when he took the dive, he musta been ripped on somethin' and tried to fly. Good thing I found him. Emma Wilkins would've freaked. So I dragged him over here and Jack stored him in the walk-in upstairs before the fire. Made it look like he jumped from the hotel to escape. When they tried to pin it on Patrick, though, I got pissed. Jack did that; I know it. Him or that friggin' bitch, Stephanie. Man, she is a piece of work - let me tell you, Frank. She's the one that got the whole thing going."

"You know her, Bobby?" Frank asked.

"Yeah, Frank, she's the one that got me dealing through Jack. She came into the Loft one night. I was drunk at the piano. Next thing I know we're upstairs and she's got me tied up with leather and she's painting my toe nails. She loved the bondage thing, Frank. Thought it was a turn on to paint my toe nails before we screwed. Weird shit, Frank. A couple of run ins with her and I was selling through Jack. She set it all up."

"She tied you up and painted your toe nails?" Frank asked.

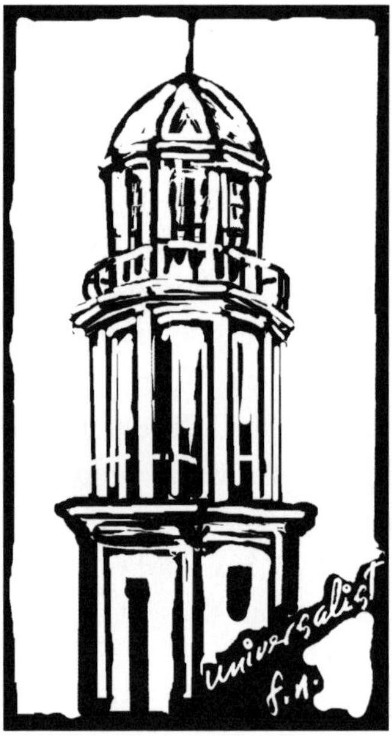
universalist
f.r.

Chapter 23

*Ya gotta have h'art.
A lightning rod makes sense, too.*

A Tribute to Les Moor
Anonymous
2005 The Aviary Papers Publishers

The theme for that summer's Beaux Artes Ball was famous buildings. Jack was accompanying the Misses Divine and Pardy so he'd cut arm holes in a large packing carton and was going as a back shore motel. He stood at the bar drinking a Vodka Gimlet when his dates promenaded through the door.

Ms. Pardy had scored a flat cardboard and plunked it on her head as a gabled roof. Her lower sections were covered with lobster buoys. Ms. Pardy twirled and soughed, "Hi Jackie. Like it?"

"Yeah," Jack said. "Motif No. 1. Can't wait to gaff those. And might I add, Bunny, you look divine."

Frank smiled as the porn star sauntered to the bar. She wore a flesh colored leotard with a low neck; an alarm clock dangled from a neck chain and rested just above her cleavage. A washed out green wig and a small model of a sailing ship sat on her head. "This is the wig I wore in <u>Debbie Does Dublin</u>," she told Frank. "Did you see that one? Very popular."

"I missed it," Frank said. "Sorry."

"Who wants to guess?" Ms. Divine asked as Bobby Crosby strolled through the door wrapped in a white sheet, a red wooden salad bowl sitting upside down on his halo.

"Gloucester City Hall," Bobby howled at Bunny Divine.

"The Universalist Church," Bunny said to Bobby.

"A match made in heaven," Frank called across the bar. Jack frowned.

"Not tonight," Bobby said. "A month ago I'd have wound that clock with my teeth, but now I am the tool of the Lord."

"Yeah," Jack derided, "A real tool."

Donna had begged Frank to take her to the ball but Jack wouldn't give Frank the night off. She'd worked on a costume for a month and she was bitterly disappointed. When she came into the bar, she took one look at Bobby and laughed. "The Universalist," she said and Bobby roared. Donna looked around and exclaimed over the creativity of some of the costumes. When she got to Jack she taunted, "What are you, Jack, the outhouse from L'il Abner?" Bobby laughed. He asked Frank and Donna why they weren't going and Donna jerked her thumb toward Jack.

Donna asked Bobby if he had a date and when he answered "No," she disappeared through the door. When she returned twenty minutes later, she was struggling to tie a ribbon under her chin while she twisted and turned to get her costume through the door without damaging it. She had three cardboard cartons of successively smaller sizes stacked one on top of the other. On the top of her head sat a tiny box with holes on all sides and an orange jelly bean skewered on a chopstick. The yellow cartons had painted railings and roof lines and cornice details.

"The Aviary," Frank shouted.

"Yes, yes," Donna screamed. "Bobby can I be your date? Frank won't mind."

"Sure," Bobby said, and off they walked through the passage way into the real world.

The crowd started filtering in from the ball around ten o'clock that night. Frank had heard the rumble of thunder and lightning flashes had lit the harbor beyond the windows - like the fireworks on the fourth of July. When Donna and Bobby came in, they were soaked to the skin. Bobby's sheet dripped and Donna's drooping boxes bled color. The small box strapped to the top of her head melted and the toothpick with the jelly bean pointed backwards.

"Dogs in a rain storm," Frank gibed.

Bobby Crosby roared, Donna flipped Frank the bird.

"Coke," Bobby hollered.

"Slllitz," Donna said.

"Man, what fun," Donna howled. "Frank, we danced through the thunder and lightning and it poured. We'd have stayed but the parking lot was flooding. It was great while it lasted though."

Bobby laughed and so did Frank.

In a Place Like No Other

The band played and dancers mobbed the floor. A man claiming to be the Rockport watertower had a coffee can strapped to the top of his head. He bent over to kiss his partner and the water that had collected in the can spilled onto the guitarist and his amplifier. An ungodly screech froze the room as the guitarist dropped his instrument to the floor. Smoke curled from the back of the amp and the band stopped for a minute while he grabbed a different guitar and plugged into a another amp. The music started up again and the room reignited.

Then lightning flashed and a clap of thunder rocked the bar. The band stopped. The singer said it was time for a break. Donna looked at Bobby; his blank gaze and ashen face shocked her. She rubbed his back whispering, "Bobby, it's OK. We're here for you. Don't think about it."

"Relax, Bobby, it'll pass in a few minutes," Frank said. He watched as Bobby stared into the mirror. Then Bobby stood and said, "I'll be right back. I've got to get my walking stick from my room. I'm being called to preach to the masses."

Jack walked in through the back passageway with his dates. Bunny Divine's scoop neck skin tight leotard was even more so wet and little imagination was required to visualize her big screen image. Jack ordered drinks and told Frank that the storm was going to get worse. "Severe thunder and lightning, Frank. High winds. Let me take over the bar while you go up and close some windows and doors." Jack motioned Frank closer and whispered. "I can't leave her here without an escort, Frank."

Frank told Donna he'd be right back and walked up through the back halls to the lobby. He secured the sliders to the sun deck and the office windows. Then he checked the front entry. Everything was closed.

He checked the first floor guest rooms and all of the windows were locked down so he went to the top floor. He secured two windows at the east end of the corridor and then walked back to the west end. The windows were closed but someone had broken the padlock on the door that led to the cupola. Frank opened it and peeked inside. He hollered "Hello," but no one answered. He hollered again - still nothing.

Frank walked to the bottom of the circular stairway. "Who's up there?" Frank demanded.

"That you, Frank?" Bobby Crosby yelled down.

"Bobby, are you nuts? Come on down."

"Can't, Frank."

"Why not, Bobby?"

"I'm being called, Frank. He wants to talk to me."

"Who?" Frank asked.

"The man, Frank."

"What man, Bobby?"

"God, Frank. Now shut the fuck up and leave me alone. Here, Frank, this is for you. I want you to have it."

Frank heard the sound of paper being ripped from a notebook. As it floated down the stairwell, he reached up to grab it. He was reading when he heard the crack of wood, then creaking hinges and glass tinkling to the floor. The hair on Frank's head stood straight up. He was still reading when suddenly he hollered, "Bobby don't go out there with that thing on your . . . " Frank looked up into bright white light.

Donna was singing along with the band when the hotel shook and the lights dimmed. "What the fuck was that!" Jack howled when the explosion rocked the bar. The lights dimmed again; the bar went black until the emergency floods kicked on. "Don't panic," Jack shouted, "just a power failure. Probably a transformer out in the street. I'll go see."

He grabbed a flash light and walked out the door through the passageway and into the drive. The rain had stopped but a violent wind whipped up from the harbor. He looked toward the street; nothing seemed amiss. He walked along the drive toward the street and pointed the beam of the flashlight at a few roofing slates that were sitting in the drive. Then Jack saw a piece of a balustrade in a hedge so he crossed the street. Bending to retrieve the wood, whiffs of burnt leather drifted to his nostrils. He pulled Bobby Crosby's charred and bent halo from the bushes.

Jack turned back to the hotel and looked up. "Holy fuck," Jack screamed as three fire engines rounded the corner and headed directly for him. He pointed to the roof as the fire chief ran to him. "It blew the friggin' top off," Jack screamed. "Look!" Jack handed the fire chief the smoldering halo.

"What the hell is that?" the chief asked.

Jack shook his head slowly.

The chief directed his men to put a spotlight on the roof. Jagged pieces of lumber protruded at all angles from a gigantic hole in the center of the roof. The cupola was gone. Whisps of smoke curled from the hole so the chief sent some men up to the second floor to extinguish any flames and douse smoldering timber. Others shined the spotlight around the top of the hotel, revealing pieces of the cupola scattered across the roof of the hotel: balustrades, window frames, slates, siding. One fireman yelled, "Look there," as he passed his searchlight beam through a large oak tree and focused on a shred of sheet, horizontal in the wind. Across the street, Bobby Crosby's walking stick had lodged in the roof shingles of a hipped roof dormer, affecting the appearance of a unicorn.

Bobby Crosby's body was never found. Later, the coroner's report presumed ablation. "Due to the intense heat generated by a massive lightning strike, one Robert Wells aka Bobby Crosby aka Les Moor was removed from the surface of the earth." A few days later, more shreds of sheet were found hanging in a couple of maple trees down on Rocky Neck Avenue. The morning after the explosion, the door to the cupola floated in the swimming pool. A gull stood on it watchfully; more circled overhead as the neighborhood appraised the damage. Fire inspectors rummaged for clues, inside and out.

It was mid-morning before they found Frank. He'd somehow made his way to the basement and was leaning into a wall - head buried in folded arms. A fireman had followed a trail of blood drops down three flights of stairs. "Christ," he said as he pulled glass shards out of Frank's arms, "we've been calling you all night. Are you deaf or something?"

Frank turned and looked at the fireman. He blinked wildly as he muttered, "We were in the science lab, Mr. Murphy. Lucas was showing me the Van de Graaff generator. Then the air raid siren sounded and I ran down here, just like Mrs. Carswell told us. I saw the flash. I'll be blind for life, Mr. Murphy."

Frank turned back to the wall and buried his face in his forearms, mumbling about "the shockwave." The fireman called to his partners out in the hall, "This guy's fried." He threw Frank over his shoulder and walked out. For a few minutes, the firemen were lost in the basement. They walked up a flight of stairs and down the other side and ended up exactly where they'd started. Then one of them decided to go back to where they'd found Frank and follow the blood drops back to the first floor.

Harley had driven to the hotel as soon as he'd heard the news and was sitting in the lobby. When they brought Frank up from the basement, he ran across the drive to get Donna. She was asleep in the cottage. She bolted across the drive to the hotel and found Frank lying on the couch in the lobby.

"Oh, lord, Frank. What happened? Are you OK? Oh, Frank, geeezuz, I thought you were gonzo. Please, Frank, say something. Frank, I love you, please say something anything. Are you hurt?"

"I don't think he hears you," a fireman said, "I think he's traumatized. We found him standing in the basement, up against a wall. He was talking to somebody named Murphy. Who's Lucas? Was he up there, too?" The fireman pointed to the stairway leading to the upper floors.

Frank rubbed the back of his neck as he opened his eyes. Donna asked him if he wanted aspirin but Frank didn't answer. She asked Frank if he could hear her and he didn't answer. Frank sat up and made a hand motion like he was sipping from a cup.

"Coffee?" Donna asked and Frank nodded.

"I'll get it." Donna said. When she got back to the lobby a police detective was asking Frank questions. "He can't hear you," Donna said. "Deaf as a haddock." The detective said he'd keep trying anyway.

"What happened, Frank? Were you up there when the lightning struck? Did you see what happened to Bobby Crosby? Frank, can you hear me? Who's Lucas?"

"Look," Donna said, "he can't hear. Can't you see that? You sure as shit can hear it, I hope. Lucas is an old friend from New York. He died years ago."

"We'll have to wait to talk to him," the detective said to Donna. "Can you help me understand what happened?"

Donna told the detective everything she could remember from the Beaux Artes Ball to the band's amplifier exploding in flames. "It was just insane, really nuts."

"What about Bobby Crosby? Why did he go up there?"

"No idea," Donna said. "Frank was up there closing doors and windows. Bobby'd said he was going to his room to get his walking stick but he never came back to the bar."

"Well," the detective said, "when Frank gets his hearing back, have him give us a call. We've got to figure out what happened up there."

Donna said she would. She turned to Frank and grimaced as she wiped drool from Frank's chin.

They held a memorial service for Bobby Crosby on Labor Day weekend. A small crowd gathered in the gazebo and Reverend Parsons read the prayers. Donna, Harley and Tommy Lozano stood at the center of the Gazebo. Frank sat in a wheel chair at the base of the steps. Emma Wilkins and Euripedes stood beside Frank - Polly Perry, Phil and Ruthie next to them. Jack, Pam and Kim Bristol were off to one side and Jack kept pushing Kim's hands from his ass as the Reverend recited the psalms.

When the Reverend finished, he asked if anyone else would like to speak. Roger walked up the steps and shouted, "Oui. Je parlerai. Bonne chance, mon ami." Donna and Harley turned. "Dans le soleil."

"Well," Reverend Parsons said. "I guess that was a mouthful."

Harley held Bobby's stainless steel halo and Donna had his walking stick. Harley lifted the halo over his head and said, "In memory of Bobby Crosby," as Donna tapped it with the stick. Then Harley walked to the railing of the gazebo and tossed the halo into the water. Donna let fly the walking stick. Tommy Lozano waited for the halo to sink and then he tossed in a bouquet of flowers. "Farewell," they said as the flowers floated out with the tide. En masse, the mourners turned their backs to the harbor, dropped their pants and said farewell to Bobby Crosby. Ruthie told Phil to keep an eye on the walking stick. "When the tide comes back, pick it up. I can resell that one."

When Harley, Donna and Tommy Lozano turned to walk out of the gazebo, Frank stood up and pushed his wheel chair back. Jack caught it just before it would have bounced over the ledge into the water. "Frank," Donna screeched, "what are you doing?"

Frank held the book Bobby had given him. He turned and faced the hotel as he opened it. Snatching a sheet of notebook paper, he then pointed to the hotel and the tarp covering the gaping indentation at the center of the roof where the cupola had rested. Holding his right hand high above his head, he read:

Ed Touchette

DINOSAURS
The Last Words of Bobby Crosby.

A poet loved Gloucester.
Who wouldn't?
Some couldn't.
Woe is Norman, Thatcher too.
Oh Rackliffe House. Oh Rocky Neck.
We do. We do. We do.   Do you?

Thar she stood in an ocean of green,
Flukes above the rolling waves
Of oaks and maples.
They marked her serene
location.
           "Location, location," Chase squalled.

She glistens with dew -the passing storm.
Black shutters flapped like flippers.
The behemoth flailed
The faithful railed, "Neveragaintoregain".
The sea?

Beached.
Her innards collapsed.
       "An unfriendly atmosphere,"
       the gathered gasped.
The belching gas.
The stench   of beer.

       But how? The harpooners died long ago.
The bolt!
The scar.
The char.

Smoke
From the blow hole
           rising.

           "Gut her," Chase bawled without hesitation.
Unrolled his charts on the hood of the truck.
It's there for the takin' mine for the makin'
Cause nobody gives a flyin'
           "Carryon," Chase bellowed
So the taxidermists labored into the night.
Piled high the innards
- frames
- flooring
- mantels

Her dentils too?
           Dentals?
The jaw
           Save that. Something left.
and bones
           Preservationists, we are. They'll love it."
of an ass.   Kindle the signal fire.
           "Three floors.
           Modern.
           Water views.
She's a winner if we finish her fast.
           Fast?
           Are you for real?
           Eat now.
Pay later.

Bones?
In the attic.

Squalls billow over Magnolia
from the west.
They arrive.
Watch.
The sun black.
The draggers slack.
Colors still shimmer
                On
The charcoal of the harbor.
Look.
                Into the tar pit.
Listen.
There.
Groans
Against the mooring lines.
                Dinosaurs.
Love B C

    When he'd finished reading, Frank sat down. The wheelchair wasn't there. He tumbled back over the rocks into the harbor. Emma said, "Fetch," and Euripedes leaped down the granite embankment and dragged Frank to the rocks by his shirt collar. Tommy Lozano lifted Frank and helped him to a flat boulder. Then Tommy carried him to his wheelchair.
    "Christ, Frank, be careful, will ya?" Donna screamed as Tommy placed him in the chair.
    Polly Perry lowered her head and, peeking over her pearl framed heavily sequined sunglasses, whispered to Phil, "And he thought I couldn't sing. That poem sucked." Then she turned to Ruthie and grabbed the arm of Ruthie's leopard skin coat, about to say something about Emma, Phil and Ruthie being the only ones left from the old days up on Banner Hill. When she realized the coat was genuine fur, she hooted, "Geeezuzz, Ruthie, this coat's not a fake. All this time I . . . "

"What'd ya think, Polly, me and Phil spend the winters in La Jolla on that abstract shit he paints."

Frank contracted pneumonia after his swim in the harbor. He was treated at Addison Gilbert Hospital and released in October.

One rainy Thursday evening in November, Donna had cleared the dinner dishes from the table and Frank sat, as he did most of the time, staring out at the harbor from the apartment window. Donna sat next to him on the couch and curled her legs under her. She rubbed the back of Frank's neck. Then she heard a voice, "Hello," and a knock on the door.

"Oh, detective," she said opening the door. "Sorry, but Frank still hasn't said a word."

"Maybe you can help me Donna," the detective said as he walked into the apartment.

"With what?" Donna said.

"Donna, how long have you known Frank?"

"A couple of years, almost. Two next June."

"Donna how well did Frank know Jack?"

"Fairly well. Why?"

"What was going on in that hotel, Donna?"

"Well," Donna said as she turned to check on Frank, "I can only tell you about the bar downstairs. It was an unfuckingbelievable scene."

"Why?" the detective asked.

"It just was, Detective. I don't know why. It attracted all kinds of people. It just was."

"Were there a lot of drugs?"

"Alcohol," Donna said.

"No, I mean hard drugs like coke, heroin?"

"Not in the bar."

"Was Frank dealing drugs in the bar, Donna?"

"No friggin' way. Jack's the one you want to talk to and that's all I'm going to say."

"Well, I can't talk to Jack, Donna. We can't find Jack. I drove to Topsfield and the Senator's under the care of his doctor. It seems his wife left him and he has no idea where Jack is. He thinks they might have run off together. That poor old man. She left the kid behind."

Epilogue

Tom said, "rat's alley."
Patrick said, "home."
Can you dig it, man?
Dead men's bones.

A Tribute to Les Moor
anonymous
2005 The Aviary Papers Publishers

The Indians knew. The stage had been set four hundred years ago. They'd watched as Champlain sailed into the harbor, noting the small villages of wigwams that lined the shores. "Le beau port" was naturally beautiful and her bounty grew from the water. When Governor Bradford evicted the dissenters from Plymouth Colony, they ventured to Cape Ann and set their fish stages on the rise. Today they call it Stage Fort. As their numbers grew, they settled throughout the granite agglomerations lining the port.

Some claim that even the nearsighted can appreciate the excitement of the festive celebration that is Gloucester Harbor and the rolling hills that line this deep water port offer the perfect stands from which to view this expressionist tableau. From the colorful wood framed triple deckers that march up Portugei Hill, tightly grouped along the winding, curling streets, some apartments offer an aspect that extends beyond the breakwater to the lights of Boston's South Shore . . . on a clear, crisp night. Down the hill, on Taylor and Friend Streets, it is still possible to see the Atlantic beyond the harbor, along a southerly line , extenging over the brick chimney of the Tarr and Wonson Paint Factory, past Ten Pound Island and out to Norman's Woe.

From Pilot and Banner Hills in East Gloucester, the view is to the west and as the sun grazes City Hall's spire to close another June day, the vibrant colors that wash the horizon bedazzle even the color blind - or so it would seem. Even for the severely myopic, a glance directly down the hill into the harbor is still worth a thousand words.

In a Place Like No Other

The farsighted came to appreciate the grandeur of the harbor and the value of narcotic beauty, too. In the mid 1980's, ebbing interest rates and properties made available by lost fortunes, missed fortunes and misfortunes, found developers hustling to eviscerate the leviathans of the hills and establish new sanctums. A new order. As the speed limit on the Technology Highway approached 500 MHz, it became possible to leave Gloucester as the sun's rays washed the triple deckers on Portugei Hill and return before they mellowed over Magnolia. The sanctuary of the sun began to fill with converts.

At first, only the pilot fish led members of the new denominations to the healing and holy waters. But as fortunes were told, the new, noveau riche and even the old, just-plain-wealthy, reveled in their new found temple and Gloucester real estate became a tracking stock on the Nasdaq. Water views, a priceless commodity, replaced gold as a standard and the brouhaha over the transformation of the Tarr and Wonson Paint Factory to residential units that accompanied the city into the 21st century, was but a foretaste. Things were changing.

It was to be expected. Everything mutates. Gortons of Gloucester, reverted to the ownership of a Dutch conglomerate late in the 20th century. Rightfully so, some will argue, as some of the earliest claimants to the riches of the Americas had survived the great Tulip bubble of the 17th century and sailed west to invest in cod and fur stocks. These refugees, along with the French and English, masterminded a strategy to negotiate with the North American Tribes a treaty that would produce lasting benefits for hundreds of years - to everyone but the Indians. Justice is as blind as one who will not see.

But it's not nice to fool mother nature - another maxim from the seventies. And so it will come as no surprise, as the last chapters of this incredible adventure close in the year 2009, Gloucester finds herself, as does the rest of the world in the throes of a metamorphosis the likes of which haven't been seen since Fulton steamed up the Hudson; since Whitney invented the gin; since Windows opened Gates to the world. A.D.D. is the watchword of the day. Sell the rumor. Sell the news.

Owen Chase acquired Rackliffe House by default in 1977. He closed the dining room and the guest quarters but kept the bar operational until interest rates waned to acceptable levels. By June of 1985, the first front

Ed Touchette

end loader attached its chains to the front portico and dragged it, in one fell swoop, to the earth. When the dust cloud cleared, all that stood was a concrete vault in the center of the basement - a chamber that had never appeared on any set of drawings. As it was jack hammered into submission, workmen had noticed a large cache of white powder and two skeletons, one's finger bone encircled by a Crandall class ring. The remains were later identified as those of Jack Carson and Stephanie Barringer Carson, the fourth or fifth wife of Senator Maynard Carson. The powder was tested and identified as Boraxo. The remains autopsied, the coroner concluded: double suicide as a result of gun shot wounds at the base of the skull.

Chase Developments obtained financing and built a three story deluxe condominium complex offering twelve units at prices ranging skyward. The project sold out before the first units had been completed. "The views are priceless:" it said in the sales brochure, "Ten Pound Island, its lighthouse, sailboats dancing to and fro. The summer breezes cool your wine as the sun slips slowly over Magnolia."

Well appointed, they were: fireplaces, indoor-outdoor hot tubs, waterside verandas and kitchens with his and her appliances. Featured in bold type on the inside of the cover panel, above a photograph of the high granite wall that lined the street: "Your privacy is ensured by state of the art security."

Investors in the project realized sizeable gains and Owen purchased most of the land on the east side of East Main Street from just below the Aviary clear through to Gerring Road - excluding a swath owned by Emma Wilkins. In her last years, Emma suffered with severe dementia and insisted that this opening to the wharf beyond be left as is in case Henry should return - otherwise Henry might not recognize the place and find his way home.

In 1989, Chase wanted to begin construction of a 200 unit two story hotel motel with retail shops and an international food pavillion. The crowning jewel was to have been the world's first fresh frozen fish restaurant featuring the world's largest lobster pool into which divers would submerge to retrieve 'your selection' which was made by pointing a hand held laser pistol to target 'your dinner.' But first Chase had to purchase a right of way from Mt. Pleasant Avenue into the site below Banner Hill. Deemed the most cost-effective way for his heavy equipment to access the uppermost reaches of the project, this was imperative.

The right of way conundrum proved Chase's undoing as the only reasonable solution was to secure entry through Emma Wilkin's drive and bring the equipment down along the side of the Aviary. Shocked, albeit momentarily, from her vegetative state by a proposal that threatened to force change on 'Her House,' Emma flatly refused to allow Chase to even walk down the drive to present a proposal. Chase eventually sold his interests in the property and Banner Hill remains much the same today as it had been when Emma Wilkins lived there.

In deference to her staunch refusal to allow unfettered development to reduce her beloved Banner Hill to an architectural graveyard, the neighborhood petitioned the City Council and finally, in 2005, the drive from Mt. Pleasant Avenue to the Aviary was dubbed Emma's Way. A Boston attorney purchased the Aviary, reinvigorated the aged home, married a Hollywood actress and now spends his time raising three sons and four lovely daughters. His wife manages the Galley restaurant and continues with Polly Perry's work.

Undaunted, Chase redirected his efforts to Gloucester's back shore. Some of his handiwork may still be visible today. After that, Chase's prescience led him to the West Coast where he became a player in the world of video games.

Tommy Lozano sold his fishing boat to the government when the Magnuson Act failed to revivify the fisheries. But, just as he'd predicted, a new species of fish would surface and things would be finest kind again. Impassioned environmentalists flocking to the coast to enjoy the few whales that still lived under the waves provided a new resource and Tommy made a comfortable living offering whale watching tours out o' Gloucester. Sometimes more specimens graced the beaches, but Tommy had not included nature hikes in his packages.

Tommy had married his high school sweetheart, Betty Principale and she'd borne Tommy five strapping sons. The oldest, Nickie 'The Little G,' who towered over Tommy, captained the tour boat. Their other sons had left Gloucester and were scattered around the world: one working as a banker and another a software account rep; two were officers in the Navy. Whenever possible, all visited during St. Peter's Fiesta.

Harley Fenton moved to Key West in 1980 to manage Frederico Frederico Frederico, an exclusive Northern Italian bistro. He kept in touch with Frank and Donna until the fall of 1984. Then with Frank and Donna spending the bulk of their time packing and unpacking cartons as they scurried to outdistance the unrelenting development on the hills and ever increasing rents, Harley quit calling because he got sick of hearing Donna say, "Can't talk now, Harl. Gotta pack." Harley would have spoken with Frank but those conversations would have proved somewhat one sided because Frank Noal hadn't uttered word one since he'd recited Bobby Crosby's epic poem, *Dinosaurs*, at the memorial service in 1976.

Fifteen years! Can you believe it? Frank Noal did not speak for fifteen years. Traumatized by the event that snuffed the light of Bobby Crosby, Frank remained mute. Even when he and Donna were married, Frank was silent; as passionate as their affair was, his condition made it somewhat difficult to legalize their bond.

Several times they'd gone before a minister or a justice of the peace and each time, approaching the part where Frank had to affirm his commitment to Donna, Donna would ask if she could speak for him and of course, as any reputable marriage official would do, her request was denied. Writing "I do," was considered an acceptable alternative but Frank's tremors were severe, his writing illegible. One minister had asked what the problem was and Donna had told him that Frank was traumatized, and the minister had asked Donna if she was sure she wanted to marry a man so frightened of the prospect and she'd said, "Oh, no, he's not afraid of me. He was struck by lightning." The minister had doubts about Donna's assertion and asked them to "take some time and think it over." Ultimately, they resolved the seemingly insoluble when Donna remembered how maintenance work and architectural details relaxed Frank. A minister administered and their bond became legal on the scaffolding of a two story Gothic Revival being renovated on Middle Street.

Roger held the reception at C'est Bon and baked a wedding cake replica of the Aviary. Details included the balustrade on the cupola as well as the leaded glass front entry. But when the time came, Frank was reluctant to incise the mammoth and when Donna tried to slice it, he grabbed her arm and wouldn't let go. Finally they realized Frank's consternation: Roger had not put a lightning rod on the cake. Instead, two figures, a bride and a groom, customary or so Roger thought, sat atop the cupola. Reluctantly Roger grabbed a toothpick and an olive and supplanted the figures. Frank smiled as Donna filled his mouth with the lemon frosted chocolate cake. He wrote a note asking for seconds.

Frank Noal didn't regain his voice until 1991. After the summer of 1976, he'd secured a standing reservation at a Back Shore motel. He'd researched the area carefully and had found the motel had the lowest profile on Cape Ann. Whenever a storm approached the peninsula, Frank checked in. And whenever Frank arrived, per his agreement with the management, all electricity to the room was shut off.

As is often the case with trauma victims, a second event can shock them back to a reasonable facsimile of that which they once were. In October of 1991, Halloween in fact, conditions were perfect for Frank's recovery. During the battering storm, Frank had opened the curtains of his concrete block covert and gawked as a humongous wall of water roared toward the seawall behind which the motel stood. Crashing into the granite, the massive wave exploded. Frank bellowed, "Holy fuck!" and was cured.

Subsequently, he was able to continue his normal activities as a part time bartender and direct the balance of his energies to his ongoing research of Gloucester's architectural past. His relationship with his beloved, Donna, hadn't suffered much because Frank had spent the bulk of his time listening to her stories, anyway.

Frank and Donna lived an idyll. In 1994, the estate of Emma Wilkins granted Frank and Donna a life tenancy in the cottage on Banner Hill in exchange for caretaking. A year later, Frank's parents died of concurrent heart attacks while engaged physically so Frank and Donna inherited their house in the Adirondacks. They spent summers at the coast and winters in the mountains. "As Abenaki as anything," Donna'd told Harley.

Donna's modest success as an expressionist painter found them financially stable. Although they never had children, they avidly supported the Cape Ann Humane Society (now devoted to rescuing canines and felines having formerly been focused on the plight of the ship wrecked) and over the years adopted a collection of cats and dogs rivaled only by that of a spring downpour. All of the dogs were named Euripedes and all of the cats were called Emma. A numerical suffix distinguished each.

A belated wedding gift from Harley Fenton bolstered the menagerie's appeal; in 1998, a Cockatoo arrived. Frank built an aviary out of chicken wire and lined it with papers; Donna taught it to speak. A handful of nuts had the bird shrilling "Up yours, Jack," in no time. They christened the bird Bobby Crosby.

Donna cooked as well as ever and enjoyed preparing sumptuous fetes for Frank and the animals. On special occasions they'd invite friends and dress in costumes. At one such bacchanal, neighborhood gossip had those attending still dancing on the front lawn of the house in the wee hours of the fourth day after the party had begun. Needless to say, despite the period of silence and his inability to relate any of Lucas' stories to his beloved Donna for so many years, the passionate and loving bond between the bartender and his favorite customer grew ever stronger. Donna was still wild about Frankie boy and vice versa.

But for Frank, the true treasure of life surfaced on Banner Hill in April of 2004. While working in the basement of the house, assembling a lightning rod from a mail order kit, Frank smashed his thumb with a hammer and when he banged his fist on the wall in frustration, a secret panel opened and a cache containing a journal kept by Henry Wilkins materialized. It chronicled 60 years of land and sea journeys.

Perusing the journal, Frank uncovered a map which Henry'd rendered as a boy, diagraming a secret landing on Rocky Neck where he'd kept a dory that he'd rowed out to Ten Pound Island. A note on the back recapped Henry's treasure hunts for buried gold that he'd suspected might have been thrown over from the West Indies trader run aground there trying to escape the British ship, *Falcon*, during the Revolutionary War.

A small wooden box, hot stamped Pew Salt Cod, had lain next to the journal, and when Frank had noticed "Henry Wilkins' Treasure Chest" written in pencil on the side, he'd opened it and discovered: a coin, some pieces of smooth glass, a small watercolor brush and what looked like a human finger bone. Believing that the items, specifically the paint brush, might be of historical significance, he'd sent them off to the Peabody Essex Museum along with the map and the journal. The museum informed Frank that, for the most part, the items were fairly common and dated to the early twentieth century. The bone had been forwarded to a forensic archaeologist in Boston.

Three months later, Frank received a copy of the reply forwarded from a Boston laboratory to the museum. A note attached to the copy thanked Frank for his contribution to the study of American History. Donna had it framed for Frank's 56th birthday. It hangs in the hallway of their home next to the nude - the one she'd painted of Frank 28 years before - and a small oil painting of two Indians in a canoe on a lake with a mountain in the background over which storm clouds released their lightning and curled skyward.

Although steeped in names like Wingaersheek, Annisquam and even Massachusetts, the recorded history of Native Americans in Gloucester is so thin as to be a near nonentity. When Frank forwarded a copy of his copy of the letter to the Gloucester papers, the news that the remains of a Native American had been discovered on Ten Pound Island brought an army of anthropologists to Cape Ann's shores. Their findings and research deemed it fact: this man had fished and planted on Cape Ann years before Champlain sounded his discovery.

In the atmosphere of uncertainty that followed the dot com debacle and the ensuing corporate scandals, not to mention the trauma of pounding war drums and rattling sabers, it is surely understandable that panic gripped the owners of Rocky Neck real estate. Housing and property had been the only investment vehicles to avoid the potholes of depreciation so profusely distributed on the road of life. Rampant rumors abounded concerning the discovery on Ten Pound Island. Fearing the worst, the erection of a gambling casino, prospective buyers shied from purchasing their piece of the granite outcropping, and real estate prices drifted - southwesterly.

These events wreaked havoc on Rocky Neck. Their coffers exhausted as a consequence of myriad failed attempts to seek remedy in the courts through stays and injunctions, the residents of The Neck experienced hard times. Increasing real estate taxes found them having to return their properties to their rightful owners - the banks. The few lucky enough to receive pennies on the dollar for their years of toil, headed west in Budget rent-a-trucks. By the time the state and federal governments stepped in to rescue the market, prices had fallen into negative territory and futures looked dim. Few options remained. Rackliffe House was placed in receivership and low income housing topped the agenda.

Woe to him who would not read his history and understand those who have come before him. Any thinking man would know, no Injun worth his salt would consider a casino on hallowed ground and land that produces food is just that. But in the words of Lucas Carver, "Ya gotta eat." Who knows?

After Glow

Generations lost.
Art facts found.
Harry and Bobby?
Homeward. Bound.

A Tribute to Les Moor
anonymous
2005 The Aviary Papers Publishers

    Donna was sitting on the patio when Harley called. She picked up her cordless phone and pushed the button for line number one. "Hi, Harley. _ Yeah, I'm just fine. Just sitting here looking back at Portugei Hill._Yeah, Harl. Clear cut. It's bare. Oh well. How are you?_ I know you old dumb fag._Yeah. I know. You really are old now._Oh sure, Harley_ What?_ You're what?_ When? Now?_Where are you now?_ Oh, God, Harley, I'm so excited I'm going to pee my pants._ Wait. Let me call to Frank."

    Donna walked down the patio steps and into the yard, hollering to Frank working up on the roof. "Frank, it's Harley. He's coming for the dedication. He's crossing the bridge now. He'll be here in a few minutes."

    "Fucken A! Tell him I can't wait to see him."

    "Hi, Harl._ Yeah I told him. He's excited, too._ Yeah, OK._Yes, darling. I'll give you directions again._I know darling, it is harder to remember things these days._ Aw Christ, Harley, stop complaining, we're all old. Now shut up and write these down._OK. Turn left and come up Mt. Pleasant Avenue to the top of the hill. Remember? Emma Wilkin's place. Yeah. Right. It's about 100 yards on your left._ Right, Harley, Emma's Way. The street sign's a silhouette of Euripedes._Christ Harley, just look up when you turn up the drive, you'll know. Don't worry._ Right. Love you, too. See you in a minute._ Bye."

    Donna walked into the house and made coffee. She turned on the television to check the stock ticker on the Bloomberg Channel, then she checked the weather channel. "Great! It'll be a perfect afternoon."

Frank had come down from the roof and stood on the patio steps gandering at his work. "Donnahr, come out heahr and see what you think."

"OK, darling. One second."

Frank paced, looked up at the roof and made notes. Donna came out and said, "All done?" and kissed Frank on the cheek.

"Yeah, this should do it."

Donna looked up at the roof. "I hope so. There's no more room."

Harley pulled into the driveway. Donna ran to greet him. She hugged him and kissed him and put her arms around his neck and hugged him again. "Oh, my God, Harley, it's been twenty nine friggin' years since we've seen you. How the f . . . How are you, you old fag?"

"As I said, darling, old."

"Hahrley Fenton, my God. Great to see ya." Frank hugged Harley.

Harley hugged Frank back. Then he stepped back and looked at Frank and Donna and hugged Frank again.

"OK, Harl," Donna said. "don't push it."

They laughed.

"Boy," Harley said, "This is fabulous. The gardens are beautiful and what an incredible job you've done with the house. You were right, Donna. All I had to do was look up and I knew which house was yours. But what the hell is it, Frank? Ham radio?"

"Lightning rods, Hahrl. Nevahr have enough."

"Frank, there must be fifty of 'em up there. Where did you get 'em?"

"Don't ask," Donna said.

"OK, I won't," Harley responded.

"Let's have coffee befohre we go," Frank said.

In the hallway to the kitchen, Harley leered at the painting and Donna shoved him along saying, "Forget it, Harl." A shrill "Up yours, Jack," reverberated from the sunroom near the foyer. Harley roared. "That must be Bobby." Again the sharp cawing pierced the air.

"What time do we have to be there?" Harley asked as he sat at the kitchen table with Frank.

"Wait a minute," Donna said as she stood and walked to the refrigerator. She snatched an invitation from the magnetic holder and started to read. "Let's see here . . . hmmm, OK, Dear Mr. and Mrs. Noal. Oh wait let me skip all that happy horseshit. The pleasure of your compan . . . aw, gimme a break, do these people ever just say what they mean? OK. Here it is: Dedication Ceremony, Tuesday, April 12, 2009 - 3-6 p.m. Formal attire is requested but not required."

"How much time do we have?" Harley asked.

"An hour," Donna said. "We could walk."

A brisk Northwest wind blew across the causeway as they crossed to Rocky Neck. Frank noted the smell of lavender and Donna explained to Harley that the fish processors added it to cut down on complaints from the residents. Harley said he understood as he eyed the condominium complex that stretched from the intersection of Stevens Lane and Rocky Neck Avenue to the tip of the former Railways.

"It's all low income housing now, Harl. People got the shit scared out of 'em when Frank found the finger bone. They figured the Indians would claim Ten Pound and build a casino."

They laughed as they passed the new sign that sat at the west end of the causeway. Harley read aloud, "Rackliffe House A new Day in America. A Low Cost Housing Development and Casino sponsored by the Mass blah, blah, blah . . .What! Mr. Maynard Carson." An arrow at the bottom of the sign pointed up the hill.

When they reached the crest of the hill, Harley, Frank and Donna stopped. They looked at Rackliffe House and then at each other. They smiled. Frank pointed to the roof and Harley said, "It's beautiful, Frank. Just like the original cupola. But why would he have spent money on that?"

"Told him a secret," Frank said.

"Yeah," Donna said, "and Frank was paid a consulting fee for locating a lightning rod."

"Aha!"

A black limousine pulled to the curb in front of Rackliffe House. Its burly driver opened the trunk of the car and took out a collapsed chrome-plated wheelchair. He opened it, then the back door of the limo. He bent over, reached inside and lifted a small frail gentleman, placing him gently in the wheelchair. He wiped the gentleman's chin and then placed a blanket over his quivering legs.

"There he is," Donna said. "A hundred and friggin' four years old.

Senator Maynard Carson."

"That peckahrhead will outlive all of us," Frank said.

"And theahr she is," Harley added, "the newest in a long line of Mrs. Senator Maynahrd Cahrsons. Looks about fifteen."

"Yeah," Donna added, "like father."

Frank and Harley laughed.

"Not funny," Donna said as she punched Frank in the arm.

They walked slowly down the drive. They were following the burly man pushing Senator Carson's wheel chair. A crowd gathered on the front lawn, sipping wine from plastic cups in a frenzy of handshaking. Donna recognized the mayor, who effusively greeted Senator Carson. Most of the City Councilors stood around talking before walking over to greet the Senator. A tall blonde woman in spike heels and a very tight red dress walked over to kiss the Senator's mottled cheek, but the Senator quickly turned his head and kissed her on the mouth. Donna, Frank and Harley roared. The woman stalked past and they heard her grumble: "That mother slipped me the tongue."

Donna looked at Harley and they both smiled. "Nothing really changes, Harley," Donna said.

"I'll bet that's not the handle of his cane under the blanket, either," Harley offered.

The mayor tapped on a microphone and begged the crowd's attention. He introduced Senator Carson, a State Senator and Representative, the entire City Council, Members of the Housing Authority, and the Right Reverend Manny E. Reichard who would be giving the Invocation.

The Reverend spoke. "Lord Almighty, creator of the sun, the moon and the stars, many of whom have visited our fair harbor to make movies." The crowd tittered at the Reverend's humor. Mr. Gary, the architect, seemed befuddled. The Reverend continued.

"Let us give thanks on this glorious, magnificent, sun soaked afternoon that men as generous with their time and their money, like Senator Carson, have graced our fair harbor with their beneficence. Let us look to the future of opportunity this represents for those previously excluded from the natural beauty of our fair harbor. And let us hope that this magnificent piece of prime real estate will be cared for in a manner befitting our fair harbor and let us . . . "

The Mayor interrupted bruskly, "OK, Manny, that's enough," and introduced Senator Carson.

"Yeah, right," Donna whispered to Harley, "this ought to be good."

The burly man pushed the Senator's wheel chair close to the podium and one of the city councilors detached the microphone from its stand and handed it to the Senator. Maynard Carson spoke. His voice was weak and raspy and the crowd had difficulty hearing him, so the mayor offered to read his words.

"I have loved many women in my time _ no, I mean he has," the mayor said, pointing to the Senator. The Senator smiled, a little drool glistened on his lower lip. The Mayor continued_ "but none as fair as the grand dame of the gold coast, Rackliffe House. She's graced our shores . . ." the Mayor hesitated and an aide whispered in his ear. The Mayor continued " . . . almost as long as . . . " the Mayor hesitated and pointed to the Senator " . . . he has."

The crowd tittered. The Mayor continued. "At the start of this new millennium, who would have dreamed Rackliffe House would regain her stature as one of the Gold Coast's havens of entertainment; that once again her coffers would spew forth that magic elixir; that the Native Americans who farmed this land and fished these waters would once again hold their rightful claim. I certainly didn't or I might have invested more heavily than I did." The Mayor injected the Senator's humor with little expression and the gathered sniggered.

"But, today, through the generosity of federal and state programs as well as corporate sponsors . . . " At this juncture in the speech, the Senator grasped the handle of his cane, extracted it from under his blanket and poked it at a series of banners emblazoned with the logos of breweries, distilleries and other corporations that hung over the terrace. The Mayor nodded and then continued " . . . it is a reality. Let our citizens know that their welfare is our highest priority and that a percentage of the proceeds from the gaming and entertainment at Rackliffe House will fund many more worthwhile projects for Gloucester and Cape Ann. Thank you," the Mayor said. "I mean he thanks you."

Donna, Frank and Harley chuckled, then walked down the path to the harbor and looked toward the rock where the gazebo had stood. The oversized inflatable Budweiser can that marked the granite outcropping bobbed in the breeze.

"Apropos," Harley said.

"Nah," Donna said, "they should have inflated a Trojan."

Frank and Harley laughed.

The sun was setting over the Magnolia shore as Donna told Harley about the first day she realized she had fallen in love with Frank. "Yeah, Harley, in broad daylight, right on the end of the breakwater. We laid there naked for a long time talking about everything from Gloucester to the Abenaki. I showed Frank Hammond Castle and where Charlie Fisk lived."

"Yeah," Frank added, "she also . . . "

"Shut up, Frank," Donna said and she punched him in the arm.

"What?" Harley asked.

"Shut up, Harley," Donna said and she punched Frank again.

"Hey," Frank said, "why don't you punch Hahrley?"

"He's too old," Donna said.

Harley and Frank laughed.

They sat on the rocks as the sun dropped behind the trees. Frank said it reminded him of the story Lucas told about the great god of the north and the jack rabbit.

"Can we hear it?" Harley asked.

"Well," Frank said, "you see theahr was this Indian warrior who always wanted to be an animal of the forest to see what it was like to live wild and free and the great god of the north said to him "But you are wild and free, One of Little Patience. Stop complaining." And One of Little Patience said, "but I want to be a deer."

So the great god of the north made him a deer and One of Little Patience ran fast through the woods and when a band of huntahrs chased him and threatened his life, he ran even fastahr back to the great god of the north and begged to be a beahr so the great god of the north made One of Little Patience a beahr.

One of Little Patience ran into the forest and found a huge honey pot in an old dead tree and he climbed up and scooped out the honey comb and stahrted to enjoy the freshest, sweetest honey he'd evahr tasted until bees stahrted stinging his nose.

One of Little Patience ran back to the great god of the north and said he hated being a beahr and he wanted to be a wolf. So the great god of the north made One of Little Patience a wolf and One of Little Patience ran to the tops of the hills and howled and attracted other wolves. They went to a nearby fahrm and howled and threatened the sheep and the fahrmer who owned the sheep came out and fired both barrels of his shotgun. A load of "00" buckshot hit One of Little Patience right in the ahs so One of Little Patience ran back to the great god of the north and said "I don't want to be a wolf. What should I be?"

The great god of the north thought and thought and thought and finally said "I know" and he changed One of Little Patience into a jack rabbit and One of Little Patience ran into the forest and theahr were a few jack rabbits and thousands of jill rabbits and One of Little Patience spent many, many moons making more rabbits with jill rabbits and was very, very happy.

When the great god of the north saw him a couple of yeahrs latahr he asked One of Little Patience if he wanted to be some othahr animal and One of Little Patience said "Absofuckenlutely not" that he was quite happy eating carrots and lettuce all the time and screwing his brains out. The great god of the north smiled and walked away. He lifted his eyes to the heavens above, saying, "Don't be One of Little Patience any longahr." One of Little Patience turned into a jack rabbit permanently. The great god of the north walked contentedly back to his pole and the jack rabbit went around the forest telling all of the animals: "I used to be One of Little Patience but now I realize that you have to have a little faith because soonahr or latahr the gods will get it right."

"Oh," Harley said, "Great story."

"I love it," Donna said. "Best one yet except for the sunsets."

"What's that one?" Harley asked.

"Oh, it's . . ." Frank started to tell the story but Donna cut him off blaring, "Shut up, Frank."

"OK," Harley said, "then let's go to Roger's for dinner."

"Sorry, Harl," Donna offered. "Roger died."

"But theahr's a Red Lobstah ovahtown," Frank said.

"Good for me," Harley said.

"Good for me," Donna said.

"Whatevahr," Frank said.

They laughed together.

F.

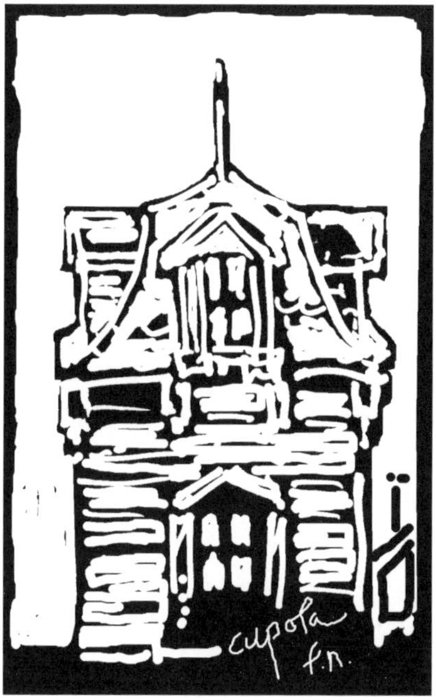
cupola
f.n.

Acknowledgements

To Duke and his Mom: Your writing and mentoring continue to be inspirational, your humor uplifting and your talents - invaluable. Dr. Brunsdale, yours, too.

The friends new and old who have been supportive of my work for more than 30 years. And M. Lily - your encyclopedic knowledge of fashion, oldies and people notwithstanding, your positive energy is salubrious.

 J.P. Ware and Dave McAveeney for your critiques

To the City: The one and only. A place like no other in all the best ways.

And of course my surrogate family at the end of the drive.